THE CONTESTANT

JOSH LANE TECHNOTHRILLERS
BOOK 1

NICK THACKER

PART ONE

KENT ISLAND, *Maryland*

Joshua Lane pulled his hands away from the wheel, feeling the vibration as the steering column reacted to the sudden lack of human control. He rubbed the itch above his left eye, then clasped his fingers together and placed them behind his back as he watched the speedometer creep upward.

75 MPH...

80...

85...

He eased down on the gas pedal, the adrenaline pumping as quickly as the car's cylinders. He tried to force the feeling of helplessness away and reason the fear back down.

But he was human, and this response was entirely normal. His eyes were observing the world around him hurtling by at a breakneck pace, and his chest and face felt the acceleration, everything in him screaming to slow down, or at least put his hands back on the wheel.

The turn up ahead was registered immediately by the optics on the car's bumper, cross-referencing the visual inputs with the onboard GPS and map data. The internal drive motor handling the steering column snapped to life, and the car eased gracefully into the turn, the autoshock system applying upward pressure to the left wheels, tossing the vehicle's center of gravity to the right and allowing the car to hit the turn without slowing.

He let out a breath of exhilaration. *This is about right,* he thought, smiling wide.

The car banked easily through the high-speed turn, and he took the opportunity to glance out the window at the Bay Bridge Marina Yacht Club on his left. Tall masts waved back at him, their owners either fast asleep belowdecks or enjoying the restful tranquility of the island's numerous forested spaces.

He understood the draw of the simpler, slower yacht lifestyle, but it was not the lifestyle for him.

Lane had chosen a more high-speed lifestyle as a Lieutenant Colonel in the United States Air Force. A programmer and software developer by trade, he had spent his time after OTS working with a special anti-terrorism unit that used the latest tech and computing to seek out and destroy terrorist cells worldwide. While most of his "action" had been experienced from the safety of a bunker in an undisclosed location, he had been on a few deployments that had gotten him up close and personal with the enemy.

All of that he had recently traded in for a hard-earned retirement pension and a lucrative career at a new tech startup, Bearbridge Consulting. Mostly working in the private sector, he had been recruited to lead a new team that would interface directly with top levels of the U.S. government.

The job at Bearbridge was the type of job his wife, Molly, liked to joke was "too cushy" and would only lead to his body growing lethargic and weak, at which point she would inevitably have to leave him.

But so far, after a week into the new job, she had not joked about his salary — or the perks it had come with.

He was driving — or at least riding inside of — one of those perks now.

The *Bear H7* was a barely-street-legal prototype created by the engineering team at Bearbridge, featuring the latest in hybrid engine and electronic drivetrain technology. He had been gifted the car as an enticement to join their team, all thinly veiled under the pretense that he would be able to help advance the state of their already state-of-the-art self-driving and self-diagnostic artificial intelligence unit.

So, after his first long week of work, he decided to put the car to the test.

He reclined the seat as the H7 hit the William Preston Lane Jr. Memorial Bridge at nearly 100 MPH, no longer worried about the car's handling or his rising adrenaline. He jammed the pedal to the floor and felt the tight constriction on his chest as the engine accelerated. His eyes swept over the sleek dashboard, checking for notifications of text messages or missed calls, hoping to have something he could ask the AI's text-to-speech feature to read to or play for him.

Instead, the bright, tablet-sized LCD simply displayed the car's current speed and outside temperature. It glowed with an orange hue, automatically adjusting the output levels to a more calm, evening tone, awaiting his input.

"Bear," he said, clearing his throat. *God, we need to change that name,* he thought.

"How may I assist you?" the car responded.

"I'd like to watch a show. Something I can finish before I get home."

There was a slight pause. *"At this current speed, I am afraid there are not many —"*

He nudged the brake and watched the car slow to a more reasonable 90 MPH.

"Here is a list of downloaded content, and if you enable internet bridge connectivity, I can tether through your phone and find additional content."

"Sure, why not?"

He waited and was impressed to see the results begin appearing on the display less than half a minute later. While the car was a marvel of the latest and greatest in automotive and computing technology, his cellphone was not — it was simply the latest and greatest consumer-grade smartphone.

The car's technology was neat. The cellular tech was the latest and greatest. But the tech he had embedded in his mind was on another level. Also still in beta, the implant was the *real* reason he had been hired at Bearbridge.

Knowing the car was not yet equipped with the ability to "hear" information from his implant, he audibly selected an option — a sitcom that hadn't aired on television in over a decade — and squinted as he realized the massive tablet screen was still somehow too small for entertainment.

"Hey," he said, a thought coming to him. "Can you pop that up on the HUD?"

He wondered if there were laws against something like that,

but then remembered that the car was still sub-classified as: *proto-type, intended for testing purposes only.*

Better make sure we give it a thorough test, in that case, he thought.

"Bear" reacted immediately to his request, and a rectangular image appeared directly in front of him on the windshield, distorted to cancel out the angle of the window itself and provide a luxurious viewing environment for the driver and passenger. At the same time, he felt the gas pedal depress as the car took over the entirety of the driving.

Okay, that's pretty cool.

As the car drove over the remainder of the bridge, another vehicle's taillights appeared up ahead. The screen immediately faded to a nearly transparent image, allowing him to clearly see the road ahead as the car deftly maneuvered into the right lane, sped past the truck, and then moved once again into the left of the two lanes.

Okay, that's even cooler, Josh thought. He had been in self-driving cars before, but congressional restrictions and manufactur-ers' legal departments had forced through rules that made "self-driving" seem more like "assisted driving."

If this was the future of vehicular travel, Josh couldn't wait.

He relaxed deeper into the leather seat, the temperature-controlled chair adapting to his form and weight perfectly. The car knew he was the only passenger, so it altered the multi-channel sound system's output toward his head as well.

As the intro credits for the sitcom began to roll, Josh took a final glance around the car's interior. The dashboard was back to its relatively empty orange glow, and the controls for the buttons and display had dimmed appropriately.

His eyes found the rearview mirror as well, and they flicked back toward the virtual screen in front of him.

Then he frowned.

His eyes worked their way back to the rearview mirror once again. *What the hell?*

He sensed movement from behind him but heard nothing but the theme music blasting through the speakers.

Another second. *There.* It *was* movement, in the form of another car.

No — another *three* cars. Directly behind him. Moving in closer.

The adrenaline that had finally abated suddenly coursed to life again. He felt his training kick in, even though his better judgment said this was most likely nothing to be concerned about.

Still, can't hurt raising my awareness levels a bit, he thought.

His hands lurched forward, grabbing the steering wheel, the seat rising to meet his back automatically.

But before he could move the car out of the way, the display screen on the HUD flickered off.

And then the LCD display, as well as the rest of the light-orange buttons and controls on the dashboard.

And finally, the car itself. He felt the sensation of lifelessness consuming him as the car died on the freeway, coasting to a halt in the left lane near the end of the bridge, only a couple of miles from land.

He turned in the seat, trying to get a look at the cars that had snuck up on him. They were black, traveling with no lights on, and every bit as silent as his.

He had shifted and rotated to his right to look through the

back windshield, so he jumped when a tapping sound on his driver-side window reached his ears.

Josh turned and looked out the window. The tapping returned, metal on glass. He saw what it was, what had caused the noise. Three times, harsh and loud.

A gun.

CHAPTER 2
JOSH

KENT ISLAND, *Maryland*

Of course, he couldn't roll the window down. The car was completely dead — all electronics black and dark. Josh noticed his cell phone lying face-up on the passenger seat. He reached for it quickly, having time only to push the side button and see the screen light up before the man at the window rapped on it harder, with his knuckles this time.

"Get out."

Josh looked up, trying to see the man's face, but it was obstructed from view by his arm and the gun he was holding.

Josh pulled his arms up, signaling innocence, then nodded. Somehow this guy was able to completely commandeer his vehicle, overrun the electronics, and cause it to decelerate automatically.

He quickly scanned his faculties and sighed as he realized his implant was still functioning. About a month ago, a pill-sized computer had been surgically installed to the base of his skull, a feat of medical and biological engineering that blew him away. He had volunteered for the procedure at Bearbridge, considering it was a marriage of all the tech and futuristic advances he had spent his life pursuing. The procedure itself was low-risk — the surgery was nowhere near as intense as brain surgery or open heart surgery. Just a few layers of skin peeled back, the object installed and wired to his skull, powered by his own body. Worst case, the pill-shaped device simply would not work as planned, and another procedure would remove it.

But the device *had* worked as planned, much to the happiness of the team and the surprise of Josh himself. He was still getting to know the device, getting to explore the ways it interacted with his mind.

The computer offered him all sorts of things — an audible HUD of sorts, able to connect to the neurological underpinnings of his brain and "speak" to him, giving him updates on heart rate, oxygen percentages in his blood and lungs, and other useful metrics.

But the real power was in using the device like a built-in AI assistant. While the device itself was compact by design, it could interface with other systems — namely, the wireless cellular grid called the mesh network. As long as there was a decent connection, Josh had the entire power of the internet in his brain.

He checked it now, excited to see that it was still functional. That meant the people who had just disabled his vehicle had not used any sort of EMP.

Localized EMP — electromagnetic pulse — weapons had been further developed over the past few years, able to kill any electronic signals in a smaller area than their more typical larger counterparts. But this was something different. His car had not simply *died*; it had been remotely *controlled*. Likewise, the car itself was far from a Faraday cage — his cell phone, also electronic, would have easily been fried if these people had used an EMP of some sort.

Which meant they had hacked his car's computer system. Since this was one of his areas of expertise, and the ostensible reason Bearbridge had hired him, he knew this was no small feat.

How the hell?

He glanced around, frantic, as the black-gloved hand waved the gun in the window again, impatient. He saw it more clearly now, thanks to the waning light of the distant streetlights. A pistol, something light and consumer-grade. Did that mean something? Was this just some typical street gang trying to rough him up?

No, he thought. *That can't be it. It can't be that simple.* His subconscious put the pieces together for him before he realized it.

He did not feel there was enough time to run a web search on the latest EMP tech — he was still getting used to controlling the device and coaxing answers from it, like a new computer user when first shown a search engine. But he didn't need the Internet's help with this one.

Not a localized EMP. Too bulky, and it would have taken out my phone. Not some random group of thugs, either. These guys are packing some heavy tech and the brains to use it.

He glanced a final time in the rearview mirror to see the three cars still behind him. *At least three people, including this guy.* Josh slowly and methodically moved his fingers over the locking mechanism on the door, relieved to discover that Bearbridge had thought it useful to install a mechanically driven lock as well as the electronic one. He pulled the tab up and heard the door click to unlock.

The door was immediately pulled roughly away from him, and

he felt his collar tighten around his neck. A hand was inside the cabin of the vehicle, yanking him upward and out. He barely had enough time to unbuckle the seatbelt, but judging by the strength in this second man's hand, he wondered if the belt would have been ripped out of its mount anyway.

"Joshua Lane?" a voice asked from behind him.

Josh was able to turn against the pressure from the second man's hand on his collar and see a third man approaching the vehicle. He was dressed in a suit, but his eyes were concealed behind sunglasses. There was no sun above their heads, and Josh wondered what sort of advanced lenses allowed this guy to see where he was going.

Two of the streetlights on the bridge's mooring towers flickered, straining to come back to life. He willed them to provide a bit more light, a bit more information that might help explain to him just who the hell these guys were.

"Who's asking?" he asked.

The man didn't respond. Instead, he reached a hand into a pocket of his black jacket and pulled out a cell phone, the same model as Josh's. He tapped on it for a few seconds, then held up the screen for Josh to see.

"This is you?" the man asked.

Josh cocked his head to the side, then tried working his neck loose. The man holding him shifted his grip, allowing Josh to breathe a bit easier, but he noticed the guy working up closer to Josh's left side, his feet about to straddle his left leg.

I could probably get him into a hold, or at least a leg lock. But then...

He didn't need to rehash the odds. Three guys visible, all of unknown ability. This one had at least the strength to pull a fit, two-hundred-pound grown man out of a vehicle, and he knew there were probably other guys just like him in the cars behind his.

"Heart rate elevated," he heard the voice in his head say. *"BPM approaching intense levels."*

He thought a response back to it. *"Thanks, NARA. Don't worry about it; I'm not going to do anything to harm either one of us."*

The company had named the device NARA — the Neurologically Activated Receiver Attachment. It was, of course, more than its name, but — as he had learned in the military — every cool science project needed a fun acronym.

He intended to keep his promise to the symbiotic barnacle riding just inside the back of his neck. If he fought, he'd easily be overcome.

"The hell do you want?" Josh asked. "And where'd you get that picture?"

The image on the man's screen was of Josh, but it was one he knew for a fact was not online anywhere. It hadn't been taken digitally, and he owned the only photo negative from which it was printed — and, apparently, uploaded.

"We need you to come with us," the man said, still ignoring his questions. "Please, follow me to the first car on the —"

"Like hell I'm going to just follow you," Josh said. "You somehow disabled my car remotely, so I know you're not just some goons looking for a fight. Tell me what this is about, and I'll consider it."

"It's a matter of national security," the man said without hesitation.

"It's a matter of — wait, what?" He had started to mock the

man's response, but something he hadn't recognized stopped him in his tracks. "You guys are government?"

He knew the drill — at least, he thought he did: lead with a polite request, flash a badge. These guys hadn't done either.

The man behind the sunglasses didn't flinch. Or if he did, Josh couldn't see it. He simply shook his head. "Not government. But it doesn't matter. You need to come with us."

Josh took a step toward his car, but the man on his left side was there with him, in lockstep. He felt the man's hot breath on his neck, noticing once again how large he was. *Probably Army,* he thought. *Smells like a Marine, though.*

"Look, dude, I'm just getting my phone."

"Unnecessary."

It *was* unnecessary since having a constantly connected computing device in his brain meant everywhere he went, he *was* a phone, but these guys couldn't know that.

"Un — what? You're kidding, right? My wife's going to be expecting —"

"Get his phone for him," the leader of the group said, waving away the goon. "It *is* unnecessary. We've just got some questions, then we'll be done, and this will all be over. We'll bring you right back here when we're finished, but if it makes him feel better, he can carry it with him."

"You can *ask* me questions right here," Josh shot back.

"I'm afraid not," the man said. "This is not a secure location. Please, we are running out of time."

Josh sighed. *This night went downhill fast.* "Fine," he said. "But tell your boy here to keep his hands to himself."

He trudged side-by-side with the hulking soldier and followed the suited man to the first car on the left. The man opened the rear door, and Josh eyed the interior. It was a sedan, luxury line but nothing terribly fancy. He had rented the same model on a trip to a conference last year. From the looks of it, it seemed to be the same year, as well.

Damn, the guys at the office are going to kill me for leaving the H7 here. It had better be here when I get back.

Josh was handed his phone a moment later, which he slid into his pocket. He then stepped into the backseat and buckled the seatbelt. There was another man in the driver's seat directly in front of him, but he didn't move his eyes from their post. Josh watched the rearview mirror to make eye contact, but the driver was intent on staring straight ahead.

He waited a few more seconds, and finally the huge soldier got into the front passenger seat, followed by the group's sunglasses-wearing leader, who got into the back seat opposite Josh. Surprisingly, the man took off the glasses as he entered the vehicle's interior, which was brighter than outside. *Perhaps they enhance low-light conditions,* Josh thought, unable to keep his mind from trying to figure out the tech.

"Hey, NARA — you got any idea what the hell's going on?"

The response was immediate but completely unhelpful. *"I am sorry. I do not understand the query."*

He sighed. While the tech itself was groundbreaking, it was incomplete. Right now, NARA depended on his cell phone's ability to connect to the mesh network, piggybacking on the device for its network capabilities. Though for the first time in history a human being had been implanted with a computing device, the onboard AI left plenty to be desired.

But that was to be expected — he was a walking prototype, a

human guinea pig. He had been hired to help the company figure out how to *make* the thing smarter, more useful.

For now, that meant the puzzle of his capture was going to be up to the wetware installed on his person — the old-school brain he had been carrying around his entire life.

Before Josh could start imagining the schematics of night-vision sunglasses in a small frame such as this, the man set the glasses on the seat between them. Josh was surprised to see they were nothing more than a simple, garden-variety pair of sunglasses.

The man leaned his face to the side, and Josh could see now why he had kept his eyes hidden behind dark glasses. A bulbous, shining scar ran from the top of the man's right eye to the bridge of his nose. It looked like it had once been a deep cut. Judging by the way his right eye rolled around unnaturally in its socket, the sheen of it almost too perfect, Josh decided that it had, in fact, been a cut bad enough to take out the man's eye.

The man continued turning his face so that Josh could see it fully. There was a bit of a blueish glow inside the car from the dash lights, and it was enough for Josh to notice the man's features.

It was enough for Josh to notice that he *knew* this guy. Still, he ran the query anyway. Silently, he willed NARA. "NARA, *focus on the face. Run a reverse image search.*"

But before NARA could provide any results, the recognition hit him.

Oh, shit.

CHAPTER 3
JOSH

"Now that we are in a relatively private space," the man began, "I would be happy to answer any questions you may have."

Josh swallowed as the car sped up, and the trio of sedans passed the prototype Josh had been driving. He tried to focus on the man's scarred face, on the man's fake eye. Every time his own eyes stopped there, they started once again and averted to a spot over his shoulder instead.

"It's fine," the man said, his voice slipping into a more casual tone. "No one knows where to look. I don't mind."

"It's... it's not that," Josh said. "I, um, I know you."

The man smiled, the bottom half of his face pleasantly contradicting the top half. "Yes, I believe you do."

Shit, he thought. *What's his name?* "I apologize; I know it's something... something 'Blake?'"

"Robert Blake," the man said. "Very good. And don't sweat it — most know my face, but my company is the name on their lips."

"*Robert Blake,*" NARA said. "*With a likelihood of 97.4%.*"

"Wow," Josh thought. *"That's helpful. Thanks, you beautiful idiot."* He kept his gaze on the man sitting across from him. *"Aetheria.* You founded it in your garage, sometime in the eighties."

"Correct," Blake said. "But it was not until recent years that we appeared, if you will, 'on the map.'"

Josh nodded along. Aetheria had made a name for itself in recent years in state-of-the-art advancement of virtual reality consoles and technology. Their claim to fame was a wearable device that could interface with a user's cellphone and provide what they called a 'layered reality.' In essence, glasses that displayed more information to the wearer, and augmented the world around them.

Many other companies had created something similar, but none were as sleek, high-powered, and yet overtly simple as Aetheria's. Josh had long thought their tech team one of the best in the business.

"Those sunglasses," Josh said. "They're not just plain-old sunglasses. They're your tech, aren't they?"

The man's smile grew. "Yes, indeed. The latest, actually, and a prototype — not unlike the one you were driving."

"I'm sure you can appreciate, then, how my boss will respond if I tell him I left his prototype dead on a bridge."

Blake nodded but didn't respond. "Mr. Lane, I asked you to come with us because I'm afraid there *is* something of national concern."

"You said security before."

"A concern that *could* lead to a problem for national security."

"Can you be more specific?" Josh asked.

"What do you know about quantum computing?"

Josh pressed his head back into the headrest. *Quantum computing? Really?* "I'm... not sure what you're asking."

Blake chuckled. "That's fair. I have it on good authority that *you* know just about all there is to know — theoretical and practical — about quantum computing. Building qubits, raising temperature requirements for successful computing, processing entanglement and coping with decoherence, all of it."

Josh frowned. "Sure, I guess. But you said it — it's mostly theoretical. It's mostly just equations and functions, propped up by hopes and dreams. There's not really anything miraculous happening, even in the big tech labs. Progress is steady, but it's slow. We've got some computers approaching 100 qubits, which is phenomenal from a *theoretical* standpoint but not from a practical one. They're basically just really fast, purpose-built computers, and that purpose is essentially to do isolated math problems."

"Right," Blake said. "But what if I told you all that's a lie?"

At this, Josh raised an eyebrow. "I would have to respectfully disagree."

"I mean, not *all* of it, but the part about there not being anything miraculous happening in the field."

"Again, I wouldn't believe you. Our progress with quantum computing is essentially a reverse Moore's Law — we're trying to build bigger and bigger machines with more and more qubits, and the problem isn't one of knowledge, it's one of funding and tech. We just need better ways to approach decoherence, specifically —
"

Blake held up a hand, and Josh fell silent. Of course he knew quantum technology — it was the *real* reason he had been hired at Bearbridge. It was the reason they had chosen him over all the other world-class programmers and software engineers. Josh operated on a level that allowed him to approach computer science from a theoretical *and* practical standpoint. He could see what others could not because he refused to look at just the pieces on the table. His brilliant mind could combine every facet of science he had studied — and he had studied and experimented with nearly all families of hard science — and combine them in new and intriguing ways.

Specifically, quantum computing was all about *small* — small, weird little particles that interacted with one another in weird ways. The object in Josh's skull was a computer, made with microscopic transistors, but it was just like a standard computer. But if they could figure out how to crack the "quantum code," as his boss liked to call it, implanting *that* tech into a human being would provide unfathomable benefits.

"You're special, Lane," Blake said, dipping into the entrepreneurial well of charisma he no doubt had within him. "You're one-of-a-kind, and that's a good place to be, most of the time."

"*Most* of the time?"

"Yes," Blake continued. "Unfortunately, there have been some machinations of late. Things that would normally not affect you. However, I came to find you in person because I'm afraid there's been a development."

"A development in what? Blake, come on. You haven't even told me what this is all about."

The car reached the end of the bridge, the driver slowed and turned to the left. So far, they were heading toward Josh's new home outside Annapolis. Maybe they would be so kind as to drop him off at home, but he had a feeling it wouldn't be that easy.

"It's a game, Josh," Blake said, his voice dropping. "And you've been chosen as a player."

Josh scowled. "Right. Okay, Blake. I'll play your game — what do you want from me?"

There was a long pause, and Blake looked at the hulk in front of him and his driver to his left, then back at Josh as if reconsidering even broaching the subject. "It's not *me*, Lane — at least not yet. This is a warning, if you will. To keep your head down, at least for the next month or so."

"What? Are you serious? You're threatening me?"

"No — again, I'm *warning* you. I can't be more specific than that, unfortunately." Robert Blake once again looked out the window at the suburban neighborhood they were passing through. His eyes fell to his lap. "I've already said too much, actually. But — and please, don't hold it against me — I'm telling you this because I hope that you'll remember this conversation when this is all over."

CHAPTER 4

JOSH

Josh wasn't sure what to say, so he said nothing. How could he *forget* this conversation? He had long ago learned to let the other party speak first and, when faced with a difficult decision, to allow the other party the opportunity to divulge more information and potentially reveal their hand. However, he had the feeling Robert Blake was a master at this very game, and nothing Josh could say would cause Blake to reveal any more than exactly what he had already planned to say.

Another sigh, and Blake finally spoke again. "My team and I have been working hard for quite some time on what we believe will be a breakthrough in quantum computing. For months, we've been perfecting a process that we think will revolutionize the entire industry."

"Wow, that's a bold statement," Josh said. "Even from a guy like you."

Blake managed a laugh. "Trust me, Joshua. If I could be

entirely honest with you, you might say it will revolutionize the entire *world*."

Josh nodded slowly. He had heard pitches like this before — *change the industry, change the world, change human life as we knew it.* All of them glamorous and romantic, all of them fated to fall short of their expectation. "Again, can you be more specific?"

Blake shook his head. "Unfortunately, I cannot. However, I wanted to tell you this in person so you will believe me when I say: we are working on something that needs just one final piece to fully solve. Something that's escaped our grasp for years but is now within reach. But hear me when I say: when I was told a bit about your hiring and what you would be able to provide Bearbridge, I was fascinated. It seems our interests may be aligned very soon."

Josh's mind raced. This man seated across from him was speaking in code, in riddles. "Who told you about me? Dalia?"

Josh knew that Ruth Dalia, CEO and founder of Bearbridge, was like Robert Blake in many ways: billionaire, owner of an innovative futuristic company, and interested in pushing the limits of science and technology. But unlike Blake, Dalia was as hands-off as they came: she rarely appeared in the office and was currently racing around the world in a luxury yacht.

His only interaction with the woman was prior to his hiring — she wanted to test a new technology her company was working on, and she thought he would be the perfect fit. It was a strange request, considering they had never met before, and he had barely heard of Bearbridge. She had mentioned that the request for his help had been upon the recommendation of others, but she hadn't told him who that might be.

"We are friends, in a way," Blake said, nodding. "Business in sectors like this cannot possibly exist in a vacuum, so we know each other well. We had a call about a year ago, and she mentioned there was something similar she was working on. When you were hired, I put the pieces together and made the assumption that you were her final piece of the puzzle."

Josh shook his head. *Final piece of* what *puzzle?* he thought. *And how much does this guy think he knows?* "Okay... yeah, they hired me, but I haven't even really gotten my rhythm yet. I'm still learning, you know?"

Blake laughed. "Right, right. The 'new employee' regimen. Guys like you don't get to play that card, Lane. You don't have to pretend," he said, taking a breath. "Look — we don't have a lot of time, and I'm sorry again to bring you in like this. I'm just interested in certain details about your contract. When does it end, what it entails after, and the like."

As much as Josh hated the cloak-and-dagger nature of the entire conversation, he loved puzzles, and he couldn't help but be intrigued. He turned to face Blake fully, then smiled. "I get it, I think," he began. "You've almost got this thing — whatever it is you're working on — solved, but you need one *final* thing, and that's me. And my, uh, *work* with Bearbridge is very closely related to what you're working on."

Blake's smile grew. "Yes."

"Specifically, you want to know what *I* know. What I can *do*. And what you think I'm going to do for Bearbridge." He knew that developing fancy new cars was only the tip of the iceberg — the consumer-facing line of products Bearbridge used to get their massive institutional investments. It was how Dalia had made her money, but he knew she was interested in bigger and better things. It was not surprising that Robert Blake already knew Bearbridge had plans up its sleeve and that those plans were related to the very thing Blake's own company was interested in.

"*Nara,*" he silently spoke to his onboard computer, "*pull up the last known location of Ruth Dalia, head of Bearbridge Associates.*"

Immediately the image of Dalia appeared in Josh's mind, along with a list of search results of articles claiming to know where the elusive billionaire was at the moment. The image and text appeared superimposed on his eyes as if he were looking at a computer screen with the opacity set to fifty percent.

He quickly scanned the articles, but none were more than just hyperbolic clickbait headlines claiming to know one thing or another about Dalia's private life.

Blake's voice caused his attention to revert back. "Precisely."

Josh's brow furrowed a bit. "Fine, I get that. This is head-hunting — but why like this? Why go through all this trouble to kidnap me and tease me with half-answers? Why not just come out and offer me a job? Hell, I like steak and wine and fancy hotels like anyone else — why not send my wife and me on a weekend getaway instead?"

Blake shifted in his seat before answering. "I'm just here to put the bug in your ear, Josh. We want your help with a project, but... we're just not ready yet, I'm sorry to say. It's a timing thing. Trust me; when the time *is* right, you'll be hearing from me."

"So that's it? You just grab me on my way home from work to tell me that soon you'll want to hire me?"

Blake shook his head. "No. While I cannot tell you the entirety of my reasoning, I can at least tell you a bit about what's to come, and how you might be able to —"

Just then, Josh felt a slight shift in the vehicle's air pressure.

He heard the ping of glass breaking in a small spot, and Robert Blake's head vanished.

Exploded.

A misting poof of blood replaced Blake's head's position on the man's neck, and Josh saw organic matter fall to the side, onto the floor of the car. Josh's own face was immediately covered in thousands of droplets of warm blood.

He screamed as Blake's lifeless torso slumped into his seatbelt.

CHAPTER 5
JOSH

"Oh, my God!" Josh screamed. "What the *actual* —"

He lurched forward as the car swerved to the left, the driver as spooked as he was. The driver narrowly missed sending the speeding car off the road and down the slope into the water, but pulled the sedan back into the lane at the last moment.

While the car made it safely back onto the road, the three remaining living passengers did not fare as well. Josh felt his torso ripped nearly in half with the centrifugal force of the change in direction, and the larger man in the front seat grunted in pain as his head smacked against the window.

Josh noticed the man had his weapon out and ready once again, though there was no immediate target to aim for. He whirled around in his seat, staring daggers at Josh.

"You okay?" the man shouted.

Josh frowned, pulling himself upright once again. "Uh, yeah. But — Blake..."

"He's gone," the man said. "And we'll all be gone like him if we don't get you back —"

He never finished the sentence. The driver swerved again, this time smashing the pedal to the floor and pulling the car in a tight arc that pointed them back toward the entrance to the bridge. Off in the distance, over the slumped headless torso of Robert Blake's bleeding body, Josh saw the dead $H7$ waiting.

"What do you mean, 'if you don't get me back?'" Josh shouted. The engine noise was deafening as the driver continued to pick up speed, and Josh had the unhelpful realization that if they had just all gotten into the $H7$, the road noise would have been diminished.

No one answered his question. The huge gunman was pressing the button to roll the window down, already poking his head out the gap to search for something to shoot at.

Two more shots impacted the car, one through the windshield and one, sadistically, into Blake's chest. Another spray of blood washed over the side of Josh's face.

"Who the *hell* is shooting at us?" he shouted.

The driver spoke for the first time to answer his question. "They must be up on the hill," he called back, pointing toward a slight rise on the left side of the car. "Probably saw the whole thing. They might be from Ravenclaw."

"*Who?*" He whirled around, trying to see through the darkness, but could not find any human-sized shadows moving.

No answer came from the front seat. That did not bode well for him, but even that lack of information gave him some clues: Blake was dead, and — judging by the cruel efficiency of the round through Blake's head — there was at least one sniper with a high-powered rifle somewhere in the dark, and they were well-trained.

It didn't really help him determine actual facts about his situation, but he got the gist of it: don't get shot, and get back to the *H7*.

At the very least, the driver was now entering the bridge once more. Within a half-minute or so, Josh would be back at his car. *Is that a good thing?* he wondered. *Will I just be an easier target then?*

Something told him that the sniper hadn't missed his first shot — that Robert Blake, not Joshua Lane — had been the actual target. Did that mean the other two bullets had been intended for the driver and his hulking friend?

The shot placement of the second and third rounds, both on the windshield and through the back side window, told Josh that was the likely scenario. They had both been pulled to the shooter's left, assuming they were on the hill and the wind was coming from the south.

They weren't shooting at me, he thought. The relief was short-lived, however, as he realized something else. *There's only one reason they want everyone else dead.*

They intended to get to *him*, and while he could have no possible idea as to why, he was certain that these people — a group called Ravenclaw, apparently — would not stop until they succeeded. They had already killed the man who had kidnapped him, and the fact that Josh was still reeling from that fact meant that his subconscious knew the truth: the shooter, and whoever they were working with, was a *far* worse outcome than staying with Robert Blake.

The car slowed as it turned and slid over the road.

"*NARA, how fast are we moving?*"

NARA's response was immediate. "*We are traveling approximately 24 miles per hour.*"

He had lost sight of the other vehicles, but this was not his immediate concern. With a slight roll of his wrist, Josh checked the door lock. Unlike the H7's futuristic mechanics, this vehicle, while luxurious, featured a simple switch above the handle.

He took a long, slow breath. *In and out.* He felt his training kicking in, felt the hyperawareness clearing his mind.

The man in the front seat turned to eye Josh. "We will head back to headquarters. We need to regroup with the rest of the team — they will already be heading that way."

Josh heard the words, but his mind compartmentalized them into a new temporary holding cell he had just created and named *Things That Don't Matter.* The man's words were useless to him — he would be long gone before the man required a response.

As it were, the man stared at Josh strangely, no doubt either confused by or in awe of Josh's calm, stoic demeanor. Truthfully, he felt adrenaline already pumping through his blood, his mind sharply taking in every last piece of information and filing it away.

Three, two...

He counted off the seconds as they sped over the bridge, approaching where the dead H7 still waited. The car was accelerating now, the bridge's span an attractive runway for the driver.

One.

He flicked the door open with one hand while grasping the handle above his head with the other. He let out a breath and lunged out of the car, careful not to let any dangly bits near the back tires of the speeding sedan.

He hit the asphalt perfectly — which is to say he hit it *hard*, nearly knocking himself out. But he fell into a practiced roll, allowing his lower legs and arms to flail naturally with the force and impacts while focusing on keeping his neck straight so as not to allow his head to smack against the pavement.

He was going to feel this one, he knew. But there had been no choice. He had absolutely zero interest in going with the flow and trusting his safety to these goons. There were no oncoming cars in the opposite lane as they drove, so he calculated the move as best he could, timing his jump so that he could get out of the car before it had increased its maximum speed and just before they passed the H7.

He came to a stop and immediately wanted to die. His head was throbbing, the blood on his face dried and caked, and the blood inside of him in all the wrong places, as if he had just been inside of a glass centrifuge vial.

Josh groaned, already feeling bruises in places he hadn't even known existed on his body. If he stood now, he would likely walk directly off the bridge, over the concrete barrier and down into the freezing water. But if he waited, the car he had just escaped from —

Too late.

He pulled himself to a seated position as the car up ahead slammed on its brakes and swerved.

Dammit, he thought. *That was a quick reaction.*

He added 'well-trained' and 'experienced' to his assessment list of Robert Blake's soldiers.

As the car started reversing and turning around, Josh stumbled toward the dead H7. He hoped that whatever electronic hacking device they had used to stop him in the first place had died with Robert Blake, or had an active time window that had now closed.

There was only one way to find out for sure, and he hustled as best he could. His eyes were playing tricks on him, placing two extra H7s in his field of view, but he forced his steps toward the middle one. Guessing correctly, he reached it and pulled the sleek metal handle.

It opened, and he fell into the seat. He pressed the car's start button before his butt was on the chair, and was elated to hear the telltale startup chime, followed by Bear's welcome message.

Thank God, he thought. The localized control device they had used on his vehicle was weak enough to be a temporary control, and had been deactivated when his kidnapper's vehicles had driven away.

The two other cars following behind him had turned around and were also barreling down the bridge's two lanes, directly toward him. The H7 was fast, but he had no desire to become prey in a three-car chase. He knew these men would simply call for help long before he could get somewhere safe.

That did not leave many options, and the best one was also by far the most dangerous. He took a deep breath as he pulled the H7 around, heading back toward the car he had just jumped from. They were going to play a game of chicken on this bridge, and that required impeccable timing and some guesswork.

He let out a breath as the car's headlights flicked on for the first time — they were past stealth, hoping to blind him now before he could accelerate past them.

He gripped the wheel, not wanting to trust this next maneuver to an artificial intelligence that held human safety as one of its highest programmed tenets. As if suspecting what he was about to attempt, Bear casually mentioned the oncoming vehicle, calculated to be moving at a speed far higher than the speed limit and thus predicting that the driver may be out of control.

Josh ignored it, pulling all his focus toward the next few seconds. He needed to get this right.

It was his only chance.

CHAPTER 6
AL-SADIR

HULHUMALÉ COAST, *Maldives*

The hundred-million-dollar yacht sat moored in the bay, the first strains of sunlight teasing the clouds over the horizon. It would be another half hour until sunrise, but Mohammad al-Sadir had been up and prepared for the day for an hour already.

He knew the weekend was approaching, and the mad dash of preparations still needed before the next week began. His assistant would be just waking, but the man had a list of to-do items a mile long already, so al-Sadir did not want to wake him early.

Besides, it was a rare day he was able to enjoy a sunrise without intervention from one of the myriad pieces of work he was juggling.

He sipped at his tea, a black blend he had found ashore in Malé from a street vendor. It was soothing, yet spiced enough to provide the necessary early morning wakefulness he desired. A balanced brew, he made a mental note to have his assistant acquire more bags of the stuff during his next shore visit.

Al-Sadir watched the gentle rocking of a smaller boat near his massive luxury yacht, once again reminded of the peace and tranquility provided by an expensive anti-rocking module. A nearly silent humming sound was the only telltale sign that he was on a boat, not in a luxury high-rise apartment.

Not that there *were* any high-rise apartments on Malé. The Maldives had been experimenting with land reclamation as far back as the late nineties, and the results were promising. The Hulhumalé project had added almost three square miles of land to the island, and already the population was booming. An expected 250,000 people would call the artificial island home by the end of next year.

Al-Sadir had come here not to get away from his work. On the contrary, he wanted to see firsthand his investment in the region, to better understand where his money was being spent. His project, a much smaller version of Hulhumalé, would also create a small island by way of land reclamation.

Only instead of adding land to host a population, this island would host *him,* and those he decided worthy. It would be a permanent home for him as well as a home base to run his growing company and business interests. While he could easily continue running the conglomerate from his yacht, he had a strong desire to build a physical, *visible* example of his massive wealth. In the circles in which he ran, the outward sign of wealth and richness was nearly as important as the actual amount in the bank.

While he would have been content amassing wealth through his investments and hard work building his business empire, many of his peers enjoyed the lazy lifestyle of living off the riches of their families' names — which meant flaunting their wealth by spending lavishly on unnecessary things.

His yacht, for example. While it was helpful as a place to run his business, he had splurged and purchased the most garish of luxury liners, ensuring that he would be seen in a positive light by his greedy peers.

But he preferred to use his wealth and intelligence to build his umbrella of business interests. To him, the ultimate legacy would be to leave behind income-producing assets instead of just an account full of cash.

Not that he had anyone to leave a legacy to — yet. He was young, handsome, and rich, so while he had no shortage of interest from female pursuers, it was especially difficult to sort through the offers and find someone who appreciated his intelligence, wit, and charm without being attracted to the lifestyle he could provide.

A voice reached his ears from the hallway. "Sir, your first appointment is already online."

He frowned, turning to his assistant and director of his private security detail, Hans, as the older man stood in the doorway. His assistant had been trained well, careful to interrupt his master only in the most gentle of ways. He would not step farther into this room unless summoned. Even better, the man was white — German, even — a visible display of al-Sadir's superiority to those close to him.

"Thank you. Everything is proceeding as planned, in that case?" al-Sadir asked. He spoke the question more as a command, and he watched as his assistant struggled for the words.

"Yes, sir, with a — minor exception."

"No exception is minor."

"Of course, sir," Hans confirmed. "I only mean that everything is proceeding exactly as you have so skillfully planned. The exception is but an annoyance. One I shall resolve with haste."

Al-Sadir frowned. He knew Hans respected him, but it was

sometimes difficult to hear the truth through the man's constant slathering of praise and acknowledgment. He could never be sure if Hans truly respected him and meant the praise in earnest, or was snidely poking fun at the power dynamic in a form al-Sadir would have trouble reprimanding.

No matter — behind closed doors, in the comfort of his own private space, al-Sadir cared little for what others in his circle of friends and peers cared. He appreciated Hans' loyalty, and that was enough for him.

"What is this 'exception?'" al-Sadir asked. "I cannot have the event delayed for even a second. Our investors will throw a fit."

"Indeed, sir," Hans replied. "No, this is not a big issue. We simply had a minor setback in procuring contestant 9."

"But you *have* retrieved him?"

"Well, sir — not quite yet. But we are on track to bring him in no matter what. When that happens, I will let you know. He will not be as rested as the remainder of the contestants, but all will be accounted for."

"Very good," al-Sadir said. "I am curious — what was the setback? Why are you having trouble retrieving #9?"

Hans swallowed, then nodded, slow to cough up the words. al-Sadir could read on his face that his answer was not going to be satisfactory. "Well, sir, there was another group that... they, well, *intercepted* #9 before your team could reach him."

"Who? And how did they know?"

"We are still working on that, sir," Hans said. "Rest assured; I will have a report for you by the end of the hour. We believe they somehow knew of the event and wanted to warn #9. Whether or not they succeeded in alerting #9 is irrelevant. Contestant 9 will be in our custody soon."

al-Sadir nodded while he stroked the remnants of a dark beard, which he currently kept clean-shaven. The sharp whiskers were even now beginning to poke through his skin. "I see. I expect to have more thorough answers in that report of yours." Again, he phrased the sentence as a command, not a question.

"Of course, sir."

Without another word, Hans turned on a heel and left al-Sadir to his upcoming meeting.

CHAPTER 7
JOSH

KENT ISLAND, *Maryland*

The H7 sang as the electric motor gave Josh Lane everything it had. He waited until the last possible moment, watching the oncoming car's headlights wash through the interior of his car and fill it with an ominous yellow glow. He noticed the two pairs of headlights following behind him, tracking their progress to ensure they would not inadvertently change his plans.

He made his move. He jerked the wheel to the right just as the oncoming sedan pulled into his lane. It was going to be tight, but an impact now would only help his car's progress.

The H7's front-right tire smacked against the curb and bounced upward, and the jolt to Lane's already leering body was massive. He held fast, however, allowing the vehicle to continue its course. He had chosen this section of bridge on purpose, as it was the point where the two suspended cables holding up the concrete platform met on this side of the road and descended to a triangle, with just enough space between them for one car to fit through.

Or so he hoped.

His violent motion had pushed the car up and over the curb, giving the H7 a bit of much-needed air, and he and his multi-million-dollar prototype vehicle flew *over* the low guardrail on the side of the bridge, right between both of the thickly wound steel cables.

It was a perfect shot; he had successfully threaded the needle. The noisy bouncing and jostling suddenly stopped as he was completely airborne, and he made it clear over the edge of the bridge before the H7's front end began turning downward.

The problem was that the *back* end of the H7 had not fully cleared the guardrail. Since he had hit the jump at an angle and the force of the impact of the front two tires on the concrete curb had slowed his acceleration considerably, and now the back-right wheel caught on the guardrail and slammed the base of the car against the edge of the bridge.

He heard the crunching sound of metal grating against the concrete, then the car stopped. He was dangling now, staring almost straight down the two-hundred-foot drop to the wide, black river below.

Josh did not have time to contemplate the situation and prepare for another attack. He saw the wash of lights fill the cabin again, only a second before the impact. The attacking sedan had swerved as well, following his lead, and it now smashed against the backend of his H7.

That did the trick, and his car was now free of the bridge. He felt the sudden sense of weightlessness, and though he had jumped from the back of an airplane hundreds of times during his career as an Air Force CRO, there was nothing like the feeling of being *forced* to fall over the edge of a cliff.

And he had to remind himself that he had never fallen from a height like this without a parachute strapped to his back.

He hoped his grasp of physics would not fail him and turn him into a meat smear on the ceiling of his vehicle.

The silence was intense, broken a few seconds later by Bear's computerized voice. He knew they had work to do in the realm of text-to-speech inflection and emotional resonance, but he could have sworn he sensed a bit of confusion in the AI operator's voice.

"Vehicle impact detected, initiating contact with the nearest emergency response —"

Bear never finished the sentence, nor did he finish his task of reaching out to the fleet of self-driving emergency vehicles that now populated metro areas. Josh had seen the approaching black canvas of water but had not been able to successfully determine his distance to it.

As such, the impact with its surface took him completely by surprise. He felt the cutting tug of the seatbelt against his chest, the liquifying of seemingly every organ inside his body as they shifted and swapped places with one another, felt the pressure behind his eyes as his brain threatened to shoot out the front of his face.

And then it was over. The splashing whitewater churned outside, but for a brief moment he was still, calm, and dry.

It was not long before the water began rushing into the cabin. He felt the chilling wetness on his feet, his socks soaking up as much as they could hold, then the water line rising to his legs.

Before another ten seconds had passed, he was up to his chest in water, and the pressure was pulling the car down quicker and quicker by the minute. He forced his breathing to steady, relying now only on his training and experience in the field, knowing that to lose sight of the end goal would spell certain death.

The water was cold but survivable. He could hold his breath for nearly five minutes under normal circumstances, four in a dicey situation. He estimated he would be good for three-and-a-half in a moment like this, and he needed to allow himself ample time to prepare his lungs.

He took in a heavy breath, then let it out forcefully but slowly. He repeated the process four more times until the only remaining air in the car was directly above his upturned head. He took in a final breath, deeper and wider this time, filling not only his lungs, but also trying to fill every last crevice available to him. He felt his stomach bulging, his neck tightening, his eyes closing. Then, when he thought there was no more room left for air, he sniffed a final burst of fresh air, his nostrils now dangerously close to the surface of the water.

"CO2 levels in the bloodstream are increasing rapidly. Exhalation recommended."

Well, at least NARA's still working, he thought.

He waited only a second to get his bearings. The H7 had sunk almost perfectly flat, so he had not been flipped upside-down. That was important to know, since everything around him was pitch-black. He unbuckled his belt, removed it, and flicked the door handle and pushed it open, the pressure inside and outside the same and thus finding hardly any resistance.

His phone was waterlogged and most likely useless, but he double-checked that it was in his pocket anyway as he slid out of the sinking car. He pushed himself off with his feet, making a horizontal line away from the sedan and staying parallel to the surface.

CHAPTER 8
JOSH

Josh swam for what felt like thirty minutes, but he knew it was actually closer to three. He wanted to get as far away from the sinking H7, both as a way to prevent the attackers up on the bridge from spotting him and as a way to distance himself from the millions of dollars he had just willfully destroyed.

He pulled his head up slightly, knowing that he was going to need a breath soon, but not yet wanting to give away his location. He knew there was little chance they would guess correctly, but there was also the chance they had a powerful light they could use to canvass the water below them. He would be easily visible then.

Therefore he needed to use his skills against them — they likely had no idea how fast he could swim and how long he could hold his breath. He assumed they were also paid mercenaries working for Robert Blake and would not simply give up the hunt.

No, they would stay on the bridge, watching the waters below for at least ten minutes, until they were sure he had drowned. After, they would split up and watch the banks downstream. A few of the smarter soldiers might even head *up*stream, hoping to catch him trying to escape that way.

So Josh had allowed the slight current to carry him along, pushing against it to gain even more speed. He had no idea how far he had traveled, but he pulled his head around and watched the surface, using the few lights from the bridge's lampposts to gauge distance. Finally satisfied, he pulled his head slowly out of the water, just enough to get a deep breath.

The coldness of the water was starting to cool his core, but it was hardly cold enough to cause him any harm, especially if he kept moving. He planned on taking a much deeper breath, calming himself down, and continuing underwater for as long as possible. At the surface, he let out two more long breaths, his lungs ready for the exertion, and plunged his head back down.

He traveled much farther this time, considering he did not have to escape a sinking vehicle, and estimated that he had made a solid half-mile from the bridge when he came up for air the next time.

He saw that the river had narrowed, and houses lined both sides of the waters. A dock was just to his left, and he swam around and found a ladder. He climbed out of the water, immediately feeling colder and starting to shiver once the night air hit his exposed skin. *Thank God it's June,* he thought. He could not imagine how he might feel if it were winter.

He walked up the hill toward the house — thankfully, no lights were on in the windows, and no motion-activated lights illuminated his trespassing. The house was a single-story, small cabin-like building, likely with only a single bedroom inside. He thought about trying to gain access but thought better of it. He did not feel comfortable anywhere near the river. The men would not give up the chase easily, even if their boss was the now-deceased Robert Blake.

He stopped then, considering something. If Robert Blake *had* been their boss, they might have been satisfied letting Josh go — after all, their benefactor's head had been smeared all over the inside of the vehicle, and it was highly unlikely any of them would be paid in full for the botched mission.

On the other hand, he had heard their words *after* Blake had been shot. They needed to "get him back" to somewhere. But where? And if not to Blake — to whom?

Blake might have been their controller, but he was not the person these men intended to bring Josh to.

And where were they going to bring me?

Blake was dead, and the men had immediately shifted gears and decided to bring Josh back somewhere. They had seemed even more eager to complete this task *after* Blake had been killed.

Another thought struck Josh: Blake had been trying to warn him about something. He had told Josh that he could not give him specific details, but that he needed Josh to remember their conversation.

If Blake couldn't give me specifics, why even warn me in the first place? Why was he adamant about speaking with me, yet didn't feel comfortable telling me anything useful?

The mysteries were already starting to stack up, and none of them made Josh feel better about his predicament. He had lost priceless technology his new company had trusted him with, he had been kidnapped on his way home from work, and he had seen a well-respected entrepreneur and technologist killed with a high-powered round.

All because he needed to warn me about something.

He continued walking, more eager than ever to get to a road to wave down a car that might help him get away. He had no plans, no ideas about where he should go. He knew that the first step in a hostile engagement was to get someplace safe, if possible, where he could better assess the situation and his options.

And here, right now, he felt decidedly *unsafe*.

He found a road quickly, and it was thankfully only a mile jog to a wider one that cut east to west through the neighborhood. He started walking along it until he saw headlights in the distance. Without thinking twice, he lifted a thumb and stuck it up and out — a signal that he was looking to hitch a ride.

While the car approached, he felt his phone move in his pocket. Frowning, he pulled it out. He had heard that cellphone technology had made strides toward total waterproof casing over the past decade, but this was still impressive. The device still worked, apparently.

The trouble was that it was completely shattered. Tiny fragments of glass cut against his fingers. He was about to toss the phone away but thought better of it. He needed to get in touch with Molly. She would expect him home at any moment, so there would be no reason for her to be concerned. But he did want to fill her in on what had happened and to make sure she was okay.

But while he could use NARA to message her or use any number of online services to reach out, NARA was not actually a cell phone, and the best way to reach his wife right now was by calling her phone.

He knew he could have NARA interface with the phone, bypassing the need for the phone's screen, but...

As the car slowed, his smile faded. *No, that won't work.* He had not considered that. Sure, since his phone was working properly, he would be able to call Molly, using it and NARA.

But it would *also* allow someone to track him. After leaving active duty service, he had traded in his security-strengthened phone for the most recent technological marvel that featured four cameras, waterproof casing, unbreakable glass — which he had just learned was far from unbreakable — and *always-connected location services*.

And it was that last feature that had him reeling. The car slowed to a halt in front of him, and he was busy looking down at his busted phone, trying to figure out a way around the last issue. He knew the technology inside and out, and he knew for a fact that if it was on, it was connected to at least a cellular tower and three satellites, pinging his device to triangulate his position. But there was another reason anyone with his phone number could reach him while the device was powered on. New, state-of-the-art near-field technology had allowed cellular companies — now down to two main providers and myriad subcontracted regional providers — to create a mesh network of interconnected devices.

What was worse, these companies all shared the devices' radio data amongst themselves, calling each one a "data bridge" that formed a nearly endless network of devices, all silently pinging each other and creating a web of connectivity. In the current world of data streaming, he had never been anywhere on the planet where he *couldn't* find a signal — whether that signal was from a cell tower, a satellite, or a nearby tablet or phone from someone he had never even met.

That was great for NARA and cell phones, but it was terrible if someone wanted to disappear and get off the grid.

The window rolled down, and Josh stepped forward. He felt

even more exposed out of the water now, knowing what this meant. He needed to get inside, to duck and hide away before —

"Need a lift?" a man's voice called out.

Josh nodded, still watching his phone. He knew full well that having his phone on this entire time meant that it had been connected to all the other devices nearby.

And *that* meant whoever had been after him could have easily tracked him through any number of reverse proxy lookups or NFT-based triangulation methods. It would not be something a kid in a basement could pull off, but these guys had been professional.

And someone had died because of it, so Josh knew they were serious.

Shit.

He looked up into the open window, suddenly having second thoughts. He made eye contact with the driver. "I, uh, actually might want to walk," he said. He needed to get away. Needed to think. He could not allow them to find him, but he could not decide whether walking along this road alone was safer than putting himself at the mercy of a driver picking up a hitchhiker.

"Sorry," the driver said. "It wasn't really meant to be a question."

Josh's frown deepened, but it was too late. A small, long-barreled pistol appeared from the back seat of the car, and only then did Josh notice the man holding it in the backseat.

He tensed, preparing to run.

It was too late. The pistol flicked upward, and he heard the gentle popping sound of the tiny detonation.

His mouth fell open, his cell phone landing next to his feet.

The screen's backlight was still on, shining through the spiderweb of cracks.

And then he started falling to the side, his vision blurred, the blood now having trouble coursing through his veins. He felt himself slowing internally while speeding up as his body fell.

NARA tried to say something, to give him an update, but the words were garbled.

He hit the ground just as everything went black.

KENT ISLAND, *Maryland*

Donovan Sloan stared at the superwide monitor on his desk in disbelief. The gently throbbing blue dot of light on the screen showed him that the reading was accurate, but his mind refused to believe it.

He verbally instructed his digital assistant to fire off a message to his coworker, Mitchell Cameron, who was out today, working from home. The assistant replied immediately that the message was sent, her cheerful British accent reminding him that he still needed to change the default AI voice.

Donovan frowned at the computer screen while he waited for his coworker's reply. He needed confirmation from someone else, especially someone who was not physically connected to the internet from Bearbridge's headquarters. Surely connectivity was not the issue — everything else was working properly — but as a career IT guy, he knew not to skip past the issues that were too obvious to be the problem. He could not recall how often a tech issue could be solved by simply unplugging and restarting a device.

But as he waited for his coworker to receive the message and double-check the H7's stated location and respond, he shook his head. He *knew* it was accurate. He had built the positioning module himself, allowing the prototype car to tap into both GPS data streams to triangulate a position *and* borrow bandwidth from the local mesh networks as well as its over-the-air connection. By triple-checking its own location in this way and averaging out any minor discrepancies, the H7's positioning software could pinpoint its location anywhere in the United States down to a single square foot.

Accuracy like this was crucial for production, as car manufacturers in the United States were heavily scrutinized by governmental bodies and had to adhere to strict safety protocols. For a self-driving vehicle, the rules were even more stringent.

As they built out the module and fed it information, it would be able to pinpoint its location in this way throughout the world, no matter where the vehicle was being driven. That was a project Donovan would tackle next year, assuming the H7 made it to market.

But right now, the data stream and the displayed on-screen position of the H7 showed something impossible. Donovan knew there could be a bug in his code, but he was not yet ready to admit defeat and dig into the module's programmatic library.

So what could this mean? The H7 was still broadcasting a signal, but it had not moved in over eight hours. But it was not at Joshua Lane's house, as Donovan expected. Lane was a new hire, a brilliant computer scientist with career military experience, and the H7 had been a proper welcoming gift from Bearbridge. He had been told to keep the vehicle as his own but to pay attention to anything that was not working properly or anything that needed further attention.

Donovan called out to his digital AI assistant once more and asked if it had Lane's number stored in its database.

"Yes, Donovan. I have both a work phone and a cellular mesh-connected phone. Would you like me to contact him?"

"Yes, call his cell. Silence the line until he picks up."

Without verbal confirmation, his assistant connected, and there was a fifteen-second pause. Finally, Lane's voice came over the in-wall speakers. *"You've reached Joshua Lane. I can't get to the phone right now, but please leave a message on —"*

"Disconnect, please," Donovan said. He was already moving on to the next strategy, pulling up a second browser window. This he dragged upward and stuck the window on his second widescreen monitor mounted above the first.

Bearbridge, as a government contractor, had access to military satellite data streams. Since the battle for control of near-orbit space had kicked off, private companies and governments alike had been continuously launching satellites into the sky for years, expanding the mesh connectivity on Earth as well as providing plenty of new video surveillance options for the countries they flew for.

Most of the public had no idea, but the United States could surveil any square mile of the planet's surface in near-real-time immediately after requesting a feed. And as long as the video feed was not requested to show restricted territory or anything the US military deemed off-limits, Bearbridge could access it as well.

Donovan dragged around the map that appeared on the second screen with a free hand, the laser and infrared beacon just beneath his monitor stand catching every motion and translating it to mouse movements. He scrolled and pinched to zoom until he found roughly the same coordinates the H7's positioning module displayed.

He looked at both maps — the feed from the H7's location beacon and the satellite imagery of the same location in real-time — and compared, finally satisfied that they were exactly the same size and position, equally zoomed. The matching images were different only in that one was just an image and had a blue beacon overlaid on it, while the other was a video feed. He saw cars and trucks working their way over the bridge between the island he was on now and the rest of the Maryland coast.

He then browsed through the supplied data streams until he found a timestamp that matched about when Lane had left the office the day before. Clicking it initiated a download and a dialog box alerting him to the fact that he was no longer going to be viewing a live stream.

He accepted, and a few seconds later the video began to play. The software had cropped the satellite's video feed to match the exact specifications Donovan had just set up, and he was now watching a video of the bridge from last evening.

Donovan played back the video at 1.5x speed, then 2x. He stared at the screen for a few more minutes until the timestamp in the bottom-right corner showed the time to be 8:15pm.

Then he pulled his hand over his mouth. *What the hell?*

He watched on-screen as Lane was pulled over and apprehended at gunpoint, then unceremoniously pushed into a black sedan, leaving the H7 behind on the bridge.

The car disappeared off the screen for about ten minutes, but Donovan did not bother to rejigger the video feed and call up another file download. He would track the sedan that had kidnapped Josh later — for now; he wanted to see what had become of the H7.

Another three minutes of high-speed video passed, and the black sedan finally returned to the bridge, only this time heading wildly back in the direction it had come from.

And a tiny figure threw a door open and rolled out onto the road. It was Josh Lane, and he quickly sat up, then pulled himself up and into the H7.

Donovan pulled his hand away from his mouth and double-clicked to zoom in as the man onscreen performed these actions. He verified that it was, in fact, Lane.

He knew that Lane had served in the military, but he had not known the details of it. From what he was watching now, it would appear Lane had been trained as a special forces soldier or in some similar high-intensity field — Donovan didn't know anything about military service, but the physical activity he was watching was surely not something a normal human being could pull off.

The H7 jumped into gear and spun around on the bridge. He watched the video in awe, shock, and a growing sense of terror.

Who the hell did this? And what did they want with Lane?

As if the previous display of physicality was not impressive enough, Donovan watched as the H7 joined in the action, first jumping the curb on the bridge's far side.

And then his breath caught in his throat as the H7 continued its course, flying *over* the side of the bridge and out over the water below.

KENT ISLAND, *Maryland*

Donovan Sloan pushed the small Hyundai sedan to the max. It was a decent car, reliable and safe.

But it lacked the power and acceleration, and he was sorely missing that speed now. He left the office immediately after seeing the video and sending it to his coworker. Cameron had not yet responded, but Donovan was not waiting around.

Josh needs help, he had told himself as he ran down the Bearbridge hallway toward the parking lot. He was no hero, but who else had seen what he had seen? He had to do *something*.

That *something* was still being formed in his mind. He thought of calling the police immediately, but they would want to see video footage, and he was not sure about the repercussions of sending encrypted government satellite footage out of the office — that had been expressly forbidden.

And if he called it in without mentioning the video he had seen, what then? The police would ask him how he knew about a car accident that had happened the night before when Donovan was supposedly not even close to the accident. They would have too many questions for him.

Besides, the William Preston Lane Jr. Memorial Bridge had been closed when he had come to work that morning. Not entirely unusual, as it seemed the bridge was in a perpetual state of disrepair and required reinforcement often. It was not the only way on and off the island where Bearbridge was located, either, nor was it a huge timesaver.

So he had driven over the bridge that intersected with the south side of the island, not giving it much thought until now.

Maybe the police were already there, he realized now. *Maybe that's why the bridge was closed.*

In that case, the police already knew about the H7's disappearance over the edge of the bridge.

So Donovan decided to check into things on his own. He knew Lane's address since his information was shared throughout the office after they had welcomed him to Bearbridge. The higher-ups at the company liked to send gifts to new employees' homes, and Donovan himself had arranged for a "beer of the month" club to be delivered to Lane's home.

He had that address up on his phone now and was navigating through the tight streets of downtown Annapolis, where Lane and his wife Molly had purchased an old house. He drove to their street and turned down it, when his phone rang.

He frowned. *Unknown Caller.* He pulled it up to his ear as he approached Lane's home.

"Hello?"

"Is this Donovan Sloan?" the caller asked.

He swallowed. *This is getting stranger by the second.* "Y — yes, who is this?" he asked.

The caller did not answer his question. *"It has come to my attention that you are investigating the disappearance of Joshua Lane. Is this accurate?"*

The disappearance? "What are you talking about?" he asked.

"I need you to leave the premises immediately. I can't get into the details over the phone, but you must trust me."

"Trust you? Who the hell even *are* you? And how the hell do you know where I am?" Donovan asked.

"Again, I can't get into details, but I need you to get away from the house as soon as possible. Can you do that?"

Donovan pulled the phone away from his ear and stared down at the receiver. *This doesn't make sense. Is this guy following me? And what does Lane have to do with any of it?*

"I hate to break it to you, man," Donovan said, watching the silent house from his side window. "But Lane's dead. I watched his car fly into the river myself. Were you aware of that?"

There was a pause on the other end of the line. *"Where are you right now? Exactly?"*

"I thought you *already* knew exactly where I was," Donovan shot back.

"Which direction are you facing?"

A quick glance toward his rearview mirror confirmed. "Southeast, roughly," Donovan said. "Why? I need some answers, man, before I just trust you to —"

"Start driving. Now!"

Donovan shook his head quickly as if trying to push away a headache. For what had to be the fiftieth time that day, he wondered what the hell sort of game Lane was up to. Who was on the other end of the phone, trying to scare him?

"Move!"

Against his better judgment, Donovan pressed the gas pedal, and the Hyundai sailed into motion toward the next four-way intersection. He moved below the speed limit, not yet wanting to commit to the strange man's request but also not wanting to miss out should the man be trying to help him.

"Where? What is this? What are you trying to —"

"I can fill you in later; just get away from the house!"

"I am! I mean, I did. What the hell is this —"

Donovan did not get a chance to finish the sentence. Before he could react, he saw an oncoming car approaching on his left side as he slid into the intersection.

Approaching *fast*.

And it was speeding up.

It was an SUV, one with blacked-out windows and reinforced steel, but he did not get more than a split-second to examine the vehicle before it collided with the driver-side door and window.

And everything in his world went dark.

CHAPTER 11
LIAM

Shit! Liam Hernandez slammed the phone down onto the top of his desk, a carryover from back when he was a kid. It was a cellphone, so there was no such thing as *actually* slamming a phone down on a receiver anymore, but the violence of it made him feel slightly better.

At least, that's what he told himself.

In truth, he was beyond disappointed and would stay that way until he had another lucky break. What could be luckier than a coworker of Joshua Lane's happening upon information that might lead to the man's whereabouts? And what could be *un*luckier than getting into a car accident outside Lane's house?

Liam had tried to help Joshua Lane's coworker, Donovan Sloan, by getting him away from Lane's house. It was a last-ditch effort, and it had obviously failed. Liam Hernandez had been tracking Lane's position as well and had also lost track of the man after he had driven the car off the bridge.

He stepped back from his standing desk and let out a deep sigh. *Think. Let's go over what we know.*

He knew that the NSA — specifically his division — had been watching Lane for a while now. They wanted to track the man's success, and the brief in front of Hernandez told him that Lane *would* be successful at Bearbridge. He was as brilliant as he was well-trained, in both military strategy and tactics and computing, and he was at the forefront of the industry.

Joshua Lane had been part of a wave of 'forced modernization' confronting the United States military. At first, the different branches had pushed against this modernization, having had a long history of success by maintaining the status quo. Still, eventually, they realized they were getting quietly and consistently beaten by other militaries. To remain number one, the military — top to bottom — was going to have to adapt and grow.

The biggest change needed was a new type of soldier. While special forces teams often had technology specialists on missions, new reports were showing that the most advanced and best-trained soldiers of tomorrow should be able to handle this technological load themselves.

That meant men and women trained to kill, but also able to get into — and out of — any situation they might find themselves in, regardless of the tech. They needed to be able to hack a cellphone, a network, a hard drive, or anything else found in the field of duty, without having to call in another specialist. The best soldiers would be the ones who could program, crack encryption protocols, and steal data while fighting off an onslaught of enemy combatants.

Joshua Lane was a perfect example of this. A man who had the skills of the best operatives, the brain of the nerdiest programmer, and the talent to put it all together on the spot.

And the reason the NSA was watching Lane was simple: the military was not quite ready to tap Lane for service, but they wanted to keep tabs on their asset. Lane was unaware that the United States was as interested in him as they were, and it was Hernandez's job to keep it that way.

At some point in the future, the US government would have a job somewhere in the world where someone with specialties and skills like Lane's would be needed. They needed people like Lane, but they had to keep him at arm's length for now. That had been the impetus behind the birth of Project Echelon — finding the top-tier supersoldiers and brilliant minds that would usher the United States into the future, and then protecting them by placing them strategically in jobs where they could thrive under the radar.

With China and Russia biting at the heels of America's military dominance but arguably already ahead in terms of technological innovation, it was crucial that the US kept its assets secret. Recruiting people like Lane and dropping them into government-sponsored think tanks was like hanging a giant banner over their heads that said, 'I'm valuable to the United States of America.'

A rash of coercive plays by these other countries, and even outright kidnappings on occasion, told the United States that they needed to be far more careful with those they deemed valuable. And with plenty of anti-American groups like ISIS finding success with highly advanced terrorism tactics, they were even more keen to keep their cards close to their chest.

That's where Hernandez's Project Echelon group came in. The NSA department had been tasked with watching a shortlist of military and civilian interests, following their progress with the organizations they worked for, and keeping tabs on their locations, movements, and communications. It was not outright spying since they were not interested in prying into their private lives, but rather a form of secret protection.

Still, no one wanted to be watched. No one deserved to be the focus of the NSA's attention 24/7, so the decision was made to keep these people like Joshua Lane in the dark regarding their own status with the United States government. They would be brought up to speed if and when it was necessary to recruit them to an overt government interest project.

Hernandez, for his part of Project Echelon, had made all of this tracking and observation easy, automating much of it with scripts and AI tools that simply alerted him to Lane's movements if Lane did something out of the ordinary. And since the man was working for Bearbridge, a government contractor, Hernandez already had easy access to the company's files and projects database. He knew what Lane's tasks and jobs were to be with his new employer, and he knew the direct coworkers he would be surrounded by each day.

Bearbridge, being a tech company first and foremost, still had tightly guarded secrets, Liam was sure. There were databases and folders on their network drives that Liam still had not gained access to. He could send any number of hackers and technicians to work on that problem — or just march in with an NSA-sanctioned military presence and demand access — but he was happy with the information he currently had.

Joshua Lane had not been at Bearbridge long enough to get involved in anything deeply secretive, Liam thought. The company was friendly with the US government, and he did not suspect any foul play or "double dipping" by selling research to America's enemies.

A casual, mildly interested watchful eye would be enough to keep tabs on Bearbridge and Josh's involvement with them.

But he had been instantly alerted when Lane had been kidnapped from the car on his way home from work the night before. Hernandez had acted quickly, alerting his team as to Lane's status, which had launched an official NSA briefing, but Hernandez's job had been simply to watch and listen. To find Lane or anyone he thought might know where Lane was going to be taken.

That was why Hernandez had found Donovan Sloan snooping on Lane's location. He had been innocently examining the marked location of Lane's prototype vehicle when he realized that Lane, too, had gone off the bridge. Taking matters into his own hands — much to the dismay of Hernandez — Sloan had raced to Lane's house just as Hernandez got an alert from one of his AI trackers.

Someone else was on their way to Lane's house.

The AI had told Hernandez that it was very likely one of the same group who had kidnapped Lane, and that they could be heading to Lane's house to retrieve Lane's personal items or computers, but it didn't matter. Hernandez knew that Sloan was putting himself in a dangerous spot.

He had tried to warn Sloan, and the man had eventually listened. But it was now too late — they weren't just on their way to Lane's house; they were there to prevent anyone *else* from snooping around. The small Hyundai would have stood no chance against the SUV, and Hernandez was already working on the satellite feeds that would prove it.

Sloan had been in the wrong place at the *very* wrong time, and now he had paid the price.

Hernandez stepped back up to his standing desk and took another long, slow breath. *Do the job,* he told himself. *The job was never supposed to be easy. But you have to do it.*

He *did* have to do it. It was not easy, and rarely fun, but he was good at it. Bad people were stopped every day by good people like Liam Hernandez, and countless lives were saved every time his job was successful. He did not know where these people had taken Lane, nor what they wanted with him, but he *absolutely* would find out.

It was his job.

CHAPTER 12

AL-SADIR

HULHUMALÉ COAST, *Maldives*

The peaceful day had shifted to an equally peaceful night, and al-Sadir lifted the glass of bourbon to his lips and took a long sip. Officially, he did not drink — he was Muslim, after all — but unofficially, especially in the comfort of his own home, he did whatever he wished.

And American bourbon was a favorite of his. The irony of it was not lost on him. Bourbon was as American as George Washington, Elvis Presley, and the Dallas Cowboys. His hatred for America — for what it stood for and represented — ran deep, but that did not change his love of the sweet, corn-laden taste of the dark alcohol.

In fact, he maintained an inventory of the booze in the lower-level smoking room of his yacht. Most of his entertaining happened on the upper levels, where the views and open-air seating added to the luxury and impressiveness. But on occasion, when meeting with a dignitary not swayed by al-Sadir's displays of richness or his outward religious motives, al-Sadir often invited them belowdecks to the more private, classier chamber.

There, he had on offer any number of fine spirits and liqueurs, as well as a cigar selection that would have impressed Fidel Castro. But his secret favorite, and the spirit he made sure was always in stock, was bourbon.

And he had no qualms about imbibing in the finer products of American industry — it was the people and the mindset he hated. The same mindset had pervaded his homeland and much of the Middle East.

The mindset that he had sworn to eradicate.

He smiled as he pulled the drink away from his lips and watched his assistant, Hans, enter the room.

"Sir, the update you requested."

al-Sadir nodded and checked his watch. *Right on time.* "Of course. Thank you."

"Contestant #9 was apprehended after a brief... skirmish."

"You mentioned this in your emailed report earlier. Does this update now mean we are back on track?"

Hans nodded. "Yes. The contestant was flown to the briefing location, where he was washed and clothed, then dropped into the cell for the —"

"Room. Dropped into his *room.*"

"Yes, of course. Sorry, sir. There, he was placed on the bed in his room and is currently sleeping soundly, with the help of some drugs."

"Quite a lot of activity for a contestant, especially considering the scope of this game," al-Sadir said, the smile on his face widening. He was pleased with Hans' work but not at all surprised. Hans was as good as they came.

"Well," Hans said. "He is a gifted candidate. Military experience seems to overtake his better judgment."

al-Sadir thought he glimpsed the briefest flashes of a smile on his assistant's face.

"Anyway," Hans continued, "I am very pleased with my team. They have performed well, and I look forward to the event's start tomorrow morning."

"As do I, my friend," al-Sadir said. "Have you found Ruth Dalia?"

For the last week, al-Sadir's team had had a terrible time trying to track down the woman behind Bearbridge Associates, the company employing Joshua Lane. Hans had a wonderful network on land, but if the woman had chosen to commute over international waters — taking a play out of al-Sadir's own playbook — she would be almost impossible to track down until she returned to civilization.

He knew full well that it could be tomorrow or three months from now.

"No, sir," Hans said. "I apologize. My team is still looking, but they are stretched thin with *Eden* about to kick off."

al-Sadir nodded. He was frustrated, as they *needed* that woman. It would make everything so much easier. But he did not blame Hans. There was only so much Hans' team could do, and the man was right — the games were the most important priority.

"Okay, understood. Please do not hesitate to retrieve her when she is found," he said. "Do not bother alerting me if it means you can save five seconds."

Hans nodded.

"Are there any further preparations needed before tomorrow's opening ceremonies?"

There was a quick pause, and al-Sadir knew Hans was running down the list of tasks and details required of him and his security team, not wanting to give an inaccurate answer. "No, sir," he said. "I believe everything is accounted for, and our live team stands by. Would you like me to confirm with the program director?"

al-Sadir shook his head. "No, thank you, Hans. I'll check in with Fatima myself, though she will likely ignore my call." He chuckled. "She truly is as professional as you, Hans — addicted to her work. Right now, she will be setting up the viewing hall for our VIP guests."

"It is not an addiction, sir, but a love for the mission."

al-Sadir laughed again. "You know, I can never tell if you are humoring me or just overzealous."

Hans looked pained, but he did not respond.

"I'm joking, Hans," al-Sadir said, rising from his chair. "We have worked together for how long now?"

"Five years, sir, and eleven more before that for your father."

al-Sadir swallowed and dismissed his assistant and head of security.

My father.

If ever there was a man of contradiction, it was his father. An otherwise great man, respected in the energy community and revered by commoners and sheiks alike, al-Sadir's relationship with his old man had been fraught with frustration.

He had built a massive empire of oil stocks and futures, as well as hard business interests in the energy sector, all with the expectation that his eldest son, al-Sadir, would one day assume his throne. When al-Sadir expressed interest in branching out into interests other than energy, his father had reluctantly agreed, sending al-Sadir to the best university in Dubai to get a business degree.

When al-Sadir had returned only a decade ago, ready to prove his worth and show his father that he was ready to take over, his father had balked, hoping al-Sadir would simply babysit the family fortune until his father's death. Never one to be satisfied in the shadows, al-Sadir — at the age of twenty-four — promptly reapportioned some of his father's funds into a new business interest for the family: reality television.

He had paid a few million dollars to a local Dubai production company to film a pilot for a show that he hoped would become the next great reality tv sensation — a live talent show that would capture the hearts and minds of not just the United Arab Emirates but all of the Middle East — and potentially the world.

The show had been an abysmal failure, and his father had never let him live it down.

But al-Sadir was as stubborn as he was driven, and motivated by the failure where most others would have been shamed and come crawling back home. Instead, al-Sadir stole more of his father's money, this time using it to build an investment company that spread the assets around many reality television products and opportunities rather than just one.

And he had been smart about it this time around, using his savvy mind and newfound business brilliance to pay dividends right back into the account he had stolen from so that his father — at first — would be none the wiser.

But by the time the business had taken off a year later and his father had discovered this second indiscretion, al-Sadir knew better than to ask for forgiveness. He had shown his father that the future of their country — of their way of life — was to separate from the hold of energy and oil and embrace the one good thing the West had created: innovation.

His culture was one of tradition, of religious zealotry and age-old belief systems that moored countries like his to the past. But the western ideal of innovation at any cost was one that he understood intuitively — it was the one innovation that had locked his country into a permanent song-and-dance with extracting oil from the ground and selling it to the highest bidder. The ability of Western civilization to innovate was paid for by the oil sucked out of the ground beneath his homeland, and his countrymen could not care less — they were happy to use the money to turn their deserts into more and more extravagant and lavish overtures to oil.

Cities that flaunted the latest and greatest in architectural prowess were still powered by the energy refined from the region's fossil fuels. Advanced tech, found in every citizen's hand and home, was still pieced together by plastic molds — a product of oil — and powered by the same batteries charged by power plants.

The Western pull of technology was addictive, and one al-Sadir had learned to wield as a weapon. It was power — literally — and he had become its most practiced apprentice.

His father had not been pleased with al-Sadir's strange and counter-cultural behavior — and certainly not pleased that his son had taken it upon himself to spend part of his fortune on frivolous endeavors — and al-Sadir found himself in a position of choosing status quo over future possibilities.

For al-Sadir, it was a no-brainer. He had never gotten along with his father, and the man had abused al-Sadir's mother and siblings most of his life. He had watched his father treat his mother like some part-time whore, nothing but a sex slave and cook. And in their culture, she had no voice — no ability to advocate for herself.

al-Sadir had thought he had been too young to do much about it, and suddenly one day, it was too late. His mother died from a stomach infection. His father had refused to bring her to the hospital for fear that the doctors and nurses would find her bruises and scars that had most definitely *not* been caused by the infection.

al-Sadir was nineteen at the time.

He enrolled in business school, keeping his father at arm's length but not yet ready to sever the ties completely. He needed the man's money and power, and when he finally graduated with a graduate degree in economics and international business, he was ready.

He had been surprised at how cheaply one could hire a professional hitman. It was only a matter of months after his father confronted him about his second theft of millions of dollars from his account when his father was found dead in his study — a heart attack that left no clues as to the actual cause of death.

And just like that, his father's interests passed into al-Sadir's name, a simple clerical matter since the older man's assets were all part of al-Sadir's eventual inheritance.

al-Sadir became one of the wealthiest men under the age of thirty in his country. And in a country with some of the wealthiest men on the planet, that was an impressive feat. He had gotten to work immediately, selling the useless vacation homes and villas around the world and consolidating his power into shell companies all run from his new yacht. He severed ties with the UAE so as not to owe as much in taxes each year, but he still paid his fair share to keep the government off his back.

Hans, like a good soldier, followed the power and remained loyal to him. If he had ever suspected that al-Sadir had paid to have his father killed, he never spoke of it. He ran a tight ship for al-Sadir, keeping the many plates spinning between physical security and scheduling. al-Sadir had many other assistants who helped in specific fields, but there was no one besides Hans who knew all of the inner workings of al-Sadir's life and business.

He reflected on the excitement that was to come tomorrow morning — the kickoff event would be spectacular, as always. Perhaps flashier than he preferred, but he knew the VIPs did not share his love of subtlety and restraint. They had fronted most of the money for this event, and — like the other events he had run in the past for other sectors — he knew that keeping the VIPs happy was priority number one.

Satisfied he had everything under control, al-Sadir walked over to the bar across from him and poured himself a refill. The smell was as intoxicating as the actual taste, and his mouth watered as he sealed the bottle once again.

Yes, he thought, *tomorrow is going to be a fantastic day.*

PART TWO

CHAPTER 13

JOSH

LOCATION *unknown*

Josh gasped and sat up. Or rather, *tried* to sit up. His lungs heaved, but every breath only brought pain and a little air. He struggled to force his eyes to adjust to the dim light, then noticed the dry, stale air encircling his body.

Air that was decidedly *not* the air from Baltimore.

"NARA, ping any listening devices. What's our GPS signal, in longitude/latitude?"

There was no response.

He squinted, frowning into the darkness as he tried to piece together anything related to the past few hours.

Or days.

In truth, he had no idea what time it was or where he was. *What happened?*

"NARA," he started again, *"what time is it? And what day?"*

Still, the computer was silent.

He remembered driving home... the H7 playing the old television show on the HUD in front of him.

The cars following him.

He gasped again as recognition finally hit. He *hadn't* been dreaming — those cars had stopped him, pulled him from the prototype vehicle at gunpoint, and shoved him into a backseat, where he had met Robert Blake, founder of the world-changing company *Aetheria.*

And then...

He tried not to recall the next part of the scene, but his mind wanted to go there. Against his well-trained conscious thought, his brain pulled up images of the man's gruesome murder. He saw the exploded head on the seat, the torso slumped over...

What the hell is this?

Josh reached out, feeling his surroundings to hopefully jump-start the recollection of what had happened *after* Blake had been shot and killed. He felt a bed — he was laying on it, the sheets still tucked tightly around its edges. A thin, useless pillow separated his back from the wall.

And the walls themselves — they were as strange as the fact that he was here in the first place. They were made of stone, but not natural. Ceramic, or something similar? He touched them. They were cool, with tiny veins of copper-tinged lines running through them. They formed a pattern not unlike a circuit board, moving in parallel lines that turned at curved ninety-degree angles.

He ran his hand along a row of these lines, still frowning as he worked to piece things together, but stopped as his arm extended fully, not yet wanting to get out of bed.

Then the memory of driving the H7 off the edge of the bridge and down into the river came crashing back to him like, well, a crash. He jolted further upright, his eyes wide. *I really did that,* he thought.

He tried to pull up the feelings and thought processes he had experienced during that split-second decision — a part of his early mission debrief training he still found helpful, especially after stressful experiences.

The fact that he was alive meant he had chosen his course of action well. But the fact that he had not, in fact, escaped whatever threat he thought still existed meant that he had failed.

But where was he now? NARA was not responding. He felt behind his head, felt the lump of hard material living inside his skin, and sighed. He almost felt relieved, but was saddened again when NARA still did not respond to his request.

They've disabled NARA. Does that mean they know about it? Why not take it out completely if that were the case? he wondered.

He had no idea who could have done this or how they would have managed it. The Bearbridge team that had given him the surgery to install NARA could not be involved — most of them had not even known what it was. The surgeon himself had confessed to Josh that he had been hired, like a contractor, to install some sort of device near the base of Josh's skull. He had laughed and jokingly referred to it as 'the ultimate tracking device.'

The only person who knew the entire story behind Josh's involvement with Bearbridge and why he had *been hired was Bearbridge's CEO,* Ruth Dalia. And since the surgery, he had not even had a conversation with the woman, as she was off yachting around the world on her luxury cruiser.

He risked putting a foot and leg over the side of the bed and pressed down. He felt the same cool, copper-traced surface that covered the wall behind him, so he pulled another leg over and stood.

He was in decent health — he had not been in this bed longer than a day or two, he guessed. He was neither hungry nor thirsty, though he knew his physiology psyche could easily mask that in favor of using his mind's resources to assess his new situation. If he were truly hungry or thirsty, he would know after his curiosity was quelled.

Josh took a few steps to the side and found another wall, then turned and faced a matching wall on the opposite side of the bed. The far wall — if he could honestly call it that — was a few feet from the end of the queen-sized bed. He guessed the room to be perfectly square, about ten feet on all sides and perhaps eight feet high. The ceiling, like all the walls and floor, looked to be made of the same material.

What the hell is this place? he thought. *Where am I?*

He was too busy examining the walls and the strange copper substance running throughout each that he did not at first notice the screaming voice at the back of his mind. When he finally stopped for a moment to listen in, he let his hand drop, stunned.

It wasn't NARA. It was his own psyche.

Something had been nagging at him ever since he had opened his eyes. His subconscious had noticed it immediately, but it logged the information away from either not believing it to be true or simply allowing itself to be more interested in other things.

But now Josh was paying attention, and he verified that his subconscious had been accurate.

There's no door.

He walked across the room and pressed his hands against the cool ceramic far wall. Just like all the others, it was smooth, cool to the touch, and had no markings or cracks or any other hints that there was a door hidden within it.

He knew that was impossible — he had to have gotten in here *somehow* — but he allowed his subconscious to have this small victory. He was trapped inside, and for whatever reason, his captors did not want even the hint of escape.

He knew his heart was beating faster than normal already, but he worked to slow its acceleration. No use working himself up; no use triggering anxiety when cooler heads would prevail.

Still, this was quite the predicament. He could not remember the last few hours — perhaps even the last entire *day* — of his life, and now he was in some strange, alien room with no doors or windows. It was as if it had been built around him while he slept.

There were other worries creeping up in his mind as well. Namely, his wife, Molly, had been expecting him at home. She would be worried, likely frantic if he did not even return her calls after not showing up at home.

With a quick brush against his pants, he confirmed exactly what he had suspected. Whoever had locked him in here had stolen his cell phone as well. He was not surprised by that, but he was surprised to see that his pants were *not* the same ones he had been wearing in the H7.

His entire wardrobe had changed. Now he was in shiny silk underpants — ridiculous in every way, and something he normally would not have been caught dead wearing — and well-fitted sweatpants that almost looked like jeans. They stretched and gave the feeling of weightlessness. Comfortable, he had to admit.

The shirt he was in fit him like a glove. It was a synthetic material, but nothing special. Long sleeves fell to his wrists, and he pushed these up past his elbows as he began pacing the cell.

That's what this is, he realized. *A cell. I've been imprisoned. But for what?*

He walked a complete circle — albeit a very small one — at the foot of his bed when something on the wall to his right caught his eye. A rectangular shape of light suddenly filled in a space on the wall.

He had never seen anything like it, though the tech had been theorized in some of his engineering circles. It was a screen, living just beneath a surface of glass, carved meticulously of whatever material the rest of the wall was made of. The effect was that of a television built behind a mirror in a hotel room — when it was off, it was impossible to see. When it was on, however, the image was as clear as the most modern high-definition television sets on the market.

It was far smaller, more in line with a computer monitor, but every bit as sharp.

He ran toward it, basically jumping a single long stride until he was face-to-face with the screen. It was lighting and dimming in procession, like an extended loading screen for an operating system.

Finally, the screen shifted to a slightly dimmer setting than the brightest it had been a moment ago, and he read the words that formed on it. They were written in all caps but with a refined and thoughtful serif font, as if the messenger was trying to put him at ease.

WELCOME, CONTESTANT #9.

CHAPTER 14
LIAM

NSA HEADQUARTERS | FORT MEADE, *Maryland*

It was a long walk to the opposite side of the building and up three flights of stairs, but Liam Hernandez knew it was worth the extra steps. A memo or email simply would not do, and besides — he could use the exercise.

Not to mention the fact that his boss, Colonel Roger Sykes, had called the meeting and expected it to start precisely on time.

Colonel Sykes had informed Hernandez late last night that he wanted to meet with him regarding the information he had found on Joshua Lane, and he wanted to have that meeting *promptly* at 0815 the next morning.

Colonel Sykes had *not* mentioned the fact that tomorrow was Saturday.

It seemed others in the building had also received similar time-sensitive, weekend-insensitive invites to meetings as well, or Hernandez was simply seeing what it meant to be driven, ladder-climbing workaholics. Every other office he passed on the way to

Colonel Sykes' seemed to be lit up, the occupant inside working feverishly.

Thankfully most of Hernandez's job could be successfully done from home, and he often did just that, so he did not fear reprimand for 'only' working a standard 9-5 throughout the week. He could log in securely through a special VPN he and his coworkers had set up, at least to take care of non-security-related or clearance-denied issues.

Hernandez reached Sykes' office and saw the area buzzing with activity. Apparently, no one else had gotten the memo that government organizations were supposed to be *off* on Saturdays, but he said nothing as he passed the desk of one of Sykes' assistants.

"Mr. Hernandez," the young man called out as he passed. He rose to meet him as Hernandez slowed down, finally pinpointing the person the words had fallen out of.

"Uh, hi — yeah, that's me."

"Great. Colonel Sykes is just finishing up with the President. He'll meet you right after. Feel free to have a seat."

Hernandez kept his face passive as if saying, *sure, just the President.* But his mind was reeling. *Why the hell is he meeting with the President? And why on Saturday? Surely the President has other things to do today, like play golf, shake hands, and —*

He was rudely interrupted from his own thoughts by Colonel Sykes' voice. "Hernandez — you here?"

He turned and saw the burly, dry-aged beef slab of a man staring at him from halfway out of his office. He nodded, pushed the glasses up his nose, and stuttered out a few unintelligible words.

Thankfully Sykes did not hear or care, and he turned on a

military-grade heel and strode back into his office, apparently not one to repeat orders *or* to wait to see if they had been received.

He got no further feedback from the shiny hipster assistant, who was already fake-smiling into a calendar app on his computer screen. Liam walked over to the colonel's office and stepped inside.

"Tell me about Joshua Lane," the colonel began, without so much as a preamble. "You saw a satellite feed that showed his location?"

Liam chose his words carefully. "I have not verified Lane's position, but I have evidence from his new employer that he was, in fact, inside the vehicle."

"As in Bearbridge, 'his new employer.'

Liam nodded. "Yeah, he started there a few —"

"I know that; I'm just surprised. I've been trying to track down his employer's location — specifically Ruth Dalia, their CEO — and none of my assistants have found anything yet. Glad you were able to get *somewhere*, I guess."

"Right," Liam said, still not sure if he was being congratulated or berated. "What do we want with Dalia? I thought Lane was the missing person."

"He is, but I'm just casting the net wider earlier. This stuff you found about him — you trust the evidence?" the colonel asked.

"I do," Liam said. "Bearbridge is in good standing generally, so we have no reason to suspect foul play. Plus, the satellite data was accessed by one of their own employees first, then he went to Lane's house to check on him."

"That's when you intervened," Colonel Sykes said. It was not a question.

Liam winced. "Yes, sir. I was trying to keep him safe — he was an innocent man, and had no reason to be involved in a situation like this."

"A situation like what?" the colonel asked quickly.

Liam knew the man was playing mind games with him, but he was in no position to argue or protest. "A situation like going to a coworker's house and getting blind-sided by an SUV hauling ass through a stop sign."

At this, the colonel actually smiled, his widow's peak scrunching up as he did. There was a long pause before the colonel continued. "Look, Hernandez, I'm not trying to bust your balls. I know you were a hell of an analyst, and your accomplishments here make most of your employees look like bumbling fools. And they're all bringing a genius-level intelligence to the table, so you can do the math."

Liam took the compliment with a simple nod and thank you.

"But I do need to nip this in the bud early before it gets blown wide open. Right now, it's us trying to track him down, and that's it. If any of the overzealous asshats in the CIA get wind of Lane and what he's capable of, this is going to be a clusterfuck."

"What he's capable of?" Liam asked.

"Yeah, his background alone makes him a very valuable patriot to *keep* on our side. Add to that he's got an IQ that matches what I see when I jump on a scale, and now he's caught up in whatever Bearbridge's top-secret project is."

This little tidbit was news to Liam. "They've got a top-secret project going on? With us?"

He knew it was common practice for government entities to partner with cutting-edge tech companies to provide plausible deniability — and reap all the rewards — of a project, but he had not known Bearbridge was engaged in one currently.

"Not us, specifically, but *someone*."

Liam sensed that this was all he was going to get from the director of his organization.

Sykes confirmed this by continuing in another direction. "What do you know about Lane's background? Specifically, why Bearbridge was so keen to get him on board that they gave him a million-dollar ride *and* a million-dollar salary?"

Liam cleared his throat. "Well, sir, I know Bearbridge is one of the US government's preferred contractors for military automotive tech. I know they're pushing the boundary in artificial intelligence and neural network algorithmic enhancement."

"Go on."

"And they say they're working on quantum computing, but I'm not entirely sure how. I do know that Lane's Air Force career as a parajumper-turned-computer-scientist means he's exceptionally gifted and well-trained in computing. My guess is that there's more than a little quantum computing knowledge on his menu of skills as well, and that's why Bearbridge was interested."

The colonel smiled again, and Liam felt himself softening toward the man. He had not spent much time with the man, as his department was considered self-sustaining and mostly autonomous and Sykes — to his credit — hated to micromanage, but he had heard stories: the colonel treated everyone around him like they were in the military. He expected results, hated excuses, and suffered no fools.

But the man in front of him now seemed to also be a wise, empathetic man, who enjoyed Liam's sense of humor. Perhaps Liam's reputation had softened the colonel first, and his boss was just doling out a bit of uncharacteristic preferential treatment.

"Everything you've said is accurate," Colonel Sykes said. "And your inference is top-notch, as I expected. Lane *was* working on quantum computing arrangements for Bearbridge. Specifically placement and treatment of qubits."

"So Project Echelon really is useful? Not just something to keep us all busy?"

"Sometimes I wish it were that simple, Hernandez," the colonel said. "But no. It's decidedly *not* simple. Project Echelon is not only real and crucial to the NSA's bottom line, it's caught the interest of the President himself."

"No shit."

"No shit," the colonel said. "He and I spoke just before you came in. I told him that Joshua Lane was nabbed, and that we're still trying to figure out by whom and where he is now. But he confirmed that while he can't yet redirect any military resources toward finding him, he's standing by for when you and your team locate him and have a plan of attack for getting him back."

Liam could not hide his surprise. "Sir? Me — my team?"

"Project Echelon."

"Yes, but sir, it's currently —"

"Currently not an official project, with a lead and budget?"

Liam nodded.

"I'm about to change that. No more 'keeping tabs' in your spare time. As of right now, I'm making this your number one — actually number *only* — priority. And I'm putting you in charge of the group. Project Echelon is yours. You've got the skillset, experience, and just the right amount of outside-the-box thinking to know it'll be one of the best calls I've made all year."

"Thank you, sir."

"I have every reason to suspect that I'll be pleasantly surprised by your success. But I'll be watching closely. The president made it clear that Lane's location and retrieval is a matter of national security, so unfortunately, you're going to have a bit of chain-of-command bullshit to deal with."

"That's fine, sir," Liam said. "I'm happy to have the oversight."

The colonel outright laughed at this. "Don't bullshit a master, son. Even though I can't stand it, I speak bullshit fluently. Adding someone like me into the mix is only going to slow things down. But I give you my word; I believe you're the right man for the job, and with that trust in your leadership comes absolute trust in your methods. The only time I'll intervene is when I have information I think you'd like to hear."

"I see. Again, thank you, sir. I truly appreciate it."

Colonel Sykes paused, looking down at his computer and back up at Liam. "On that note," he began, "I just might have something interesting for you."

"I'm all ears," Liam said.

LOCATION *unknown*

Josh stared at the screen, not believing what he was seeing.

Contestant 9? What is this, some type of game show?

He strode across the tiny room once more, trying for a moment to ignore this strange computer monitor and once again see if there was a way out. Since the screen had appeared seemingly from out of nowhere, perhaps there was a new door or window that had appeared on one of the walls as well.

Of course, no new access points had shown up in the last few seconds — the walls were still as sealed as they had been the moment he had awoken. He stepped back over to the screen, this time leaning in toward it a bit more.

Suddenly a horizontal slot opened beneath the makeshift screen, and a thin tray slid out toward him. He frowned as a full-size computer keyboard, complete with a number pad and half-height keys, lit up on the tray.

Okay, this is getting weirder and weirder.

He had no other choice. He placed his wrists up on the tray, testing the keyboard's responsiveness. The butterfly-style mechanics felt natural to him, and the height of the tray was perfect for a standing desk arrangement.

He shook his head quickly, as if tossing away any idea that he might be complimenting his quarters. He did not want to get used to this — he wanted to figure out what the hell it was all for.

The keyboard's backlight throbbed gently, emanating a glow in a color that perfectly matched the typeface of the words on the screen. Josh stood in front of the screen, typing a few words here and there both to test the keyboard and to pass the time. He could not help but consider the fact that every time he had explored this room, one of its secrets had been revealed to him.

Surely it couldn't hurt to type a bit, just to see what might happen?

The screen dimmed, and the words disappeared, a moment later replaced by new words. A list:

1. *Food*

2. *Water*

3. *Exit*

Josh pulled his hands back and placed them over the back of his head, a longtime tic of his when his mind was working to piece something together. He interlocked them, then rubbed his fingers through his short hair, massaging his scalp and urging his mind to put the pieces together.

He smiled. *Surely it can't be that easy, right?*

He removed his hands and placed them once again on the pop-out keyboard tray. He waited for a few seconds, still trying to analyze the message on the screen, as short and simple as it appeared to be. Specifically, he looked for intent — like all computer programs, some human being had programmed this application, whatever it was. They had created the *if-then* loop or logic function that led to this specific message, and they had programmed it in the exact language he was seeing here now.

He had to admit it *did* seem a bit too simple.

He spoke aloud. "I guess... *exit.* I'd like to get the hell out of here. As he spoke, he tapped the 3 on the numpad and waited.

At first, nothing happened, and he wondered if he needed to give the input a return or 'enter' to solidify his choice. But before he could even hover his finger over to that key, the screen dimmed, and the words faded out.

A second later, the same message he had seen earlier reappeared.

WELCOME, CONTESTANT #9.

He chuckled. "Well, it was worth a shot." He had wanted to exit the *room* he was trapped in, of course, but the program or applet or whatever he had been interacting with had given him the choice of exiting that particular *menu.*

Testing that theory, he started typing his name on the keyboard. The program did not care what he typed; as soon as he struck the second key, the menu appeared once again:

1. Food

2. Water

3. Exit

"All right, all right," he said softly, unable to help himself from conversing with the machine. He couldn't do it silently as he could with NARA, but he had taken to the idea of conversing with his machines. "Okay, you outsmarted me. Probably knew I would try to be clever. But are you hiding any other little secrets? Like, maybe where I could find a *door?*"

Of course, nothing happened after the verbal cue, so he tested one of the other two options besides *exit*. He pressed the number 2 on the numpad, and he heard a tiny latch clicking to his right.

His eyes flicked over to the area just as another small section of the ceramic wall opened. This was a square section, and a flap of the wall on a hinge fell forward and down, stopping at ninety degrees from where it had begun. Then a snakelike, semi-opaque tube fell out a few inches.

"You have got to be shitting me," Josh said. The end of the tube held a spigot nozzle, the kind found on the lids of some sports drinks. He walked over to it and gently tugged at the hose.

It pulled out about a foot, and he leaned down a bit and put his lips over the nozzle. He sucked in, and ice-cold water immediately hit the inside of his mouth. It was clear, delicious, and — as much as he hated to admit it — it hit the spot.

He drank for almost a minute, going slowly so as not to make himself sick, feeling the dehydration his mind had been hiding from him appear and then immediately start to wane. He drank until he was sufficiently full, then released the straw. Ten more seconds passed, the hose retracted itself into its miniature cubby, and the square top lifted back into place with a final click.

"Got it," Josh said. "I'm a hamster in a cage — I drink from a water spigot and do tricks for your enjoyment." He spun a full circle in the small space at the foot of his bed. "Mind telling me exactly who *you* are, though? Hello?"

He waited. Nothing. He let out a sigh, then walked back over to the computer. He hoped to find out if the food selection in this prison was as refined and tasty as the water had been, but he would not have been surprised if, continuing the "hamster on a wheel" theme, the food slot would only drop massive sunflower seeds onto the floor.

But before he reached the computer terminal, the screen shifted and morphed another time.

This time, however, it was not words that appeared on the screen but a *person*.

A man's face appeared in front of him on the computer monitor. *"Hello, contestants,"* he suddenly heard blare out from hidden speakers, the words perfectly matching the movement of the man's mouth. *"Welcome to Eden."*

NSA HEADQUARTERS | FORT MEADE, *Maryland*

Liam waited as Colonel Sykes prepared to launch into the second phase of their meeting. He sensed the information Sykes had was delicate, as the older gentleman walked over to the door again and double-checked that it was closed. To further sell the importance of the next thing he was about to say, he actually closed the blinds on the floor-to-ceiling window next to the door.

He gave a quick glance around the room, as if to ensure there were no cartoon villains hiding behind a fake potted plant, and then he let out a long sigh.

"What do you know about Eden?" the colonel asked Liam.

Hernandez squeezed his eyebrows together. "I'm guessing you don't mean the biblical home of Adam and Eve," he said.

"I do not. No, I'm referring to *Escape from Eden*, the, uh... television show."

"That game show that's not actually watchable anywhere?" Liam asked. "It's streamed via a dark net service that's only available to a few with a very specific dedicated IP address."

"Yes, that one."

"Well — that's about all I know, sir," Liam said. "It's more a rumor than a fact. Guys downstairs sort of joke about it, like it's some sadistic television show for the super-rich, yet it's also somehow defied government espionage efforts to hack. Most people I've talked to don't even think it exists."

Of course, most people don't seek out entertainment options on the dark web, either.

Liam had heard a few people mention it, mostly in the same breath as other Internet-based conspiracies, like the Dead Internet Theory, in which some people believed that the internet as it currently existed was effectively 'dead.' That no new human-generated information had actually been added to the web for some number of years, and most of what humans interacted with on social media sites was artificial intelligence-created content or social updates written by bots.

The rumor was, of course, absurd, but it gave Liam and folks like him — people with a knack for problem-solving, a keen intelligence in the technological and networking realm, and a stressful day job — something to laugh about at lunch.

The *Escape from Eden* theory was similar. Apparently, there was a television show that pitted people against one another, trying to solve puzzles or something. No one could corroborate the claims one way or another, but some of the more conspiracy-intrigued pockets of the internet population said that those behind it were a sinister group with bigger plans, and that only the world's elite were invited to watch it. No one knew *how* they watched it, of course, but there were theories.

One such theory was elegant in its simplicity: that the producer of the show sent out a link directly to the viewers they wanted to invite, and the link would only work from their IP address. While simple, it was also fraught with problems. The world's most wealthy individuals did not happen to be the most *computer-savvy* individuals — surely someone would have accidentally let one of these links slip.

Another theory was that the viewing of the show took place only in person, in protected and isolated chambers that the viewers were invited to. This theory was more plausible, but it still left holes and made Liam think the entire idea of a secret reality show was too far-fetched to be true.

And no matter what, the traditional web — the Internet most people were familiar with — only postulated theories. No actual hard evidence of such a show — real or staged — had been found. Liam knew there was an entirely *different* web, accessible by the more tenacious web browsers, called the Dark Web. It was possible this *Escape from Eden* show could be there somewhere floating around, but it had never interested him enough to research it.

But Colonel Sykes was no fool. The fact he had mentioned it meant something. "I hate to be blunt, sir," Liam said, "but I have a hard time believing something like this could even be true."

Sykes smiled, but it did not reach his eyes. "I do, as well. And yet, in all the years I've served this country both overseas and from the comfort of my own office, I've seen some things that I *wish* couldn't be true. Things that I would not have believed to be true, even though I was staring them in the face."

"You think this *Eden* thing is real?" Liam asked.

Skyes hesitated before answering. "I don't know. But what I *do* know is what the president just told me. He asked me the same question, and then told me to check my email. Another group, I'm guessing the CIA or even a black-ops military cell, sent over a dossier on a man named al-Sadir. I haven't gone through everything yet, but the initial brief I read fits the profile of someone who might actually be able to pull something like this off."

Liam's eyes widened.

"I've already forwarded it to you — I want this to be the first rock you check under, because the intelligence is good. I have a hunch, and my hunches are rarely completely off-base. If this guy actually is behind something like *Eden,* and it's real, well... I think it's a good place to start looking."

"You mean you think this al-Sadir guy might be behind Lane's kidnapping," Liam said.

"I do. It makes sense, too — if *Escape from Eden* is real, and there's a group of power-hungry rich assholes hoping to get their hands on the information in Lane's head, al-Sadir would be perfectly poised to take advantage of that."

"That makes sense," Liam continued. "If al-Sadir wanted to make a ton of money exploiting geniuses like Lane, this is a good — if not sick and twisted — way of doing it."

"My thoughts exactly," Colonel Sykes said. "So start there. It could be nothing, but in that case it'll be quick and painless to find that nothing, and you won't have wasted a lot of time. On the other hand, if al-Sadir knows *anything,* he'll have left clues."

Liam was nodding along as if to agree with Sykes, but internally he was reeling. *How the hell am I supposed to track down a guy named al-Sadir and just hope he's made a big enough mistake to find it? If al-Sadir was even a bit smart, he would have carefully covered his tracks. Not to mention he'll see a guy like me coming from a mile away.*

"Don't worry too much about the tracking part," the colonel

said, nearly reading his mind. "I've got assets in place that I can tap and feed information to you. You can redirect the assets as you see fit, but this way the professionals can do their job — all you have to do is figure out what the data means. Put the pieces together."

"That I *can* do, sir," Liam said, the smile returning to his face.

"Good. And I know you can. As I said, you'll have pretty much carte blanche to launch this investigation. Hernandez, if there's something you need, even if it's your own personal Death Star, I'll be far more pissed if you don't ask for it than if you do ask and it turns out to be a ridiculous request, understand?"

"Got it. No Death Star."

"Unless you can make a case that it's warranted for your investigation. But other than that, I'm here to make sure you get what you need." He cleared his throat. "And that includes personnel. *Do not* hold back, got it? The President of the United States of America wants Joshua Lane found and brought home safe and sound, and I intend to move heaven and earth to make sure that happens."

"In that case, I intend to as well, sir," Liam said.

The colonel extended his hand and they shook. Not another word was spoken, and Liam left the colonel's office feeling optimistic.

Tired, weary, and downright terrified, but optimistic.

LOCATION *unknown*

Joshua Lane stood, transfixed, watching the computer monitor as the man appeared onscreen. He was young, perhaps mid-thirties or about ten years younger than Josh, and he had distinctly Middle Eastern features. He kept his beard trimmed close, but it was thick and likely needed daily trimming. His hair was slicked back, but also in a way that said his hygiene was of the utmost importance.

He seemed to be wearing makeup, but in the way a celebrity on camera or an actor would wear — subtle, bringing out the depth of his eyes and the stark features of his jawline and forehead.

Josh could feel the charisma emanating through him even onscreen.

"I truly hope you are all comfortable," he continued. *"Our contestants are extremely important to us — without you, there would be no Eden from which to escape."*

He paused, chuckling.

"Oh, and I suppose I should explain our game — we call it

'Escape from Eden,' and it is, well, exactly what it sounds like — a game, one in which you, our contestants, must complete tasks and solve problems in order to win your freedom."

Josh was reeling, but he could not take his eyes off the computer screen. The camera work was as slick as the man speaking, cutting between shots, revealing the side of his face, then the front, then a sweeping pull shot that showed the man standing on a wide, empty stage, a huge lit backdrop behind him.

"You have been chosen because of your exceptional skill and brilliance in the world of computing technology. Your skill set will be necessary to gain your freedom, and your refusal to comply or your failure to complete the tasks will result in your elimination."

Josh frowned.

"The game began this morning, about one hour ago. By now, most of our contestants have completed the first simple task: interacting with Eve, our friendly computer system. She is in charge of each of your chambers, as well as your continued comfort as you work to solve the problems she will give you. Some of you have explored the menu system and its delivery of food and water upon your command. Some of you have even questioned the system's obvious lack of another necessity — a restroom option."

Josh felt himself nodding along. *Now that I think of it, I do need to pee.*

"The cleverest among you noticed that your water is delivered from a sanitary tube from the front wall. Likewise, a similar tube is available for waste disposal and can be found on the back wall of your room. You simply must approach the area and the wall will reveal the tube automatically. We wanted to give you each as much privacy and decency as possible, considering, so you have my word that the room's cameras will not be recording whenever you must

take care of business. Eve will ensure this, so as long as the waste tube is out, the cameras are off."

Josh did not at all feel more comfortable at this revelation, but he was at least relieved to discover that there *was* a way to relieve himself in here.

"Your interactions with Eve so far have been rather eye-opening and have already given her — as well as our viewers — insight into your problem-solving skills. She has assigned you scores, as she will upon completion of each problem, and those scores will help our viewers determine where to rank your likelihood of... Escape from Eden."

The man on the screen seemed smitten by this turn of phrase, but the pause lasted only half a second. *"My name is al-Sadir, and I will be your host for this iteration of the game."* He turned to another camera, as if addressing the viewing audience rather than the contestants. *"The final phase of our opening ceremonies is to reveal the result of the first trial."*

The screen faded and cut, the man disappearing from view and soon replaced by a shot of the interior of a room.

Josh recognized the room immediately. It was *his* room.

No. He squinted, examining the room closer now. It was not *his* room, but it was one almost exactly like his. The walls were the same strange, ceramic material with copper lines running throughout them. A bed, unmade with a pillow lying in the center of it, sat in the middle of the room against the back wall.

But the sole difference between Josh's room and the one onscreen was readily apparent: there was a man lying on the floor of the room next to the bed, curled into a fetal position. He was crying, and Josh could see the man's lip quivering. His hair was disheveled, unkempt, and while he wore the same comfortable clothing Josh had on, this man had pulled against the fabric, ripping the shirt in two places and yanking the legs of the pants up past his calves.

There was no sound, but Josh did not need to hear — this man was struggling, the anxiety and terror so obvious on his face Josh could almost hear his wails through the silence.

al-Sadir's voice continued while the camera zoomed in on the man on the floor of his chamber. *"Contestant 4 has, unfortunately, failed the first trial. He is now scheduled for elimination."*

Josh felt bile rising in his throat. His conscious mind had not yet even considered what 'elimination' meant, but something in his subconscious must have. He wanted to vomit, but he could not remove his eyes from the screen.

The man must have been listening to his own screen and in-ceiling speakers as the host, al-Sadir, explained the elimination process. He sat up slightly, the fear in his eyes palpable, and stared across the small room at the tiny computer monitor. Josh could not see his screen, but he imagined the man was watching himself on it.

He pulled himself to a seated position, then jumped up from the floor, landing on the bed. He was trembling now, shaking so hard it was visible through the camera and monitor. Something had excited him, terrified him even more than he had been before.

Josh felt panicked, and everything he tried to do to calm himself down failed. He wanted to look away, for fear that his subconscious knew what was about to happen.

But he could not. Something dark inside of him knew that he *needed* to see this. He *needed* to know how it would end for Contestant #4, so as to hopefully prevent a similar fate from befalling him.

Perhaps 'elimination' was simply getting booted from the game. Perhaps the man's wife and kids were just outside the door, ready to congratulate him on trying, to take him home to console him.

Josh knew he was completely wrong, and he knew it even before the floor onscreen in the other contestant's room began to light up with a bright orange hue.

NSA HEADQUARTERS | FORT MEADE, *Maryland*

"Thank you all for joining me here," Liam Hernandez said, trying to address the people around the table at once. "I know you don't know me personally, and you are confused as to why I called this meeting for a Sunday afternoon."

A couple of people nodded, but no one was outwardly hostile.

He took a breath, then continued. "Truth be told, I'd much rather be at home with my wife and kids, also. But this really is a matter of national security."

"Hence why we're meeting here, I presume," said the man to Liam's left. Lieutenant Colonel Roger Witherspoon was the military appointee Colonel Sykes had recommended to Liam. Apparently, a great strategic mind, he could not only lead other men into battle, but he had seen no shortage of battles himself. Judging by the scars that marked the man's hands and face, Liam was not about to disagree.

"As tongue-in-cheek as it may seem to have a meeting about something related to *national security* at the *National Security*

Administration headquarters, it really just sort of happened that way. Our intelligence led me to snoop around a bit, and lo and behold, now it's an NSA-sanctioned mission."

"What *mission,* exactly?" a woman across the table from him asked. She was Jocelyn Potter, a world-renowned quantum computing expert, working as a consultant with the NSA. She worked down in the 'dregs,' the subterranean bunker-like level of the NSA where the massive servers and banks of networking computers lived, as well as the army of ponytailed engineers who babysat them. Someone like Liam rarely had a reason to venture down there, and he shuddered to think about what it might be like to have to *work* down in the dregs regularly. No windows, outside access points, and miles of fluorescent lighting.

"I'll get to the details momentarily," he said, wanting to keep the meeting on track. He was no power-hungry dictator, but he needed to make the point that he was — and would remain — in charge of this ragtag group. "First, I need to express to you all the importance of this meeting, and the ones that will follow. As I mentioned, I would not call you all here on a Sunday if it was not one of the most important meetings you all will attend this year."

He paused and got the expected result. There was no literal scoffing, but the looks of disbelief on the four attendees' faces were palpable.

"Yesterday, I met with Colonel Sykes upstairs." He noticed Jocelyn Potter's eyebrows raise slightly. She knew who Sykes was, and she knew he was not one to waste time on pet projects. "What's more, my meeting with Sykes was bookended by meetings with the President."

At this, there was an *actual* scoff, this time from Curtis Lee, the Asian-American man seated to the right of Lieutenant Colonel

Witherspoon. Lee was a transplant from Hong Kong, but he was a well-known corporate hacker and 'white hat' cyber espionage professional, currently heading a small department at the NSA focused on artificial intelligence applications for cybersecurity.

"And lest you misunderstand, I am referring to the President of the *United States*."

"What could *we* possibly be needed for in that case?" Jocelyn asked. She quickly flicked her eyes at the others. "I mean... no offense."

Roger Witherspoon laughed. "None taken. I've actually made a career out of being just off center stage, trying to avoid the limelight. That's what special forces and lots of black ops does to you after a while. You start to get used to it. And hell, nothing good ever comes from being the face of an operation."

"Unfortunately, your reputation let you down in that case," Liam said. "Sykes recommended you personally, and the President affirmed it. You're the right man for the job."

"Which is?"

"Right," he continued. "Roughly two days ago, we got word — verified by our intelligence — that a man named Joshua Lane was kidnapped. I doubt any of you will know his name, but —"

"He's with Bearbridge, right?" Jocelyn asked. "Fantastic scientist. If anyone's going to break the theoretical qubit limit in applied quantum computing, it's him. And he's married to a woman, Molly Lane, who almost equals his accomplishments in computing. Graduate of MIT, then on to an academic career in chemical computer science."

She paused, then looked at the rest of the group. "Sorry, Molly was a force of nature when I was at MIT. I never knew her, but everyone knew *of* her."

Liam smiled at her. "I meant *most* of you won't know who he is. But yes, you are correct. Joshua Lane was kidnapped on his way home from Bearbridge, actually. Taken by an unknown force, but we believe they are extremely well-organized. They were able to track him, remotely disable his vehicle, and coerce him into their vehicle." Liam skipped a few details, knowing that this was spelled out in the reports that sat in front of each member of the team. "The important thing about Joshua Lane is that he is a member of what we at the NSA call Project Echelon — a group of the top echelon of civilian and military scientists and citizens that we believe will usher in the future of modern computing and technology."

"Echelon, huh? Fitting."

"Yeah, and most of the members of Echelon, including Lane, have no idea they're in the program. It's a way for the NSA and the US government to keep tabs on those we feel... well, those we think need to be watched."

"But not in a *breach of privacy* sort of way, of course," Lee said, snickering.

"Of course not." Liam did not let his smile waver. "Lane is as top-tier as it gets, but if word leaked that we're watching his progress, or if we gave him a cushy, visible job with the government or military, the rest of the world — who, I assure you, has programs *just* like this one — will be very curious as to *why* we're interested in him."

"So you keep your interest in Lane on the down-low," Lieutenant Colonel Witherspoon said. "But at the same time, you can keep track of his progress on whatever cool thing he's cooking up."

"Precisely."

"And since it's a matter of national security, going all the way up the chain, we need to assume that he was kidnapped *because* of the very thing he's been 'cooking up.'"

Liam pushed his glasses up his nose. "Yes, exactly. He was sniped by Bearbridge to work on a project, and while we don't have the details of that project just yet, I expect to by tomorrow morning."

"But you have an idea as to the nature of that project," Curtis said. "Don't you?"

Liam's breath caught in his throat. He nodded. "Yes. Yes, we do."

"You believe he is working on a quantum computer that can host an artificial intelligence."

LOCATION *unknown*

Josh watched the screen in horror and fascination. Horror, because the man on the screen was going to die. Fascination, because he simply could not make himself believe that what he was seeing was true.

The man writhed on the bed, sweat beading on his forehead and falling to the sheets beneath him. His body was twisting, turning each second, as if he were trying to escape a bad dream. Lane imagined that he was absolutely trying to escape a bad dream.

The floor continued to heat up, judging by the color of the ceramic, which now glowed with a bright-red intensity. He also noticed that the walls were also painted bright red with heat.

What the actual f—

"As you will see on your monitor, contestants," al-Sadir's voice continued, *"Contestant #4's elimination process has begun. Typical elimination takes anywhere from one to three minutes."*

Lane put a hand over his mouth. He felt tears forming in the corners of his eyes. He felt for the man — how could he not? Who the hell could do something like this, and why?

He did not understand; his mind would not allow it to make sense. He knew what was happening, but it was an understanding on a cerebral level. He could not get to the point where he fully accepted what his eyes were telling him.

He screamed, beating fists against the wall. "Let me out!" Lane shouted. "Let me out of here, *now!*"

He pounded the section of ceramic he thought must have had a door cut into it. *I had to have gotten in here somehow,* he told himself. *I've seen that weird tube thing pop out of the wall — and the computer screen and keyboard.*

He assumed there *had* to be a door here, but his vision was starting to blur as he panicked. He scraped against the wall, hoping to let his fingers find purchase on something resembling a crack, a line, a score that meant he had found a door. From there, he could pull on it. He could work it until his fingernails bled, ripping them out one by one as long as he could make progress.

But Lane found no lines, nothing signaling that there was so much as a crack in the perfect ceramic wall.

He had no choice; he turned his attention back to the man onscreen. Contestant #4. He was crying profusely, rocking once again but this time on the bed. The tears fell and sizzled on the sheets, eliciting a tiny dot of steam each time. The man pulled his arms up and around him and squeezed, hugging himself, but quickly removed them. The heat had built to such an intensity his own clothes were no longer working to protect him.

Lane knew it would be less than a minute now. He refused to watch. He turned around and sat on his own bed, on the far side, away from the monitor, and cried. *What is this?* he wondered. *Who could do this to another human?*

He had seen plenty of death, plenty of killing. But all of it had been while serving overseas, while performing his duties, and working to eradicate evil in some twisted corner of the globe. It had all felt *proper*, then. Or at least normalized. As if it had been sanctioned or planned. Evil rises, good prevails. Good triumphs.

He had thankfully not had to witness evil's rare victory. He had not seen helpless children slaughtered, had not been present when Islamic terrorists beheaded women and innocent men. He had heard of these things, even seen pictures and video footage, but had never had to witness it firsthand.

Now, he was forced to watch, and the reality of the situation was haunting. He was in the *same* situation. He had been brought here against his will, taken from his normal, easy life, taken from his wife. He had been placed in a literal *hell* — even the fires of Dante's inferno seemed to have made an entrance in this poor man's cell. This contestant, likely every bit as innocent as Joshua Lane, had been given a death sentence. And for what? Had he not interacted with the computer system appropriately? Or at all?

He had refused to play this dark game and was currently paying the ultimate sacrifice in a room exactly the same as Lane's.

What would happen if Lane also refused to play this game? Obviously silent protest only ended in disaster. Was there another option besides agreeing to these sadistic terms? Was there another option for Lane besides pretending to play along, even though the rules seemed to be explained *after* it was too late?

He knew he was brilliant — he had a mind that sometimes worked faster than he realized. He often had a problem he was trying to solve that was eluding him, then would take it to bed with him and wake up with a solution. Sometimes, unfortunately, that happened in the middle of the night.

But he *always* found a solution. Would he find a solution to this predicament? A life-or-death situation with terms that changed every moment? Could he even do that, considering the immense pressure?

There was only one way to find out, and panicking and scratching his way out of this prison was not it. He needed to think. He needed to understand what they — what this 'host,' al-Sadir — wanted from him and the other contestants. Why *they* had been chosen. If he could find the answer to that question, he might be able to bypass the terror and destruction of human life.

But he had nothing to start from. He had been given *nothing* in the way of pieces to start putting together. The puzzle itself was impossible to solve because he had no pieces to start with.

He made the mistake of turning around quickly, mostly to satisfy his curiosity to see if the screen had changed. It was still completely silent in the room while al-Sadir was not talking, so he had no audio cues to go off of. He let his eyes dance over to the screen.

He wished he would not have done that.

Smoked filled the room. The man onscreen was dead, lying on his back on the bed. Bits of his clothing and skin were charred, burnt as the heat in the room reached a temperature high enough to begin igniting clothing, sheets, the pillow. Flames licked up the back wall near the man's head.

And then... the man moved.

Lane's jaw dropped, just as the contestant's mouth opened. He was groaning, crying out, one last attempt to cling to life.

It was pure agony. Lane watched, helpless, as the man lifted his head one final time, then let it fall back, now finally perished.

Lane struggled to maintain his composure, but the tears were flowing freely now as the second revelation hit him. He had refused to acknowledge it, but as the man's face had lifted, in full view of the hidden camera inside his chamber, Lane knew it to be true.

He *recognized* the man.

CHAPTER 20
LIAM

Liam looked at the younger man for a long moment. "Yes, Mr. Lee. I believe that is the case."

While Lee appeared to be a rough-around-the-edges hacker, his youthful face only adding to the punk attitude, some of the papers he had published on the theoretical limits of artificial intelligence and neural networks were considered the gold standard, and while many computer scientists and engineers worked their entire lives to disprove his theories, they were nothing short of reverent when it came to the man himself. He was only twenty-eight years old but already making waves at the NSA.

If they were able to somehow come across documents, project files, plans — anything at all — they might be able to get a peek into what Lane had been doing prior to and immediately following his recent onboarding at Bearbridge. No one in the room doubted it was related to intelligence, specifically in the 'artificial' sense, and most of them already suspected he had been hired to help Bearbridge finish a first-stage quantum computer.

Quantum computing was all the rage now, and most of the world's largest tech companies had publicly revealed their quantum projects, each claiming it was slightly better than the previous company's. Liam personally believed that any of the major computer companies that had *not* revealed anything only meant they were trying to keep their work a secret.

As it were, the first company that could show real results from quantum technology was nearly guaranteed a seat at the table regarding the next-generation military projects, as well as the massive amounts of funding that would follow. Any company able to create a usable prototype of a quantum computer, even if for just a singular problem set, would be all but guaranteed long-term funding. Liam knew of many such problems a quantum computer would be perfect for. For example, the incredible amount of logistics and supply chain data the US Army needed to make its decisions needed to be parsed, processed, and organized. Because of ever-changing variables, the moment current technology and human administrators spit out an answer, it was already out of date.

There were already companies working toward this very goal, and some had nearly succeeded. IBM was already selling access to its cloud-based quantum computer terminals, but each problem set needed to be painstakingly coded and built from the ground up. Google and Apple had similar programs, but each had taken a different approach when it came to building out their technology and who would be able to access them.

The holy grail of quantum computing, and the reason Liam had invited Curtis and Jocelyn to the team, was a true artificial intelligence.

"Do you actually think Lane has figured it out?" Lee asked.

His voice was calm, but Liam could almost feel the frenetic energy in the kid — he was excited to be here, to be a part of this.

"I cannot say with absolute certainty. But we know his background, his training in the Air Force and subsequent rise as one of the world's best programmers. We know Bearbridge headhunted him and offered him a salary a prince wouldn't refuse. We don't know yet what they are asking him to do, but we highly suspect it involves quantum technology, which Bearbridge is involved in, and artificial intelligence."

"We're years away from being able to run a true AGI inside of a quantum machine," Lee said matter-of-factly.

"Why is that?" Roger Witherspoon asked.

Lee seemed perplexed for a moment, then annoyed, but the look vanished as soon as he began talking. "*My* expertise is in artificial intelligence. But the limitations of artificial intelligence are not *software* related, they are *hardware* related. We have the software capability to build out an entire library of *libraries* of pre-programmed responses far larger than anything the world has ever seen. This would be more than enough material to load into a Turing-level machine as programmatic responses that could mimic, potentially even fool, the average human into believing that the machine was alive."

Liam nodded. "Right, like a chatbot."

"Far more intelligent than a chatbot," Lee said. "But in a sense, yes. If there were a dedicated team of programmers and statisticians large enough, this would be easy work. But the problem — the real reason no one would actually fall for this and call it a true general intelligence — is that the *hardware* and *firmware* on the machine itself would be far too slow to parse through all possible responses and display one that appears to check all the boxes for intelligence."

"Like the old chess computer. The one that beat Kasparov?"

"Yes, exactly," Jocelyn said, taking over for Lee. "Deep Blue beat a human, but it was nothing more than a library of responses with a program that it ran to determine the best *possible* response given a certain situation. The delay between responses was massive. At one point longer than twenty minutes. Even with the massively faster central processing units and RAM we have today, the hardware becomes a bottleneck. It simply is not possible."

"Without a quantum computer, you mean," Witherspoon said.

"Well, yes," Lee answered, a small smile snaking upward from his left lip. "That's why I said it was impossible — there *is* no true quantum computer available for this sort of work. Not yet, anyway."

CHAPTER 21

JOSH

Josh knew who that man was, the man who had died right in front of his eyes. Though a computer monitor had streamed the murder into his room, the room itself — the bed, the pillow, the walls — had been exactly the same as Josh's. It had the desired effect on Josh for that reason: he was absolutely terrified.

But his fear had grown to heights he had never experienced when he realized that he recognized the man who had been killed. He could not recall how or why he knew the man's face, but there was no doubt in his mind: he *knew* this man from somewhere.

But from where? His mind raced. *Have I met him before? Seen him in person or on television?*

Any answers he could glean from this situation might help him understand the larger situation — the answer as to why he was here. Why he had been kidnapped and placed into this cell.

He knew it was a game. He had been told as much; he was a contestant in something called *Escape from Eden,* which sounded like the name of a twisted reality show. Reality television was still all the rage, although most of the popular shows had moved from cable television channels to online video streaming sites. The typical viewer of these shows watched television differently today — they sat on their couches with a tablet in-hand, watching any number of streams piped onto the television in front of them as well as onto the smaller screens on their laps. Human attention spans had been dropping for decades, a few seconds at a time. Still, the trillion-dollar entertainment industry had done its best to keep up, offering bite-sized "showettes" instead of the half-hour or hour-long presentations of a decade ago.

As well, they split their content into bite-sized, shareable chunks, then spliced together a nonstop run of individual sound-bites from each 'show' to create an ongoing stream of entertainment. There was no published schedule — people dropped into the stream whenever they felt like it, and the algorithmic recommendations engines each viewer had been training for years simply spliced an automated episode of content it knew the viewer would enjoy.

It was immediate, incredibly well-adapted, and addictive. Lane and his wife Molly had never watched much television, with the exception of a few old shows they had on in the background while cooking together. In his mind, the world had moved on — the couple preferred real-life experiences to artificial ones, and even the best 'reality' entertainment seemed contrived and scripted.

But this — *Escape from Eden,* or whatever it truly was — was something different entirely. The man's face was real, his contortions not contrived, his body actually *there.* He had been murdered, and Lane had been forced to watch it happen. For a moment, he had considered that it may have been a deep fake — a video of a person made to look like someone else.

But in order for that to have been true, he knew there had to be a *real* person acting beneath the digital mask — and he had seen the flesh ignite, seen the charred remains of the clothing, melted and stuck to the body beneath it. He had as much an eye for that sort of thing as anyone, and everything within him told him it had been real.

That man, whoever he may be, had died. It had not been fake.

A *true* reality show.

Lane shuddered.

But back to the matter at hand — who the hell *was* he? Lane scoured his brain for an answer. He knew he *should* know; the recognition was real, and therefore the answer was somewhere within him. He needed to think, to get away and figure this out, but the very fact that he was trapped inside the same sort of room that had literally just turned into an oven was very disconcerting and caused his mind to feel like mush.

Think, Josh, he told himself.

Before he could start unpacking everything that had just happened, the man calling himself the host appeared once again on the screen, his smile still plastered across his slick face.

"Hello again, contestants," he began. *"Eve has informed me that Contestant #4 has been eliminated. His room is currently being scrubbed and reset, but rest assured, we will not add another contestant as challenger. That means you all have survived the first test and have made it to the next round."*

Josh started pacing again. He could not bear to stare at this man, nonchalantly explaining the situation as though someone had not just been brutally murdered. He wanted to scream, to lash out and destroy the computer monitor, but he could not help but feel that he also needed to keep his mind clear, to take in whatever information this man, al-Sadir, said, if by chance something he said might prove to be useful to him.

He paced reluctantly, listening to al-Sadir's words.

"The next trial is scheduled to begin soon. Eve will display the trial on your screen when it begins. All of you, save for Contestant #4, have explored the room appropriately and found the hidden keyboard, through which you may interact with Eve."

He paused, then turned to address another camera. The feed kept up, cutting to the new angle, this one from the left side of al-Sadir's face. He continued turning, facing this camera now.

"As always, contestants: good luck."

Josh stopped walking, standing still in the middle of the floor now, waiting to see if al-Sadir was finished. His subconscious was racing now, plowing through a field of possibilities at a breakneck pace, running off without the rest of him.

That was a good sign, at least — it told him that there was *something* to process. Even though he could not understand what exactly it was working on, he knew there was a problem being solved. It was how his mind worked, how it always had worked. Even as a 'gifted' kid in math class, he would sit and stare at a problem, frustrated that he could not force the answer to come into the forefront of his mind. He would work through the structure of the problem as he had been taught, not understanding or feeling as though he was making progress.

And then suddenly, as if by magic, the answer, fully formed and ready for his hand to write it down, would pop into his brain. He often could not keep up when his mind began to work this way, knocking down one problem after another, the solutions flowing through him without slowing. His hand would cramp as he scratched the answers onto the paper, and inevitably he would look up minutes later, realizing he had somehow finished almost an hour before the next-fastest student.

He felt his mind doing this now, felt it putting pieces together that he could not even describe. All he needed to do now was wait; his brain would supply him with an answer that — hopefully — would help him make sense of things.

The question now was whether or not that answer would come before it was too late.

The computer terminal faded to black, then immediately the onscreen image changed again to text.

His eyes flashed over to it, reading the words as they appeared.

CONTESTANT #9, CONGRATULATIONS.

PREPARE FOR THE SECOND TRIAL.

HULHUMALÉ COAST, *Maldives*

Mohammad al-Sadir was exhausted. He was descending toward the master suite at the far end of the spacious yacht, but the cavernous boat would make that a five-minute walk. He had been awake for more than twenty-four hours, but his work was not yet finished. Playing host of the games was a tiresome task by itself, but playing host to all manner of issues and problems that cropped up in his business at the same time was going to kill him.

He momentarily considered placing Hans in charge of the games, having him step into the host role, a position Hans would be able to pull off well. But that would jeopardize al-Sadir's relationship with the viewers, who would no doubt ask questions about al-Sadir's whereabouts.

The games were a perfect example of the extreme loyalty and discretion required by those in power and having enough wealth to attend. These were no figureheads; they demanded al-Sadir's presence and calming voice because they had paid for the games with their own money. Their wealth was on the line, and any weakness

— any chinks in the armor of the brand loyalty he had painstakingly built over the years — would mean lost trust. It was unrecoverable, and for al-Sadir it meant there was no other option.

He would play host, as he always had, and he could command his growing empire at the same time. His assistants would continue to do their jobs, as would Hans, and he would remain protected and functional, at the expense of good sleep.

al-Sadir was met at the door to one of the suites onboard the massive yacht by his best friend, the slightly younger Ahmed Ibn Kahn. Kahn fell out of the suite in a drunken stupor, nearly colliding with al-Sadir.

Disgusted, al-Sadir pushed Kahn away but grabbed the man's face, holding it tightly with his hand. "What is this, Kahn?" he asked.

Kahn tried to focus, but his eyes rolled around. "I — I... we just... yeah," he stuttered.

al-Sadir sensed movement, and saw behind Kahn into the room. Two very young-looking women sat on the bed, both giggling, both barely clothed.

al-Sadir waited, knowing he was not going to get any further explanation but wanting Kahn to offer some semblance of an apology. None came, and al-Sadir pushed the man's face away. "This is an embarrassment to your father, friend," he said.

"I want... father should see... you want?"

al-Sadir could not parse the drunken syllables, but he didn't need to. This man was too far gone. "Kahn, you came here to learn from me, *brother*. To one day be at my side as we grow this business together. I did not want to share it with my own siblings, for they were not worthy. You, I thought, *were*. Have you changed your mind? Because you are changing mine."

Kahn seemed to register some of his words, but his eyes still rolled. "No!" he spat. "Fun... just... bit of fun. All well, tomorrow," he slurred.

"All will *not* be well tomorrow. The games require my utmost attention and concern, and my business must not be interrupted by... whatever *this* is. You must learn to control yourself, or you risk losing your reputation. Worse, you threaten mine."

Kahn blinked a few times, and the girls behind him giggled. One of them urged him back into the room with a soothing call.

al-Sadir shook his head. "So be it. Finish your own games before you ruin mine. I will give you another chance, but I urge you caution, friend. See that this behavior does not continue while I am footing the bill for it.

A flash of realization came over Kahn's face. He nodded, and al-Sadir couldn't help but think he had somehow gotten through to the younger man. *Good,* he thought. *I cannot have this consume any more of my attention.*

"I must sleep, Kahn, and so should you. Your role in these games may be small, but it is important. If you fail, I will have no choice but to request your resignation."

Another nod, another solemn look on the man's face.

"Good," he said, already moving down the hallway toward his bedroom. He sent a text message to Hans to have the head of security set the onboard AI to listen into his friend's room, alerting Hans whenever there was gratuitous noise. He hated snooping on his friend, but he needed to sleep well. Any noise must be stopped before it emanated into al-Sadir's room, and by having the AI doing the listening, he felt better about the whole thing.

He reached his quarters and entered. The room was immaculate, both in stature and cleanliness, just as he required. He was

not one to flaunt his wealth and status more than what was absolutely necessary, but he had also decided that *having* that sort of
wealth meant he should at least be able to enjoy a perfect night's
sleep. The mattress and sheets were high-end and cost more than
the rest of the beds on board combined.

And the room itself was the epitome of security and high-end
technology. He could commandeer the yacht from in here, and the
wall-sized screens made watching the waves roll past almost as
good as the real thing up on the bridge. There was even a hidden
passageway upstairs, as well as a hidden exit that led to the galley.

It was his and his alone. On the rare occasion he hosted female
companionship, he slept with them in one of the luxurious guest
suites but always retired — alone — to his room.

He wanted nothing more than to sleep as long as his body
wanted, but the viewers would be expecting him to begin the
festivities early the next morning. He also needed to check in with
Hans to get an update on anything that may have transpired
overnight, and to see if there were any pressing business matters to
tend to.

For that reason, he spoke aloud a command to the yacht's
onboard AI. "Please set my alarm for 5:45," he said.

*"Alarm is set for 5:45. Do you require an audible command as
well?"*

"No, thank you," al-Sadir said. The bed was equipped with a
motorized alarm system that would gently vibrate starting a few
minutes before he needed to wake, increasing in speed and intensity until he couldn't help but wake up. It was more than enough
to awaken the light sleeper, but al-Sadir used the technology as
little as possible, preferring to wake with the light of morning
instead.

With nothing else to tend to for now, and looking forward to a few hours of good sleep, al-Sadir instructed the AI to lock his doors and turn out the lights.

He sighed, took off his clothes, and was asleep a few minutes after his head hit the pillow.

CHAPTER 23
LIAM

As much as Liam had wanted to stay at home and sleep through the day, he also wanted to find Joshua Lane. As such, he had decided to stay at the coffee shop near the NSA campus for an extra hour, hosting his early-morning meetings from a table in the back of the room.

The first of these meetings had taken place with Curtis Lee, the resident white-hat hacker and AI expert Liam had invited to the team. Now, he was meeting with Colonel Witherspoon and Jocelyn Potter, trying to figure out what the next steps for their search should be.

"Any updates, Colonel?" he asked as soon as Witherspoon reached the table he and Jocelyn were seated at. He had sent a follow-up email yesterday afternoon to the Lieutenant Colonel asking the man to begin putting a mobile unit together, assuming they would eventually decide on where to send it.

"Please," he said, pulling out his chair and taking a seat. He held a steaming cup of black coffee in his hand that he placed on the table. "Call me Roger. This doesn't need to reek of formality, like everything else I'm forced to do all day."

Liam smiled. "Sure thing. Were you able to pull some men together?" he asked.

"I was. It's a group of Rangers, so they're plenty well-trained for whatever we might throw them into. We're keeping this one off the books, too, so it helps that they're familiar with some of the more... *black* missions."

"Perfect," Liam said. "I wish I had a better update, but we still don't know where to send these guys."

Roger shook his head. "Doesn't matter. We'll find Lane and where he's being held, and my boys will be ready to drop everything and suit up. We'll be wheels-up within four hours of the orders, guaranteed."

Liam raised an eyebrow. "That's great. Thank you." He turned to Jocelyn. "Anything interesting pop up on your front?"

As the resident expert in quantum computing — a field Lane would have been working in with Bearbridge — Liam wanted to know if anything exciting, interesting, or otherwise important had transpired.

"Well, nothing I've looked into much, but do you know Robert Blake?" she asked.

Liam and Roger frowned simultaneously. "He that rich tech guy with the messed-up face?" Roger asked.

She nodded. "Yeah. Founder of Aetheria, has a fake eye. They've been so far ahead of the game in virtual reality and wearable tech that some people think he's got a special phone line to God."

Roger chuckled. "Sure, if God's a capitalistic megalomaniac."

"What about him?" Liam asked.

"Well... he's dead."

"Shit. Really?" he asked.

"Yeah — police think it was foul play, too," she continued. "Reports I'm seeing say that a bullet took his head clean off, but there wasn't a weapon found in the car."

"He died in the car?" Roger asked.

"Yeah, but it wasn't a car accident," she said. "Still, he was found in the car. As well as the... remains. Of his head, I guess. Enough blood and stuff that they assume he was shot — but he was in the backseat, hunched over."

"Christ," Roger said. "That's sick."

"Interestingly, he was found in Baltimore. Not more than an hour-and-a-half from where Lane was kidnapped."

Liam felt his blood run cold. "Wait, do any of the reports have a picture of the car? The one Blake was found in?" As he spoke, he was already digging his phone out of his front pocket.

Jocelyn beat him to it, nodding again as she pulled her own phone out. "Sure. I think, anyway. Let me find the first news report of it. Why? You think it could be related."

Liam swallowed. "I'm ready to turn over any rocks we come across. We've got no other leads, and this feels too serendipitous not to be related."

Roger looked at him strangely.

"I didn't mention this yesterday, but I know you've all seen the satellite video of the cars on the bridge. The *H7* from Bearbridge, the cars that showed up and nabbed Josh..."

Jocelyn put her phone down face-up on the table, and Josh saw a grainy picture of a black sedan, the license plate blurred out. Police lines ran around the length of the vehicle, and cops and forensics teams stood in the area just past the car. The headline for the article was expectedly tongue-in-cheek and tasteless, if not pithy: *Tech Founder Found Dead.*

Josh leaned in and examined the vehicle, squinting as he tried to capture every detail. Even without being able to see the plates, he had no doubt in his mind that this was the same vehicle that Josh had entered after being accosted on the bridge.

"This is it," he said. "I'll have the guys back at HQ cross-reference it and pull plates from the police database. We'll be able to track it back to the bridge, I'm sure. But I know for a fact that this is the exact same car."

"Lane was in that car," Roger said.

"He was," Liam said. "He *left* the car, got back to the *H7*, and drove it off the bridge. Whatever happened to this particular *after* that, we don't know. But I'm starting to have some ideas."

"Yeah," Roger said. "There were two parties. This one, and one that came later. The later party apparently won. They found Lane in the river and disappeared. Then moved the car with the dead, headless Blake inside, and got rid of the driver."

"But not before taking out the *other* guy who saw this stuff," Liam said. "Donovan Sloan, that guy who also worked at Bearbridge — he was snooping around as well, and they followed him to Lane's house and took him out then."

He was now speculating; there was no way at this point to corroborate the claims. And while he was no detective, he knew that having a workable hypothesis was the first step in making sense of otherwise unrelated clues.

The Sloan case was still an ongoing investigation. The Baltimore Police Department had been ready to write it off as a standard-fare fatal accident, but Liam, through some manipulative string-pulling, had managed to get them to infer that there might be more to it. They were doing a full autopsy, forensics were investigating the vehicle, and he would be able to access the report in a week's time when the teams finished their work.

But the piece that he was now confident of was that Blake's death was *absolutely* related to Lane's kidnapping. He did not know how or why, but Blake had been with Lane shortly before his own death. The killer had moved the car, taken out the driver and anyone else still in the vehicle, but left Blake to be found later.

Why? Surely it was not an accident; they were not sloppy. These were professionals they were dealing with. But why not hide his body? Why leave it for someone to find, only to lead to another — far more in-depth — investigation?

Maybe that was it, he thought. *Maybe they wanted the cops to focus on Blake, to use up resources that would otherwise be used to find Lane and look into Sloan's death.* By creating a distraction with the death of Robert Blake, tech icon and billionaire mogul, they could more easily hide in the shadows.

It was a good working theory. Good enough, anyway. But it only added more questions.

The most important one was the one he knew was now nagging the others at the table, as well.

Why was Joshua Lane with Robert Blake?

LOCATION *unknown*

Josh couldn't help but feel excitement growing. Regardless of the current situation — being held captive in a murderous game — he *loved* puzzles, especially those involving computers. His mind was still working through the events from before, and he was still trying to place where he had seen the man who had perished.

But his attention was now drawn to the screen, where dots in a seemingly random configuration began to appear. He walked closer, watching the dots fade into existence. He quickly counted seventeen of them, then eighteen and nineteen, when they stopped appearing.

He waited. A minute passed. *Is this it?* he wondered. *Am I supposed to understand what this is?*

Josh wished for the hundredth time that NARA was still working, still able to send him help. Although he knew that even if NARA were up and running, it likely would not be able to connect with the outside world.

He turned his head to the side, hoping that a different perspective — usually a requirement for solving computational or programmatic problems — would help. But the dots just looked... even more random.

He turned his head to the opposite side, then almost all the way around so that he was looking at the screen upside-down. It was like the computer equivalent of a Rorschach test. *What do you see in the dots, Lane?* he imagined a therapist asking him.

"I don't see a damn thing," he said aloud. No one answered, of course. If Eve, the digital assistant, had been listening, she was not going to give him any help. Though that did not prevent him from trying. "Hey, computer... uh, Eve. You there?"

Surprisingly a response emanated from the tiny hidden speakers above him. *"I am here, Contestant #9. What may I help you with?"*

Josh's eyes flicked to the ceiling. *Where have I heard that voice before?* It was recognizable, not just one of the many generic off-the-shelf voice assistants he had heard. He couldn't place where it was from, however.

He thought for a moment. "Well, I'd sure like to go home. Can I just... leave? Maybe you show me where the door is?"

"I am sorry, I am not permitted to reveal the location of the exit to any of the contestants."

Josh frowned. It seemed this digital assistant had inadvertently revealed useful information to him. He wondered if that had been on purpose.

"Right," he said. "Worth a shot, I guess. Anyway, *Eve,*" he continued, testing whether or not using the machine's name would change the nature of her responses, "I am confused as to the nature of this puzzle. I see dots, but I don't really know what to do with them."

"I am sorry, I am not permitted to give solutions to the problem sets to any of the contestants."

Well, he thought, *fat bit of good that did.*

But he still did not understand the problem. What were these dots supposed to represent? And if this were the 'problem set' Eve had referred to, what the hell was he supposed to do with them?

Suddenly the screen flashed again, and a line appeared, connecting two of the dots on the bottom-right corner of the screen. It stayed there, then a number appeared immediately above the line, next to a word: *DISTANCE* $= 23$.

His frown deepened, but a thought popped into his mind. He tapped the return key on the keyboard, and the dots disappeared, replaced by a blinking cursor and what appeared to be a text editor.

He typed 'HELLO WORLD' in the prompt and hit return. Immediately the same message appeared below the typed words, repeating his message. He typed something else next.

$2 + 3$

The result, 5, showed up on the next line down.

"Okay, we're in a simple command prompt," he said to himself, muttering the words. "No idea what language we're using here, but..." his voice drifted away as he began typing once again. He wanted to explore this system a bit to see what he was working with. Was Eve connected to it as part of the server? Was she an app that ran simultaneously, or was one isolated from the other?

He had a feeling they were connected — that would be the easiest way to allow her to know what was going on in the rooms, as well as allow her to control things.

But his curiosity was piqued, and he felt he needed some clarity. He quickly typed a command.

sudo -u root ls

He wanted to see a list of all the files and directories on this mysterious computer, but the response was not quite as helpful as he would have hoped:

Sorry, user ROOT is not allowed to execute '/bin/ls' as root on HOST

Interesting, he thought. "So I can't even root in, even if I knew the password." He would not even be able to brute force his way into the server, at least not like this. Still, he had gleaned a bit of information from the computer.

He was communicating with the server successfully — that was a huge step. The command prompt was Linux-based, or at least shared similarities. That was good, as he was comfortable in that environment. He guessed this was an SSH terminal, which meant he could still do a bit of digging without needing root access.

Suddenly Eve's voice came back into his ears. *"Contestants, the second trial is about to begin. You will have 24 hours to complete the task and find a solution, and the clock starts now."*

A timer appeared overlaid on the screen in the bottom-right corner. It had started at exactly twenty-four hours and was already ticking off the seconds.

"Shit," he said, still muttering, "looks like Eve wants me focused on the task at hand."

He hit the key commands to exit the terminal prompt and was not surprised to see that the window disappeared, replaced once again by the strange dots. The two that had been connected earlier were no longer connected.

...complete the task and find a solution. His mind churned through her words. She had revealed earlier that there was in fact,

a door into and out of his jail cell. He still had no way to tell whether or not she had let that slip due to a programming error or if the digital assistant simply did not care if he knew.

But now she had said something else: his task was not just a task, but one which *required his finding a solution*. It was like some programming problem, and he started to think back over the years of his training.

Suddenly the dots in front of him made a little more sense. It was not a pattern he was supposed to recognize — these dots were arbitrary. But the little line connecting two of them, complete with a descriptor of distance and a number next to it, made him think of an old programming puzzle.

The *Traveling Salesman Puzzle*, he thought. It was a famous early twentieth-century computing puzzle that had iterated and morphed over the decades into all manner of subproblems and theories. The essential problem, at its core, was simple when represented as a question: how can a hypothetical traveling salesman reach all of his designated cities — the dots on the screen — as quickly and efficiently as possible?

Of course, the solution itself was anything *but* simple. The reason this particular problem was used in computing still today was that it was a great test of a system's resources and the management of those resources. Brute-forcing an answer to the problem was only possible for a handful of 'cities,' otherwise the possible routes the computer would have to run through to find the most efficient route would exceed the capacity of processors even running in parallel very quickly.

He remembered the math: the permutations for all the ordered combinations of cities would be $O(n!)$, where the time it would take to find the best answer would be a factorial of the total number of cities. Even with nineteen dots on the screen, to brute force a solution with an algorithm would take *far* longer than twenty-four hours, even with the most powerful computer on the planet.

Josh stepped back, then sat down on the bed. He needed to think, to process, but there was already too much thinking and processing happening in his mind. He needed to *rest*, but then again he felt as though wasting time would get him nowhere.

And even if he solved it, would he do it fast enough? He shuddered as he thought of the poor soul in the other room, the contestant who had refused to participate in the first trial.

What would happen if he completed this problem but not quickly enough?

As he sat on the bed, his thoughts turning back to the man who had not solved the previous problem and had paid the most horrific price for it, Josh tried to force himself to focus. There must be a solution to this problem, or Eve would not have presented it. But he had never had to solve it himself — worse, there were *already* theoretical solutions for it. Why did they want him to solve it as well?

Suddenly his head shot up. He stared at the screen a few feet away from the edge of his bed, and his mouth fell open.

The Traveling Salesman Problem was no longer the subject of his concern. His mind had finally pulled forth an answer to the *other* problem he had been struggling with.

He knew who the man was.

He knew the man's face, the man who had been burned alive in his torture chamber nearby.

He didn't just know the man's face; he *knew* the man himself.

CHAPTER 25
LIAM

"I may have a fix on a location, sir," Curtis Lee said. He stood up from his terminal, which consisted of his personal laptop set on a milk crate on a folding table in the corner of Liam's conference room. It was a terrible excuse for a standing desk, but Liam had to admit it fit the stereotype of a "professional hacker."

Curtis brushed his hair to the side to keep it out of his eyes, then walked over to where Liam was seated in front of his own computer. Liam was currently typing an email to Colonel Sykes about their progress, so this was perfect timing. If what Curtis had found proved to be accurate, he might be able to earn even more favor with Sykes — never a bad thing.

The newly formed team was gathered in the conference room. "What's up?" he asked, his eyes following Curtis as he approached Liam. He spun the small office chair around and sat backward, his hair dropping back over his eyes.

He blew it up and away from his face this time. "So I was

trying to figure out a link between Blake and Lane," he began, "but I figured, why not start with Robert Blake himself?"

"Right," Jocelyn said from next to Liam, "like track his location leading up to his interaction with Lane, and eventual death?"

"Uh, not really," Curtis said, frowning. "I figured that sort of spy stuff would be left to the, uh, *spies*." He flashed a glance at Liam.

"I'm not a *spy* either, Lee," Liam said. "But go on."

"Right, sure. We all work for the NSA, but we're *totally not spies*." He laughed but continued. "Anyway, nah — my specialty is hacking, right? So I... hacked."

"You hacked *Robert Blake?*" Roger Witherspoon asked. "How the hell did you gain access to a famous tech guy?"

"Well, I didn't. Not exactly. Hacking isn't just slinging shell scripts around and brute-forcing into backdoors with a black ski mask on, guys. It's problem solving. And more than anything else, it's *psychology*."

Liam nodded. "Yeah, that tracks. Hacking is about *people*. After all, we're not trying to access a computer for the computer's sake. We're trying to gain access to something that will help us learn something about a *person*."

"Exactly," Curtis said. "So anyway, I knew Blake would have his fingers in just about everything at his company, Aetheria. And even if I couldn't get access to someone or something that *he* was directly involved with, someone at Aetheria would have something informative on *him*. And *that* person might be, you know — a bit lazier when it comes to security and privacy protocols."

Liam was nodding along but getting impatient. "I'm assuming you found that person?"

Curtis's face broke into a wide smile. "Oh, I hit the jackpot. I gained access to a low-level tech who works there part-time. He was running a site-wide backup of their email software, as well as the internal company email database."

Liam was already getting excited. "You gained access to all of Blake's *email?*" he asked. That would have been better than he could have expected.

"Woah, slow down," Curtis said. "No — not all of it. As I said, this was just a backup. It was also an iterative backup, only adding the new data that had been created in the past twenty-four hours. But long story short, I was able to find this guy's access key and password in an unencrypted data dump he logged later that day. From that, I got into the backup files, decoded the email folder, and found a couple of emails to Robert Blake."

"All without being caught?" Jocelyn asked. "That's *damn* impressive."

She smiled at Curtis, and Liam could have sworn there was a spark of flirtatious interest between the two youngest members of the team.

"Uh, no..." Curtis said. "Not without being caught."

"What?" Liam asked. It was not the end of the world if they were found snooping around in a company's system, but it would require getting the NSA's legal team involved, as well as a friendly judge who owed them a favor.

"I mean, *I* didn't get caught. I'm using layers of VPNs and proxies, so there's no way they can trace this stuff back to me, personally. And us. But they *did* see it. Someone saw that there was an unidentifiable IP logged into the system for a few minutes, and they blocked access. Very likely, they'll start poking around and try to figure out who hacked them and how. But that's neither here nor there."

"I'd say that's *both* here *and* there," Witherspoon said.

"It's fine," Liam said. "They'll be on a wild goose chase, and besides, we're not trying to cause any harm. We're just... taking a few legal liberties to skip ahead. It's very likely this info would have taken weeks to access through proper channels, especially since Blake's death is now the subject of a murder investigation."

Curtis' smile widened. "Thanks. So, to recap, I got access to Blake's emails from only a twenty-four window, give or take. Most of those emails were boring business shit — reports, financial updates, yada yada. But there was one..."

Jocelyn leaned over the edge of the table, her chin resting on her hands, elbows on the table. Liam once again caught that glint in her eye. *Kids,* he thought, rolling his eyes.

"It was from a man named Kahn. Ahmed Ibn Kahn, to be exact."

Liam immediately started typing.

"Don't bother," Curtis said. "Unless you're searching the dark web. He's a ghost in real life, but fire up a DeepMesh Browser with the VPN config I'm running, and he's all over the place."

"We're the NSA, Lee. We have access to DeepMesh, but we'll have to bypass —"

"All the firewalls and run everything through a virtual server that fakes its location, yeah. I did that."

"Just now?" Roger asked.

Curtis looked at the older man as if *he* were a ghost. "I've been here for an hour and a half. The hell you think I was doing?"

Liam motioned with a hand for Curtis to continue. "Get to the good stuff, then, Lee. You've got a captive audience."

The kid's smile returned full force, and he launched into the explanation. "He's the son of a wealthy banker. Not royalty, but he hangs out with royalty. Loves to party, which is why his footprint's all over the dark web. Drugs, alcohol, hell — he's even purchased weapons for a party, what I'm assuming was an absolute rager. All of it, of course, untraceable using the ledger of some obscure Middle Eastern tech company's blockchain-backed currency. But he doesn't care about privacy, which is how it's easy to find him. He's all over the equivalent of social media over there, flaunting gold jewelry, said weaponry, hundred-dollar US bills, all of it."

"Sounds delightful," Liam said.

Curtis raised his eyebrows and shrugged. "What can I say? You guys are old. Kahn sounds like a lot of fun if you ask me."

"What's his relationship to Blake, then?" Roger asked.

"He emailed him a week ago. Blake responded, and the email chain was in the data dump I stole."

Liam waited, knowing they were finally getting answers.

"The email from Blake was simple: *not interested*. But the email he was responding to was a bit more... colorful."

"How so?"

"I forwarded it to Liam, so you can all read it in-depth later. But it spoke of a game — a competition, featuring the best-of-the-best from around the world. All hoping to be victorious and come out on top — again, really colorful stuff. It was encrypted, of course, but Blake's response wasn't, and it left in the text from the thread."

"So... a game?"

Curtis took a breath. "Best of all, there was a link. Again encrypted, once again requiring some finesse and skill to open unless you were the designated recipient. But I — *of course* — managed to open it."

At this, he opened up his own laptop and set it on the table, turning the screen toward everyone now gathered around Liam's seat.

Liam read it along with everyone else. It was a video, a simple textured background with a single logo superimposed on top, gently rocking and swaying with an invisible breath of wind.

Escape from Eden.

CHAPTER 26
LIAM

NSA HEADQUARTERS | FORT MEADE, *Maryland*

"I want this stream up on the screen!" Liam said. The entire room had burst into motion; every person suddenly urged into action by the words *Escape from Eden* that had appeared on Curtis' laptop.

Liam was busy working the controls of the ancient projector screen at the far end of the conference room. In a world of holographic videoconferencing technology and at an organization that prided itself on being able to know anything that happened digitally around the world at all times, Liam almost laughed out loud that this conference room still only had a drop screen mounted to the ceiling, with a tabletop projector sitting on the massive oak conference table.

But what they had just found was no laughing matter, and right now, their method of viewing it did not matter. "I want it on the projector screen, stat," he said, "and I want it there *constantly*. This is a loading screen or a preview or something. Maybe they took a commercial break — I don't know, and I don't care. I want it streaming 24/7 until we know for sure."

"But that's — this is an encrypted *stream*," Curtis argued. "I can't just add in another access point, and then another. They'll see the nodes, see that there are at least two more computers requesting the feed, and if they decide to check the locations of these IP addresses —"

"Lee," Liam said. "Come on. You're telling me you can't bypass all that? Run the traffic through eighteen proxy servers and anonymize our access?"

"I mean... yeah, but they'll still see that we're trying to access it, and —"

"*Lee*. Do it. I need to see this. Maybe it's nothing, but I want to know. And hell, once we figure out what it is and if it leads us to Lane, we can turn it off. Unless they've got NSA-caliber surveillance running on that feed, they're not even going to realize we're watching."

Curtis was already working, moving to the laptop that sat on a shelf near the projector screen. Each of them had been given limited access credentials to the NSA network, and he signed in then began navigating to a private browser and then to the website.

"So — this Kahn guy," Jocelyn continued. "Is he our primary suspect? If he's the one behind this... *Eden* thing, is he our lead to Joshua Lane? And why are we so interested in this *Escape from Eden* show? It's just a television show, right?"

Witherspoon spoke up, too. "And if what they're doing is *real*, that's a big deal. Why didn't Robert Blake report it? Call the NSA, the CIA, *anyone*?"

Liam didn't need to answer. They all knew why: blackmail.

While Curtis Lee had been phenomenally helpful in gaining access to Blake's emails, they had not seen the entire chain of communication between Kahn and Blake. He was positive there was something earlier in the chain that would answer that question accurately. But he was positive that Blake had kept things quiet because Kahn — and whoever he was working for — had dirt on Blake.

Liam considered his options. As a career NSA employee, he had been trained from early on to keep his cards close to his chest, even amongst his own team. It was not an outright rule, but there was an unspoken expectation at the National Security Agency that you could never fully trust anyone, and playing "information games" with coworkers was almost a requirement.

Still... this was *his* team, and Sykes had told him to run it the way he wanted. Liam was not a fan of withholding helpful information from others just for fun, and Sykes had not told him their meeting was confidential.

"Hernandez," Roger said. "You still with us, bud?"

Liam glanced from one member of his team to the next. He could tell them. He *had* to. He stood up and cleared his throat. He liked to move a bit when talking things out, and this bit of talking certainly required some activity. "Okay, listen," he began. "This is the NSA. You get it. Here, information is considered currency. The more you have, the more *power* you have. But by giving that information away to others, it's almost as if you no longer get to spend it elsewhere. I say all of this to assure you all that I am not purposefully withholding information because I don't *trust* you, but because it's my nature."

Roger chuckled. "Son, you've just described every branch of every armed force of every nation. You don't need to apologize to us, and — in the interest of getting this show on the road — skip to the meat."

Liam nodded, ignoring the mixed metaphor. "Thanks. Okay. Well, I was talking to Colonel Sykes, and I mentioned that the president was interested in finding Lane. That's true, but he *also* told Sykes to look into something for him."

Curtis turned from the computer in the corner of the room to face Liam. "I'm assuming this 'something' has something to do with Joshua Lane."

"That's my assumption, yes," Liam said. "Specifically, the president, through Sykes, has tasked us with finding out what's up with some weird little theorized dark web reality show called *Escape from Eden*."

Jocelyn rolled her eyes. "Should have just led with that, sir," she said.

"Perhaps so," he said. "But yes — to answer your question — I *do* think *Escape from Eden* is our link to Lane. And if this guy, Kahn, knows something about it, I think we need to have a chat."

"Any idea where he is?" Witherspoon asked.

"Working on it," Curtis said. "But the teacher wanted some fancy special video, so you're gonna have to wait."

Liam smiled. "Don't make me keep you after class," he said. Then, turning to Roger, "the president's still looking into it, apparently. If there's information on al-Sadir, the guy he thinks is behind all of this; he's going to pass it through Colonel Sykes and then on to us."

"al-Sadir?" Curtis asked. He stopped typing and turned to face Liam once more. "*Mohammad* al-Sadir?"

Liam blinked. "Yes — yeah, why? That's the name the president passed on to us. He told Sykes he has some intelligence groups gathering information on *Escape from Eden,* and that al-Sadir might be a person of interest."

Curtis laughed. "Yeah, you definitely need to work on that 'withholding information' shit. Man, if you would have just told me that earlier —"

"What do you know?" Witherspoon shot back. Liam sensed this older man was growing tired of the briefing and info dump and wanted to take actual *action.*

Curtis typed a few more words, then used the laptop's trackpad to drag a window to the other screen, which was the projector display. A gigantic, slowly moving version of the *Escape from Eden* graphic appeared onscreen. "Ta-da!" he said. "Anyway, yeah — Mohammad al-Sadir. Rich playboy, eager entrepreneur, sexy yacht owner."

"What *about* him? What else do you know?" Witherspoon asked.

"Oh, you know — nothing much. That's all public knowledge I found while snooping around a few minutes ago, and it's all public knowledge. But the best part? I think he's best friends with our guy, Kahn."

"That's perfect," Jocelyn said. "So al-Sadir's behind *Escape from Eden,* or at least the president — whose intelligence gathering *I'm* not going to question — thinks so. That's good, right?"

"Sure," Curtis added, now seated in front of his own laptop on the oak table. "The problem is, he's a ghost. There's *nothing* about his current location. He's got a freaking *Wikipedia* page, but he's not on any social networks. No way to trace him with any sort of expectation of accuracy."

"So where does that leave us?" Liam asked.

"Back at square one, which is why I mentioned that I have a possible location."

Liam had nearly forgotten that their conversation had started with Curtis saying as much but motioned for the kid to continue.

"al-Sadir may be impossible to track down — he's wealthy beyond measure, so he's no doubt hired a fleet of guys like me to keep his online presence nonexistent. But his friend, Kahn, is nowhere near that sophisticated."

He made a point of sliding his computer around slowly, dramatically, to reveal a social media post by none other than Ahmed Ibn Kahn. "Check it out," he said, reading off the post. "'*Nothing like hanging with friends in high places.*' As I said, he doesn't have a presence on any *popular* social media accounts, but he's got a little profile on a network on the Dark Web."

Liam examined the picture. It was a shot of a beautiful sunset, with a large, doughy-looking man of Arab descent smiling at the camera through sunglasses. He was shirtless, wearing board shorts and flip-flops, and his arm was around a petite, young girl.

And Kahn was standing on a yacht. It was unmistakable — he saw the railing behind the trio, the cerulean waters of whatever ocean they were in beyond the group.

"Could we be so lucky as to —"

"As to have a reflection of the boat's name in Kahn's glasses?" Curtis asked. "Turns out, we *could* be so lucky."

He messed with the image onscreen a bit, then enlarged it. It was still pixelated — technology had not increased to the point of adding perfect data into places there was none to begin with — but imaging software had at least advanced to the point of calculating the probability of a neighboring pixel's hue. In this case, it had taken the reflection of Kahn's sunglasses and enhanced it enough to see that there was lettering against the wall in front of Kahn, off to the side a bit.

"It's the name of the boat," Curtis said. "And I don't have the programming chops Jocelyn does, so I'd bet she could whip up some fancy AI tool that could make a better guess. But the good news is we can see half of it."

"I can see that," Liam said, hardly listening. They had just been given a major clue. It was a thread, and it might lead them nowhere, but they were going to track it down. "Looks like the letters *A-T-I-U-M,*" he said. "That's the last half of the word, I think."

It was good enough to start down the rabbit hole. He knew the servers downstairs could be spun up to search their databases for purchase records for sizable investments like yachts. That was standard fare for catching embezzlers and tax evaders, and the IRS often requested information just like that. In the interest of completion and thoroughness, the system would have all known purchases of all known yachts in its massive bank of drives, at least somewhere.

He did not even have to mention it to Jocelyn. "I can find it," she said. "I'll run a search downstairs, see if there's any match for a vessel of that name, or at least those letters making up part of it."

Liam nodded. Curtis pulled the computer back toward his lap, obviously ready to start looking for the next clue. "How long?" he asked.

She shrugged. "Maybe an hour?"

He nodded. "Great. Get it done." He turned to Curtis Lee. "You can help her out with an online search. Anything related to the yacht, Kahn, or al-Sadir that you can dig up."

Curtis smirked. "Way ahead of you."

"Great," Liam replied. "In that case, go with Jocelyn. She may not need the help or the company, but I need to discuss our plan with Colonel Witherspoon about what we'll be doing once we *do* find this yacht."

Curtis stood to leave, and Roger Witherspoon pulled up a briefcase onto his lap and unclasped it. Liam was surprised to see not a laptop inside but a thick ream of paper.

"I'm a bit old-school," Roger said with a wink. "But my plan's solid as ever. Check this out."

CHAPTER 27

JOSH

LOCATION *unknown*

Josh's mouth fell open. He had known the man who he had just seen murdered on the computer monitor. Dr. Nazem Moussaf was a world-renowned mathematician and computer cryptology expert. Josh had met him once at an Air Force training, though they hadn't spent much time together.

Who are the rest of the contestants? he wondered. *Why were we all brought here against our will?*

And why are they killing us if we don't obey?

Josh sat back on the bed, rubbing his eyes. This was all becoming too much to bear, though he suspected that was all part of this game as well. It wasn't just about who could solve these problems — it was about watching the contestants solve problem sets under immense pressure. The *pressure* was what mattered, not the *solution*.

They need us for something, he realized. *They want us to prove our worth.* The people behind this 'game' knew they were all geniuses — knew they were all experts in something related to computing and technology. So they wanted their genius for something, but they needed to understand how they would all act under pressure.

Josh considered the problem facing him now — not the existential problem, but the one waiting for him on the computer screen. The Traveling Salesman Problem was easily solvable, in that one simply needed to put in an equation and then wait for the computer to do the work. The issue was that larger versions of the traveling salesman problem could render CPU resources of even the largest supercomputers useless for too long a time. Working through all the permutations of the routes in a brute-force way would cost a lot in terms of energy and bandwidth. Some weaker machines couldn't handle the load at all, and would simply time out.

That meant the answer Josh was looking for needed to be elegant — the people running the show wouldn't care that their computer could solve the problem — they cared whether or not *Josh* could solve it, and whether or not he could give their computer an elegant enough equation to solve it in the allotted time.

Without knowing exactly what computer specifications he had available, that meant there would still be plenty of brute force and guesswork happening.

He stood, trying to remember the classes he had taken years ago that covered the problem. It was often taught as a theoretical exercise meant to lead to a discussion of computing power and Moore's Law. He remembered the algorithm to brute force a solution — literally a way to tell the computer to trace each route one at a time, measuring the distance between each, for every single possible route on the map that connected all of the dots. Then, the computer could put the routes in order from longest to shortest or vice versa. It was an elegant solution from an algorithmic standpoint, and it was considered the foundational solution to the problem. Once the programmer understood this algorithm, they could build one that was more complicated but faster or more streamlined later.

He frowned, trying to ensure he knew each of the steps and the exact code he would need to write.

His embedded computer chip would have been helpful in this situation, but only if it could connect to the outside world. While NARA was helpful at scanning the memories that existed in his mind before the chip had been implanted at the base of his skull, only the memories he had formed *after* it was added were considered complete and retrievable.

Human memory was strange — while most people considered memory storage and retrieval working the same way they watched a movie, by queuing it up and pressing play, the reality was that memory worked in far stranger ways.

It was malleable, unreliable, and often completely wrong. In the '90s, an experimenter named James Coan even proved that it was possible to plant 'false' memories. He gave a booklet detailing fictitious events to his brother, including in it a story of Coan getting lost in a mall. His brother, after reading and 'remembering' the story, believed it to be true. He even added in his own slight changes — what they were wearing, what they were talking about when it happened, and more.

Josh's interest in memory began in grade school when he tried to develop an eidetic memory through practice and experimentation. It had failed, so when given the opportunity to implant

NARA into his head, he knew it was just the sort of leap forward he wanted to be a part of.

Josh's memory was good, but it was far from eidetic or photographic. Therefore, he was most excited about NARA's capabilities on that front. Early tests using NARA's storage capabilities were promising — Josh still had not been able to force NARA to store an image or scene into memory on command reliably, but he often found that by concentrating extremely hard on one thing — a long string of numbers, for example — NARA would assume the memory was important enough to store it. He then only had to subconsciously ask for its retrieval and the image would be superimposed directly in front of his eyes.

It was indistinguishable from magic, and when Josh had learned about it, he was giddy.

But he had learned of the Traveling Salesman Problem long before he had NARA implanted in his head, so in this moment, he truly was on his own. He remembered the basics and assumed he could figure out the rest once he started working.

He walked over to the computer and the flat, lit keyboard appeared again. He placed his hands on it and started typing.

Line by line, code swirled through his mind and out his fingers, appearing onscreen. He had remained in the terminal window, using a break character that would only start a new line rather than enter the program and clear the screen. He had a few missteps, but after ten minutes of work, he had written what he remembered to be the correct code for solving the brute-force version of the algorithm. He took a few extra glances over the screen, then pressed return on the keyboard.

He shrugged as the screen changed, and a progress bar appeared. *Let's see how close I got,* he thought. He had no idea if he was going to get another chance or not. If he were wrong — if there was a typo in the code — would *Eve* just kick it back to him for him to try again? Or had he sealed his fate the moment he had pressed return?

The progress bar began filling to the right, and he frowned again as he watched its speed. He assumed the progress bar was *Eve* trying out his code against the traveling salesman problem, but it was moving far too fast.

His brute force approach on a problem set of this size should take many minutes on a powerful computer — this seemed to be only taking seconds.

What sort of supercomputing power are we working with here?

He wondered what *Eve* had up her sleeve, wondered how the people who had built this place planned to handle the immense amount of computing power required for not just one solution but many, as each contestant finished their own version.

Josh stepped back from the screen and waited for the progress bar to finish.

A new message suddenly displayed on the screen.

Solution correct. Total elapsed time, 9.32 seconds.

Josh's jaw dropped. He had solved the traveling salesman problem with the basic brute force algorithm. That part wasn't a surprise. What was amazing to him was how quickly *Eve* — the computer he assumed was behind all of this — had been able to use the algorithm to find the solution. It didn't seem possible, and yet here was confirmation right in front of his face.

He doubled down on his feeling from earlier. *They're using us for something. They need us to solve some complex computing problem. And they have the tech to be able to pull it off.*

Josh would not have considered himself a genius, but he did

know as much as anyone about his particular domain. His background in quantum computing, as it related to cryptography, made him one of the world's foremost experts on the topic.

Could this knowledge be what they're after?

They wanted his brain — his mind — for some reason, and they had built a supercomputer to help determine if he was fit for the job.

It was all speculation now, of course. His best guess was still that — just a guess. He had no idea the true reason why he was here — why Dr. Nazem Moussaf had been killed and why others just like him were sitting in their own torture chambers, solving an already known problem for their strange host.

But Josh *was* a problem-solver, so left with only a few pieces of information, he would try to put those pieces together the only way they made sense. It might lead him toward finding a way out of this place. He had solved this game, but his gut check told him there would be more. He barely remembered the solution to this one, so what would happen when he was faced with a problem he wasn't familiar with?

What would happen when the problems got trickier?

He shuddered, thinking once more of Dr. Moussaf and his terrible fate.

CHAPTER 28
AL-SADIR

"Sir, they're moving," Hans' voice called out.

The large German was still booming through the yacht's hallways, preparing to enter al-Sadir's study, but he had forecasted his news. *Which meant it was urgent*, al-Sadir thought.

"Come in," he said. Hans entered, repeating the statement. "Moving where?" al-Sadir asked.

Hans' brow furrowed as he examined his small tablet. It seemed even smaller in the giant's hands. "Looks like they are preparing a raid," Hans said. "Still in Baltimore, but the military contingent working on this has a 'team in place.' His words," he added.

al-Sadir rubbed his chin, looking up from his own tablet.

"Have we tracked down Ruth Dalia's location yet?" he asked.

Hans shook his head. "No, sir. I apologize — it's likely she is aware that we are attempting to track her down. Do you think she somehow knows about Lane?"

al-Sadir thought for a moment. "No, I don't believe so. She

probably wants to maintain as much plausible deniability as possible. It's happened before."

"Yes, and those times we have had knowledge of their location and maneuverings, so we were able to get to them before they reported it or fled."

"I'm aware," al-Sadir said. "Which is exactly why I'm *very* interested in tracking her down. She's the only loose end we need to tie up. If she somehow manages to convince someone of the invitation to view, we could have more than just the NSA on our tail."

"The US President —"

"I *know* the President is interested in finding Lane as well, Hans," al-Sadir snapped. He calmed himself down and rubbed his temples. "What are the odds a mark for participating in the games is part of some top-secret project there? We could not have known about it beforehand."

"I just mean we should be more careful going forward," Hans said. "Perhaps we drop the search for Dalia, so we can focus our resources on *not* causing more US organizations to join their search for *us*. She may not have even told anyone about us yet."

al-Sadir considered this. "Perhaps. I'm not convinced she is just taking a pleasure cruise, though. If she is intending to stay out of reach because she *knows* we are looking for her, that only means she will certainly call it in and tell someone about us once she surfaces again."

He paused again, then looked back up at Hans. "Is there more news about the NSA group?"

Hans nodded. "Yes, but it's worse. They know of the *Solatium* as well, so they will come directly here. I believe they found a record of Kahn's social account — they know he is close with you, so it would be a wise move to examine his online presence. I did see a picture he took of himself, on the yacht. My guess is that they found this as well and somehow connected it back to us. In any event, they will be coming here, looking for you. I can call our own team to bolster my security presence, but at the end of the day, this is still just a boat, and I am unsure of how many mercenaries I can have here in time."

"Right."

"And if they *do* come here..." Hans' voice trailed off for a moment. "I know we have discussed options, but sir, there is no way it can end well. Failure means your capture, or worse."

While al-Sadir was not about to jump to worst-case scenarios, he nodded solemnly. He did not want to give the impression that he did not understand the gravity of the situation. Truthfully, he was impressed. Hans' meddling in the NSA's security systems for the past few years had paid off. The German brute of a man was anything but when it came to knowledge of computers. He could hack almost anything, given enough time, and al-Sadir had resourced him enough to provide whatever capabilities the man did not already have.

The result was an NSA network that, to this day, still had no idea there was a tunnel breach allowing access to the cursory surveillance systems around their offices.

But cursory access was all al-Sadir needed or wanted. He just wanted to keep tabs on any American wanderlust, any teams that thought it might be prudent to try to track him down.

This effort had paid off in spades — al-Sadir knew Hans' information had been gleaned from the camera and audio surveillance devices the American National Security Administration had installed in their facilities and connected to their closed intranet server. And since no one in any US government body could justifiably track and monitor internal communications of one of their own agencies without severe scrutiny, the intranet devices simply saved their data to local hard drives, to be accessed only in instances of a break-in or if someone needed to reference a conversation that had transpired.

So Hans' team of computer experts had successfully added an invisible upload link to the intranet's line, one that compressed and sent all the terabytes of video and audio data it received to a satellite uplink that only he could access.

Now, Hans could surveil any and all of the private conversations taking place in and around the NSA headquarters buildings, assuming those conversations were in range of a local security camera. Most of the offices had no such security inside, and none of the NSA's computers were connected to this system, so there was no chance of Hans intercepting classified files or data, but that was not the point.

The point was to find and root out exactly what he had just found: a conversation that had transpired in a *less* private location within the NSA's walls — namely, a conference room.

"Good work, Hans. You are sure of what you heard?" al-Sadir asked.

Hans nodded. "I did have to use lip reading intelligence software to compile best-guess reconstructions of some of the audio, but yes. I am sure."

"I see. What are your suggested maneuverings?"

al-Sadir had, of course, already planned for multiple contingencies, including something like this, but he knew that Hans' expertise would be wasted without at least hearing the man out.

"I suggest we all leave at once, sir," Hans said. "You, me, Kahn, and we can dispose of his... escorts on the island before we reach the airport. We must leave with no delay. We can continue receiving updates as we travel, of course, so we will not be deaf or blind. I will feed you updates as you request them or if anything requires your attention, but until then, you can be at ease knowing I am taking care of our forthcoming visitors."

"And how exactly *do* you plan on taking care of these visitors?" al-Sadir asked. While Hans was a gifted security expert, both knowledgeable enough to handle a hacker's breach *and* physically well-trained enough to handle himself in a gunfight, he was but one man. Hans' team of mercenaries and cyber experts was really just a collection of contacts spread out around the world. al-Sadir kept them all on retainer, so they could be tapped for service at any time, but the truth of the matter was that on the yacht, a single man had responsibility for al-Sadir's safety and protection.

"I have already sent out a call for a team to prepare to meet up with us, but I have yet to tell them a location in case our new visitors are also monitoring *our* communications. I am assuming you want to be near *Palem*, correct?"

al-Sadir nodded. It wasn't impossible that the NSA — the world's foremost experts on computer hacking and systems — could be listening in, but he knew it was highly unlikely. To do that, they would have to know *what* to listen for and how to find them.

"Perfect," Hans continued. "I will tell them to prepare and head to our *Palem* facility, then await further instructions. My assumption is that our visitors will scour the yacht and look for any clues that may lead them to *Palem*. Most likely, they will find some."

"They will, indeed," al-Sadir said.

"Sir?"

"I like your plan. Thank you, Hans. You have once more proved your worth. However, *we* will be traveling alone. You and me only — not Kahn."

"You intend to leave him behind?"

"He has once again disobeyed my orders, and his cavalier ways have directly led them to us."

"I agree."

"As such," al-Sadir continued, "I intend to show him just what a lack of loyalty earns. He wants to galavant around with his play-things on *my* dime, to spend this time ignoring his role of one day taking over for me; that is his choice. I have given him more than enough chances."

"So you will leave him here to die?"

al-Sadir was not sure if Hans' words were meant as a slight, but he assumed the best. "No, Hans. I do not believe these American soldiers will strike to kill. They want *me*, and they need me alive, just like I need one of *them* alive to tell us about this top-secret project of theirs. So they will board and search the yacht, but they will not kill anyone who does not put up a fight. It is a risk, but one worth taking. We can leverage this for our needs."

"I see. But he may reveal the location of —"

"*Palem* is not the end game, Hans. They will find it, no matter what we do to conceal its existence. A secret this large cannot be kept forever, and while Kahn forced our hand, this was always part of the plan. Send your team there, and have them prepared to fight. But with one small change."

"What change, sir?"

"The team's size — whatever it is now, double it. Tell them to be ready for engagement."

CHAPTER 29
JOSH

LOCATION *unknown*

The moment the solution was flashed on Josh's screen, the lights in the room changed. The built-in recessed LEDs shifted in hue to a bluish tone, a calming, soothing color that immediately gave Josh pause.

Oh no, he thought. *I just solved the puzzle. But that means...*

Eve's voice reverberated through Josh's room, and he knew she was addressing *all* the contestants, not just Josh. *"Contestant #9 has succeeded in finding a solution to the problem. Time elapsed is thirty-seven minutes, nineteen seconds from trial start. Solution time is 9.32 seconds. Contestant #9 is victorious and shall receive immunity from the next trial."*

He swallowed. *Had the previous victor received immunity?* He could not remember hearing anything about that, but perhaps that first trial was really just a way to introduce the contestants to the game. This, for all intents and purposes, could have been the *real* first trial.

And he had solved it, apparently faster than the others, but...
who had *failed* to solve it?

As if reading his mind, the computer monitor shifted again to a
view of another room, this one also identical to Josh's. He still had
no concept of the larger space they were all in, or if they even *were*
all in one space separated into identical rooms, but he assumed so.

As he watched the space come into view, he noticed that the
room was actually only close to identical — it was a mirror image
of his own. The bed was on the opposite wall; the computer screen
there set into the wall on the other side of the room as Josh's.

And it was easy enough to tell that this was not Josh's room
because there was another person sitting on the bed.

They were sweating profusely, muttering something to themselves. He frowned as he watched the woman's lips moving, her
long, reddish-blonde hair drooped over the front and sides of her
head, her mouth barely visible.

No, not a woman, he thought. Once they rolled their head
back and the hair fell from his eyes, Josh saw that the sole occupant of this other room was a man, a frail-looking older gentleman
whose features were slightly effeminate.

And once again, Josh recognized him.

It was another computer scientist, this time a professor of
computer science and conceptual algorithms from Stanford. He
was more well-known to Josh than Nazem Moussaf, even though
he had never met the man.

His name was Roger Eberly, and he had multiple PhDs from
multiple universities, was often cited in research and scholarly
journals for his work in reverse-engineering algorithmic social platform functions, and had — the reason Josh knew of him — had
been contracted for the past decade or so to work with the Air

Force on a groundbreaking new technology that would be able to automatically pilot drones and launch attacks on enemy nations.

And, once again, there was no sound from the room itself. Eve had turned off the functionality, and Josh had no choice but to watch Eberly's mouth move, the incoherent ramblings of a man who knew what was coming next.

Josh felt the same remorse, the same fear and trepidation he had felt watching Dr. Moussaf, but he still could not pull his eyes away.

Eberly's lips moved along, a repeated pattern of opening and closing his lips, just as Eve's unnaturally calm voice broke in.

"Contestant #2 has failed the last test and shall now be eliminated."

Josh held back the tears, but the emotions were there, just beneath the surface. Sure, he did not know this man personally, but that didn't matter. It was a *man*, a human being, a person who probably had a family and friends and interests and —

He stopped the thought process as he realized something about Eberly's mouth. It wasn't just moving in a weird, repeated pattern.

He was speaking the same *words* over and over again.

Strange, Josh thought.

He was not a lip reader, but it seemed like one of the words was the number *one*. He watched carefully for a few more seconds as the room began to turn slightly orange.

Eberly's sweat intensified, but he did not move from his perch on the bed. He seemed to *know* what was coming, almost seemed to be inviting it.

It reminded Josh of the videos of the Vietnamese Buddhist monk, Thich Quang Duc, who had self-immolated at a Saigon intersection in 1963 to protest the persecution of his fellow believers.

The stoicism in the man's face registered in Josh's mind more strongly than his shaking hands, his sweat-filled brow, and the strange ramblings.

Two, four-five-three. One.

Josh saw the words again, complete with a slight pause between them. He was watching for it now, and it was obvious to see that they were, in fact, numbers. Repeated. Five of them, over and over again.

One, two, four, five, three.

One, two, four, five, three.

Josh frowned as Eberly's head began to shake softly. His long, stringy hair fell back in front of his mouth, and he paused the strange incantation of the four numbers to try to blow the hair off his lips. It did not work, and Josh could almost hear the hot air escaping the man's chapped lips.

He gave up and began reciting again, the same numbers, the same order.

Josh tried to imagine him saying something else. *Could it be something else instead? Words instead of letters?*

There were plenty of options for English words that might look the same as saying a string of numbers, he knew. But it made sense that this man would be reciting numbers — he had been a mathematician and computer scientist.

But did it? *This* was how he wanted to die? Reciting a strange incantation of numbers that made no sense.

And with whom was he trying to communicate? There were only the contestants themselves and whoever might be watching — if the man in charge allowed anyone to watch it — outside of these walls. Was he trying to talk to someone out there? To convince them to stop this?

Josh had to admit that repeating *one, two, four, five, three* over and over was a terrible way to convince anyone to do anything.

That meant it had to be something else.

And it had to be meant for someone who would understand it.

One, two, four, five, three.

EAST OF MALÉ | *Maldives*

Liam Hernandez did not like the plan. He sat buckled in the military helicopter across from Lieutenant Colonel Roger Witherspoon, commander of this operation. There were five other soldiers in the chopper as well, the five special forces soldiers Witherspoon had called in, who would be led on the ground by a man named Nathan Symonds. They were fully geared up and ready for a war, by the looks of it. Witherspoon had also reached out to a friend of his in charge of a private mercenary group called *Ravenclaw*. He was standing by in southern Europe, preparing a team that would be able to get to Witherspoon in under five hours.

To be fair, Witherspoon's plan was perfect, considering the time constraints and variables — Liam just did not want to be a part of it. He had hoped that by being tasked by Colonel Sykes to run point on this mission to retrieve Joshua Lane, he would be able to stay back at the NSA headquarters, safely tucked away behind numerous layers of protective steel, concrete, and military security.

But that was not to be. He had been told by Witherspoon in no uncertain terms that his presence was crucial here. He would stay in the helicopter, which would hover a mile away from the soldiers' insertion point, running the communication lines between himself, Witherspoon, and the rest of the team back in Maryland. Curtis Lee and Jocelyn Potter had set up a semi-permanent base of operations in Liam's conference room, and both had assured him that they would be ready for anything.

He sincerely hoped so. He had not joined the NSA to fly around in military helicopters, hunting down a Middle Eastern derelict halfway around the world. And to top it off, he was exhausted. They had taken a jet to an American air base in Sri Lanka, and from there, hopped on the helicopter that would drop them at their destination.

Liam took a deep breath, then raised his chin toward Witherspoon. "Everything on track?" he asked.

Witherspoon smiled, then nodded. He spoke to him through the headset they were all wearing. "Relax, Hernandez. Piece of cake. It's a single yacht in the middle of the ocean — best guess is they've got one, maybe two grunts playing security guard. They don't stand a chance against my boys."

"I..."

"What's more, I don't leave things to chance. It's why I'm still alive long after my card was punched. Five of these guys is about four too many."

"I know," Liam said. "It's just... my role —"

"Is crucial, son," Witherspoon said. "Don't get in your head about it. I'm here to control the on-the-ground stuff. You're here to make sure I've got any information that your hacker kid might dig up. Usually, it's not the way we do things, but this operation is happening at the speed of light, remember? We need to know if there's any movement from our mark — both to alert us that they're on to us and to make sure we're keeping tabs on them. The internet age made all this crap infinitely more difficult, so trust me: you need to be here."

"I still think I could have done that from Maryland."

Witherspoon was shaking his head before Liam could even finish. "Nope. Not an option. I have to be one-hundred-percent eyes-on with my guys. That means playing God from this chopper. I can't be worrying about fiddling with technology, too. That's your only job — it doesn't sound like much, but it is."

Liam swallowed, but nodded. He knew this already — it's what they had hashed out back in the conference room. Curtis and Jocelyn had found the yacht: a massive luxury liner sailing under the Latin name *Solatium* — solace. It had been purchased by a sheik, given to his son, then sold a few times until landing in the hands of a man named al-Sadir — the very man they were after.

Thanks to al-Sadir's friend's loose grasp of social media and modern tracking technology, they had a very good idea as to where to find the yacht.

And Witherspoon had put together a flawless operation to *take over* that yacht.

The plan was simple: full-force, smash-and-grab operation to bring al-Sadir, and possibly his friend Kahn, into US custody. They could interrogate him for as long as it took, knowing that al-Sadir needed to get back to his sadistic *Escape from Eden* game. He would crack quickly, eventually giving them the location of Joshua Lane and the other poor souls imprisoned with him.

And if that did not work, they would repeat the same process on Kahn — the man had already fumbled secret information; it was Witherspoon's professional opinion that he was likely to do it again, especially if a bit of nudging was involved.

They had traveled all day, leaving immediately after Witherspoon had drawn up the plan and Sykes had approved it. Both men were eager for action, and Liam could not argue with that. After half a day of supersonic flights, they were finally here.

The chopper pulled up, having reached its destination. All Liam saw was inky blackness; it would have been mid-evening back in Baltimore, but here it was still over an hour until dawn. He yawned, even though it was nowhere near bedtime.

Witherspoon barked orders to the men in the cabin and they jumped into action. One of them pulled three personal submersible propulsion vehicles from duffel bags that seemed too small to be able to hold them. Liam knew from Witherspoon's briefing that these were military prototypes, state-of-the-art technology that was not available on the open market. Each was capable of reaching speeds of nearly twenty miles an hour underwater and powerful enough to haul two or even three men chained in tow with one another.

Another man prepared the diving gear — miniature scuba tanks that held just enough breathable air to get there and back — and flippers.

Finally, a third man checked the weaponry they would be carrying. An assault rifle for each member and two magazines of ammunition that would not stop functioning after being submerged. Each man also carried a personal sidearm and a combat knife.

To Liam's untrained eye, it seemed like a *lot* of firepower, especially for an operation to take out one or two civilians and some unsuspecting guards. Still, he was reminded of Witherspoon's preference — be more prepared than they would have deemed necessary.

The soldiers finished their preparations and waited for Witherspoon's order. He had organized this mission down to the second, and he watched his dive watch with scrutiny. After a minute of hovering over the empty section of the Indian Ocean, he held up a hand with five fingers splayed out. He counted down one at a time.

Three, two, one.

"Go time, boys. Get it done."

The soldiers grunted a quick response, and the first of the men threw open the chopper door, then fell backward out of the open space.

Liam's voice caught in his throat, and he watched as the soldiers, one by one, disappeared.

"No going back now, Liam," Witherspoon said. "Let's hope we're in and out, just as planned."

Liam gulped again, but nodded.

No going back now, indeed, he thought.

PART THREE

CHAPTER 31
NATHAN

Captain Nathan Symonds assessed the situation. It wasn't that he hated the situation; it was just... off. Something about the whole mission seemed haphazard, thrown together. As if Witherspoon had simply woken up that morning and decided to throw some Rangers into a battle.

And if that *had* happened, not a lot of hours had ticked off the clock so far *this* morning — it wasn't even five o'clock yet — which meant Witherspoon must have really put it together last minute.

Symonds was a seasoned veteran, so he knew this wasn't actually the case. Witherspoon was likely under immense pressure to get results *yesterday*, to put it in military speak. That meant rushing out here, scrambling the men he knew he could trust to do it right and dumping them in the broth that was the ocean surrounding the Maldives.

He knew the men he was with now, all swimming toward the massive luxury yacht floating just up ahead. He had worked with most of them before, on some mission or another, in some random location around the world. He had to admit, this was not the worst-planned one, and Witherspoon's track record spoke for itself. The man was nearly a legend, someone who had figured out how to play the politics game in Washington and somehow still keep his troops happy.

The mission today seemed easy enough, and that's what had Symonds worried. The easy ones on paper always turned out to be the challenging ones for reasons no one could have predicted. They were certainly prepared for anything, both in their training and in their load-out, but that didn't matter. *No plan survives first contact with the enemy.*

He motioned with a free hand to the man to his right, a First Lieutenant named Bryson he had never deployed with. The kid seemed sturdy enough, at least for this smash-and-grab.

Bryson sped off to the right, flanking the yacht with two other men behind him. A lone soldier followed Symonds' path through the dark waters, and within another minute they were at the built-in ladder that would allow access to the lowest deck of the yacht.

He pulled his dive mask back and let it fall, a lanyard holding it now while he pulled off his fins and clipped these also to the carabiner on the strap. He would only don these if the mission was a success — if they needed a quick exit, there wouldn't be time to get dolled up in scuba gear once more.

The man behind him followed him up the ladder and onto the deck, where he immediately crouched and waited for Symonds' order. Symonds watched the deck facing the opposite direction, as eye contact was not needed. He waited thirty seconds and then spoke, his voice barely above a whisper.

"Team One, in position. Team Two, awaiting your confirmation."

A paper-thin computing device inside a waterproof bag strapped around his thigh translated the near-grunts into an intelligible voice, then encrypted it and sent it out to his teammates. This message was sent through an ad-hoc network that wouldn't appear on any network scanners currently on the market, but it was short-range. If any of his men got more than a hundred feet away from him, they would be out of range.

Since he planned to stay near the center of the yacht for this very reason, he suspected there would be no trouble with communication.

Team Two's leader, a man Symonds had served with for years, responded almost immediately. *"Team Two, in position."*

He didn't hesitate. The sooner they kicked this off, the sooner they could all get back, dry off, and get a *real* night's sleep. "Go," he said.

The man behind him dashed off to the nearest door and slid it open. This was the access point to the inside hallway, and it was unlocked.

So far, so good.

He heard the confirmation that Team Two had also gotten inside successfully. He jogged to the open door to rejoin his second, making sure his assault rifle was in hand as he pulled himself through the hatch.

"No movement so far. Moving toward the stairs at the aft section."

Witherspoon's plan, approved by Symonds, had split the yacht into upper and lower sections, each to be explored by a different team. Symonds and his sole team member would stay on this main deck, eventually working down to the belowdecks level, while

Team Two would start upstairs and explore the bedrooms and lounge on that level.

The entire procedure should last no more than five minutes total, at which point anyone on board would be found by the teams and apprehended.

But it did not even take one minute for the first group of people to be found.

"We've got people. One of the guest rooms. Permission to enter?"

"Do it."

There was a crashing sound that Symonds could hear through the hull of the yacht, and he and his teammate waited for the sound of gunfire.

None came.

Soon, the voice came back through his in-ear. *"Uh, you — you guys need to come see this. We got him."*

Symonds' heart sank. That was never good news, not in the line of fire. "Affirmative, but we'll do a quick sweep through our section first. You safe?"

"We're fine. Hurry up."

Symonds was now more intrigued than he was worried. This was uncharacteristic, but it didn't sound ominous. His men had not stumbled upon a gun-wielding bad guy.

But that did not mean they were out of danger. There was still a large yacht to poke around in, and that meant many small nooks and crannies, perfect hiding spots for *other* gun-wielding bad guys.

They made the rounds in another few minutes, then headed up the stairs to the second level to join Team Two.

Two of the men were waiting for Team One at the door, and Symonds knew the third would be inside, gun out, making sure their capture stayed put. Symonds now spoke using his voice's full volume. "What's this about, soldier? You had me spooked for a minute."

The two men apparently couldn't contain themselves any longer. They burst out laughing, almost in sync with one another. Symonds frowned as he walked up closer to the open door. He wasn't about to let his guard down.

When he reached the open door and peered in, he couldn't help himself either. In his years of service, he had come across many things. Some of them horrifying, disgusting, and downright cruel, some of them strange and macabre.

But he had never seen anything like... this.

"What do you think, boss?" a man behind him asked. He heard the voice through his in-ear almost in real-time as the words were spoken. "You taking first crack?"

CHAPTER 32

JOSH

LOCATION *unknown*

It was time to move. Time to act.

Josh could not get the words out of his mind. The numbers.

One, two, four, five, three.

Twelve-thousand four-hundred fifty-three.

He was not sure if the numbers were meant to be a single string or separate digits. Dr. Eberly had only spoken them as singular words, but the man had been dying — literally. Who knows what was going through the man's mind as his prison cell erupted in broiling temperatures?

Josh could not shake the thought, however, that Eberly had been trying to tell him something. He had seen the look in the man's eyes as he died — as he stared straight into the camera, straight into Josh's soul.

That had been his next clue. Josh had watched the man die, erupt into flames as his long, stringy hair had gone up first, followed by his dry, loose-fitting clothes. The entire time, Roger Eberly had stared at Josh.

Josh knew there was no way for Eberly to *know* Josh was watching. He must have been as much in the dark about who else was in this sadistic 'game' as Josh was, but the very fact that he was staring at the camera told him something.

He knows what this is, Josh had thought as the man perished, the numbers still on his lips.

One, two, four, five, three.

He *knew* where the camera was.

Josh looked up, examining the ceramic-like walls and ceiling, trying to pinpoint where the hidden camera was. He had seen Moussaf's room as well, and the angle, proportionate to the layout of each room, even if inverted, was identical.

That means there's a camera here, as well, Josh thought.

He knew that had to be the case — why wouldn't it be? — but he had yet to *see* the camera.

Fiber optic technology had been a slow-but-steady industry for the past three decades, and Josh had heard a little about heat-shielded camera tech being added to expensive security systems and the like. He assumed similar tech must have been at play here, but he was still stunned that there was *nothing* in the ceiling or top of the front wall that indicated a recess for a camera lens, even if near-microscopic.

So the fact that Eberly had been staring *right into* that very camera, impossible to see with the naked eye, had told Josh what he knew to be the case now: Eberly somehow knew about the camera and where it was located.

Had he helped build this place? Had he consulted for their computer system, for Eve herself?

It was impossible to know, but Josh felt as though this clue *had* to be useful to him somehow.

And the numbers — they had to mean something as well.

Josh paced again, apparently his de facto nervous tic while locked up here. He reached the computer's console just as it shimmered to life; Eve's soothing voice piped in once more.

"*Contestant #9,*" she began, "*you have immunity from the next trial. In addition, you will not be allowed to witness the trial or other contestants as they compete. However, because of your victory, you have been awarded an extra meal.*"

He frowned, almost smiling. *Seems like the torturous computer lady is willing to go to great lengths to ensure my comfort,* he thought.

As the screen shimmered back to its grayish-black hue, a slot opened in the 'front' wall, near where the tube for water had appeared. A tray slid into the room, then a tiny erector set-like robotic contraption lowered the tray to the floor.

On it was a two-inch-thick steak, still steaming, with grill lines that appeared to be too perfect to have been cooked by a human.

His frown deepened, but his stomach won out. He finished pacing and walked to the tray just as the robot arms slid back into the walls and disappeared.

He followed their movements, coming up next to the wall with his eyes only inches away. His fingers traced the lines around the area where the slit had just re-closed, and he felt the miniature lines.

It was nearly perfect, but now that he knew where to look, he saw the rectangular slits carved into the ceramic, almost perfectly flush with the surrounding wall.

Almost.

If he hadn't known where to look, he never would have been able to see the lines.

So this perfect little room isn't so perfect after all, he thought. *I'd bet there's even a door somewhere.*

He picked up the steak and dropped it onto the bed, for the moment ignoring his stomach. Right now, he needed to think.

He needed to take this opportunity — the unknown number of hours of freedom he had just 'won' — to get out.

Josh nodded. *That's right,* he thought, as if confirming his own subconscious's desires. *I'm getting the hell out of here.*

He walked over to Eve's terminal and tapped at the wall. The keyboard appeared as expected, as well as the original prompt he had seen on the wall, but he was a bit surprised to see anything at all.

Since he was not allowed to watch the trial unfolding around him, he was surprised that Eve had been programmed to allow him to interact with her at all. To a group of world-class computer scientists, having a bit of free time with a supercomputer like Eve seemed like a *bit* of a security risk.

And that was exactly the security risk he hoped to exploit.

He had not spend his career in hacking — white, grey, black-hat or otherwise — but hacking was really just a form of computer science in itself, and one that had its roots in the exact same sciences Josh *did* have expertise in.

His last few years in the Air Force had him working with the world's best specialists, all trying to understand the fickle nature of human behavior as it related to the non-fickle, *finite* behavior of computers.

They had been trying to find the answer to the question: how do we build a super-soldier capable of not only killing anyone who might get in their way but *also* capable of breaking into wherever those people may be?

In the past, these soldiers would have been equipped with state-of-the-art communications gear meant for one thing: interfacing with the nerds back home who could hack into the computer-based security systems and panels.

Now, the US Military wanted to get rid of the need for that gear. They wanted to get rid of the need for a group of soldiers and a group of nerds.

They wanted that soldier to be capable of doing whatever it took to gain access to secured facilities *and* kill everyone inside.

It was not enough any more to force one's way into a bad guy's lair, steal their hard drives, and get out, all while shooting over one's shoulder, Rambo-style.

Technology and firmware hardening had made situations like that not just implausible, but downright impossible. Now, soldiers needed to not only gain access to high-security places but also be skilled and knowledgeable enough to know *what* to steal, *how* to get it, and *where* it would be located.

Josh was the Air Force's first answer to this. He had already been close to retirement, so his services would not be used for active-duty missions, but he had been one of the first graduates of just such a program, in charge of training the next generation of super-soldiers. The bioenhancements the US military had been planning were not quite ready for this group, but they were to be the first-ever truly 'enhanced' military operatives in the world.

Until then, the Air Force program Josh had run was charged with creating the most brilliant, technologically savvy, brute-force-capable strike team on the planet, even without the need for futuristic enhancements. Their training should allow them to enter any enemy fortification, with or without technical security implements, and then get out without a trace.

So Josh was not *just* a brilliant programmer. He was not *just* a sought-after expert in the field of biocomputing and future technology.

He was more than capable of escaping from a room and gaining access to the computer that controlled this place. He was *uniquely* suited to doing just that.

That thought steadied his mind, but it also terrified him.

He had not been brought here by accident. There was something sinister happening here, and not just the overt brutal murders of his fellow prisoners.

Something deeper, bigger. He knew he had been brought here for a reason, and he was afraid he knew *exactly* what that reason was.

He was brought here *to* escape. They knew exactly who he was, exactly what he was capable of.

And he was going to play right into their hands.

CHAPTER 33
JOSH

LOCATION *unknown*

Josh was an accomplished hacker, capable of taking down a network from a single access point or breaking into a remote email server with nothing more than a laptop. But that was child's play in the black-hat world of computer hacking.

The most successful hackers throughout history knew their history, as well. Their exploits paid homage to the greats who came before, and for Josh Lane, that meant knowing in detail their methods and mindsets, the reasons they had been successful, the methods the hacked used to further secure and protect their systems, and the history of how hacking led to advancements in the fields of IT and computer security.

He was not just an expert in hacking as a way to gain entry and the history of hacking — he was an expert in the human psychology that led to *why*.

He suspected, then, that this "free pass" he had been given, the successful completion of the previous trial that led to his temporary freedom to sit with his own thoughts, had also been planned by those behind *Escape from Eden.*

Josh considered what this meant. They had kidnapped him, brought him here — wherever that was — and forced him to compete in strange computer-related trials. But they had also put him up against other professionals and experts in related and similar fields. Computer scientists, security experts, and any number of others.

Two of those men had perished onscreen in front of him, and while the field of deepfaking was rapidly taking off and could have explained the horrific video he saw, he had a feeling these men had truly died.

And now he had won a trial, giving him a moment of respite from the terror of it all, but for what reason? They must have known he would not simply sit back and wait for the next trial to end. They must have known he would try to fashion an escape.

They would know he would try exactly what he was trying now.

His hands flew over the keyboard. In a previous life, he preferred keyboards with a tighter press, a taller key, and never in a million years would he have chosen a flat, light-based display keyboard like this one. Still, it took almost no time at all for him to grow acquainted enough with the uncomfortable position and the no-tactile-feedback style to be able to type almost as fast as he was capable of.

He gained root access in fifteen minutes; a simple recursion exploit that allowed him to pull back the curtain on *Eve*'s capabilities. He had assumed the female-sounding AI was more than just a program running on a server, and he had been correct.

Eve seemed to be the operating system itself, as "her" fingers were everywhere in the system. He saw calls to her subroutines, full-fledged apps and programs, built-in libraries, and, finally, exactly what he was looking for: an *external* library called by one of her subroutines in an obscure folder tucked away wherever the mainframe CPU lived.

The biggest problem with most hacks was that the hacker needed to have a *target*. To put it simply, in order to find something on another server, one needed to know exactly *what* they were trying to find. It was never as simple as just poking around and stumbling across scores of credit card and social security numbers.

So he searched for a common library he was familiar with, one often called by programmers to translate a high-level programming language into machine code — something every computer system had to have — and found the references that proved it was there. Then, he studied the calls to this library and found one that interfaced with the system's MAC address. The Media Access Control address was a core requirement for basic internet access, allowing a machine to be labeled on a larger network.

He added a few lines of code to the library file that pinged this MAC address and discovered a little more about the system. Soon he discovered that *Eve* was, in fact, synonymous with the network itself. Strange in that whoever had built *Eve* seemed to be reinventing the wheel.

There were already solutions for this sort of network firmware and software. Oracle, Google, and any number of commercial enterprise-level networking solutions existed on the market, not to mention smaller installations like Merlin that could perform what this iteration of *Eve* was doing here.

It was overkill for what even the largest organizations would have needed, and no IT professional he knew would *choose* to build their own version of this firmware when plenty of good, tweakable options existed on the market.

But this was not just a run-of-the-mill company. *Escape from Eden* was some sort of sick, twisted game show, but the organization behind it was clearly working on something far more serious. They had wanted *Eve* to have a presence in every nook and cranny of this server, but why?

In places like this, where it did not even matter, why have an artificial intelligence installed as both the firmware and software in charge of running the server? And while he recognized what the firmware was intended for, he did not recognize its particular implementations of it. It was peculiar: elegant code in some places and convoluted in others. As if he were reading a book that had been automatically translated by a computer program from another language.

He had never seen anything like it, but then again, he had never seen anything like *any* of this.

Confused but not deterred, he continued on, filing this piece of the puzzle away for future reference. He examined the rest of the filesystem, taking a quick glance at everything available to him. As expected, he could not see everything *Eve* — or whatever this actual network was called — was hiding. Like most systems, this one had been properly compartmentalized into components that interacted with one another but did not share full access. Like branches of a tree, each branch was related to one another, but only through the main trunk.

He knew gaining access to this "main trunk" would take hours, at least, and he did not want to risk a breach of this magnitude, alerting whoever was watching the server's vital signs. Something like that would almost immediately alert a good security expert that someone was attempting to back-door their server, and he knew the countermeasures they would be able to deploy would be far better prepared than he was.

So he stayed in the lane he had already accessed, hiding his work as best he could. He used his root access to change the updated timestamps back to what they had been prior to his actions, and deleted log files of the changes themselves. Another core study of professional hackers was in learning how to disguise the fact that they had been in a system in the first place. If the ultimate goal was to steal information, when that information had been successfully retrieved, leaving no trace they had been there in the first place was the icing on the cake.

And Josh knew his life might depend on his covering his tracks. He still could not imagine the nature of his being here, nor could he imagine that those who had taken him were ignorant of his abilities. He had to proceed with the expectation that they would *expect* him to try to hack in, but he had to proceed nonetheless.

The downside, of course, was that he might be wrong, and his insubordination here would simply lead to his horrific death.

He wondered if it was a risk worth taking, but only for a moment. He knew himself better even than he knew computers, and there was no way he was *not* going to try to escape.

It was in his nature. He would try to leave this place, and he would most likely succeed.

EAST OF MALÉ | *Maldives*

"Is that... what I think it is?" Liam asked.

Witherspoon was watching the feed from Captain Symonds' head-mounted camera. From Witherspoon's briefing, Liam knew that Symonds wore a specialized computer on his person that would collate his team's video and audio feedback, as well as use an ad-hoc local network to keep them all in communication, since the open ocean was the only place on the planet not currently interconnected with the worldwide mesh network that cellular technology had introduced.

But Symonds also wore a tiny antenna on the back of his helmet, which was more than powerful enough to connect back to the hovering chopper, over a mile away and far out of sight. Through this connection, Liam and Witherspoon were getting a near-realtime update on the status of the mission.

Witherspoon snickered. "Everyone's got a kink, I guess," he said.

Liam's mouth fell open. He saw the back of the head of one of the Rangers, currently inside the bedroom on the yacht and holding his assault rifle in front of him. He was aiming at a very large, very out-of-shape man on the bed, arms affixed to the two bed posts by way of some rope or straps.

And he was also *very* naked.

He had a ball gag in his mouth, and his eyes were wide, the whites of them visible even on the grainy screen. Surrounding him on the bed were two young women, both cuddled close to the naked man and both scared out of their minds.

In one of the girls' hands was what appeared to be a jump rope. On its end was some sort of fuzzy attachment. Liam's eyes fell back to the man strapped to the bed and saw long red lines running diagonally across his chest and belly.

Liam could not pull his eyes away from the scene, and he heard through his own headset the cackles and laughing of the men in and near the bedroom.

"Is that him?" Witherspoon asked.

Liam waited a moment, listening in to the other feed he was attached to — the one that connected him to Curtis and Jocelyn back in Maryland. The response from Curtis was immediate.

"Affirmative. We're looking at Ahmed Ibn Kahn, best friend of Mohammad al-Sadir."

"Best friend of, uh, a very specific sort of punishment, as well," Witherspoon added.

Liam was no prude, but he had never expected to see something quite so... private. Certainly not in real-time video, taking place before his eyes.

Onscreen, Kahn's face softened, then his eyebrows shifted down into a glare.

Symonds spoke through the headset. *"Go ahead and take out*

that ball from his mouth. Let's see what this guy has to say for himself."

Another soldier chimed in. *"Shit, man.* You *take it out. I ain't going anywhere near that thing."*

"Matheson, your ass has been in far dirtier spots than that ball. And I've got pictures."

"Cut it out. Get over there and take it out," Symonds' voice said.

There was a deep audible sarcastic sigh, but the soldier — Matheson — walked over to Kahn and pulled the elastic band connected to two sides of the ball. The sex toy fell to the man's neck.

Symonds stepped into view on the screen. *"Ahmed Ibn Kahn?"* he asked.

The doughy man nodded.

"Where's your buddy? al-Sadir?"

Kahn's glare deepened into a scowl. He mumbled something unintelligible.

"Save it, pal. I know you speak fluent English. You got two choices: talk, strapped to a warm, comfy bed with your little friends here, or talk, strapped to a very cold metal chair in a very isolated room."

Kahn didn't move, save for a single swallow. His gigantic throat bobbed, the red ball gag moving up and down as he did.

"Yeah, I know. You were just enjoying yourself, nothing to worry about, all that. But trust me when I say I really don't want to be here any more than you want to come with us. So let's get this done quick, all right? We know all about your friend's show. Escape from Eden, is it? Cute name. Where the hell is it? Where's al-Sadir?"

Kahn spat. "You will never get what you want."

"Mmm, maybe not. But this would be a good start. Where is he?"

Kahn paused, then looked at each of the soldiers in the room. When his eyes returned to face Symonds, Liam felt the man's eyes boring through the camera into his own soul. A strange sensation came over him, a chill. *What is that?*

Liam was not sure what was happening — while he was a highly trained NSA operative with plenty of experience, he was not a soldier. He had never been on a mission like this, hovering out at sea in a helicopter, awaiting the results of a team of armed troops.

He was having a hard time getting his bearings. He was an analyst, a data geek. He wanted to take things apart and see how they worked, then extrapolate numerical possibilities that might lead to another clue. At most, he wanted to feed information to the boots on the ground.

He rubbed his eyes as he watched and listened in. So far, everything had gone off without a hitch.

Maybe that was the problem?

He looked to Witherspoon. If the Lieutenant Colonel was feeling a sense of unease, there was no evidence on his face. He still wore the same wry smile he'd had on when the video feed started.

"You will never get what you want. You do not want al-Sadir. You do not want Escape from Eden.*"*

"Try me," Symonds said.

"Fine. You think it is that easy. You are wrong. al-Sadir is a busy man, so even I have a hard time keeping track of him. But if you want him, I would look where the show is being filmed."

"And where is that?"

"Jakarta."

"Indonesia?"

"Where else?" Kahn asked. *"Plenty of willing, able-bodied workers at a cheap price. Plenty of tech for the studio work."*

Witherspoon cut in, speaking directly into Symonds' ear. "We need more than that. There are nine million people in Jakarta."

"Can you be more specific?" Symonds asked.

"I can take you there."

"I bet you can, big boy. But I'm not sure we're friends yet. I can't trust you. Why don't you tell me exactly where he is first?"

"Let me go, and I will tell you."

"Tell me, then I'll let you go. I'm not sure you're, uh, in a proper position to negotiate."

Kahn spat again. *"You know nothing, American."*

"I don't need to know a lot. I've got a big gun." At this, he stepped up closer to the bed, pulling his assault rifle around and sticking the end of the barrel hard into Kahn's left foot. *"Tell me where he is."*

"Fine," Kahn said. *"He is north of the city, not far from the airport. Tanjung Burung Village, a coastal community. There is a complex there, something called Palem. It is actually a film studio, and that is where you will find al-Sadir."*

Symonds seemed impressed, and he motioned for his men to leave the room, all except for Matheson. *"Get him untied,"* he instructed Matheson. *"I'll get his other arm."* Turning back to Kahn, he said, *"Get dressed. You have two minutes."*

"Dressed?" Kahn asked. *"What — what is this? We had a deal. You would let me go."*

"I will let you go, asshole, I just never agreed to when. But we

might need to clarify a few things. We might need a bit of help finding this place called Palem. Who knows, we might need a lesson in... sadistic sex acts. Get up and get dressed."

"We are going there now?" Kahn asked, incredulous. "And what of them? My... companions?"

Liam saw the girls squeal and cower when Matheson and Symonds approached the bed and Kahn's straps. They both got off the bed, but neither moved from the room.

"This is a luxury yacht, and it's completely full of supplies and food. I think they'll be just fine for a bit."

Kahn's glare returned, but he pulled his large body up and into a seated position. *"What should I wear?"* he asked. *"I do not have the proper attire for Jakarta."*

Symonds laughed. *"That's a future-Kahn problem, my friend. For now, I'd put on a swimsuit. That'll be far more appropriate, at least for the time being."*

LOCATION *unknown*

Josh had made considerable progress, and not a moment too soon. He had successfully changed the settings he needed to proceed through Eve's programming.

His first task had been to code a simple loop that caused any 'phoning home' to reroute to a log file, which would be deleted every minute and recreated. This allowed him to make changes without the risk of pinging some security alert that would tell someone on-site that there was a rogue operative messing with their filesystem.

After he had accomplished this, he navigated around the folder hierarchy until he found a file full of functions that seemed to be the routing that told Eve which libraries and programs to pull in, and when. This would allow him to see generally how Eve made her decisions, and if there were any useful applications of that, he could start down that rabbit hole from this file.

It only took him a few minutes of browsing the file's structure before he found something that would be helpful. He could not easily dismantle Eve or take her offline, as that would immediately inform the security here that there had been tampering. He also could not change any code in this file, crippling Eve, for the same reason — but also for the reason that changing this file would likely be very easy to spot.

So he had decided on a less invasive alteration of Eve's files, at least for now. By following the routing information in this functions file, Josh was able to trace the hierarchy to the correct repository of subfolders and files that he needed.

He opened a few of these files using the terminal's text-based editor, browsing the code to determine he was in the right place. After another few minutes, he changed a few commands and reworked some functions in this file and a few others, and he was done.

He needed to wait for the internal reset of this subroutine, which he had figured would take about five minutes. With nothing else to do except wait it out and see if his changes would work — or if he would be summarily executed for tampering with the system — he was about to exit the terminal prompt.

But Josh paused, another idea coming to him. He felt for NARA's casing with a free hand, wondering if there was something in Eve's source that would help get it back online.

He once again found the functions file he had been working from and browsed again, this time looking for different types of references. Near the bottom of the file, he found a small array that had some intriguing entries in it.

The array in the file was called from another subfolder and a file within it, and inside this file, the array listed a handful of variables. None of the lines were commented, which he assumed would be the case, but that meant playing around with these was risky — he could not be sure that what he was doing would work.

He used the up and down arrows to scroll through the file until he came across one variable simply called foreignObject. The current count of the variable was set to 1.

By his logic, from what he could figure, Eve's system monitored and controlled access to any number of devices on its wireless intranet. He saw variables that were obvious, like officeRouter1 and mainlevelPrinter and a variable that counted the number of cellular phones on the premises, so he assumed that foreignObject was a count of any devices Eve did not initially recognize.

He changed this variable to 0, then added a line of code that would effectively pass this object through as an allowed device. In short, he hoped it meant that Eve had been preventing his device's access to her intranet *or* connecting with any internet module that might exist here.

He saved the file, exited, then took a seat on the bed.

And waited.

After a few minutes, the screen blinked. There was no confirmation of anything, but Josh had to assume that his changes had taken effect and the subroutines had restarted and resolved themselves.

Or... he would probably die.

After another minute or two, he sensed something strange. His mind felt rejuvenated, alive. He was familiar with the feeling and his fist was cocked, ready to pump it in the air when he got confirmation.

"Your heart rate is 86 BPM, and your internal temperature is holding at 98.9 degrees Fahrenheit."

He let out an audible *whoop* as he realized he had been right: Eve had been blocking access to his internal device, but it had not been *deactivated*. All he'd needed to do was tell Eve that the device was allowed on its network.

And then the *first* thing he'd changed in Eve's system proved to be successful, as well. The screen set into the wall displayed a massive wall of text, and NARA, in Eve's voice, began reading it in Josh's head.

"Preparing mini-cut of Escape from Eden *promotional video. Contestant Room #4 and #8 requesting restroom access. Contestant Room #10 requesting water access."*

He sensed NARA confirming each request as they came in, immediately. He told the device to accept any requests as quickly as it could — emulating the back-and-forth of Eve's interfacing with her own internal "superiors." It was all happening at the speed of light, so there was likely a one- or two-second delay taking place now, but he was hoping no one would notice.

He sat back on the bed, stunned. *It worked. It really worked.* He had been hoping to commandeer Eve's decision matrix, the "brain" of her operations, in order to view and accept — or deny — any request that came in from his room or any other place in the facility. Normally Eve would receive these requests and allow them on her own, using her powerful AI to control the "yeses" and "nos" of each.

But he had rerouted these requests to his own terminal, in his own room. And when NARA had come back online, he had been able to "hear" these requests in his own mind, read from the internal screen on which they were displayed.

The commands were constant, a steady barrage of speed-of-light requests, but they were all answered in the affirmative. Since

Eve was a computer system that seemed to receive a request only to have the subroutine it was calling launched upon her acceptance, Josh found no reason to deny any of them. In other words, he was just placing himself between the requesting device and Eve, like a casual observer.

But he had the ability to *deny* any of these requests, as well. He told NARA to scan through the rapid-fire requests coming in, and listed a set of keywords he wanted to be alerted to, then told NARA to process the remainder of the requests automatically. This he could run effectively as a background task, not being interrupted unless a request was passed to Eve that included one of the keywords.

After this was completed, he got back to work. Now that he had regained access to NARA, and he had wireless access to Eve herself, he laid back on the bed and closed his eyes. One of the most miraculous features of NARA's tech and its tight integration with his central nervous system was that he did not have to actually be awake in order for NARA to work. The pill-sized computer was just that — a computer that did not need its host to be awake. He had to be alive, of course, but he could be unconscious and the little CPU in his brain would still be functioning.

On the bed, Josh tweaked a few more functions in hidden folders deep within Eve's filesystem. He made these changes carefully, as he knew the more he meddled, the more likely a bug would reveal itself or his actions would interfere with the system's functioning altogether.

Mostly, he browsed. He read, consumed, and made mental notes — literally having NARA store them in his mind — about Eve and how she worked. It was a relatively painless process to discover her general feature-set, since at her core she was just an operating system, and most operating systems functioned similarly. He focused on the intricacies that made Eve special, trying to gain knowledge of her more interesting abilities.

Finally, after about half an hour of poking around and making minor tweaks here and there, he felt ready.

Before he could do anything else, however, NARA flashed an alert in front of his eyes.

"Request; System Access:" it began. *"EFE Trial Completion. Solution attempted, trial passed: Contestant #10 victorious."*

Tanjung Burung | Indonesia

Liam listened in as Lieutenant Colonel Roger Witherspoon and Captain Symonds discussed the op. *"We're a go; on my mark,"* Liam heard through the chopper's headset.

He was exhausted, mentally and physically, and after sitting for hours in a helicopter in the Maldives, catching a six-hour flight to Indonesia, and then once again embarking on a borrowed Army Black Hawk, he thought he'd never fly again.

He pulled upward, forcing his back straight, and felt a few areas pop in relief. It was hardly enough, and he knew he would likely sleep for a day after all of this.

"I still don't know why I need to be here," he said, knowing his comms would send the message down through Captain Symonds and his team as well.

Symonds laughed. *"It's trial-by-fire, baby,"* he said. *"How do you think we all learned? No one trained for this — Witherspoon just picked us up one day and threw us into the pot."*

Witherspoon smirked. *"You boys act like you've never been*

trained, that's for damn sure." He turned in his own seat and faced Liam. *"You get used to it, son."*

Not really an answer, Liam thought, grimacing as his knees locked up. He wanted to stand up and at least walk around, but with both doors open on either side of the chopper, he knew he would likely just fall out and die.

Maybe that would *be better.*

"We're setting down about a mile from here," Witherspoon continued. *"You keep moving. Once you're in position, get out and walk the perimeter a bit; I want a full brief of the security we're dealing with. Ravenclaw should be here already, sending ten men. I'm waiting their commander's word, but expect them to be in position shortly after you are."*

"Roger, Roger," Symonds said. Liam heard a few other men snicker.

The plan was simple: They would drop off their prisoner, Kahn, at a location he had given the mercenary group, gagged and secured to a chair in a locked warehouse. The mercenary group would be sending two men to watch Kahn later. He would be held captive until they no longer had a use for him. They did not need him on this mission, but they also did not want to let him get away in case he had more information about the *Palem* facility or if al-Sadir was not here.

After dropping Kahn off, the pilot would drop off Symonds' group, then fly out around the village of Tanjung Burung, staying low over the water and well out of sight, while Symonds and his men would take local civilian vehicles in toward the land owned by al-Sadir, about a twenty-mile rectangle of space with a massive white building at the center of it.

From there, they would do their best to sneak into the building, recon, and look for any sign of al-Sadir or Joshua Lane, as well as any other obvious kidnapping victim.

Back in Baltimore, Liam's two team members, Curtis and Jocelyn, would continue watching the live stream of *Escape from Eden*, taking notes and researching anything and everything that might be helpful for Liam and Witherspoon and his men.

So far, they had been mostly quiet — they had split duties, allowing the other to get a quick nap in — and their only updates were that there had been another trial, another death. While brutal, it had not given them any new insights as to what al-Sadir's ultimate goal was.

And that played into Liam's greatest fear: that al-Sadir *had* no ultimate goal. That the man was the ultimate supervillain — deranged, brilliant, and fabulously wealthy, intent on simply watching the world burn. He hoped he was wrong, but everything seemed to point to that being the most plausible outcome.

Why else would he be kidnapping top-notch computer scientists and putting them through an evil set of trials? Why else would he have cooked up this sadistic reality show and streamed it for the world to see?

Nothing made sense.

Still, as he considered this option, it also didn't seem to click. He was missing something — they were *all* missing something. He needed to figure out what that missing piece was, and he needed to do it before anyone else died.

And *that* was why Witherspoon had brought him along. Witherspoon was every bit as in the dark as Liam, and since Liam was in charge of the overall mission to bring Josh Lane home, he was needed here. He knew it, as much as he did not like it.

As the chopper descended slowly, working toward the north

side of the small peninsula where Witherspoon had told the pilot to bring them, he hailed Curtis and Jocelyn on their separate channel. "Hey guys — we're getting close to go-time here. Any update?"

There was a pause, but a few seconds later Jocelyn's voice came on. *"Hey Liam — funny you should ask. Curtis went for a bite to eat for us, but I've been watching. It's been nothing but a black screen for hours, but just a few minutes ago, al-Sadir popped up and started talking, flashing that evil grin of his."*

"What about?"

"Curtis mentioned that it's probably on a significant delay — movie business stuff, I guess — so I was going to take notes and ping you if anything significant happened. But right now, it's just al-Sadir bragging about how cool his show is. Like he's talking to the audience, but a small audience of 'benefactors.'"

"Like people who are *paying* him to put this shit on?"

"That's my best guess. Makes sense he wouldn't have the resources to do it alone, especially if he's skated under the radar for so long. But he hasn't said anything useful yet."

Liam laughed. "He hasn't revealed these benefactors by name, then, huh?"

Jocelyn's laugh returned from the other side. *"I wish — nope, nothing that easy. I'll keep you posted."*

Nothing that easy, he thought. He shuddered. He remembered the op to bring in Kahn, the friend of al-Sadir they had found on the yacht.

It had all seemed too easy. Too simple.

Why? Kahn had even barely resisted when Symonds had asked him where al-Sadir was located. For obvious reasons, Witherspoon had pressed his men into action immediately, moving them all toward Indonesia with the utmost speed the United

States Army could provide, no doubt calling in any number of favors. He had wanted to get the jump on al-Sadir, to catch him before he could discover that Kahn had been captured and they were after him.

"Actually, he just said something... weird," Jocelyn's voice rang through his ears once again. He saw Witherspoon's mouth moving but could not hear the man's words. They were on separate channels now, and Witherspoon was busy giving the go orders to Symonds and his team.

That meant they were in position and now moving toward the central building Kahn had called *Palem.* He needed to flip back over to that channel, but Jocelyn was in the middle of saying something.

"'...attention to the next *scheduled event for this afternoon,'"* she said.

He tuned in, listening along as she parroted what al-Sadir was saying on the broadcast. He frowned, trying to make sense of it. It seemed al-Sadir was *not* talking about the regular version of *Escape from Eden* — he was introducing something else. Another episode of a different nature?

He shook his head, just as he heard Witherspoon bark a command, loudly enough for him to hear over the rotor wash and through the headphone cups.

"...move move! Let's move, boys! Get in there and stop this maniac!"

Jocelyn's voice was far louder and easier to understand. *"... This is my* Palem *facility, where I am now located. My team has informed me —"*

Liam gripped the headset's microphone. "What?" he shouted. "Informed him of *what?*"

He watched the feed from Symonds' camera as the man trotted forward across the swaying grass of the field separating the parked car he had just exited and the facility in the distance. He moved slower than he should have, dragging something next to him — Kahn, who appeared at the far edge of the camera's vision.

He reached out and grabbed Witherspoon's shoulder as Jocelyn repeated what she had just said. He had missed it, trying to alert Witherspoon at the same time as trying to urge her to switch to the main channel.

Witherspoon brushed his hand away, then looked over at him as if he were nothing but an annoying kid.

Onscreen, Symonds and two other men, flanking him, reached the *Palem* studio building.

Jocelyn finally switched over, just as Witherspoon realized Liam was trying to get his attention.

"*— shit! Shit! They* know! *Guys, they* know *you're coming!*"

Her voice was frantic, hysterical. Witherspoon barked orders through the headset, the comm translating them to static and back before reaching Liam's ears.

"*...high-alert, boys. You heard her — all of you should remain on high—*"

Witherspoon stopped mid-sentence and sucked in a breath of air as the feed from Symonds' camera changed drastically, now jittering and bouncing. The display turned bright white, and the camera adjusted, showing the sky above the facility and suddenly nothing else.

There were shouts, voices Liam couldn't place. "*Man down! Man down!*"

"*Fuck, what the fuck was —*"

Another man's voice was cut off, and the feed from Symonds'

camera showed a blur of activity as another soldier raced across Symonds' view from the ground. He made it almost to the opposite edge of the screen when he, too, fell. A splash of what could only be blood landed on Symonds' camera, and Liam winced.

Witherspoon was still shouting instructions, this time to the pilot of the Black Hawk. Liam tried to make sense of the instructions, but his mind was reeling. He was an NSA employee, not a damned soldier. What the hell was he supposed to do? How was he supposed to remain in control of the situation when he could not even figure out *what* the situation was?

The feed settled to an ominous blank whiteness as the shouting over the comms subsided, replaced by Witherspoon's repeated requests for an update.

None came.

No one spoke.

Over the public channel, Liam heard Jocelyn's voice next. *"Oh, my God... Oh, my — fuck. What the fuck. Liam, are you there? Liam — they're... they're going to attack you."*

"Liam, they know... they knew everything."

CHAPTER 37
AL-SADIR

Tanjung Burung | Indonesia

"...And I believe our final trial will commence this evening," al-Sadir said, a smile plastered on his face. He was addressing the cameras arranged around the stage, all facing him. There were no human operators — *Eve*, his state-of-the-art artificial intelligence, had a module onboard that tracked and pulled focus during live presentations such as this, and the camera equipment was programmed to respond to the computer's direction.

It was a modern-day television set, designed by the latest Hollywood engineers and funded by the very men he was currently addressing. None were in the room with him, as nearly all of them were agoraphobic, paranoid, and hated leaving the comforts of their own million-dollar homes. al-Sadir knew this, so when he had started putting together the plans for the *Escape from Eden* concept, he had built a small soundstage here at *Palem* that would mimic a much larger, live-attended reality show.

Selling the concept to the men watching came down to showing them that the show was legitimate, that they were able to pull off what al-Sadir had promised. They wanted the reality show to *be* a reality show — no paid actors, no script, nothing but trials and contestants. They wanted a positive return on their massive investment, and the way al-Sadir promised to deliver that was twofold.

First, he would actually come through with their request. They wanted to find an answer to a problem they each shared. This common ground was the one thing these rich oligarchs from around the world had in common, and while the countries they each hailed from were at each others' throats, bickering and threatening one another in a merry-go-round of jingoism and aggression, these men had temporarily put their differences aside to accomplish a shared goal. al-Sadir's job was to deliver that result, that solution, to them.

Second, al-Sadir would provide them a good return on their investment by streaming the *Escape from Eden* television show through a few specific channels on the dark web. Each of these streams was tracked by Hans' infiltrators, watching these feeds to see who stumbled across them. Over the three seasons his *Escape from Eden* had aired, its rumor and presence on the dark web grew exponentially. What began as a few handfuls of watchers and only relatively minor downsides for the contestants had become a few *thousand* today, with obviously dire consequences for those contestants who failed. Hans' team was tasked with picking through these streamers to determine who they were.

al-Sadir then sought out some of these viewers and identified their real-life persona. If they were a good fit for the small group of oligarch benefactors, al-Sadir would massage both parties with a brief introduction, feeling out their fit for this group. In this way, he kept a revolving door of wealthy patrons feeding the *Escape from Eden* system. More money meant more reach, and more money meant everyone was happy.

Lately, the *Escape from Eden* franchise al-Sadir had started had been controlled by a different group of wealthy benefactors — a small handful of like-minded individuals had paid him a *massive* amount of money to set up a slightly modified version of the game, intending to use it to find the best candidate for their own project.

The other upside of Hans' digital investigations came from turning up those potentially *against* his program. Governments and some large private corporations were the natural culprits, and by offering a free stream to the world by way of an internet undercurrent mostly accessible to only those in the know, he could easily identify who might be watching in order to attempt to bring him down.

By hiding in plain sight, he was able to get a read on his possible enemies long before they intended to reveal themselves.

His smile deepened as he considered what he had accomplished. Only three years into production, and he had already earned his benefactors *trillions* of dollars. He got to pocket billions himself, which was no small prize.

He would need to grow his team soon. Hans was brilliant and capable, but he was only one man. Through his networks of mercenaries, technicians and engineering teams, and other paid staff, Hans had maintained control of the logistics of this operation, but it was bad business to expect that Hans would be available forever.

Besides, those under Hans' employ were growing ever more curious as to the nature of their work. They had compartmentalized each division into silos, but the most clever among them would no doubt start to wonder what their work was being used for.

He sighed, then turned to the camera on his left. Immediately responding, *Eve* pulled the lens inward and rotated it a bit, all the while gently panning to the right to keep al-Sadir's body in frame.

"So, without further ado, I want to call your attention to the *next* scheduled event for this afternoon. Hopefully, you are all ready for an exciting turn of events — one we did not anticipate this early in the tournament, but which we are no doubt ready for."

He paused and took a breath. "As you all know, your generosity knows no bounds and has provided for the phenomenally exciting entertainment you have been watching. However, what is repeated becomes mundane, and there is no *excitement* in the mundane." He stretched his arms wide in a practiced flourish, knowing that *Eve* was reacting in kind. "I wanted to surprise you, and what better way to do that than by presenting an *unexpected* sort of reality show? What better way to thank our generous benefactors than by surprising you all with something you are not prepared for?"

He turned now, waving a hand behind him. Immediately the stage lit up on the edges, the light from numerous LED fixtures illuminating a frame in the center of the wall. On this wall, a video flashed to life, the frame rate synced with the cameras,' and a wide shot of the bright, sunny exterior of the building al-Sadir was now in appeared. It was a nondescript building, looking like some sort of distribution warehouse, with tall, white brick walls and no windows.

"This is my *Palem* facility, where I am now located. My team has informed me that there are to be visitors — a group of American soldiers who intercepted our *Escape from Eden* stream — coming by shortly."

He waited, watching the video as the drone footage zoomed in on a row of three doors on the side of the building, all steel and windowless as well.

"With any luck, my own security forces here will be putting on a show you and I get to appreciate. No scripted battle scenes, choreographed fighting, and fake explosives, my friends. What you are about to witness is every bit as real as the rest of the *Escape from Eden* program."

He saw the camera switch to that of another drone, this one flying even higher and farther away from the building. He could see the square mile of emptiness around the building and the small, dotted huts and shacks of the rest of the sleepy coastal town far off in the distance. He had purchased twenty square miles of land here, placing his *Palem* studio right in the center.

He knew they would have privacy here, and had even filed with the municipality that he would be filming a war movie, in case any concerned citizen heard gunshots. Every detail had been accounted for, and al-Sadir could not have been prouder. He and Hans had slaved over every aspect of this event, and he knew it would impress his benefactors.

He turned back to face the center camera as he spoke again. " I have been so excited to surprise all of you with this next episode, so please — sit back, relax, and enjoy the show."

al-Sadir winked as *Eve* faded up the music through the soundstage's speakers, and he held the position until the cameras' red lights blinked off.

CHAPTER 38
JOSH

The keyword 'contestant' had forced Josh's auto process to halt, allowing him to read the request and respond. He could not tell what the request was actually *asking*, however.

Shit, he thought. *I guess we'll find out.*

He confirmed the request, and immediately the screen in his room flashed back on just as the lights dimmed to a calm, bluish hue.

Eve's voice rang through the speakers.

"Contestant #10 has succeeded in finding a solution to the problem. Time elapsed is ten hours, 3 minutes, and 17 seconds from trial start. Solution time is 43.0 seconds. Contestant #10 is victorious and shall receive immunity from the next trial."

Josh watched the screen as the view of the winning contestant, a woman with long, auburn hair, appeared. She seemed relieved, but he could easily see the lines of stress on her forehead and matching streaks from tears on her cheeks. She swayed back and forth and looked to be one gentle puff of air away from collapsing.

Another alert came into Josh's mind: *"Request: Contestant elimination routine."*

Oh, shit.

He knew what it was asking. There had been a few requests auto-accepted by NARA in the background, but once again his keyword alert system had forced a halt to the requests coming in.

He knew now that these requests controlled, among many other tasks, how the show *Escape from Eden* was aired. Rather than a human video switcher, the AI itself handled the requests and acceptances of the different shots, preloaded videos, and cut scenes — the same things Josh had seen on the screen.

And Josh had inadvertently put himself between the request and the AI's response, meaning he was now *in charge* of determining the losing contestant's fate.

He almost declined, but hesitated. If he declined, this contestant would likely be saved — for now. But it would break the logic of the larger game's routine, and it would definitely not go without notice. There were real humans watching this show, he assumed, and they would know that something was awry when the losing contestant was not named and eliminated.

But to accept it...

Could Josh actually approve the request, knowing it would cause the contestant — whoever they were — to die in pure agony?

He could not make that decision knowingly. And to turn off his little hack, to allow Eve to make the decision for him, would end in exactly the same outcome he feared most. It would be no different than making the call himself.

He took a deep breath, acutely aware that the longer the camera slow-zoomed on and panned around Contestant #10, the more confused and curious the human viewers would become.

They would wonder if something had happened to Eve, had caused it to slow down. The AI had not skipped a beat so far, so they would naturally wonder why she was taking so long to play the 'elimination subroutine' now being requested.

"Contestant #4 has failed the last test, and shall now be eliminated."

Josh was now exclusively in charge of another contestant's life or death, and he was unable to determine what to do next. To confirm the request — the expected and predicted outcome that would not ruffle any feathers of the people behind this "game" — would kill Contestant #4. But to deny the request, thus saving the contestant, would only prolong the inevitable: he was sure they would be eliminated anyway, and this route would mean Josh's meddling in Eve's system would no longer go unnoticed.

Either Contestant #4 — whoever they were — would die, or they both would.

In a utilitarian world, the easy answer was to confirm the request and watch Contestant #4 die onscreen.

But Josh was far from utilitarian. The correct answer, morally, was not one that caused the least amount of quantitative damage. That was too simple, too broad a brush. No, he was better than that.

He was about to choose his response and have NARA send it to Eve when the screen suddenly shifted.

Josh frowned. *I didn't see this request,* he thought, quickly running a search and scanning the most recent requests. There were all sorts of minor, random requests logged — lights turned on or off, television screens changed to different channels, and the myriad requests of the surviving contestants, like restroom breaks, food, water, and the like. There was even an automated oven in a kitchenette somewhere on the premises that was hooked into Eve's server, and a request had come in about it.

But all of these requests had been silently and swiftly passed on to Eve, as they had not hit one of his keywords. They were also mundane, ordinary, and did not require his attention.

But this latest change of pace — the screen shifting to something else, something brighter, as if it were a video of the area just outside the compound he was in — had not triggered a request at all. It had been manually entered.

It meant someone else was able to program the feed that others were watching, apparently. Josh had full control of any *automated* requests that came through, but not anything manual, from another human onsite.

That made sense, he realized. Eve was a computer — an incredibly adept artificial intelligence — but she was a computer nonetheless. Every computer had a creator, a manager, a *human* element maintaining control.

He tried to consider what that meant, but his mind was being pulled in a million directions. NARA seemed to be urging him along, trying to get him to make a decision. The screen shifted again as whatever camera's view he was watching brought its vision into focus. He saw the outside clearly now — it was a drone's camera, and it began switching between a few other drones. He saw them descending, a whitish building far below growing larger.

NARA tugged at him again, and he considered what this meant.

He snapped to attention once again, ignoring the monitor for a moment.

Find it... come on, he willed. *Please be there.*

And then... *yes.*

It was there. Just as he'd predicted, the request to continue the elimination of Contestant #4, albeit offscreen, had arrived.

The system wanted to continue with its previously calculated marching orders, knowing that the bigger picture was to eliminate contestants who had not succeeded in the previous trials. Even though the television cameras had been commandeered by whoever was running the show for the human viewers, the system knew it was supposed to eliminate Contestant #4.

Well, plans change, Josh thought.

He declined the request almost immediately, passing the decision on to Eve.

There was no time to react, no time to wait to see if his little insubordination had gone unnoticed, but it didn't matter. He had saved them, for now.

Now, it was time to leave.

Tanjung Burung | Indonesia

Captain Nathan Symonds surveilled the area immediately in front of him. The drones had descended from out of nowhere, and there were three of them spaced evenly between his current position and the front of the building.

And they were attacking.

Matheson was down, lying still on the ground about fifteen feet to his left. He was not sure if the man was dead or injured, but it was clear Matheson was out of the fight.

Three shots soared over Symonds' head, their close proximity to his ears the only sign they had been fired. The drones, large quadcopters with two onboard cameras, were also equipped with simple weapons systems. He was familiar with the design, created by the Israeli military for surveillance and as a first line of defense. Their fore-mounted gun was nowhere near as powerful as any standard-issue modern assault rifle, but it did not need to be: getting hit by one of the tiny rounds still left a mark.

And if one of them hit a fleshy, unprotected patch of skin, the victim was out. Matheson had borne the brunt of two of the drones' attacks, and Symonds had been helpless as the man was peppered with miniature, near-invisible rounds.

And that was hardly the worst of it.

"We got company to the north, too, boss," came a man's voice through his headset. It was Bryson's, and Symonds dared a look over the boulder sitting in the field he was currently using as protection.

He saw Bryson running toward the water line, unable to parry the onslaught of another drone. Toward the building, Symonds saw another man laying prone in the field — again, he was unsure of the man's current status.

"Let's pull back and try to concentrate fire at these assholes, one at a time," he said. He tried to keep his voice steady, calm. No need freaking anyone out — they all knew that they were under attack. "And we could really use those ten grunts from Ravenclaw, Witherspoon."

No reply.

There was movement to his left again, and he saw a man jump and run back toward the road, where there were a few rusted-out cars parked. It was as good a place as any to regroup and try to turn the tables on the automated defenses, but before the man reached the cars, Symonds saw something else.

More drones were racing toward the man's location, but from the opposite direction. They had been hiding amongst the shacks and shanties nearby, and he saw at least four of the things open fire.

His man didn't stand a chance. Symonds saw a fine mist of blood envelop the air around the man, and he stumbled forward and dived toward the car. It was too late — he was still five feet away from any sort of protection, and the drones simply encircled his body and continued their barrage.

Symonds looked away. *Fuck. This is not going well.* He assessed the battle — so far, two sets of drones, at least eight in total, were flying around and attacking. None had seen him yet, but they were already starting to pair off and start flying in concentric circles to seek out any enemy combatants still alive.

We're severely outnumbered, he realized. He whispered into his comms. "We've got activity here, and that's just the automated defenses," he said. His back was to the boulder, and his eyes looked left to the north, toward where he knew the chopper was spinning down. "Keep that bird hot — we may need an evac."

"Already working on it," Witherspoon's voice shot back. *"We saw the drones. What's your status?"*

"Fucked, mostly. I've got three men down, at least one KIA. Certainly at least two more injured. Sir, we don't have the firepower to get these little dicks out of the sky, much less into the compound and take out any *real* security forces."

He knew Witherspoon already knew this, but it was worth saying out loud. *We haven't even seen* human *soldiers yet.*

"I understand. Stay sharp for a few more seconds, I'm working on another plan."

Symonds considered his own capabilities and preparations. He had a full load-out, including a sidearm and Ka-bar, as well as two frag grenades. Nothing that could work against these flying machines.

Except...

"Hey, listen up," he said, as much to Witherspoon as everyone else still listening in. "I may have a way out of this, but we're going to lose comms. If we don't try, though, these little bastards are just going to follow us around until we're just pulp. We need to end this, now. Got it?"

He didn't wait for a response. "Here's the plan: I've got a little gift from the science lab back home. A localized EMP device — it's got enough juice to take down a half-square-mile of electronics, but you know what that means."

Anything requiring power, including his phone and radio, as well as a handful of other battery-powered components he was carrying, would be fried. Some of them might survive and be able to be recharged, but their communications would certainly go down.

Witherspoon crackled back into his ear. *"I'm working on getting backup here. There's a Rangers unit not far from here, but I'm not sure of their status. I put in a word that I might need their help, if they're willing to give it, but I'm going to double back with the group leader and see. Best case, they're a couple of hours out."*

Symonds nodded. "Got it. So it sounds like this is the best plan we've got."

"Right now, it's the only one we've got. Do it."

Symonds swallowed, then checked his load-out again. He grabbed the car battery-sized device from his pack, thankful that it was mostly empty space inside. It was a bomb, but unlike standard explosives, this was an electromagnetic bomb. While there would be a very real, albeit small, explosion, the damage would be mostly felt to any and all electronic devices in the immediate area.

The problem was the device had been designed for use in a small space — certainly not outside, where the effects had nothing to bounce off of and react with. He had carried it along because most of their travel would be vehicular, not walking, where weight and size were an issue. Still, it was the only option they had.

But that meant he needed to corral the drones into a small enough area that the bomb would defeat them.

So I get to be human bait, he thought. *Wonderful.*

If Witherspoon knew this, the man had not said anything. Likely because he knew it, *and* he understood there was no better option.

"Okay, Symonds," he said aloud, "here goes nothing."

He stood up, device in hand, his gun in the other, and started waving and shouting at the drones still patrolling the area.

CHAPTER 40
NATHAN

Tanjung Burung | Indonesia

The drones flew toward him, the buzzing of their tiny rotors whizzing as they picked up speed. They had a target in sight.

Nathan Symonds was that target.

He wanted to squeeze his eyes shut, wanted to block out all the world and ignore the oncoming onslaught, but he needed to focus.

He needed to see them coming, to better judge his next move. Symonds lifted the small device and gave it a quick once-over — for the third time. *If it's going to work, it's going to work,* he thought, silently repeating the mantra a friend of his used to say all the time. *And if it won't, it won't.*

It wasn't exactly calming, but it helped him nonetheless.

He tossed the device about fifteen feet away, toward the building, targeting the location he assumed most of the drones were heading. They wouldn't fly directly over him — their weapons systems couldn't swivel around to point directly below them — so this was as good as it would get.

The timer on the EMP device was set for three seconds, a number that had seemed short when he'd first thought this through but now seemed like an eternity.

He waited.

A flash of light burst forth from the device, and Symonds fell to his rear end. A popping sound came next, but he hardly heard it over the whine of the drones' collective motors and rotor wash.

Then, immediately after, the sounds ended. The drones' rotors stopped, and the objects fell straight to earth.

Symonds' headset would be useless now, but he left it in place, subconsciously hoping that the device had been far enough away from him before detonating that it had left his communications intact.

He dared a peek around the boulder and ran a quick count. He saw five drones littered on the ground just past the boulder, and two more were still flying but clearly damaged. They jumped and sputtered in the air, trying to right themselves. One finally crashed near Symonds' boulder, and did not move again.

That leaves one, maybe two more. Two I can handle.

He stood up, then checked his comms once again. Still nothing, but that did not surprise him.

He saw a man jogging over to his location from almost near the end of the building. It was one of his own, but he couldn't tell who it was. He squinted, trying to make out the man's figure. *Campos?* he thought. It could have been the short Mexican-American soldier, but he needed to wait until —

The man brought his weapon up and immediately started firing, *directly* at Symonds.

What the fuck?

He dove back behind the boulder, back to safety. The shots

peppered the boulder as Symonds confirmed that the man had in fact been firing at *him*. *What the hell? Why is Campos firing at me?*

He needed to act, needed to move. He groaned aloud — *why can't this shit be easier?* — and came to a knee, getting his weapon ready. Thankfully there were no electronics on the assault rifle. While the military was constantly testing new futuristic weaponry that used electronics for distance measurement, wind speed, and automatic targeting, he was thankful that those prototypes were still stuck in the lab.

"Campos!" he shouted. "What the hell, man? It's me!"

He waited. He heard footsteps approaching, knowing Campos had closed the gap.

"Campos, I'm coming out. Hold your —"

Campos fired again, this time a round embedding into the dirt beside Symonds' foot.

"Christ, man! Stop it! It's *me*!"

He rolled to the opposite side and came up firing, getting the man he thought was Campos in his sights only half a second after the man had stopped firing his own rifle. He hit him in the thigh, sending him to his knees.

It stung Symonds to shoot at his own man, but it stung less when *another* half-second passed and he realized it *wasn't* Campos.

The man was short and stocky with a similar build to Justin Campos, but when he saw his face, he knew he had been mistaken.

In that case... he raised his rifle again and fired three more shots, acting before the Campos lookalike could recover.

The man fell, and Symonds frowned. *What the hell is going on?*

If there were any drones still orbiting his location, they were now high enough in the air not to be a problem. He couldn't hear any of their flitting and whirring sounds, but even if he could, it would not have been his main focus.

"Who the hell are you?" he asked, knowing the dead man wouldn't answer. He approached cautiously, hoping to get an ID or name or something he could glean insight from on his uniform. Instead, the man was wearing fatigues with no telltale insignia whatsoever on them.

Symonds reached the man's side, careful to lead with his rifle, and started kneeling.

Just then, *another* shot ricocheted over his head — right where his head had been only a second prior.

Once again, he hit the deck, dropping to his belly next to the fallen soldier. He twisted around to see who was shooting at him this time.

His mouth fell open.

Okay, this is getting ridiculous.

There was not *one* shooter, but five. Five men, all dressed exactly like the soldier Symonds had just dispatched. All five were approaching in a semi-circle, each far enough apart that shooting at one would immediately aggravate the rest, and Symonds knew he could not get more than a few decent shots off on one man before the others took him down.

The man in the center of the line was smiling. He watched as they approached, as they drew nearer to his position in the open field.

This was, to put it bluntly, *not* the way Symonds had envisioned the situation playing out.

He lowered his weapon, knowing he was outmatched and

outgunned, and spun a slow circle, taking in the processional. From the corner of his eye, he saw movement and turned fully around. *Four* more men had appeared behind him, also moving toward him slowly. Each had an assault rifle as well, and each was pointed directly at him.

He did the math. *One man down on the ground next to me, four more coming at me, five behind me.*

Ten men.

Ten Ravenclaw *men.*

Symonds turned back around and addressed the smiling mercenary. "You — you're with Ravenclaw?"

The man's smile never faltered. He nodded.

"Your man shot at me," he said. "Why? You're not here to help? At Roger Witherspoon's request?"

Finally, the man's smile faded, replaced by a thoughtful expression. Then he raised his rifle closer to his eye and pulled the trigger.

"No," he said. "I'm afraid not."

Symonds screamed, but it was too late. The *crack* of the rifle blast took him by surprise, but the impact of the round surprised him even more. He fell backward, landing on dirt just inches from the Campos-looking Ravenclaw soldier.

The soldier's bloodied face was the only thing Nathan Symonds could focus on as his world faded to black.

CHAPTER 41

LIAM

Tanjung Burung | Indonesia

Liam jumped out of the helicopter, which had barely had a chance to spin up again in preparation for an emergency extraction. Witherspoon had informed the pilot to stay put, countermanding his previous order to be prepared to retrieve Symonds and his team.

Liam was frantic; from what he could gather, there *was* no more 'Symonds and his team.' After Symonds' EMP device had detonated, they'd lost contact with the man.

But they hadn't lost contact with one of the *dying* men laying on the ground near the *Palem* building; his comms had not been affected by the localized EMP, and he was still transmitting.

And what he was transmitting directly into Liam's and Roger Witherspoon's ears was terrifying.

It sounded to Liam like a battle. *After* the drones were supposedly nullified, he was hearing assault rifle blasts, both bursts and single shots. There was nothing to distinguish between the different weapons or the firers through the single-mic communications system, but Liam knew enough to be troubled.

"We need to check on them," he had shouted at Witherspoon.

Witherspoon had only nodded, pulling his sidearm from its holster. Liam took that as a sign that the older man was already thinking along the same lines, already preparing something.

"What's the plan?" he asked. He hoped Witherspoon was not just going to head toward where the battle had gone down, only a pistol to protect both of them.

They exited the chopper and met on Liam's side. "I told him to keep it hot!" Witherspoon shouted. "Our help from Ravenclaw should be here any minute — I don't know why they aren't already, but until they get here, we're it!"

"Do you have another weapon?" Liam asked. He didn't *want* to run toward a battle carrying a gun, but he'd much rather be armed than not.

Witherspoon shook his head but was watching the side of the building, about half a mile distant. "Let's get over there at least, then we can see if any of the other comms come back online. I'm not engaging their guards unless it's self-defense. We're obviously outnumbered, but they might be working their way through the field in the opposite direction.

"And besides," he added. "Ravenclaw should be here any minute to help us out."

Liam swallowed and followed Witherspoon's lead. The older man was in insanely good shape, and he nearly sprinted the half-mile to the *Palem* facility building. Liam did his best to control his breath and heart rate, and even still, he had trouble keeping up.

At the edge of the building, Witherspoon looked upward, and

Liam followed his gaze. "Cameras," he said, no longer having to shout over the helicopter's rotor wash, which was still beating a constant rhythm but now far enough away to not be a distraction.

"Too late now," Liam muttered.

"True, but they don't know *we're* here. And I hope we can keep it that way. I need you to stay here, keep watch on your six. There was movement up in the field, so we can't let them go all the way around the building and sneak up behind us."

"Okay," Liam said, glad not to be sent into the fray without a weapon. "But where are you going?"

Witherspoon turned and smiled. "I'm going to see if the door's unlocked."

Liam did not share the old soldier's confidence, but then again, there was really nothing better to do. They could have waited in the chopper, but even Liam's confusion as to their men's status would be too much to bear. Better to be here, ready to provide assistance, when the Ravenclaw mercenaries finally showed up.

Liam saw Witherspoon moving up the side of the building. It was possible that they were being watched on the security feeds, but it didn't matter anymore. The cat was out of the bag, and the *Palem* facility guards were already marching around the premises.

Witherspoon stopped at the doors that marked the middle of the building, and waited a few seconds. Then, he reached out and pulled on the door's handle. Liam saw that it was locked, and Witherspoon tried the next one.

The third door in line opened, but it wasn't from Witherspoon's hand. He jumped back, crouching in front of the second locked door. Liam's breath caught in his throat.

"Shit," he whispered. His palms were sweating, his heart rate accelerated. He wished once again that he had never left Baltimore, but he also wished he at least had something with him to protect himself with.

Four security guards, all armed with assault rifles and looking like they were more apt to be fighting a war than protecting a film company, spilled from the doors.

Witherspoon fired, reacting swiftly, but the guards were ready, likely already knowing his position from the cameras. The first guard ducked and rolled, and the second and third guards out of the door fired while Witherspoon tried to dodge.

Liam saw the man fall, rolling sideways as blood began pooling around him. Liam pulled a hand over his mouth, shocked by the gruesome display and how quickly it had happened.

Roger Witherspoon lurched to the side, coughed, and then died.

He was once again reminded that he was no soldier — he was not supposed to be here, not supposed to be leading a group of men into battle.

...And now he was alone. Completely unarmed, completely isolated. He had been leaning on Witherspoon for the man's experience, but his safety net was bleeding out in front of his eyes.

He turned, hoping to run from the four guards that were now making their way toward him, but slammed into the chest of a mountainous creature that had snuck up behind him.

It was another man, this one wearing all black and rising to a height nearly a foot taller than Liam. He bounced back, looking up into the man's eyes.

Liam was about to ask a question when the man lifted his right hand. He saw the pistol, saw the man pull the trigger.

His mouth fell open. *It wasn't supposed to happen like this,* he thought.

He formulated words, formulated a response, but before his mouth could move, he fell to his knees, then onto the hard-packed ground, face-first.

CHAPTER 42
LIAM

Tanjung Burung | Indonesia

Liam's eyes were closed, but sound began filtering into his mind. He heard words, voices. All around him, bouncing off one another like they were in a cavern, difficult to split apart.

Eventually, his brain began to parse them, to assign them locations and stylistic differences enough to understand that there were three people present. Two men and a woman surrounding him.

Am I lying down?

He could not tell if he was even *alive*, much less where he was located. He tried to wiggle a finger but found resistance there. He could not tell if his hands were fastened down or if his mind simply would not pass along the order to his body.

"He will wake up, but his body will be frozen in place until we give him the other shot?" one of the men asked.

"Correct," the woman answered. She was stationed at his feet. He was horizontal, apparently laying on something. *A bed? A table?*

"But he can hear us?"

"Potentially," the other man's voice said. "Eventually, yes. His mind must be awake, but the drug severs all voluntary control he'll have over his person."

"Forever?"

"Well... Perhaps a few days, a week?" the woman answered. "We're still working on the details of the anesthesia, but the human body was designed to be mobile. His muscles will eventually atrophy to the point of uselessness, much like a coma patient. But because his mind is actually functioning properly — albeit without the voluntary muscular control — he will decay far more rapidly. We've been able to keep subjects alive for up to six months in this state, but they quickly decline upon waking."

There was a scoff, a laugh. "It won't come to that."

Liam could not believe they were talking about *him* as if he were not there.

"Give him the shot. We aren't keeping him alive to let him devolve into a vegetable. We need answers."

"Yes, sir."

The woman's voice moved away slightly, so he assumed she was the one now preparing this "shot" to give him.

There was a brief pause and then the pinging sound of something falling onto metal. He had not felt a thing, but the woman confirmed that the job was done.

Another minute passed, with neither of the three people speaking. Finally, Liam's eyes fluttered open. The room was sparse, with hard tile walls. The ceiling was made of some hardened material as well, and there was a bright light directly above him. The three people were mere blobs, the light blocking out any noticeable details.

"See, it's already working," the woman said. "He will awaken and function normally, but it will take perhaps an hour."

"Perfect," the first man said. "Thank you — that is all."

It was a way of dismissing the woman doctor, and she nodded and left the room. Liam heard a door open and shut, and the two men still in the room leaned closer.

"Mr. Hernandez, I presume?" one of the men asked.

He tested his neck muscles by trying out a nod. It worked.

"Perfect," the man said. "I do apologize for questioning you under these *extreme* conditions, but you have to know you forced my hand."

Liam frowned. "al-Sadir?"

The man smiled. "You *did* find me, after all. Wonderful. I would have preferred to meet under slightly different pretenses, but — what the hell, as you Americans say."

The other man chuckled.

"Hans," al-Sadir said, addressing the other man. "Please continue with the show — the next segments of mine have been pre-recorded, and I no longer require your assistance here. Check in with the security team, and please let me know if there is any trouble."

Hans nodded and left the room as well.

al-Sadir's eyebrows furrowed in a look of concern. "I'm afraid your friend did not make it," he said.

"My friend? You mean Witherspoon?"

"Oh, right. Well, all of them. Your crack team of soldiers, their commanding officer. But between the drone footage and that of my security cameras, the show really was as intense as I could have hoped."

Liam swallowed. *They're all dead?* His mind raced. What was he doing here? And why was he still alive?

"I needed someone to answer a few questions," al-Sadir continued, "and I was stunned to learn that *you,* of all people, were among those outside of my complex. So I had Hans' team bring you in."

Liam could not make sense of this — of any of it. "How — how do you know who I am?"

al-Sadir seemed to have anticipated this question. "Liam Ortega Hernandez, Director of Future Security at the National Security Administration. Unmarried, no children. Girlfriend, but you are in the "off" stage of the "on again, off again" style relationship. You have a cat, because a dog requires too much attention. Am I close so far? We can get into your private bank account information, your social security number, your current address. However, I don't have all day."

Liam's mind reeled. "Y — yes, that's all correct. But... how?"

"Hans — my head of security — is very good at what he does. Or, rather, he is very good at *hiring* those who are good at what they do. And, as it turns out, there is no place better for finding private and secret data than your company, Mr. Hernandez. The NSA is chock full of information just *waiting* to see the light of day."

"You *hacked* the NSA?"

"Hardly," al-Sadir said. "You of all people know how difficult that would be. At least from afar. But Hans is much more 'hands-on,' if you will. It's almost not a challenge at all to gain access to your facilities in broad daylight, so long as the information checks out. And a bit of social engineering and knowing your way around a computer gets you into your server farm. After that, it's just a matter of knowing where to look and how to retrieve it.

"Now, the *real* fun stuff is not on those servers, as you well know. But those servers *do* control the intra-network security of most all of the NSA centers, as well as the headquarters building in which *you* work, Mr. Hernandez."

Liam's blood ran cold. *Of course.* This man did not *need* to hack the NSA, nor did he need to steal data at all. "You installed something there, didn't you? Something that uploads data otherwise never accessible to the larger web?"

"Precisely. Hans himself planted the device, and it's nearly invisible. No network footprint, since it's not technically *on* your network. It's simply copying the data as it passes through, then uploading it to my cloud. So I've been watching you, and I've been watching your team.

Liam swallowed again. He knew the truth about al-Sadir's claims. It was *theoretically* simple — from a computing standpoint — to gain access to NSA servers and data. The large databases of information that were not deemed top-secret or classified were stored in a physical data center, and while there was a baseline of protection over the data layers, the NSA's main security methodology came down to *physically* securing the buildings the data was stored in.

If someone could successfully gain access to the building, the data would be up for grabs with only a passing knowledge of computer science.

Still, they were the *NSA.* They had never been hacked. There had been attempts — hell, they even had an entire division dedicated to onsite security for the NSA organization itself.

"That's impossible," Liam spat. "We've never had a breach like this. *Ever.* The NSA's computers and server farm are locked down tight."

"Of course they are!" al-Sadir said, seeming to enjoy this turn in the conversation. "However, you and I both know how simple it is to fake a background check, or — in this case — *pass* a background check. You have how many employees?"

Liam thought through the implications. "This man — Hans, you said? You're saying he gained access by becoming an *actual* NSA employee?"

"Temporarily, yes," al-Sadir said. "Then he wiped record of his employment from the same servers he accessed."

Liam shook his head, happy that his physical faculties were returning. "But how did he manage to sneak a device onto the premises? It's not like he could have just ordered an Amazon package to be delivered to his office. If we're thorough anywhere, it's in peripheral and device management. Hell, we can't even get through with a *cell* phone."

"But all of the equipment one would need to install and activate a monitoring and transmission device is already *on* the premises," al-Sadir said with a frown, as if disappointed Liam had not already come to this conclusion.

Liam closed his eyes and sucked in a breath. *Of course. It would be as simple as that.* The NSA building he worked in even had what they called "The Graveyard," a conference room-sized closet full of old gear and networking devices that employees and staff no longer had a use for. Not all computers could be safely refurbished and released to the outside world, and yet it would be a waste to just destroy every single laptop and cell phone that was a few years out of date.

So, like most government organizations and large bureaucracies, the pile of discarded equipment grew larger over time, not smaller. It would be a simple affair to snatch a small listening device, fashion it onto an old router, and use a microprocessor to run a barebones OS on the whole thing.

"So, during our reconnaissance of your team, I was ecstatic to learn that you would be visiting *Escape from Eden*, as well."

"So..." Liam said, his voice nearly a whisper. "It's real? The show? What we've been watching back in Maryland is not some sick joke? A theatrical performance?"

al-Sadir smiled. "Brilliant, isn't it? Hide something like this in plain sight? I mean, it's not like we're live streaming through a cable company. There must be *some* semblance of secrecy, which is why we chose the Dark Web as a funneling tool. But it's enough that it causes a rumor to grow, to blossom, to *spread*."

He leaned farther over Liam. "Yes, Mr. Hernandez, *Escape from Eden* is *very* real. And I am ecstatic to show you just *how* real it is."

LOCATION *unknown*

Joshua Lane felt as though he'd just run a marathon. And he knew the feeling, too — he and his wife had participated in quite a few runs together since they'd met. But he had not done anything nearly that physically taxing; the feeling was in his mind.

He, combined with NARA and Eve, had processed over a thousand minor requests since he had taken control. Most of these had gone straight through without his knowledge, but it still seemed to be having an effect on his mental state.

He stumbled, blinked a few times, and then forced himself to stand upright again. The sheer amount of data passing through his brain — thanks to the artificial computer spliced to his spinal cord — was incredible. And it wasn't completely passive. He realized that his mind was still processing each request, at least subconsciously.

Was that a feature or a bug? he wondered. It seemed to be mentally taxing, but it also could have something to do with the fact that he had just saved Contestant #4 from certain death.

But there was no time to relax, no time to rest. The endgame was here, and judging by the battle taking place onscreen, he needed to move before the man running all of this had figured out that Contestant #4 was still alive.

His first move was to examine one of the dozens of requests that were coming in each second. They were all parsed the same way, their syntax matching what he had seen of high-abstraction programming languages. Most of the words read like English, but he knew that they had been created by Eve's monitoring system, spread throughout the intranet-connected facility he was in now. That meant each request *was* code, in a sense.

It did not take long. He found the common variables — usually nouns and pronouns — and pieced together his own request.

The next step was trickier. He needed NARA to fake a submission, routing it *out* onto the intranet and then letting it hit Eve's monitoring suite, only to be sent back to him and NARA for confirmation or denial.

That meant he needed to pass the correct envelope, as well. He scanned through the prior requests, eventually landing on one that seemed to fit the nature of the request he wanted to send. He opened it, amazed at how quickly he, aided by NARA's technology, could send and receive messages on the system. It was almost as quick as thinking.

He had no time to geek out about the tech, though. He ran a quick command on NARA's built-in text-based terminal and told the computer to open the envelope of the request, and then he copied the data stream and pasted it into a new file. He changed a few key variables, then saved it again.

Finally, he sent the request.

There was a lag time of only a few milliseconds, but to Josh it felt like an eternity.

The request came back, hitting Eve, and thus NARA, almost immediately after.

My God, he thought. *It worked.*

"NARA, pass on the request as confirmed," he thought.

The request was passed on to Eve's system, and he waited the excruciating three or four hundred milliseconds for the response.

The response came.

A click.

Where before there was just a strange, ceramic-looking wall, there now appeared a rectangular crack from the floor to a few feet below the ceiling.

A door.

He almost cried. It had worked! He had been successful emulating a computer-generated request in Eve's system.

The implications were absolutely *enormous.* He now had a way to *completely control* Eve and her systems, at least while connected via NARA to her intranet. And it was wireless, so he could move around the facility without even needing to stop and check a device or console as he moved.

And move he did. Josh wasted no time exiting the room, looking left and right before proceeding into the hallway. His chamber was one of many, and in the hallway he could see that there were outlines of doors on this side of the wall — likely so that any human captors walking the length of the hall knew which door was which.

He slunk into the shadow of his open door, waiting for any sounds and wondering if there were any guards or security presence here before realizing he did not *need* to guess.

He fired up the same console he had used before, this time saving even more precious seconds by loading the previous request and envelope. He changed the text a bit, operating at the speed of thought, and then fired it away to Eve.

Immediately in his mind, he saw a video superimposed on his vision. It was a split-screen view of the two cameras monitoring this hallway; one faced him, and one stood at the opposite end, facing outward.

Unbelievable, he thought. *I'm like a god.*

He could now see anyone coming this direction.

In a similar fashion, he ran toward the second camera, telling NARA to run a request to search Eve's system for any and all cameras in the building, then set up a feed to display whenever he approached one.

He could now see around corners. And in all directions. At the same time.

He ran faster, no longer needing to worry about taking someone by surprise. He could see them from afar, and he used it to his advantage.

At the opposite end of *this* hall — one strikingly similar to the one he'd just left — he slowed. It seemed the back corner of the facility had been where his cell was. There were two hallways perpendicular to one another, meeting at each of their ends, forming the outer two edges of a square building.

He heard noise here, though. The lights were a bit brighter in this new hallway, and he assumed it was a sort of office or administration wing. There were voices reaching him.

Shouting?

It sounded like two or more people, at least one of them upset about something.

He tried to find a feed showing any other human in one of the rooms off this hallway, but there were no cameras in whatever room they were in.

The volume of the shouting grew, then subsided. But it was enough. Josh could hear the voices more clearly now, at least well enough to determine that they were in the second or third door down, on the right side. The building seemed to have four similar-sized hallways — two in an "L" shape that housed the contestants, and two more that were well-lit, housing the offices of whoever worked for this sadistic operation.

He assumed the large, square-shaped space in the middle was the soundstage he had seen shots of on his room's monitor, or otherwise a larger, gym-like space for events or something.

But Josh didn't dwell on it. He could have browsed Eve's system for a camera feed of the interior of the larger space, but it was not his priority right now.

He needed to find out who was in that room.

The voices rose again; more shouting. Someone sounded hurt, in pain.

And he needed to do it *now*.

CHAPTER 44
LIAM

"Why am I still alive?" Liam asked. "You killed my men, as well as a decorated US military officer."

al-Sadir had left Liam strapped to the table for fifteen minutes, but then he had returned, the large, hulking man named Hans in tow.

"Roger Witherspoon?" al-Sadir asked. "He was a washed-up old grunt, wasn't he? Hans looked him up before you all came, just to make sure that if he somehow... didn't *make it*, no one in your government would come looking for him."

"So you just killed him?"

"Consider yourself the lucky one, Liam," al-Sadir said. "It made good viewing to have our drones take out your team, and I'm sure my viewers would have loved to see you fall as well."

"So again — *why am I alive?*" Liam tried to steady his voice and grit his teeth, but he was no soldier, no operative. He knew it came across as sniveling fear instead.

"I need answers, of course."

"Answers to what?"

al-Sadir smiled. He turned to Hans, who produced a tablet from behind his back and slid it in front of Liam. Suddenly the table crunched forward, lifting Liam's torso while simultaneously lowering his feet. It was transforming into a chair, lifting and lowering in two separate places.

The entire device lowered to the floor, and Liam watched the screen as Hans held it out in front of him.

He saw the same rooms he and his team had seen before, and he knew he was looking at an *Escape from Eden* contestant.

Suddenly Joshua Lane appeared onscreen, pacing from a lower corner to the center of the room and back again.

"This is your man," al-Sadir said. "The one who has all of America's espionage and covert ops divisions all hot and bothered."

Liam didn't say anything.

"And why is that?" al-Sadir asked. "Why is it that when Hans' team grabs *this* man from a street in Baltimore, suddenly your service is on high alert? Suddenly the *President* himself is interested in tracking him down?"

Liam swallowed. *He never should have mentioned to the group back at headquarters that Sykes and POTUS were involved.* But how could he have known that the NSA itself was listening in, and a device in its server room sending that message out to al-Sadir?

"It seems to me that I've somehow got my hands on a man who is *far* more interesting than I initially believed. You see, we wanted Lane because he is believed to be the world's foremost expert on quantum mechanics when it comes to microscopic computing. That's a mouthful, of course, but I'm sure you understand where I'm going with this."

"You kidnap scientists and pit them against each other in a life-or-death battle," Liam said.

al-Sadir's eyes lit up. *"Yes!"* he cried. "Precisely. And what a group of scientists we have this round! My viewers are ecstatic for the event, not to mention the bonus round of entertainment your men provided."

"You already know then that Josh is of interest to us," Liam said. "You just explained why. So why am I here?"

"I merely told you what *you* know I know. I'm interested in what I *do not* know. I'm interested in the tech inside Josh's skull."

"The... what?"

He saw Hans tighten the grip on the tablet, and Liam watched as the man's knuckles hardened and turned white.

"Let's not make this difficult, Liam. I need that *tech*, but it's useless to me until I understand *what it is.*"

"I have *no idea* what you're talking about, man," Liam said. He was telling the truth. *What the hell did he mean by* tech *inside Josh's skull?*

al-Sadir nodded at Hans, who removed the tablet from view. His hands came back a few seconds later, this time wielding a butane-powered blowtorch, with a piezo ignition button screwed onto its top.

Liam gulped a breath of air. "Look, man," he stammered. "I — I don't know what you mean by *tech*, but in his skull? You mean his brain?"

Hans smiled, then flicked the igniter on the torch and the tiny flame shot out toward Liam's face. He felt the warmth of the blue flame already licking against his lips.

"I'm telling the truth!" Liam shouted.

al-Sadir shook his head. "Not good enough, my friend," he

said. "I know you're good at what you do. *The best*, even. Your reputation at the NSA precedes you — just like Colonel Sykes told you in his office."

Liam squeezed his eyes shut.

"Sykes mentioned the tech then, too. Do you remember? 'Bearbridge's top-secret project?'"

"Yes, but he never told me what it was! I swear!"

al-Sadir watched him, the man's face a mask. Liam felt his eyes welling with tears, and he knew what was coming next.

"I'm sorry, my friend," al-Sadir said. "I truly despise people like you — you play dumb, assuming I'm *dumber*." He motioned to the large man next to him. "Hans, proceed."

Hans lowered the torch, still burning, and isolated one of Liam's fingers. The flame immediately turned orange as it connected with his flesh.

Liam screamed, surprising himself with the volume. The pain was incredible, worse than anything he'd ever imagined.

"No! Pl — please!" he shouted. "Stop!"

Hans held the butane torch there for an excruciating three more seconds before al-Sadir waved him off.

al-Sadir raised his voice. "I am no longer playing games, Mr. Hernandez. The next words out of your mouth had better be an explanation — an explanation as to why you are here, trying to retrieve Lane. And, eventually, what is it that we found near the base of his skull."

Liam sobbed, the pain he was experiencing somehow still growing and spreading. His finger was as good as gone, but he could not bring himself to look at it. "I..." he started, his voice weak. "I was asked by Sykes to put a team together to get Josh Lane back."

"Yes, I am aware of that."

"He told me Lane was important to national security."

"Is that what he said?" Hans asked, the torch always bobbing menacingly just in sight.

"He — he told me the President himself wanted Lane back," Liam said. "That he was a crucial asset for our project."

"Project...?" al-Sadir asked.

Liam knew what he wanted to say, but to say it would be to reveal classified information. However, Liam's life was absolutely at stake now, and he assumed al-Sadir and Hans already *knew* what he was going to say next.

"Project Echelon," Liam said, wincing. "It's a sort of brain trust, but the members don't know they're part of it. We're keeping tabs on them because of one thing or another — their intelligence in general, but usually because of their particular experience and knowledge in a certain domain."

"And Joshua Lane's domain?"

"He's — he's a computer genius," Liam said. "But you already know that, don't you?" He sat up a bit, catching a glimpse of his smoking, fried finger. The pain was insurmountable, but talking seemed to keep his brain focused forward. He felt a slight adrenaline rush as the anger he felt bubbled to the surface. "You already know that, because you *kidnapped* him and stuck him in your sadistic game."

al-Sadir didn't respond.

"You guys are pitting them against each other, and they're all obviously brilliant in their respective fields. All your contestants have genius-level intelligence already, and you're killing anyone who loses? Why? What purpose does that serve? How the hell can you justify —"

Before he could finish, Hans leaned in with the torch. He pressed down harder this time, the white-hot flame nearly invisible as it neared Liam's charred finger.

He screamed even louder this time, sobbing and choking through the smoke and smell of burning flesh. The bloodcurdling wails emanating from his mouth must have reached every corner of the facility, but no one came to his rescue.

There *was* no one to come to his rescue — anyone inside the *Palem* studio not working for al-Sadir was locked up in a chamber already.

His scream heightened, and he nearly passed out as Hans moved to the next finger. He started in from the tip, slowly and meticulously burning down the entire digit, one excruciating millimeter at a time.

al-Sadir once again stopped Hans. "I do apologize for the intensity, but you must understand that we are running out of time. And I did not ask you to ask *me* questions, now did I?"

Liam shook his head, tears dripping down the sides of his face.

"Good. So I ask once more — what is Project Echelon, *really?* Why is Joshua Lane currently the world's most-wanted man? *What is in his head?*"

Liam's heart sank. He knew how this would end. He was not going to be believed, simply because these two men — his *torturers* — had already *chosen* not to believe Liam was out of the loop. They *needed* him to know, and they would kill him either way.

"I — I don't know," Liam said. "I wondered that myself," he said, truthfully. "I didn't ask Sykes because it's not my business, and that's how these things work. Hell, I wasn't even sure there *was* something going on with Lane. I figured it could just be Sykes' typical need-to-know personality."

"The little bug in his head," Hans asked. "It is pill-sized. Is it a tracker? I have never seen anything like it, but it must be a tracker."

Al-Sadir jumped in. "Yes, we deactivated it, of course, but we were afraid to remove it — what if it were some sort of dead man's switch? Remove it and it detonates, and everything — including Josh — is vaporized? We could not take that chance. So what *is* it, Mr. Hernandez?"

Liam swallowed, and he was acutely aware of how dire his situation was. His tears were flowing freely now, and his body was shaking. He felt nothing other than the numbness of the pain, still throbbing.

"I wish I knew," he said. "I truly wish I knew."

al-Sadir waited, then realized Liam was done speaking. His head fell, and he stepped away from the table-turned-chair. "I see," he whispered. "I, too, wish you knew."

He nodded at Hans, then walked toward the door.

Hans' smile widened, and he lifted the torch again and got to work.

LOCATION *unknown*

Josh stopped just outside the door.

He had heard the same *clicking* sound he had heard when he'd left his own room, but he had not caused it.

Instead, he found a request logged by NARA from only a half-second prior. The door had been opened automatically by NARA — the artificial intelligence apparently working to control the rest of the building as well.

No human had logged the request, at least judging by the headers in the envelope, but the result was the same. The door swung open, thankfully also moving outward into the hallway, giving Josh something to hide behind.

And out walked the man he had seen onscreen — the man behind all of this.

Josh felt his heart catch in his throat. He wanted to scream. He wanted to rush the man, to take him down.

But his subconscious prevented it. He steeled himself, waiting for the man to turn toward him and recognize what had happened, that one of his captives had escaped.

But the man did not turn in his direction. He walked silently out of the room and headed down the lit hallway toward the other rooms.

Josh had not been spotted.

He quickly told the camera facing him to run an automated shutdown and restart sequence, citing 'updates required,' in case this man also had immediate access to the feeds, but Josh doubted it. NARA itself was groundbreaking technology — and, he suspected, the reason he was here in the first place — and Josh was the only person to his knowledge who had it installed.

Surely this man, a glorified reality television host, had no such implant.

Still, Josh was cautious. He forced his mind to slow, his breaths to follow suit. He needed stealth right now; he needed to maintain his ability to move around this place without anyone else knowing anything was *out* of place.

There were more screams coming from the open door. He swallowed, suddenly remembering the horrifying and brutal things being done to the prisoners here, and he made a decision.

Whatever evil's behind that door will die today, he told himself.

He needed the next few seconds to be timed perfectly. The person inside the room was obviously torturing someone else, judging by the screams, and while every fiber of his being told him to rush in and start using his *other* training, he needed to wait. He needed to trust NARA, who was showing him that the camera view on the far side of the hallway was tracking the man's progress toward it, the open door obscuring Josh just beyond it.

He needed to wait another few seconds. The television host

needed to be far enough away that any noise Josh made moving into the room would not alert him. But he needed to do it all quickly enough so that the door did not close —

No, he thought. *I don't* need to worry about that.

He sent a request in, and the door in front of him stayed open. Whoever was inside likely had no idea the door had not shut again, but even if they did, it was a risk worth taking. He still had no view of the inside of this room, but he needed to move. He had no better options.

The host ducked into another opening door, and Josh made his move.

What he saw inside horrified him.

There was a man about Josh's age, strapped to a chair-like contraption in the center of a tiled floor, with a hulking human-shaped object above him. The hulk had a blowtorch in his hands — the same kind Josh and his wife had used for running a camping stove.

And the blowtorch was on and currently being used to cook a very different thing than Josh wanted to see.

He winced, but pushed forward anyway. He did not bother looking at the victim — he needed to get to the man currently trying to cook the prisoner.

Josh reached him in three strides, and it was only during the third stride that the man seemed to realize someone else was in the room.

The man turned his head, but the torch continued blasting the prisoner's hand.

Josh leaped forward.

He struck the hulk of a man in the chest, tackling him away

from the bound prisoner, and together they fell into a heap on the floor.

Josh was already moving before the other guy seemed to know what was happening. He slunk sideways, ignoring the screams and wails of the prisoner just above him, and slammed the heel of his fist into the meathead's chin.

The man grunted but shifted sideways faster than Josh thought was possible. Apparently the guy was trained as well, and Josh moved to his left, trying to get to his feet before the monster did.

The blowtorch had rattled away and was rolling toward the now-closing door, but it was still lit, the governor valve either not present or not caring that it had been jostled around. Josh eyed it but kept his focus on the man now rising to his feet.

He stood about six-and-a-half feet tall, well over Josh's head. And he seemed to be made completely of muscle, his rippling biceps surging through his long-sleeved shirt, which had a few tears in it.

He rushed Josh, swinging before he had maintained his balance.

Josh used the off-balance attack against the man, sweeping a foot and ducking just as the man's beefy fist passed his head.

The man tripped and fell, and Josh lunged.

He jumped on the still-lit torch while the man in the chair wailed in pure agony. He tried to ignore the sound, but the cacophony only added to his stress.

Thankfully, it also forced his mind to focus, the adrenaline to surge through him. He felt time seem to slow down, the constant barrage of requests seem to come in less often, a handful of them taking center stage as NARA alerted him to their arrival. He scanned them subconsciously, discarding them and letting Eve handle the bulk of them, but for one:

"Request: Eve server access: Room 4B."

Josh's heartbeat increased. He needed to stop this — all of this.

"Request denied," he told NARA. *"Send another request: Close door to Room 4B, lock it. No manual access."*

He was moving toward the behemoth now, holding the torch. Josh didn't know if the request would work, but there were more pressing issues to tackle at the moment.

He brought the torch up just as he slid *beneath* the end of the chair and the wall around the legs of the man. The torch provided a temporary relief — the man was not stupid, and did not want the thing anywhere near him — but Josh was also faster. He lifted the torch again as he caught his feet, standing as the man began turning around.

Josh was there, waiting, as he thrust the torch up and toward the man's neck.

He wasn't trying to burn him.

He was trying to *maim* him.

The move worked. Josh felt the singed flesh give way almost immediately, as the soft part of the man's jugular fell to the white-hot metal of the butane torch. He continued pressing inward, hoping to get a good sever of the artery before cauterization took place.

Or, if that didn't work, he hoped it hurt like absolute hell.

A few more requests came in, pinging NARA's and his attention, but he ignored them. There was nothing more important right now, and he continued his plight against this torturer. He held the torch steady for a few more seconds, the man pulling and shrieking and generally losing all semblance of control, and then he fell, clutching his neck.

Josh held tight to the torch — a weapon, the only one he'd had in some time. To let it go would mean his death, most likely — but focused on the trapped prisoner.

He saw the straps connecting the man's arms and feet to the chair, and quickly undid the side that had not been charred. The man was groaning in pain, but he moved his left arm over and undid the straps on his right side delicately while Josh pulled the straps free that were holding his right foot.

The big man on the ground was clutching his neck still, but he was standing up, slowly. He was in severe pain, but he was alive.

Josh needed to change that, but he also needed to get this guy free and out of the way.

He fought with himself, trying to decide what to accomplish first when a request hit NARA.

"Request: elimination routine of all remaining contestants."

PART FOUR

LOCATION *unknown*

Josh shouted down at the prisoner on the chair. "Can you walk?" He didn't need to shout, as there was really no noise outside of his own head. But the noise *in* his head was deafening.

The request had been manual.

The man on the floor was very quickly getting his legs back underneath him.

And he had no idea who this other man was and why he was being tortured. His hand was mangled, charred, and missing fingers, but it seemed the wounds had been cauterized by the same mechanism that had caused them.

Josh walked over to the hulking giant holding his throat, and swung the butane torch out and struck him in the forehead. He fell back but wasn't out yet. Josh kicked him hard in the side, dodging the man's hand as it fought to grasp Josh's foot.

He wheeled around again, bringing the butane torch down and smacking it against the back of the giant's head.

This time, he fell quiet.

"Hey — can you walk?" Josh asked again.

The guy in the chair nodded. "Yeah, I can walk. My hand's wasted, but I'm fine otherwise." He sniffed back tears, and Josh could not imagine how much pain he must have been in.

"Good," he said, lifting the man out of the chair and helping him catch his balance. "We need to run. They're eliminating all of the contestants."

The man rose to his feet, unsteady at first. "Wait, what?" he asked. "H — how do you know that?"

"Look, I really don't have time to explain it fully. Just trust me. If I'm going to shut this down, we need to —"

"You can shut this down?" the guy asked. Josh was annoyed, but to his credit, the man was moving toward the door. "Like, you know the system?"

Josh reached the door to the room just as the large hulk of a guard behind them rose to his feet. He was bleeding profusely from his neck and chin, but he clearly was not dead. *Damn,* Josh thought. *Next time I'll make sure he's down for the count.*

He pulled the smaller man through the open door and placed a request of his own. *"Shut door. Lock it, manual override only."*

The automated door immediately swung closed and he heard the telltale *click* of the lock engaging. Then he heard the sound of meaty fists banging against the other side. There were no shouts, as he assumed the man's severed throat was preventing that, but Josh knew he was probably trying.

"How the hell did you do that?" the man next to Josh asked.

"Come on," Josh said. "We need to get —"

"No," the man said suddenly. Josh wheeled around, ready to smack the guy. "You're Lane, right?"

Josh blinked.

"I — I'm Liam Hernandez. National Security Agency. I'm here to get you out."

"Out of *where*, exactly? I'm a little in the dark as to where we are."

Liam nodded. "Place called *Palem*. We're in Indonesia."

"Got it. Okay, you ready?"

"Not really. Can we just... figure this out first? As I said, I'm here to find *you*. To rescue you."

Josh raised an eyebrow as he sent a few requests through NARA. He did not have time to have a conversation with his self-proclaimed rescuer, but at least he was able to multitask. "That's, uh, great," he said. "Thanks for the rescue."

Surprisingly, Liam smiled. "I mean, that's what I was *supposed* to be doing. Thanks for coming over here." He paused, taking a look up and down the hallway. "How the hell did you get out? Those weird cells they were keeping you in — they didn't seem like the sort of thing you can walk in and out of."

Josh returned the smile, "Yeah, they're not. Look, I appreciate the attempt, but it's really not a good time to catch up. Help me shut down this shitshow, and we can debrief all day."

Liam nodded, and Josh started jogging toward the room he'd seen the other man disappear into. At the same time, he ran through the requests being logged in Eve's system. Many of them were automated, as had been true so far, but quite a few were now showing a *MANUAL* flag.

Someone's working in the system, running the show by hand, he realized. He thought about attempting to lock them out of their account, but he did not even know where to begin. It's not like he could see a list of currently logged-in users. Besides, he did not have root access to Eve's overall system.

Instead, he threw as many requests toward Eve as possible, each countermanding the manual orders just after they were placed. He hoped that whoever was working in the system did not notice that just after they changed something or ordered Eve to do something, it would be changed back seconds later.

He pulled up a camera feed of the hallway and watched as he and Liam progressed toward the door.

"You here alone?" Josh asked.

"I — uh, I am now," Liam said.

Josh sensed there was more to this part of the man's story as well, but he dropped it. "And NSA — that's not traditional. Why'd they send you?"

"I was an analyst but moved up the ranks. Got put in charge of the rescue mission, and my military cohort sort of dragged me along."

"Right," Josh said. "And I'm assuming that 'military cohort' didn't make it this far?"

Liam nodded again.

"Okay, look," Josh said, shifting the conversion to the more immediate focus. "The guy that runs this place is right inside that door."

"al-Sadir," Liam said.

"Okay, al-Sadir. Anyway, I think he's the one who's got his hands on the controls. He's been trying to get Eve to eliminate all the contestants, but I've been fighting him off. However, if he figures it out, he's going to lock *me* out of the system."

Liam looked like Josh *had* just smacked him in the face. "Wait. *You* are fighting him? How?"

"I've got a helpful friend," Josh said. "Let's just leave it at that for now."

"The thing in your head," Liam said suddenly. "The, uh, *chip*, or whatever it is. al-Sadir was asking me — *torturing* me — about it."

Josh frowned, considering this. "Yeah, that's the one." He stopped along the wall, thinking. *If al-Sadir brought me here and accidentally deactivated NARA, then tortured this NSA guy about it, it means he doesn't have any idea what it really is.*

That was good news, at least in the whole scheme of things. *He wants to know what it can do. But why? Why not just ask me? Why not just torture* me?

"What's the plan, then?" Liam asked. "We just go in and rush al-Sadir?"

Josh shook his head. "No. *I* go in and rush al-Sadir."

CHAPTER 47
JOSH

PALEM FACILITY

Tanjung Burung | Indonesia

It wasn't much of a plan. But Joshua Lane had been in plenty of situations where the carefully crafted plan fell apart, and he had to adapt on the fly, making things up as he went along anyway.

And he had never had to plan for "trapped in a sadistic reality television show with a crazed lunatic trying to kill everyone."

So he was just trusting his gut. Or, rather, trusting the data he was receiving from NARA and Eve.

"I need you to keep running down this hallway. Same direction. Down there, where it turns, you'll be in the wing where they were keeping us."

He needed to find the place the requests were coming from. With any luck, al-Sadir was there now, manually putting them in and fighting against Josh's efforts. He had NARA trace the routes of the requests, hoping she would be able to isolate which particular routing switches they were bouncing off of. Perhaps they could narrow down the exact location by measuring ping time latencies or something.

It was a long shot, but it was the perfect thing to have a computer work on. She would be able to measure the minuscule differences in timestamps between the request's pings.

Maybe.

"Those rooms that... burned people alive?" Liam asked.

"Yes," Josh said. "And if al-Sadir gets his way now, they'll light up again, and every single one of the remaining contestants will die."

"So what do I do?"

"Help them. I don't really know what that's going to entail, but if I can get their doors opened, I'll need you to lead them out of the building."

Truth be told, Josh didn't *know* what to tell Liam. The guy was a wreck, his hand a mess of blood and charred flesh. He shuddered as he imagined it. *Poor guy didn't even have time to pass out,* he thought.

Liam nodded and ran off.

"I have narrowed down the possible location to a room at the opposite end of this hallway," NARA told him.

"Good," he replied. *"With any particular level of certainty?"*

"Impossible to say."

Well, he thought. *Better than nothing.*

He hoped he had a good idea where he would find al-Sadir. He was constantly fighting against the man's manual overrides, his trying to persuade Eve to continue with the *elimination* routine. Josh was able to shut the requests down and bury them beneath more, unrelated requests, hiding them from sight because he could work at the speed of thought.

Josh stopped outside the room, imagining what he would find inside. al-Sadir would be at a desk, furiously working the keyboard as quickly as he could type or using voice activation. Both slower than Josh's setup, but with one massive advantage: al-Sadir's computer would be connected to the network, hardwired in.

And if he realized what was happening, that Josh was able to connect to Eve via the wireless transmission of NARA's tech, he could shut down his access in an instant by simply shutting down the wireless network itself.

He needed to hurry. He wanted to move slowly, stealthily. But he knew he would not be taking al-Sadir by surprise. The man would be just inside this door, sending requests like a madman, but he would *also* be waiting for Josh. He would know by now what had happened, that a contestant had escaped and that person was toying with Eve's system.

There would be no way to sneak up on him. No way to get the jump on him, at least physically. Unfortunate, too, because Josh knew he would have the upper hand in a fight with the man he had seen on the *Escape from Eden* screens.

That means we're fighting this one digitally, Josh thought.

He paused outside the door, sending one final bombardment of requests. These were all the easiest, most mundane requests he could think of — turn on and off lights in the rooms at the far reaches of campus, both inside and outside, restart printers and devices connected to Eve. They were requests only meant to bog down the system. If someone were watching in, checking the logs, they would be confused for at least a second or two.

And Josh was using that second or two now to send one final request. A request very similar to the one he had used to escape his own room.

Open all the contestants' room doors.

He felt the confirmation ping in his mind almost instantly, also satisfied to receive a secondary message after. A request had come in to continue with the elimination routine — the same one Josh had been fighting against the whole time, but this time Eve had failed it entirely. Since the doors were being unlocked, the elimination routine could not be confirmed.

It was a failsafe, Josh realized. The rooms had been specially designed to contain the fiery inferno caused by the eliminations, which meant a bunch of open doors would challenge the integrity of the building. It would make the hallways vulnerable, and Eve would not allow that until the doors were fully closed and sealed again.

But whoever was sending the elimination routine request would have to back up, *lock* the doors once again, and then send the request for elimination a final time. And they would have to do it all manually, wasting precious seconds, precious *focus*.

It was a window just large enough. He asked Eve to unlock the door in front of him — *al-Sadir's* door — and it clicked open immediately.

For a moment, he wondered why al-Sadir had not put the request back in — why the man had suddenly stopped worrying about the elimination routine. Josh knew that he would have been able to re-lock the contestants' room doors and resubmit the elimination request.

But he also did not have time to waste. He clicked the butane torch on once again and gripped the bottle. He pulled the door away and stormed inside.

Joshua Lane entered the room like a bull, seeing red, torch lit and leading him inside. He let NARA handle the low-level requests that shot around his skull, moving toward the hunched figure seated at a table in the far corner.

Until, suddenly, the requests *stopped.*

He tried hailing Eve's server, tried pinging the IP address.

No. al-Sadir had done it.

He understood now. al-Sadir had shifted his focus when Josh had unlocked all the doors. He had changed gears, worrying about how to eliminate all the remaining contestants to how to deal with Joshua Lane.

And he had apparently figured it out.

al-Sadir had cut Josh off. He had removed his only tactical advantage.

NARA displayed the return message from the ping command, confirming his fears.

Error: no address found.

Shit.

He tried a few more times, but NARA's response was the same each time. Josh — and NARA — was no longer able to access Eve.

But his focus shifted to the person hunched over the terminal across the room. He gulped, panicking.

It was *not* al-Sadir.

The woman sitting there turned around slowly. He saw her short hair, realized that her features and frame were just similar enough to al-Sadir's that he had mistaken them at first. But as she turned, the requests stopped.

This woman had been sending the requests — *not* al-Sadir. This woman was the one who had been playing with him.

Who had been *toying* with him.

She was a distraction. All of this was part of al-Sadir's misdirection. Part of his plan. While Josh fumbled around in the dark, trying to make sense of this place and how to control it, al-Sadir had his henchmen — and women — working against him.

All to buy al-Sadir more time.

This time, the curse actually escaped his lips. He reared back and roared at the woman, who was now eyeing him cautiously.

"Shit!"

PALEM FACILITY

Tanjung Burung | Indonesia

Just go help people, Liam thought.

No shit, Sherlock. And how, exactly, *do I help people?*

He had torn down the hallway, looking around frantically, waiting for something to happen that would clue him in on what the hell he was supposed to do next.

He wasn't mad at Joshua Lane. The guy had just been trying to help — and he certainly rescued him from further torture and likely death — but his hand was in excruciating pain, causing him to not be able to focus.

He wasn't mad at *Josh,* he was just *mad.* He wanted to shove a knife into al-Sadir's eye, and he definitely wanted to get out of this place.

He knew the best choice was to follow Josh's instructions and try to help the poor souls trapped inside these rooms... but it was also the last thing Liam wanted to do. He just wanted to run — to get out of here. To get back to the helicopter and hide in its backseat, praying for somebody to stroll by who happened to know how to fly the damned thing.

That he was essentially marooned in a strange country halfway around the world, with a vehicle he couldn't even drive as the only way out, caused him to want to give up.

He stopped, leaning his good hand against the wall, and took a few breaths.

Get a hold of yourself, man. While it was true that Liam had not joined the NSA because he was a people person, he certainly wasn't a *bad* person. He didn't want these innocent people to die, and he certainly wanted the terrorists behind this place to go down. But he was the last person on earth who should be wandering these halls, putting up a fight.

He was supposed to be the guy running the show from afar, just like Curtis and Jocelyn were now. He should never have listened to Witherspoon. He should be back in Fort Meade, safely seated at a table with computer monitors all around.

That was why he had joined up; *that* was why he had chosen to use his brilliance for good.

He shook his head. But to be here, in the midst of all this, the fact that *Escape from Eden* was actually real? He almost couldn't believe it.

No, he *actually* could not believe it.

What was he supposed to do now, anyway? These walls had the outlines of doors on them, but they were all locked. He had pressed on one of them, wondering if it was a push-to-release mechanism hidden in the latch, but the door didn't budge. He couldn't get his fingers in the crack enough to try to pull outward, either.

It was no use — the stupid things were locked, so he was just wandering aimlessly in the very prison he had been observing onscreen.

He started walking again, his pace much slower now. He didn't want to run into any of the mercenaries who had captured him the first time. He wondered how long he had been unconscious, if the soldiers were even still out there. If so, al-Sadir would have them patrolling outside the facility, making sure no one could escape. But did that mean there were also guards *inside*? Was he walking around a labyrinth, blindly following the maze of hallways until he inevitably stumbled onto somebody wanting to shoot him?

And where were the Ravenclaw mercenaries? He knew Witherspoon and Symonds had set it up with Ravenclaw and confirmed that there would be a team in place, ready to go.

Either that had been a total lie, or they had been stood up.

Or...

Could it be? Had they walked into a trap? Had al-Sadir somehow predicted their move and hired the very team *they* had been hoping would help them? It made sense if what al-Sadir said was true. If his man had somehow gotten into the NSA's server rooms, while he wouldn't have access to *everything*, he would certainly have access to the unclassified projects and meeting agendas, as well as their last-minute plan to recover Joshua Lane.

And the mercenary crew they would hire to help.

It seemed they had been played. But how deeply did the deception go? How far ahead of them was al-Sadir?

Liam had reached the end of the hallway, only a few steps remaining before the hallway turned sharply left and continued. What was the plan here? If all of the doors in the hall suddenly sprang open, was he supposed to play the role of Moses, here to guide them all out of proverbial Egypt?

He wasn't sure he even knew the way out of this facility — and even if he did, what would be waiting for them outside?

He pressed his back against the wall at the end of the hallway, waiting, watching for any movement or shadows dancing in his vision.

At this point, he had held his breath, not realizing he was even doing it, and his hand brushed against the doorway near his right side. His palm passed over an invisible mechanism inside, and he heard a slight click. A hiss of air sounded as the door fell open an inch, then stopped.

Liam frowned, glancing down at the door. Sure enough, it was open. He waved his hand in front of it again as if not believing he had somehow figured out its trick. In reality, he knew that Josh must have successfully accomplished his mission. He looked up and down the hallway and saw that *all* the doors were now unlocked.

Liam swallowed, pushing away his fears for one more moment, then pulled the door open wider.

Here goes nothing, he thought.

PALEM FACILITY

Tanjung Burung | Indonesia

He closed the distance from the door to the woman. In two strides, he was breathing down her neck. There was confusion in her eyes, but it quickly shifted into fear.

"Where is he?" Josh roared.

Joshua Lane was not a physically intimidating man, but the anger, rage, and exhaustion had all culminated into a wild-eyed expression and burst of adrenaline that seemed to do the trick.

She shrank back, lifting her forearm in front of her for protection. He felt the cold canister of butane in his hand, squeezed it tightly. It was a blunt weapon, but it was the only weapon he had.

And he wouldn't hesitate to use it.

"Where *is he?*" he repeated. He watched her eyes, tried to identify any clues that might lead him to al-Sadir's location within the facility.

"He... he is dead already." The woman's voice was heavily

accented; he guessed German or Austrian. *She thinks I'm talking about Liam.* She must have been in the room with the giant torturing the NSA man before escaping back into this room where she had been putting in the manual requests.

As she spoke, Josh saw the computer behind her — a monitor set diagonally on a tabletop. He saw an open terminal prompt window, saw a red-outlined light-reflection keyboard illuminated on the desktop in front of the monitor window. He queried NARA and confirmed that no more manual requests had been submitted. This woman was, indeed, the person he had been fighting with.

Which meant al-Sadir was not here. Had he already escaped? Was he already on his way out of the facility?

He needed to act; he needed to find a map or layout that would tell him what possible escape routes al-Sadir might use.

Josh shook his head. "I'm not worried about *him*," he snapped. "He's going to be just fine. Where is —"

"But he *will* be dead," she said. "*You* will be dead. Everyone here will be dead. It is only a matter of time."

Josh leaped forward, flipping the butane bottle up and spinning it a half-turn so that he held now held the tip of the torch and igniter attachment. He swung the heavy steel canister around, connecting with the woman's jawbone.

There was a sickening crack, and the woman stumbled backward and fell to the floor.

She shrieked in pain. Josh felt no remorse. "I'm going to ask you *one more time*," he said through clenched teeth. "*Where is al-Sadir?*"

He watched her response. She pulled a hand up slowly, shaking, grasping the edge of the table and clamping onto it to pull herself up. It was slow, painstaking, and he had to wonder if she was trying to buy time. He saw a large purple welt forming on the left side of her face, saw the fear in her eyes.

"You're not just an employee," Josh said, leaning down but holding the torch up over his head in a threatening pose. "You actually *believe* in this. You actually think you're doing the right thing."

She glared up at him, still half-crouched on the floor. She wiped spittle from her lip and nodded once. "We will change the world. We will do something no one has ever done before."

Josh smirked. "Sounds like *another* German who went down in history for thinking along those same lines. He, too, thought he could change the world." He paused, shifted on his feet. "I guess, in a sense, he did."

"He is no *Hitler*," she whispered. "We are not Nazis."

"Where is al-Sadir? I'd love to ask him myself."

She shook her head, anger clouding her face. The welt had already grown, and he wondered if he had broken her jaw. She seemed dizzy, confused. Either he had done some damage, or it was all an act. "You will *never* catch him."

"What was al-Sadir doing here? And who's behind the *Escape from Eden* game? What was the purpose of these trials?

"To find the best."

He smiled again, shaking his head in disbelief. *Of course* that's what she would believe. *Of course* that's what al-Sadir would tell each of his acolytes and disciples. They all truly believed in the mission, in the cause. Of course they wanted to find the best, and of course they had been brainwashed into thinking *this* was the only way.

He knew of al-Sadir's charisma — that had bled through even the computer screen in his chamber. He only imagined how much stronger it would be in person. Is this how he had coerced these people to build all of this? Is this how he had convinced everyone working for him to follow his every order, even when it included burning people alive and torturing them?

He took a step back, his eyes turning to the computer terminal. The woman stood between him and the computer station, and he suddenly realized why she hadn't moved.

She was no longer afraid of being attacked; she was ready to die for her cause.

"What's on the machine?" he asked. He wished he was still connected to the local network here. He could have NARA log in remotely, jump around the hard drive and explore a bit just to see what she was ultimately working on. Surely she wasn't still here *just* to slow him down. She had to be doing something — something al-Sadir had left her here to complete.

He glanced at the computer screen but was too far away to see.

At least with his own eyes.

"NARA, can you zoom in on the screen?"

NARA superimposed an image of the computer screen over his eyes, larger than the screen was in real life. There were sections of text on the screen that NARA was unable to interpret, and these she left at the original focal length, which made them blurry to Josh's eyes.

But his onboard AI processor was able to make some best-guess assumptions about many of the strings of text in each of the windows and dialog boxes on the monitor, and Josh scanned these quickly.

He found one string in particular of interest.

INITIATE   SHUTDOWN   SEQUENCE: PALEM FACILITY.

Beneath that was another term, the results from the command she had entered.

CONFIRMED. INITIATE SHUTDOWN AND FACILITY DESTRUCTION.... 18:37.

The number at the end of the string results was moving. Josh didn't need NARA's enhancement ability to know that it was a countdown timer.

The woman's body language and facial expression told Josh everything he needed to know. "This isn't just going to shut down the computer systems, is it?"

A sly smile stretched across her face. He moved toward her; she cowered but didn't slide out of the way.

She was protecting this terminal. Protecting what she had done.

"al-Sadir's burning this place to the ground, isn't he? With all of us still inside."

She didn't shrug. Didn't confirm or deny his accusation.

"Cancel it. *Now.*"

She stood up, facing him, still shaking, the welt on her face now covering the entire left side. It stretched from the bottom of her jaw to her temple and almost as far forward as her left eye.

Her grin grew, though he could see the pain it caused her. This woman was committed. She was going to do whatever it took to execute her leader's orders.

"Last chance," Josh said. "I'm not going to warn you again."

She spat. "It *cannot* be stopped. You will *never* stop him."

Josh held the butane canister in a firm grip, this time aiming the bottom of it toward the woman's head. He swung hard, aiming for the woman's left temple. The corner edge of the cylindrical tube struck hard, immediately sending her to the floor.

She was out cold, either dead or seriously messed up.

Josh didn't care to find out.

He needed to find al-Sadir.

PALEM FACILITY

Tanjung Burung | Indonesia

Josh needed to reconnect to the server. It was his only option now. Having NARA implanted in his brain was helpful, but she was but a mere extension of his own brain. He didn't know his way around this facility, and during his digital battle with al-Sadir's technician, he had not had time to pull up a map and save it locally to NARA's extended storage.

He wanted to find al-Sadir, of course, but he doubted the man was going to stick around for long. It was likely he was leaving or already gone, since he had slowed Josh down. If Josh could find a map of this place, he might be able to figure out where al-Sadir was headed, perhaps even find his planned escape route.

Josh's mind kicked into gear. He knew a portion of the layout, knew that some of the rooms along this hallway were torture chambers, the same prison cells where he and the contestants had been kept. And he knew that the newcomer, Liam, had emerged from a room nearby. But that room and the ones he had passed and found the woman inside were not the same sorts of ceramic-walled chambers where he had been kept.

He hadn't seen stairs anywhere, so his assumption was that the facility was all on one level, and if he worked his way around the perimeter, checking each of these rooms, he would eventually find some sort of server room.

He wanted to find Eve, wanted to reconnect into the intranet, and dig around a bit.

He checked the room next to the one he had confronted the woman in, as well as one across the hall, finding only empty offices. Apparently, al-Sadir ran a skeleton crew, as he had so far only seen the hulking giant of a man and the slight, thin woman who had been controlling Eve on the network.

At the end of this corridor, he came to a set of double doors that opened into the hallway, and he pulled the handle of the first one. It swung open easily. He entered and knew immediately he was in the right place. Surrounding him on all sides were computer racks, thousands of blinking lights, the gentle hum of disk drives spinning, and the whine of fans working to keep everything cool. He even felt a slight temperature change as he entered, a rise of a few degrees as he stepped into the warm, dry room.

His eyes were already dancing over each of the racks, trying to identify what each unit or machine was in charge of.

He saw a rack to his left packed with GPU processors — they would be earmarked for running the graphics and video production for the television show. Next to that, standard-grade CPUs, which could be purchased off the shelf. Likely these hosted the cloud and online components for the company, but it was certainly possible Eve's files would find a home there, as well.

It was possible, of course, that her files were *completely* remote and off-site. If that were the case, Josh wouldn't be able to do much without access to the network. He figured this was unlikely, however, due to the sheer speed of response Eve had been maintaining. Even the fastest mesh networks would have a baked-in delay due to distance.

And he didn't *need* to access Eve again, just the local servers. He wanted to reinstate the interface between NARA and Eve if possible, only because of the power he felt controlling both computers. But it wasn't his top priority.

He wanted to find al-Sadir.

Moving along, he noted a bank of cables configured by color, running to and from different patch bays along the faces of the racks. These, he knew, were related to the mesh network and localized intranet, handling all of the digital communication throughout the building, as well as its access to the outside world.

If Josh had been carrying a laptop, he simply could have unplugged one of these cables and inserted it into his computer to gain access to the servers.

But his computer was attached to his brain. There was no port on the back of his head. NARA was hardwired into his own brain using fiber filaments, and unless there was some sort of wireless or near-field technology broadcasting close by, she was basically just another voice in his head.

He racked his brain. *Think, damn it.*

He was running out of time. If al-Sadir was still here, he needed to find him. If he had already left, Josh needed to see where he was going. This Liam guy was with the NSA, which would be helpful in tracking the man down, but Josh didn't want to lose the opportunity to find him *today.*

He snapped his fingers, suddenly realizing he could set up an 'ad-hoc' network, a local wireless band that would broadcast only as far as the strength of the emitting signal allowed. Something that would only be useful to connect the CPUs in this room — not something he would be able to access from outside this room. It would have to be close range, literally line-of-sight. NARA's onboard receiver was microscopic too, as it often relied on a stronger emitted signal than most built-in integrated network cards could provide.

But it was the best idea he had — it was the *only* idea he had.

Josh fumbled around the room, coming closer to examine some of the computers in the rack near the entrance. He shook his head, not seeing the type of machine he was looking for at first. Taking a step back and looking over the entire room, he finally noticed it.

On a table near the far side of the room sat a large, angled touchscreen monitor, sloping downward into the desk. A simple rectangular folding mouse sat next to it.

The days of desktop PCs were all but over — many companies and organizations had opted for setups much like this one, where a rack — or a room full of racks — housed the actual computers and processors, with individual terminals around the facility that could access it. It was a simpler, more elegant way of handling the networking for large enterprises, but Josh knew people who used similar setups at home as well. They packed a closet with a half-sized rack and installed monitor control terminals throughout the house or used 'floating' tablets and devices that connected wirelessly.

Josh walked over and grabbed the black rectangle on the table-top. He curved the mouse into his palm, feeling it coil beneath his hand like a metal snake. The terminal's screen woke and presented him with a logo. He used his left hand to touch the screen itself, watching it change from the logo to the operating system's home screen.

He saw a desktop, icons, a taskbar, some menus.

Thankfully, graphical user interfaces had not changed much during the second computing revolution. Most of the upgrades that had transpired had been in the hardware or biological spaces — new ways of interfacing with machines, better haptic feedback systems, machines and devices that were constantly connected to the cloud.

And the future held neurological enhancements like the one Josh had in his brain.

Josh navigated to an icon that looked like a cogwheel — the settings pane for this particular machine. He navigated to the network preferences and saw what he was looking for in an instant. Using his left hand to poke at the screen and his right hand on the mouse, he navigated through the submenus until he had set the parameters for his ad hoc network.

He needed it to be a 'pass through' network — to send its wired connection outward into the immediate space around the machine. Hopefully, there was a strong enough wireless chip in the terminal that NARA could pick up on it.

He waited, watching the small wheel spin as the computer followed his instructions.

NARA recognized the new network first. *"New network has been found. Would you like me to connect?"*

Josh confirmed. Immediately he felt a surge of data, similar to how he had felt when he had first accessed Eve remotely. He waited for NARA to make sense of where she was in the new network, to understand its configuration and limitations.

It took all of .008 seconds.

"I'm connected via near-field, though it's weak. I don't detect any larger mesh capabilities."

"And you won't," he muttered to himself. "I'm not going anywhere, though. We just need to find a layout of this place."

"It appears this terminal is set up for general-purpose communications maintenance and security."

Perfect, he thought. Knowing NARA would be able to work far faster than he could with a mouse and touchscreen, he gave her some instructions and parameters to use to search through this machine's local drive. He doubted the permissions settings would allow him to browse the entirety of the servers in this room, but if he was lucky, he just needed to look through the files stored locally on the machine this terminal was connected to.

In just over a second, NARA returned a few promising results. The screen changed and showed a folder hierarchy with the search results selected.

Josh skipped the first one, as its file name was just a string of numbers separated by an underscore. Perhaps it would be helpful, but he was going for speed, and the second file on the list seemed promising.

It was called *cc_int_ext_locations,* with an image extension after.

PALEM FACILITY

Tanjung Burung | Indonesia

Josh studied the map for a split second. While NARA saved the file, he pulled it up on the screen briefly, just long enough to ensure it was what he thought it was. He recognized hallways and corridors, internal rooms, prison cells. Each of those was labeled with a number; there was nothing descriptive about what their purpose was.

But he knew he was looking at a map of the building he was in now. As the title of the file signified, he could see small triangles that had been superimposed on the map, each marking the location of a security camera in and around the premises. The bases of the triangles pointed in the direction each camera faced.

al-Sadir — or whoever was running his security — would have seen anyone coming from a mile away. No wonder Liam had come in alone; he must have run the gauntlet to get inside. And he had implied that he had *not* originally come alone. Had his men been gunned down by a security force out there?

Josh still wanted to debrief with the man, to figure out why he was here in the first place and what had transpired outside.

But he had what he wanted. He no longer needed the map displayed on the screen — he had a copy of the file stored in his head. Possibly his favorite feature of NARA's technology was the ability to interface with his brain's own memory storage system. While he couldn't recall the onboard library of files stored in his head without NARA's ability to decrypt and tran-scribe them, with her help, he *literally* had a photographic memory.

He told her to display the map in front of his vision, and she immediately complied. Now armed with the knowledge of a route through the facility, he began closing out of the settings tabs on the terminal.

Then he frowned.

The dialog window displaying the handful of search results NARA had found on the drive came to the foreground once more. He was hovering over the button to close the window but hesitated.

He cocked his head to the side. He looked at the first file on the list — the one he had skipped over previously.

Why is that familiar?

The recognition suddenly hit him as he read the file aloud, slowly.

One, two, four, five, three. The filename started with numbers: 12453.

The file itself was a text file, but the title of it included the same numbers — in the same *order* — that Dr. Roger Eberly, Contestant #2, had been mouthing as he had been burned alive.

Josh tried not to recall the memory of that scene, but it was already there. He saw Eberly's lips moving well after the throes of death had started, the same five numbers repeated over and over.

One, two, four, five, three.

Dr. Eberly had been trying to tell him something — trying to get a message to whoever might be watching — and Josh had stumbled upon it.

Why had the computer returned this file with the others in NARA's search? The search query she had run was a custom GREP command meant to narrow down any possible results to fit a few parameters and keywords: *map, blueprint, facility, security,* things like that.

And she had searched for *image* and *video* files — the logical file types for carrying image-based data inside. A text file should not have been returned, and he verified in the search query above the window that she had, in fact, excluded these sorts of files.

Perhaps...

He was running out of time, but now he was intrigued. He double-clicked this text file, and it opened immediately. He saw right away that it was gibberish. This is what he had expected — NARA would *not* have returned a simple text file, even though it was labeled as such. The search query she had used wanted images, documents, other file types that could hold images within them.

He paused, thinking. Quickly, he changed the extension of the file to a common image format. A dialogue window popped up, asking him if he was sure he wanted to do it.

Yes, damn it.

Archaic technology baked into operating systems like this often got in his way — thanks to NARA, he often worked faster than the machine wanted to go. Trying once more, he double-clicked the new image file, and it opened.

At least, to a point. Another dialog box appeared on the screen, signifying that the file was corrupt or damaged.

He tried again, choosing another popular image extension.

This time, he double-clicked it, and a simple image viewer program opened.

Progress, he thought, smiling.

And then, the file appeared onscreen.

It was *not* gibberish, nor was it corrupt or damaged.

It was, in fact, an image. Specifically, it was a scan of a piece of white paper filled with a handwritten list of names.

There were two columns, names on both sides streaming down the page. The handwriting was scratched, scrawled as if done in a hurry. A few names toward the bottom of the second column were impossible to decipher, the handwriting slipping away into mere squiggles and flat lines. Whoever had written down these names had been in a major hurry.

It appeared the names were split into two columns for a reason: on the left-hand column, Josh recognized his own name, as well as the man who had been mouthing the very numbers that had led him to this file: Dr. Roger Eberly. Perhaps Eberly was the man who had scrawled this last-minute document and scanned it in. He was a renowned expert in computer security systems, so uploading something like this remotely, hiding it in a filesystem for someone to find in the future, would have been child's play for him.

Josh supposed he had even ensured a search query on this terminal would return this particular file, as well.

Perhaps that was the point of all of this — perhaps he had *wanted* someone like Josh to stumble upon it, to find his last words.

The implications of it were *massive*. Whoever had placed this file here had somehow discovered the list of contestants — each and every one of them. Josh saw Dr. Eberly's name, as well as a few other renowned computer scientists and physicists.

Eberly must have been involved in the creation of *Escape from Eden*. Perhaps he had been working on the project without realizing what it was, what the stakes were. That seemed likely to Josh. This al-Sadir guy was cunning — he would have hired contractors like Eberly to finish the project, using them for their smarts, keeping each party in the dark about the true nature of the sadistic game.

Josh immediately had NARA store a copy of this file as well, saving it in its decrypted image format. He kept the file name intact in case he needed to recall that string as well. Once again, he was about to finish closing the dialogue windows and programs onscreen when his eyes fell to the bottom of the list.

Josh shrank back in horror. He had been scanning the list from left to right; first name in the left column followed by the name in the right. While he knew the left column was the list of contestants, the right column was a list of names whose purpose he did not understand.

He did recognize some of the names on the right-hand list, however. The late Robert Blake, owner of *Aetheria*, the same man who had been assassinated in the seat next to him some unknowable number of days ago.

And he recognized the name of his boss, the owner of Bearbridge, Ruth Dalia. It was concerning that she would be on a list like this, but even that was not what had caught his attention.

No, he was staring at the last name in the left column, the *contestants'* column.

He knew the name of the last person on the list — and the person who owned it — intimately, because he was married to her.

The last contestant in the *Escape from Eden* game was his wife.

PALEM FACILITY

Tanjung Burung | Indonesia

Liam peered inside the first door that had opened as he passed it. There was a bed sitting against the back wall, centered across from the doorway. Nothing else on the floor or on the walls. A man in his mid-50s sat in the center of the bed, streaks of dried tears running down his cheeks, red rimming his eyes. He stared back at Liam, terrified.

"It's... okay now.," Liam muttered. He wasn't sure he believed his own words; what else was he supposed to do? "You're safe now — the game's over."

The man didn't move.

Liam felt a sudden sense of urgency. "Look, I don't care if you trust me or not, but this door might shut again at any moment. You can follow me as I help get the others out, or you can wait here and see what happens. Your call."

He waited for another second as the man started to stir, but then Liam started moving again. He reached the second doorway and nearly bumped into an older gentleman wearing tiny circular glasses far out on the tip of his nose. He was short, squat. The rotund gentleman was wearing the same outfit he had seen onscreen, marking him as a contestant.

Liam repeated the short monologue and the older gentleman nodded. He was obviously better able to mentally handle what was happening than the first man Liam had discovered.

"Who are you?" the man asked, his voice heavily accented English. Liam guessed the man was Russian, but he didn't recognize him.

"Name's Liam, but we need to keep moving. I'm supposed to get all the people out of here and corralled so we can..." he let his voice trail off. *So we can... what?*

The Russian man repeated the question. "Then *what*? You do have a plan to get us out of this evil place, yes?"

Liam cocked his head to the side as he motioned for the man to follow him to the next room. As they continued, he noticed the man from the first room had finally poked his head out of the doorway, his eyes still wide and scared.

"More like a plan to *make* a plan," Liam said. "But I figure the farthest away from these rooms we can get you, the better."

"You will get no argument from me," the Russian said.

Satisfied that he was at least doing what Lane had requested, Liam continued working down the hallway.

The fourth door on the left side of the hallway sat open, but the room was empty. Not even a bed sat against the center wall. A thin layer of soot covered the floor, and it didn't take long for Liam to realize what he was looking at. He convulsed, nearly vomiting, but continued onward.

He decided he didn't need to poke his head all the way into

the doorways — the contestants were starting to come out on their own, a few on the opposite side of the hallway and some in front of him on this side. He guessed there had to be about a dozen remaining contestants. All of them congealed into a blob of frantic humanity at the end of the hallway, waiting for Liam to approach. Questions began flying, and Liam caught at least three different languages.

He held his hands up, trying to calm everyone. "My name is Liam Hernandez. I work for the National Security Agency, and I'm here to help. For now, we just need to get away from this place. We could all still be in danger. We don't have time to go through everything, but rest assured, you'll get answers."

You'll get them when we get them, he mused.

"First, we need to find an exit. Does anyone know their way around this place?"

Heads shook.

He knew there were still mercenaries nearby, the same group that had killed his team. Perhaps still waiting outside, or trying to get inside to finish the job. It was possible they had fled, taking al-Sadir with them, but Liam had to operate as though the threat was still present.

A sadistic thought nagged at the back of his mind. What if this, too, was all part of al-Sadir's game? What if this next phase was one of the challenges he had planned for *Escape from Eden?* The mercenaries had gotten the jump on Liam's team — obviously paid by al-Sadir but told to pretend otherwise. Liam's team had walked into a trap set by al-Sadir. He wondered if all of this was a setup — that somewhere in the belly of this terrible place, they were being watched by al-Sadir with sadistic glee. Liam and the remaining contestants would get their hopes up, only to be cut to ribbons by the mercenaries.

Don't think like that, he told himself. *Just get to the next checkpoint.*

Josh had told him to help the others — he had done that. He had freed them, at least — helped them get into the hallway where they were that much closer to being free. But now what? Josh hadn't told him what to do after — the man seemed to know what he was doing, so why hadn't he told Liam what to do?

Liam wanted to keep moving — to wait for Josh could be the death of them all. His best option was to head back the way they had come, since he knew there was an exit on that side of the building. But again, he worried that the mercenaries might just be waiting for them outside. Was it better to hide inside?

He was thinking through all of these options, trying to put them in order in his mind and let his problem-solving skills do the dirty work of providing him with their best chance of success. He chewed his lip, staring at the floor as more questions from the contestants flew in his direction.

He looked up, prepared to admit that he didn't know what was happening, that he didn't know what to do, when another contestant's face caught his eye.

He squinted, trying to examine the woman in the dim light. He thought he recognized her but couldn't place exactly how he knew her.

Or why he *would* know her. He knew most of these men and women were renowned computer scientists, and even though he worked for the NSA, he didn't recognize many of their faces.

But her...

And then it hit him.

No... it can't be...

The woman stared back at him, their eyes locking. He knew who she was. She knew he recognized her, as well.

She stepped forward, pushing aside the round Russian scientist and moving toward the center of the hallway, toward Liam. There was a question on her face, and she didn't need to voice it.

He asked first. "You... you're Molly. Molly Lane."

She was crying now, the tears that had welled up no longer small enough to contain. She let them fall as she moved closer still to Liam.

She nodded, finally finding the words. "Is Josh here?"

CHAPTER 53
JOSH

PALEM FACILITY

Tanjung Burung | Indonesia

Molly is here.

The recognition nearly knocked Josh off his feet. He stood, shellshocked, standing at the desk and staring at the screen.

He moved his jaw side to side, his mouth open then closed again, completely numb as he stood at the computer station. NARA was busy delivering observations and instructions into his mind, but he was ignoring each of them. He couldn't focus, couldn't think straight.

Molly is here.

It didn't make sense to him at first, but on another level — a *terrifying* level — it also made *perfect* sense. While Josh got a lot of the credit for being the US military's prized possession when it came to cryptography and computer systems, Molly was nearly his equal in these fields, though she had taken a different career path. Opting instead to go into academia, she had accepted her fate as a researcher and educator who would likely never achieve the distinguished veneration as her husband.

But recognition had never been Molly's goal — she wasn't in it for glory or fame. She wanted to change the world not by creating new technology but by creating new *technologists*. She used her brilliance to teach others, to research the cutting edge and then distill it down to a level anyone could understand, and then equip the next generation of technicians, engineers, and scientists.

Yet she was very highly regarded in academic computer science circles. Her list of publications dwarfed Josh's, and many institutions fell all over themselves to try to get her onto their lecture circuit each year.

She had given up a high-paying job and great benefits in exchange for her dream job — doing the work she knew and loved. Josh had taken up the slack financially, opting to take the high-paying position at Bearbridge. Both were impressive technologists that any company in the industry would bend over backward to acquire.

And al-Sadir had planned to pit them against each other.

Josh couldn't believe her name was on the list, and yet it made a cruel sort of sense. She was his equal in many areas within the field of computer science and technology, but she excelled in areas Josh considered himself somewhat lacking in. Mathematics and chemistry — at least as they related to computing and technology — were some of her areas of expertise that Josh couldn't compete with her in.

It told Josh that whoever was truly behind these games — whether it was al-Sadir or someone else — was trying to find the best in the world at something related to those fields. They wanted the best of the best and would go to any lengths to find that person.

But for what? What project could be so important to someone that they would not only set up a horrific contest, pitting the world's best computer science minds against one another, but completely eliminating — *murdering* — those who did not make it through?

The second realization struck him almost as hard as it had as the first, and only a moment later. He suddenly knew *exactly* why they had structured the competition this way.

It wasn't just about finding the best. It wasn't just about weeding out the lesser minds in order to come up with the perfect candidate for whatever sick and twisted program they were cooking up. It was about eliminating the competition.

If this contest had succeeded, they would be left with only one winner. Only one man or woman capable of taking their project to the next level. They would have the mind they needed; they would completely own the person. If they were capable of *this*, they would be capable of coercing that person into helping them, into doing their job for them. Into building whatever it was they wanted built.

Perhaps they had brought Molly here to act as leverage against Josh, and vice versa. Perhaps if either husband or wife won, they would keep the other alive in order to maintain power over them.

He didn't understand it yet, but he knew they were *deadly* serious about finding someone to help them accomplish their goals.

And if they had succeeded, there would be no one left on earth capable of stopping them.

PALEM FACILITY

Tanjung Burung | Indonesia

Liam saw movement behind Molly's head. The group of contestants was splitting down the middle, pressing their backs against the walls on both sides of the hallway. He sensed someone was entering the hall from around the corner, but the lights were still too dim to see clearly.

Until they stepped into view.

He heard gasps, a few shouts. He pressed Molly back against the wall to his right, next to one of the doors a contestant had come out of.

The newcomers were a smaller group of the same Ravenclaw mercenaries Liam had run into outside — the Ravenclaw team that was supposed to be here helping *him*. Three men, each wielding an assault rifle and pointing them at the group.

He froze. If this was it, there was no way to fight back. They had no weapons, and none of them were trained in combat anyway. These were scientists, civilians. Innocent men and women.

And he had failed Joshua Lane.

He heard Molly's sobs as she, too, noticed the mercs. One of them began barking orders. "Everyone stay where you are. Do not move. If you move, you die."

The man who had spoken dropped his assault rifle and put a hand to his ear, listening in to instructions from someone delivering them remotely. *al-Sadir?* The mercenary nodded once, then started scanning the crowd. Liam moved forward and to the right, careful to do it slowly enough none of the mercenaries would notice. He pressed his shoulder against the wall, trying his best to use his frame to cover Molly's body.

Maybe they won't notice she's here, he thought.

The mercenary continued glancing around, stepping a few feet toward the group. He was looking for someone, and Liam had a feeling he knew who it was. He wanted to whisper back to her, to urge her caution, to not move or breathe or do anything that might attract attention to herself.

He knew she was scared out of her mind; he didn't need to tell her anything, didn't need to urge her to be quiet and stay hidden.

The mercenary squinted through the dim light, his eyes landing on each of the contestants one at a time. Liam saw their backs, their shoulders shaking, shivering in terror. These people had gone from being trapped inside their own personal oven to being trapped in a hallway filled with gunmen.

Finally, the mercenary's eyes landed on the same man Liam had rescued previously, the roundish bespectacled Russian scientist. "You," the mercenary grumbled. He pointed a meaty finger toward the scientist. The man gulped, tears also streaking down his cheeks. "Jakob Antonov?"

The scientist nodded.

"Come with us."

The man took a half-step forward, his eyes darting to Liam. Liam wanted to shrink away, to become part of the wall. He hoped the mercenary hadn't noticed.

Too late. The mercenary glanced over at Liam, then smiled. "I didn't notice *you* there. You're the man we captured earlier, aren't you?"

Liam didn't answer.

"Looks like you've already been interrogated a bit." Liam saw the mercenary's eyes drop to his hand, noticing the bandage that was covering his missing fingers. A sudden burst of rage filled Liam's mind, consuming him. "What the hell do you guys want?"

The mercenary flicked his eyebrows toward the scientist he had called out. "Him, obviously."

"For what?"

"This project has been moved into the next phase," the mercenary explained. "Thanks to your team and your man on the inside, my boss was not able to finish the last phase. No matter — we'll still get him what he wants."

One of the mercenary's partners rushed forward then and snatched Antonov's elbow, pulling him back toward the end of the hallway. A few murmurs of surprise and fright reverberated through the space, but most of the contestants were too terrified to speak, to call attention to themselves.

"So... you're going to just kill us all?" Liam asked. "What good will that do?"

The mercenary frowned as if questioning why he was even

having this conversation in the first place. He lifted his assault rifle and pointed the barrel toward Liam's chest. Liam felt his heart drop, pounding through his body. He swallowed, backed into Molly. Still, he kept his shoulders squared to the wall, kept his body in front of her.

"For *you*, I suppose it *would* be a waste," the mercenary said. "You're not a contestant; you're not one of the people here who could actually help."

The mercenary pulling the scientist away suddenly stopped, his head falling to the side. Looking directly at Liam...

No — looking at the woman behind him.

"Boss," the mercenary began, "there she is." He flicked his head to the side; not willing to let go of Antonov's elbow or his assault rifle.

The mercenary holding his rifle at Liam's chest smirked. "I understand now. Acting the brave soldier."

Liam stared down. The man was half a head taller than him, and built like a tank. Not that their physical matchup would matter at all — one round fired from his gun would be enough to take Liam out of the fight for good.

He forced his mind into gear, trying to come up with some better idea than to just stand in the way of an angry mercenary.

"Move." The mercenary stared at Liam, unmoving, but he shook the tip of his weapon. Liam understood the motion perfectly well. *Slide away from the wall.*

Liam shook his head, gritting his teeth. *I guess this is my last stand.* He wondered where Josh Lane was — if the man had found something he could use to take down these mercenaries. Their backs were to the corridor behind him; perhaps if —

"Grab her, and let's get out of here."

The mercenary who had taken the scientist nodded, marching over to Liam's position and plucking Molly from the wall as well. She tried to fight back, pounding the man's chest with closed fists, but she eventually realized it was futile as she saw both of the other mercenaries pointing their rifles directly at her.

None of the other contestants moved. Many of them were looking down, their heads focusing on the floor.

Liam watched as the man holding Molly and Antonov rejoined his partners and continued walking back down the hallway and veering to the left, out of sight.

"What of them?" the second mercenary asked his leader.

"al-Sadir's going to bring this place down on their heads," the man said. "Ten minutes from now this place will be rubble."

The man next to him nodded, but the leader wasn't done, apparently.

"*But* I don't want there to be any chance these guys get away. Put a few rounds into each of them and be done with it."

Liam's eyes widened as the man immediately stepped two feet to the side, putting more distance between him and the contestants, then opened fire.

The contestants all starting screaming at once, but they were already falling. It was a mad dash for cover, but the only cover to be found were other writhing bodies. Humans flopped into one another as the massacre took place. Each of them fell, some leaning on others and bringing them down as well.

The mercenaries turned, then left the hallway.

PALEM FACILITY

Tanjung Burung | Indonesia

"NARA, how much time do we have left?"

NARA responded immediately. "*11 minutes, 14 seconds.*"

"Give me an alert at ten minutes, five minutes, then another alert at two minutes and one minute."

"*Affirmative.*"

Josh needed to get to Molly. He had all but forgotten al-Sadir — his new priority was to find his wife. To get her far away from this place before the end of the countdown.

But if there was any chance he could re-establish a connection with Eve, he needed to try. He was exactly where he needed to be to pull it off; it was just a matter of whether or not NARA could find a way in once again. He didn't have time to manually exploit the server in root mode, so he hoped that al-Sadir's helper, when she had severed his connection earlier, had not thought to reestablish new secure access keys and permissions for the system users.

He might still be able to access Eve's network, but only if there *was* a wireless network still up and running.

He worked quickly, typing with his left hand while navigating through dialogue windows with his right on the mouse, all while querying NARA for specific questions. Her library of knowledge gave Josh the ability to look up strings and commands in just about any language in an instant, and he had come to rely on this feature quite a bit.

He had never thought he would have to rely on this feature as a matter of life or death, however.

"It appears you are trying to gain access once more to the wireless network of the facility," NARA began. Josh was busy digging through the hierarchy of folders stored on this terminal's drives, and the words barely registered. *"I still have connection to the ad hoc network, however, and —"*

Of course. His mind was running a million miles an hour, but it was running in a thousand different directions. On the one hand, he was still shaken up by his encounter with the woman in the other room. He was still interested to know what al-Sadir's ultimate goal was.

And, of course, most of his conscious mind was focused on coming up with a plan to find Molly.

He hadn't even considered that NARA could essentially do all of this work on her own since she still had a way to create a direct connection with this machine.

He issued the command, cutting her off. "Try using the same root user access we had before, ping Eve's server and see if she is able to find *us* through the ad-hoc network."

It took half a second before Eve's voice entered Josh's mind, piggybacking on NARA's technology. *"Hello, contestant number nine."*

He didn't bother responding — he had bigger problems to worry about than being polite to a computer program. "Eve, can you reestablish my connection to the wireless network here?" he asked out loud.

"Negative. Your temporary user name and address have been permanently blocked."

Josh shook his head. *"NARA, reinstate our connection by creating another user account on this machine. It will reset your network Access, but give it the same permissions as before."*

NARA confirmed, and Josh waited the excruciating 4.5 seconds to hear the results. He hoped that by creating a cloned user account, NARA would be able to trick the network access points into thinking he was a brand-new user that simply had the correct password and access parameters as before. It would be no different than logging into a mesh network on a laptop the network didn't recognize — as long as it accepted the credentials, he would be good to go.

There was a brief clip of static — the sound of NARA's network card overloading her circuitry for a moment before resetting — then Josh heard Eve's voice once more.

"Welcome, contestant number nine. How may I help you today?"

Josh let out a sigh of relief. He was already moving, heading toward the door. He needed to find Molly, to find Liam. He needed to get out of here. He turned left and ran down the hallway, hoping this building was, in fact, rectangular shaped all the way around, the hallways connected. He didn't want to have to trudge all the way back up the hallway he had come from and turn left. If he was right, this was a shortcut to Liam.

He fired off requests to both NARA and Eve at the speed of thought. NARA displayed the map of the facility, once again overlaid on his vision, while he urged Eve to give him access to the security camera feeds once more.

She complied, and he saw each feed in front of his eyes as he approached each camera's location.

It was a trippy feeling, running toward a camera while watching the feed in full stereoscopic vision at the same time, but he blinked and forced his eyes to focus on the hallway. He wanted the map and the closed-circuit feeds to be there for a reference point, so he dimmed their views until they were all but invisible, viewable only when he focused on them.

"Eve, can you find any interior cameras that show movement?" Josh asked. *"Narrow the movement down to recognized human motion."*

He was sure there was a command for this in Eve's programming, but he didn't know what it was. Still, she was a capable AI — she would be able to interpret his request.

There was a delay, 1.3 seconds. Another camera view appeared over his vision. *"I have found three views, each depicting different angles of what I believe to be the same scene. Location is —*
"

Josh stopped listening as he watched the scene unfold. Eve cycled between all three cameras, and he saw that it was, in fact, three angles that showed the same thing. A group of people in the hallway. He thought he recognized Liam Hernandez among them. He was standing with his arms up, palms out.

Josh's blood ran cold. Every one of the people around him was standing in a similar fashion — all looking the same direction, all terrified.

He squinted just as the camera cycled once more, this time showing the same thing but from the opposite direction. He saw Liam's face, now near the back of the crowd, in grainy, pixilated black and white. There was not enough light in the hallway, and these were not expensive cameras. But it was enough to understand what was happening.

In the foreground of this angle, Josh saw three men, each wielding an assault rifle. Each dressed exactly the same — black fatigues, long-sleeve black shirts, belts with a sidearm and magazine holster attached.

Soldiers-for-hire.

And there was a fourth person with them. A small, roundish man, his elbow held fast by one of the mercenary's viselike grips. The mercenaries were sliding slowly to the left side of the hallway, toward a doorway, perhaps. He couldn't see what they were aiming for.

The camera view cycled again, and he saw a wide, expansive shot from the middle of the hallway, this time with Liam just to the left, the mercenaries and the roundish, glasses-wearing contestant even farther to the left side of the screen. The fisheye lens distorted everything, giving it a warped appearance.

Josh focused on the mercenaries.

That's when he saw it. He had missed it at first, because of the way the mercenaries were standing. The largest of them had been standing directly in front of another person, a fifth person in their group.

Much smaller, almost petite. He recognized her frame even before he could see her face clearly, but then as the mercenaries stepped into frame, it came into focus. He knew in an instant where he was headed.

His legs picked up speed, and he looked through the different superimposed images in front of his eyes and saw that he was nearing a diagonal section of hallway. He hadn't expected a diagonal slant in the building's layout.

At least he was still heading in the right direction, but the hallway seemed impossibly long. If he was right about where the mercenaries and the other group of people were, he was twenty seconds away from turning right once more and stumbling directly into their backs.

His feet pounded, no longer worrying about stealth or surprise. He needed to get there.

He needed to get to Molly.

PALEM FACILITY

Tanjung Burung | Indonesia

Josh ran like his life depended on it. In a way, it did. The men had taken his life from him — they had exited the hallway, disappearing out of sight with Molly. The three mercenaries were out of sight for an excruciating ten seconds before a new feed was superimposed on his vision — this one from outside the facility. He watched as the last mercenary in the group closed the double doors behind him, locking them by waving a key over a keypad. The other two veered left and headed away from the Palem facility over what appeared to be a large, open field.

His wife and the other contestant were in tow. He watched the feed as he rounded the corner to the right. The mercenaries disappeared from view completely then, the cameras only capturing the area around the immediate vicinity. He finished running the length of the shorter diagonal strip of hallway, noticing the double doors the mercs had gone through off to his left, but turned right and faced the new hallway.

And all he saw was a massacre.

Bodies were strewn everywhere — contestants, obviously. There were a few people moving, trying to crawl or slide along a floor that was now slick with blood, each trying in vain to get away from the mess of death. He gingerly stepped over an arm, a leg. Slight groans reached his ears, but there was nothing he could do to help those still living.

He knew it wouldn't be long. All of these people were as good as dead already.

He had enough medical training to seal a few wounds, wrap some gauze around the larger bullet holes, but there were no tools here, no equipment. He had no antiseptic wipes, no way to suture and stitch a wound closed.

He continued walking, looking for Liam Hernandez.

He had considered trying to have NARA and Eve open the locked doors and leave the facility to follow the soldiers, but he sensed they were as good as gone as well. The mercs would have an exit planned.

He wondered what that exit would be: helicopter? He hadn't seen anything on the external feeds, but then again, he hadn't cycled through all of them. Perhaps he could have Eve display those feeds now while he searched for Liam's corpse.

He was feeling helpless, his hope of retrieving his wife diminishing. At the very least, he needed to find Liam, to see if his only ally here might still be alive.

None of the bodies on the floor of the hallway were that of Liam Hernandez. That fact gave him a sense of reassurance, but only briefly. He didn't have time to search the entire facility — if Liam was not here, he hoped he was close by.

He checked his position in the hallway and compared to what

he remembered of the scene from the camera feed. He looked to the left — to the doorway there. It was open, and he pulled the door wider. He heard the low moan of a man in pain.

Liam was there, sprawled out on the floor, both his hands covering a blood slick on his leg.

He looked up at Josh as he entered, his eyes wide with confusion, terror.

"I — I'm sorry. I tried..."

Josh ignored him. He ran forward, kneeling and placing his own hands over the leg.

Liam chuckled. "It's not my blood. My hand hurts like hell, but I'm okay. I was able to sneak in here when they started firing, and I guess they didn't see me. But they... they took her," Liam stammered.

Josh nodded. "I saw."

Liam frowned. "How? How do you know what's going on?"

"No time, man. We need to get out of here, get a message out to the rest of the world." Josh assumed this man had not been working alone; Liam had told him as much earlier. He assumed there would also be a team back home, offering mission support, communications help, something like that.

Liam nodded. "I have a team back at NSA headquarters. We haven't had a way to contact them, though, since our men here were killed. There was communications equipment in the chopper but..."

But the chopper won't be here anymore, Josh thought.

He now understood how the mercenaries planned to leave — they had known all along that Liam's team would arrive via chopper, so they had planned an ambush, killing Liam's team and capturing him, hoping to use the group's own vehicle as their escape vessel.

He helped Liam to his feet, then quickly checked the bandage around his hand. It was still bleeding and would for some time, but there was nothing more he could do here.

"First order of business: we need to get away from here in..." he checked with NARA. "Seven minutes."

"You're going to have to show me that trick sometime," Liam said.

Josh smiled. "I will, I promise. Guy like you will love it, too."

PALEM FACILITY

Tanjung Burung | Indonesia

Josh and Liam raced out to the hallway, each of them holding one of the two surviving contestants they had found. There were no other contestants in the hallway still alive, and though Liam wanted to stop and check each of them for pulses, he knew Josh was correct in his assumption: there was no time.

Liam knew Josh needed to get outside to track down Molly and al-Sadir, though he feared she was already long gone. Where would they take her? al-Sadir was still alive, still at large. Though he had not seen the man with the mercenary crew, he assumed he would be pulling the strings from somewhere remotely. His right-hand man was dead, but al-Sadir would be able to direct his mercenary teams from anywhere in the world.

And the fact that those mercs had taken Josh's wife as leverage meant only one thing: al-Sadir wasn't done yet. Whatever this *Escape from Eden* game was intended to accomplish, al-Sadir was not ready to call it quits.

Josh was urging Liam faster, moving him hurriedly through the hallway toward the same exit in the diagonal section the mercenaries had left through.

Josh whispered something to himself as they walked side-by-side. At first, Liam thought he had been speaking with the man he was holding — a wounded male contestant.

"What did you say?" Liam asked.

"Seven minutes, thirty seconds," Josh said, his voice a bit louder now.

Liam's frown deepened. "Seven minutes, thirty seconds until *what?*"

Josh shook his head quickly, then let out a sigh. "Sorry, there's a countdown timer in my head. I'm just making sure we've got enough time to get clear of the building."

Liam's eyes widened. "Clear of the building? Lane, what do you know?"

At this, Josh stopped completely and turned to face Liam. "All I *know* is that we've got just over seven minutes to get clear of the building."

Liam wished for a better explanation, but it was clear Josh was playing at urgency. Whatever he knew — whatever he thought was going to happen — they didn't have much time to get away.

Josh began moving again, quicker this time. Liam's hand was throbbing, and there were other areas of his body seemingly afflicted, but he pulled the woman he was helping up higher on his shoulder and followed after Josh Lane.

They reached the doors to the facility, and Liam followed Josh through, the door miraculously unlocking and opening just as Josh appeared in front of it. The sun outside was blinding, and it took a moment for his eyes to adjust. He kept his head down, trudging forward with Josh and their contestants. They reached the edge of the field, still smoking with the remains of drones and Liam saw where the soldiers they had brought here had fallen.

This whole thing is a cluster, Liam thought. *What mess have we gotten into?*

He turned to examine Josh, now a half-step behind him. The man's face was haggard, no doubt due to the insane stress he had experienced as a contestant in the *Escape from Eden* game. Still, he felt the man's sense of duty as well, a stubborn resilience Liam saw in the man's squinted, determined eyes and thin mouth.

They traded leads as they worked their way across the field, coming to an abandoned vehicle. They continued toward the road that led back to town before Josh spoke again. "Do you have a way to contact anyone? A way to get a message out?"

Liam thought for a moment. He wasn't carrying his cell phone, and all of their communications equipment was in the helicopter the mercenaries had stolen. He shook his head once.

"Fine. We need to get to town. Find the first corner store we see. We'll leave these two there — nothing we can do for them a local won't be able to do as well."

"Even an unlocked phone is going to require a few hours of setup time," Liam muttered.

While cell connectivity blanketed the globe thanks to the mesh network, individual corporations running regional access points required background checks and credit pulls before new devices were allowed full access. It was a trade-off after the digital security and privacy war, which had led to governments around the world passing legislation to ensure safety and privacy for citizens.

Liam, working for the NSA, knew all too well that most of

these laws and implementation were handwaving. The NSA didn't care what the average citizen did, who they talked to, what videos they downloaded. They weren't listening to every single phone call, scanning every single message sent over the mesh. They had bigger and more important work to do, and the last thing they cared about was what some soccer mom sent to her friends on Friday night.

But over the years, the public outcry and fear about foreign hackers stealing identities and information had become an uproar. The developers of computing and mobile technology, as well as infrastructure providers the world over, had eventually been forced to add useless steps into their protocols to assuage the average citizen's fears. It was security theater, designed to appear legitimate and lend credibility to the entire process. Making people *think* they were safe was the goal, not *actually* making them safe.

Most people knew that background checks and credit pulls could happen in a split-second these days, but there was a feeling that the longer it took for a device to be granted full mesh access, the more secure the system was.

Josh met his eyes. "Just get me an unlocked phone. I can handle the rest."

Liam swallowed, still unsure of what Lane was planning. His determination was evident — this man was going to track down his wife, that much was clear. But how? It had to have something to do with the chip in the man's head, but Liam still knew nothing about it. It was the object of desire al-Sadir had been torturing Liam to find out about, and it had something to do with Josh's ability to interact with locked doors and find his way through a foreign facility.

Liam looked down the road, already seeing two bodega-like shops with signs jutting out over a dirt path that ran parallel to the road. Both would be viable options, carrying any number of small tech devices, wearables, and phones.

He also noticed the stark contrast between the open field they had come across and the Palem facility, compared to the gentle business of the town they were entering. Children played in an alley to the right. Bicycles crossed their path, their baskets full of groceries or wares of some sort. In a second-story window, a woman hung clothes out to dry.

And then he felt it. While watching the idyllic village in front of him, a gentle rumble began behind him. Vibrations flew up his lower body and settled in his stomach. The woman he was pulling along stumbled, her hand barely able to contain the blood gushing over it from the gunshot wound in her side.

The rumble increased in intensity, and he and Josh stopped in the middle of the street. One of the bicyclists stopped as well, looking past them at the Palem building. They watched the white building as its walls began to collapse.

The building's outer walls fell inward just as an explosion rocked black smoke and fire into the air above it. Liam fell backward as the earth shifted, and he dropped the woman on the path. He pulled himself up to a squat as the Palem building completely disintegrated, debris now filling the air and hurtling toward them.

"Glad we left," Josh said.

Liam shook his head in disbelief.

Kohod

Tanjung Burung | Indonesia

Josh ripped open the packaging around the phone's external card. Modern mobile phones didn't need such an archaic storage device, but these old disposable phones had resisted the urge to evolve for almost two decades. The tiny card acted not just as a storage device for additional space on the phone but as a side-loaded operating system allowing any phone it was installed into to be attached to a particular regional network. In this way, an unlocked phone could move around the globe, accessing the mesh network at will, provided the user credentials checked out.

But Josh had no interest in waiting for these user credentials to be sent back to the server, bounced around for an hour or so, then approved. He didn't have that kind of time.

After seeing the facility he had been held captive in disintegrate and explode from within, he and Liam had set the contestants they had been helping by the front door of a small bodega-like shop. Vinyl stickers on the glass windows insisted they would be able to find some sort of mobile technology inside, and Liam spoke with the proprietor of the establishment about getting medical help for the contestants, while Josh frantically looked around the store for a phone.

Thankfully, the phone was charged to half its capacity — more than enough to power on and get its basic peripherals working.

NARA identified the new device immediately and asked Josh if he would like for her to connect to it.

He bypassed the phone's setup features, instead allowing NARA to dig her fingers into the operating system directly and use the kernel to access the built-in radio to act as a "handover" to the mesh network.

Within seconds, Josh had a working cell phone.

In actuality, between him, NARA, and the device in hand, he had a working mesh connection. It wouldn't work exactly like a phone, but it allowed him access to the network — which was all he needed.

Liam returned, confirming that the store owner would call medical professionals. Since there had been an explosion nearby, no one would bat an eye as to why there were two injured people sitting in front of this building. And Josh planned to be long gone by the time whoever arrived realized that the two contestants had been shot, and had NATO rounds embedded in their sides.

Josh was already walking out the front door while operating the phone. Using NARA's terminal, he had the AI run a search for local flights leaving in the next half-hour, then had her find the quickest route to the closest airport. Soekarno-Hatta International Airport sprawled out on the northwest side of Jakarta, but it was too far away on foot. Fortunately, there was a municipal airport only about ten minutes away if they ran. They could cut that time down if they could find a ride.

Josh was halfway up the street, heading toward the denser part of Kohod, when Liam caught up to him. He felt a hand on his arm, and he slowed, suddenly remembering that he was not alone in this journey.

"Lane," Liam said quickly. "Listen, I know you've got a plan and all that, but I'd love to know how —"

"I've got a chip implanted in my brain, at the base of my skull. Interfaces with my entire mind. NARA is what we're calling the operating system. And NARA's got a low-level artificial intelligence running constantly, and can perform pretty much any interfaced task, especially when I have a connection to the outside world." As if trying to underline his haste, he lifted the phone up and shook it a couple of times.

Liam's eyes widened. "That's what al-Sadir wanted..."

"al-Sadir *and* whoever helped him run this sadistic tournament," Josh added. "There's no way he did that all himself."

Liam nodded, and Josh watched the man work through the implications and ramifications. This man worked for the NSA, so Josh knew he wouldn't have to explain how the tech worked — Liam would just trust that it did.

As it turned out, Liam was quick on the uptake. "So you've used the radio in the phone to bounce a connection from the unlocked card to NARA, and now *it's* connected to the mesh network. But you can't use the phone's browser or other features, so you're still limited to whatever she has onboard in your skull. I'm guessing at least like a shell command or something, which NARA then reinterprets into whatever language it's running in?"

Josh raised an eyebrow. *Wow, the guy nailed it.*

"That's pretty damn cool," Liam muttered.

"And I can't wait to tell you all about it and show you what it can do," Josh said. "But we've got a flight to catch."

He started walking, surprised that Liam began jogging. He really didn't need to convince this man of NARA's capabilities, it seemed — he just trusted him; Josh liked that.

"Mind telling me where exactly we have a flight *to*?" Liam asked.

"That's what I need your help with," Josh said. "I need to contact your team back at the NSA. Do you have a secure line? Maybe an email address? We can set up a chat, something NARA can do from a terminal."

CHAPTER 59
JOSH

"Let me know when you're ready; I can give you the secure portal address."

Josh nodded, only half-listening. NARA was busy interfacing with the new phone, which meant *Josh* was busy interfacing with the new phone. He saw its loading screen shift as the mesh-connected phone began its startup procedure for the second time.

Once again, NARA bypassed it and sent Josh's information. The first time he'd booted up the phone, NARA had installed the necessary permissions to accept a new account, and the reload would allow NARA to actually input those credentials. The phone flashed a welcome message, and Josh heard the audio greeting. *"Hello, Joshua Lane!"* a chipper voice rang out from the phone's tiny speakers. *"Would you like to use your existing mesh credentials to add this device to our network?"*

Josh shook his head while NARA worked her magic. The kernel on the device was baked in, and the radio that created its connection out to the mesh network was built into the firmware. Everything else was just an operating system on top that could be subverted. Josh's goal wasn't to *hack* the phone; it was to simply make it think it was the same phone he had left back in Maryland.

Thankfully, smartphones were anything but *smart.*

A few seconds passed, and NARA gave him a new alert. *"Device is ready for use."*

He told NARA to open another shell window, this time with a remote connection available. He pinged the servers of his company as a test and got a positive response back instantaneously.

He looked up at Liam. "Okay, we're in. Where am I going?"

Liam gave him an IP address, as well as a root username and password. "That will get you into my office. My team will be monitoring all channels, but it could take them a minute or two to see the message. I'd bet they're dying to hear from me, though."

Josh nodded. He understood the protocol. This was a rudimentary chat window now, and whoever sat at the other end of this connection would be on a computer constantly monitoring the network. A notification would be displayed on their screen when he messaged, and it might take a few extra seconds for the team member to pull open their own terminal and connect into the chat as well.

Surprisingly, it only took ten seconds. A message appeared in front of Josh's eyes.

> *This is Curtis. Liam, are you there?*

Josh flashed a smile and watched as Liam let out a deep sigh of relief.

"Curtis?" Josh asked.

Liam nodded quickly. "Yeah, he's one-half of the team back at headquarters. The other's name is Jocelyn."

Josh was already formulating his response.

> *This is Joshua Lane. I'm with Liam Hernandez. The rest of the team is down, and outlook is grim.*

He was about to have NARA send the response when he decided to alter the last sentence. *No need to be pessimistic.*

> *We are safe, away from the facility. They have my wife, and we need your help.*

He sent the reply. Only three seconds passed this time.

> *How can we help.*

Josh was relieved and happy not to have to answer a thousand questions. They would know he was stressed; more so now that al-Sadir had Molly.

> *They're in the same chopper Liam arrived on. Do you have a way to track it? Satellite?*

Five seconds passed.

> *Negative. Not without a bit of setup. We can get traffic control information, but it will take time.*

Josh was thinking through alternatives when one appeared on the screen in front of him.

> *Suggest working out from the location. We can calculate fuel range based on estimated capacity.*

Of course. It would be that simple — they were in Indonesia, surrounded by water, and even a large helicopter like that would have limited range. Far less range than a plane, and to his knowledge, the helicopter had not refueled before taking off.

> *Perfect,* Josh replied. > *Let me find our exact location.*

This time the reply was instantaneous, as if Curtis had been formulating the response the entire time Josh was thinking.

> *We have your location. Says you are connecting to the mesh via a phone in your name in Kohod, Indonesia. Close to Jakarta.*

Josh raised an eyebrow and looked at Liam. "Smart team you've got," he said.

Liam laughed. "It *is* the NSA. And they're not interns."

> *Give us five minutes to draw some circles on the map,* Curtis continued. > *We should be able to get some best estimates for at least a refueling spot. From there, we can narrow further.*

Josh agreed, then addressed Liam. "We're going to figure out some best-guess spots for the chopper to land for refueling," he said. "Curtis and Jocelyn will be able to work on that faster than I can. Best we can do is wait for them to get back with us, but if you've got any ideas or suggestions —"

Liam's eyes widened. He snapped his fingers. "What about the yacht?" he asked.

Josh frowned.

"Sorry, you don't know about that. Well, this al-Sadir guy has a yacht. We found it, thanks to a friend of his boasting on social media. The yacht itself is burned, but we might —"

"— Be able to find record of it in nearby ports!" Josh said.

Liam nodded excitedly. Josh liked this guy — the man was injured and in dire need of some medication and painkillers, but he was every bit as enthusiastic as Josh about moving forward.

"Give me the details, and I'll have NARA search for any public records from nearby ports. Hopefully, that stuff won't be encrypted."

"It shouldn't be," Liam said. He gave Josh the name of the vessel and the information his team had found on it and Josh had NARA perform the search.

He noticed the battery on the phone had already diminished by ten percent and wondered how much longer they would have connection to the outside world. Of course, they could always go into a store and buy another, but he wanted to keep moving toward the airport.

"The big guy, the one who did... *that* to you," Josh began, motioning toward Liam's wrapped hand.

"It is unfortunate," Liam said, shifting. "He was al-Sadir's right-hand man, I think. At the very least, he was the guy who snuck into the NSA and planted a listening device."

"Wow," Josh said.

"Yeah, we're not proud of it. It's going to cost me some paperwork. Anyway, if he's still alive —"

"I doubt he is," Josh answered. "But if so, he'll be long gone by now." He shook his head. "And I don't want to meet him again unarmed. Especially after the hit I gave him — he won't be happy waking up to that kind of a bump on his head."

Liam let out a breath. "Let's hope the Palem facility came down on top of him, then."

Kohod

Tanjung Burung | Indonesia

Five minutes passed. Josh and Liam were already into the northern district of Kohod, heading southwest. They had tried finding a taxi, and Josh had even seen the lit logo of popular ridesharing company *Thum* in the windshield of a passing sedan, but he had no way to download the company's app in order to organize a ride.

He was frustrated, feeling hope diminishing, when NARA pinged him again. *"Receiving incoming transmission."*

Josh immediately focused on the small dialog window in the corner of his vision. It came into focus, as if turning up the brightness on a monitor screen, and a bit of the world disappeared around him as he watched the blinking cursor.

A second later, NARA flashed Curtis's response from the NSA.

> *We may have a match. Got a lot of false positives, but we were*

able to zoom in a few high dynamic range satellite imagers onto your location.

Josh squeezed his eyes shut. *Yes.* Curtis and Jocelyn had come through for them — they had somehow figured out how to get access to one of the many satellites orbiting, watching the earth from high above. He shouldn't have been surprised — if anyone could pull it off in so little time, it was the National Security Agency.

> *Point me in the right direction,* Josh responded.

There was a pause.

> *Lane, if the satellite's AI is correct, it's narrowed the search with 87% accuracy to a location about 50 miles northwest of your location.*

Josh stepped onto the sidewalk. Liam paused behind him, no doubt surprised that Josh had stopped moving. To the outside world, he probably looked like a crazed mumbling tourist, talking to himself and lost in his own thoughts. He suddenly realized he needed a way to inform other humans around him that he was 'locked in,' transmitting back and forth with an artificial intelligence in his own mind. A hand signal, perhaps.

The world's not ready for something like this. I'm not ready for something like this.

> *That's perfect,* he responded. > *What's the problem?*

He thought back to the camera feeds and superimposed their locations on the map of the facility as it stood before exploding. The helicopter would have been heading out in a north-northwest direction, so Curtis' findings checked out. But what was 50 miles to the northwest of the Palem facility? What would await them there?

He assumed it would be difficult to get a flight directly to that location, wherever it was. Curtis would be concerned as well, knowing that finding a vehicle to drive them the distance would set them back hours.

"Liam, you can get us a private flight, right?" Josh asked aloud. "Even if it's a single-prop, our best bet will be to fly directly there."

Liam nodded, picking up on the fact that Josh was actively conversing with his team back in Maryland once again. "Not a problem. Any airport around here will be able to get me a direct line to an international ATC dispatch. I know the protocol for getting through to someone back home who can expedite everything."

"Good," Josh said. "If we can just find a *ride* to the airport, we can get moving again. Sounds like your team has narrowed in on a possible match for the chopper."

"That's fantastic!" Liam said, joining Josh as he started walking toward an intersection of two larger roads. "Where, exactly?"

The response flashed on Josh's screen as Liam asked the question.

> *It's a military base, Lane. One that's not exactly friendly to outsiders, especially Americans. The Way Kambas Proving Ground is a top-secret installation we are not supposed to know exists. It's on Indonesian land, but controlled by the Chinese.*

Josh's heart sank. > *That's where the chopper landed?*

> *Yes. We can trust the satellite's onboard AI. I saw some of the false positives it sent over; most of the images were of something besides helicopters. This one checks out, though. Stand by.*

Josh didn't want to stand by. He wanted to rip his hair out, wanted to scream.

He wanted to find his wife. al-Sadir had taken her somewhere close by, and they had gotten extremely lucky in being able to find a possible place. They had asked for a stroke of luck and had gotten it. To lose them now was infuriating.

> *We can sneak in,* Josh responded. He knew how it sounded, knew the desperation in his words would come through even a simple terminal command window. He waited, already knowing what the response would be. Liam was tugging at his elbow, trying to get an update. He waved him off and held up a finger.

> *Lane... it's impossible. See the image I just sent.*

NARA pinged him with an alert at the same moment, then opened an image that had come through the phone's connection to the mesh network. He examined it, seeing the unmistakable silhouette of a black helicopter, military, top-down, centered on the image. Around it were tiny black dots framed by white halos.

Personnel. Crew.

He was looking at a military airport and command center. And it was bustling with activity.

Josh knew in an instant Curtis was correct — gaining access to this facility was going to be impossible, at least on his own or with Liam. They needed a surgical strike team, one trained in extraction.

He could have done it, at least at one point in his career. He had done missions like this before, snuck into private and secure spaces to retrieve something of value — a high-ranking official, a strategic business partner, even the son or daughter of some rich sheik in the good graces of the US military.

But this was different. He was not in a plane, preparing to jump out its rear end. He had no chute, no way to stealthily fall onto the base from high above. No way to perform a HALO — high-altitude, low-opening — fall onto the Way Kambas facility.

And he had no team, no equipment. What would he do if he *did* find Molly there? If he could somehow locate her, free her, then what? How in the world was he supposed to get all three of them out, safely and securely?

He stopped once more, tears welling in his eyes. al-Sadir had moved too quickly, been too prepared. He knew this was all a game to him — literally and figuratively. This last phase, while likely not part of al-Sadir's overall plan, was certainly a contingency plan — one al-Sadir had enacted flawlessly.

He had left the facility in the hands of one of his techs, the woman who had toyed with Josh as he stormed through the halls looking for al-Sadir. It had bought him enough time to get away with the only thing Josh could imagine providing him enough leverage — his own wife, Molly.

And he had watched the mercenaries dragging out another scientist as well, which told Josh that the game would continue. al-Sadir had everything he needed to accomplish his goals. He had a scientist to help him with whatever project warranted enough money and resources to build something as evil and thorough as *Escape from Eden.* A project so big — so important to someone — al-Sadir simply could *not* stop.

And Josh's assumptions had proven true as well. al-Sadir had taken Molly not because he was acting out of spite, seeking revenge for ruining his facility. He had taken her because he wanted leverage over Josh. The computer scientist he had in tow was likely brilliant, someone useful to al-Sadir for the project.

But the *true* price — the person al-Sadir *really* wanted — was Joshua Lane himself.

Whether for the knowledge in his head or the enhanced tech implanted there, Joshua Lane was al-Sadir's priority target. He had taken Josh's wife in order to ensure Josh kept his sights on al-Sadir.

In short, al-Sadir was going to get what he wanted. Joshua Lane would find him, would track him down.

And Josh knew he would visit the ends of the earth to get his hands on the man who had kidnapped him and his wife — which was exactly what al-Sadir wanted. This was not over — far from it. al-Sadir wanted something Josh had.

al-Sadir had shown his hand, and Josh was going to play right into it.

CHAPTER 61

JOSH

Kohod

Tanjung Burung | Indonesia

"We can't go there now, Lane," Liam muttered.

"Curtis said the same. It's impossible, a suicide mission. We're not set up for it."

"No, but we *can* be. Once we get back to Maryland, I'll reconnect with my team and Colonel Sykes; he can pull some strings to get a strike team ready. Maybe even get a jump on it all on the plane ride home."

Josh shook his head, rubbing his temples. "No," he said. "We're not going back to Maryland. We don't have the time for an intercontinental flight... even if we used the time wisely and planned an entire mission, it just puts me that much farther away from Molly."

"Josh, we've got teams that can —"

"That's fine; I know we can put the team together. I know it doesn't have to be me; I trust that. I trust you."

"Then... what is it?"

Josh looked at Liam as they stood in the street outside a modern-looking pharmacy. People brushed past them as they entered and exited the store. Everyone seemed nonplussed by the explosion of the Palem facility, as life had quickly returned back to normal.

"I'm working with Curtis on something else."

Liam frowned.

"I know we can't get to the chopper, so we can't get to Molly and al-Sadir. He's stayed a step ahead of us the whole time, and if pitting your own mercenaries against you was one contingency plan, it tells me he's shrewd enough to have a dozen others. There's no way you and I are going to sneak over there and take the one thing he knows he has as leverage against me. She'll be locked down tight."

"Right... so, what are you getting at?"

"It means we're going on the offensive. We've been playing defense this whole time — trying to get me and the others out of that facility. Trying to catch al-Sadir, trying to track down Molly. But he's going to have plans in place to prevent that from working. So we need to take down something valuable to him."

"Okay, I'm on board. What are you thinking?" Liam asked.

"I sent Curtis a copy of a file I found on the servers back at the facility. It had all of us contestants listed. Obviously, I want your team to track down their next-of-kin, to figure out who they were and what their specialty was in computer science."

"Maybe Jocelyn can figure out what al-Sadir is ultimately working toward. Why he did all of this."

Josh nodded. "I also want them checking out another list in that same file. I think it's a list of people al-Sadir was working with

— or at least a list of people interested in the *Escape from Eden* game.

"The viewers..." Liam said.

Josh cocked his head sideways.

"My team and I were able to determine that *Escape from Eden* was being broadcast on the dark web. Obviously, al-Sadir had structured it as a sort of reality show. Sadistic, but it fits the premise we are all familiar with — a lot of contestants, slowly whittled down to one winner."

Josh nodded along. "That tracks. But why even broadcast something like this, exposing al-Sadir and his team? It was the very thing that gave you and your crew the lead that led to finding me. Why take the risk?"

Liam answered. "The feeds of the game were as secure as we've ever seen. al-Sadir's tech lead — the guy whose head you smashed back there is world-class. Runs teams of contractors and hackers who are also world-class, from what the NSA has been able to gather. These guys would be the best of the best, the very types of people the NSA would want to keep tabs on.

"All that to say, they did their homework," Liam continued. "They did everything right. If you wanted to broadcast something like this over the darknet, only allowing it to be viewable by those on a short list who had access, this would be the way to do it. We got lucky in that al-Sadir's buddy led us to him. Even luckier that my team was able to find and track the stream as it shifted from one dynamic IP to the next."

"So this list could really be a list of the viewers al-Sadir created *Escape for Eden* for?"

Liam thought for a moment, then nodded. "Sure — why wouldn't it be? What else could the list mean? But this all implies that you recognized a name on that list, right? Otherwise, it could just be a list of low-level employees who happened to be in the facility at any given time."

"Right," Josh nodded. "I did recognize a name. Maybe more than one, though I have to cross-reference it with known entities. I think a couple of them were tech bigwigs — people like Robert Blake."

Liam's eyes widened. "Robert Blake? The same guy who was killed three days ago in Baltimore?"

"One and the same. And I had a front-row seat to his execution."

Liam shuddered. "Sorry to hear that."

"Thanks. He was trying to warn me, I think. His men pulled me over on the bridge, coerced me into his car. I don't think he was trying to harm me, but he felt — rightfully, now that we know what happened — that he was in danger. Or that I was. Ultimately, I think he was trying to tell me about the game."

This was clearly news to Liam, who leaned forward, listening intently. "What did he tell you?"

Josh gave him the gist. "Just that he thought something was going to happen that I was going to be involved in. He was going to tell me more, but..."

"al-Sadir's guys took him out."

Josh nodded. "Anyway, his name was on the list. But it was another name that caught my attention. Ruth Dalia."

"Your boss at Bearbridge?"

Josh looked down at the ground. He nodded slowly. "She knows something about this. She's the person who led the project to develop the implant that's in my head now. NARA — Neurologically Activated Receiver Attachment — Dalia's the one who had the vision and attracted me to the project. She gave me a prototype self-driving car as a bonus, and I'm convinced its onboard AI is the same one they used in the *Escape from Eden* game, one they called Eve.

"Anyway, some members of her implantation team weren't sure they wanted to test NARA on me, but she and I both wanted to see what would happen. She thought I was the perfect candidate because of my expertise and prior experience. I wanted to try it out because... well, because I'm somewhat of a geek when it comes to stuff like this."

"Seems like it worked flawlessly," Liam said. "How many others did they operate on?"

Josh shook his head. "None. I'm the only one, as far as I know. And it worked *far* better than expected. I know I owe you an explanation, a demonstration. Again, it will have to wait. But rest assured, it's going to blow your mind."

Josh winced at the analogy after discussing the untimely demise of Robert Blake, but Liam didn't seem fazed. "Got it. So you think if we track down your boss, we'll be able to get some answers? Perhaps even get some leverage on al-Sadir himself?"

"That's exactly my line of reasoning. Curtis just responded as well. They're on board, already working. I gave them the name of my boss' yacht. Seems like boats have a funny way of betraying their owners, lately."

Liam laughed. "Could we be so lucky as to once again use a yacht to track down a person of interest?"

"Here's hoping." Josh smiled. "By the way, I never thanked you appropriately for saving me."

He stretched out his hand, then pulled it back awkwardly as

he saw Liam's massacred wrist. His missing fingers bled slowly from beneath the wrappings on his right hand.

Liam looked at him sheepishly, then flicked his eyebrows up. "An *appropriate* handshake will have to wait, I'm afraid. Let's just get your boss tracked down. I know you've got some questions for her. I do as well."

CHAPTER 62
AL-SADIR

Indonesia

al-Sadir watched Molly Lane's face as the chopper landed. He smiled at her, meaning for it to be calming, reassuring. He almost laughed. As if he could *possibly* reassure this woman.

"Where are we?" Molly shouted toward him. He couldn't hear the words — he hadn't given her a headset — but he could read her lips.

Her face was tear-streaked, eyes red. His mercenaries told him that she had screamed almost the entire way to the chopper. He had been waiting there for it all to play out. Not his desired outcome, but one he certainly still had control over. As soon as the Ravenclaw group had located Jakob Antonov and Molly Lane, they were off the ground and heading toward their next destination.

"Somewhere safe," he said. He didn't bother repeating it — she was confused, as if she were about to ask another question, but he ignored it.

They were at the Way Kambas Proving Ground, a Chinese military installation that the Indonesian government pretended didn't exist. It was a short hop over to Singapore, just a bit south to Jakarta, and most of the aircraft here would have no trouble getting all the way to mainland China if need be. While some of the crafts here were considered prototypes, earning this facility its name, it was effectively just a Chinese Air Force base.

Most importantly, it was filled to the brim with loyal Chinese soldiers and airmen, ready and willing to protect al-Sadir and his prize. They didn't know why, but they had been told that al-Sadir was a VIP and would be protected at all costs.

If there was any dissension in the ranks, fear would be the motivating factor in keeping them in line. No one wanted to upset the Chinese government — least of all its loyal subjects and military personnel.

He felt safe here, though he couldn't stay long. He had appointments, meetings. Some scheduled prior to this, some he had to arrange while waiting for his soldiers to grab Molly Lane.

The NSA had gotten a bit too close to him thanks to Kahn, and he had to change plans. Still, he had been surprised to learn that the NSA man they had captured back at Palem knew nothing of the device in Joshua Lane's brain. What was it? What did it do?

A man like Joshua Lane would not have some useless device implanted at the base of his skull. Whatever it was, it represented a leap forward in technological innovation.

And al-Sadir wanted it.

He would complete his *Escape from Eden* task, ensuring the project came to fruition, but he still had his eyes on the ultimate prize. That technology would give him an edge. It would prove to himself that he was far better than his father. It would be the very thing separating him from all the others like him — rich, intelligent businessmen who were constantly vying for power amongst one another.

With this technology, whatever it was, he could rise to the top.

He would be no one's lackey. He would work for no one. Al-Sadir had big plans, and they didn't involve hosting game shows, no matter how well they paid.

He wondered what Joshua Lane was doing now as he stared across at the man's wife. He knew the man had hardly even had time to recover from his own exploits in the facility, but would already be planning how to hunt down al-Sadir. He *would* come for him — he would come for his wife. al-Sadir knew it, and Molly knew it.

Next to her, the Russian computer scientist sat with his arms cuffed in front of him on his lap, his head hanging. The man was defeated, worn. He had no tears left to cry — it was likely the man considered himself already dead.

He would be, soon. No matter the outcome, Joshua Lane would either succeed or not, at which point this man would be useless to him. He didn't think he needed more leverage beyond Molly Lane, but al-Sadir was not in the business of taking chances. It was easy enough to grab Molly and Antonov, so while he had his eyes on Joshua Lane ultimately, this man could potentially help with the next phase of the project.

Right now, al-Sadir just needed to keep moving.

He stood up as the rotors spun down, motioning for Molly to follow.

She hesitated, but finally stood as the doors of the chopper swung open and five uniformed Chinese military personnel stared in at them.

One of them ran forward and leaned in, speaking loudly over the sound of the rotor wash. "Welcome, al-Sadir," he said in clipped English. "The Director thanks you for your service. He is excited you have made it here with the package intact."

Al-Sadir nodded, hopping off the edge of the chopper and onto the tarmac. The man behind him grabbed Molly and pulled her forward, yanking her out. When she hit the ground, she stood, wavering.

Al-Sadir held out a hand, waiting for her to place hers in it. When she did, he clasped it tight and pulled her close to him.

"I'm sorry it's come to this," he said. "I trust you understand what this all means."

She nodded, the tears returning.

"Follow instructions, and you stay alive. Do anything stupid, and you *and* your husband both die."

She swallowed.

He reached forward and put his finger under her chin. Her skin was soft, and al-Sadir felt a rush through his body. He had not expected this, but it could prove to be an interesting distraction, one he could even use to further persuade Joshua Lane to remain loyal to the cause.

He shivered as he considered it. *Maybe there will be time to... play.*

He looked down at Molly's grief-stricken, terrified face. "And I will *not* make it quick."

NEAR UMM SAID

Persian Gulf | Qatar

Liam and Josh pulled the boat to the left to dodge a rising swell. The rented motorboat was nothing special — certainly nothing expensive. It was old, but the motor worked and the engine was powerful enough to zip them across the channel without fuss.

Josh sat in the bucket seat to Liam's left while Liam navigated through the increasingly choppy waters.

After twelve hours of travel, leaving from Jakarta, then landing in Dubai and finally Doha, they had almost reached their destination. The boat had been waiting for them in Doha, reserved and paid for. The small city of Umm Said, south of Doha, featured an idyllic lighthouse still in use today. They had launched from a spot 200 meters south of the lighthouse, aiming for a spot about a half-mile offshore in the Persian Gulf.

Their destination had come into view five minutes prior, and Liam held the wheel steady as they approached the massive vessel.

The *Athena*-class boat, from *Nebula Yachts*, stretched out in front of them. Reasonable in terms of luxury yachts, the vessel was considered small, a mere 130 feet long. During the trip, Liam and Josh had plenty of time to study the yacht's layout, its capabilities, and what they might expect when they boarded.

The flight had also given Liam time for the very thing he had needed most: rest. He had slept for five hours straight, then napped again a few hours later. There had still been plenty of time to catch up with the duo back at the NSA and to connect with Josh and discuss plans.

As Josh had promised, Liam had been incredibly impressed with NARA's technology. The fact that the bionic interface worked so well was a testament to the direction the world was heading. There were still ethical concerns, and some necessary upgrades and enhancements the onboard AI in the operating system needed, but Liam could tell Josh was ultimately very happy with how well the system worked.

Liam's mind still raced with the possibilities. *To have unlimited memory... to be able to recall any information just by looking it up on the web with a simple thought...* The implications were astounding, and Liam had not even given it the necessary time to think it through.

Most of the time they'd spent together had been discussing what their plan was when they found Josh's boss. The yacht had been harbored for a few days at Umm Said, but it had disembarked earlier that morning. With any luck, Josh's boss would be on board, unaware that she was about to be visited by an NSA director and one of her own employees.

They had not bothered to stop for any sort of weaponry — Josh didn't want the situation to devolve into a dangerous hold-up.

They had decided not to use force to approach Dalia — she was harmless alone, and there was still a chance she was not involved in this.

Dalia was divorced, choosing to focus on her career rather than her personal relationships. If she was lonely now, it didn't show. The times Josh had spoken with her, she seemed happy, content running one of the world's most innovative tech companies.

Though she was probably within five or six years of retiring, the woman had not seemed to slow down at all and was constantly making news, either through her personal investments or from her company's accomplishments.

But as he had disclosed on the plane, Josh wasn't feeling the pride of working for such a luminous figure. Like Liam, he wanted answers — wanted to know why al-Sadir had built all of this.

He wanted to know why he had been taken, why al-Sadir's team had killed Robert Blake.

Pieces of it made sense, but both men were still blanking on the big picture.

Liam piloted their boat right up next to the larger vessel, aiming for the flat deck extending out over the water at the aft section of the luxury yacht. This boat was a bit smaller than al-Sadir's, but it was still unbelievably large. Liam wondered how one single person could be comfortable in such a massive space. He knew there would be a light crew on board as well, handling the actual piloting of the boat, navigation, cooking and cleaning, but it would still feel as though she lived in solitude.

Josh was standing now, and threw a line over a post to pull the boat close enough to reach the landing deck. He tied off and stepped over the edge onto the yacht's deck, then climbed the steps as Liam turned off the motor and followed suit. Standing now on the aft deck that extended around the entirety of the massive vessel, Liam felt himself in the presence of incredible wealth.

A massive hot tub sat in front of him, half-covered by a sprawling top deck that was lit by recessed lighting. The deck they were standing on extended forward into an open-air bar and lounge, and a doorway to a deeper hallway sat beyond that. To his left and right were outdoor seating and lounge chairs, and music emanated from hidden speakers, blasting an oldies tune he hadn't heard in fifteen years. Josh leaned in close and whispered. "We need to take her by surprise. We're not here to punch and scrape answers out of her, but I won't be upset if she gets a couple of scratches on her."

Liam just nodded. He followed Josh toward the bar section, knowing that his partner was aiming for the doorway at the end, recalling the layout of the yacht. While each could be customized by the purchaser, most of the time the general layouts were kept the same across the model, only the furnishings and decorations changing between each boat.

They reached the open-air lounge, and Liam caught sight of rows of high-end scotch and other liquors. In another world, he could see himself sidling up to the bar and mixing himself an Old-Fashioned.

Or, more likely, some hired bartender would appear out of nowhere and make the drink for him.

Josh stopped ahead of him, standing to the side of a set of comfortable-looking armchairs. Liam paused, hearing the noise as well. A click, coming from the door.

It was opening, first a crack, then wider. The door was thin, single-core, and had no ornate window on it. This door was merely for keeping weather out. Normally, it would stay open, blending into the wall behind it.

It opened fully, and Liam saw her standing in the hallway. Ruth Dalia. Smirk on her face, signs of age stretching across her forehead as she looked at the two men quizzically.

"Joshua Lane," she said softly. She turned to Liam. "And I'm not sure we've met."

"Name's Liam."

Liam didn't feel particularly polite. This woman was playing a game, toying with them. He wasn't quite sure *what* exactly that game was, and it seemed Josh didn't either, as he fidgeted beside him. Suddenly Liam heard movement, the pounding of footsteps; he whirled around just as four men appeared from both sides of the deck they were on, previously hidden.

More mercenaries. Each of them was brandishing an assault rifle. Each of them aimed at Liam and Josh.

Well… hell.

Josh raised his eyebrows and spoke to Dalia, his voice calm, his mouth a thin line. "It seems you weren't as surprised to see me as I thought you might be."

"Surprised? Sure. But that doesn't mean preparation was not in order."

"And what sort of *preparation* is this?" Liam asked. "Seems like you fear for your life. Why would that be?"

She eyed Liam with an intelligent shrewdness that suddenly struck fear in Liam. Her voice was even, measured.

"Perhaps you can tell me."

NEAR UMM SAID

Persian Gulf | Qatar

His mind raced. How did she know? How was she prepared for this? Josh couldn't understand how Ruth Dalia had so smoothly prepared for their arrival. How long had the mercenaries been here, waiting as their boat approached, waiting for them to climb aboard? Had they been here all night or for just the past few hours?

She was moving toward them now, offering them seats. Josh's mind was in turmoil, and it was causing his senses to blur. He was trying to think through what to do next, and he couldn't even see straight because of it.

They had made a plan — one he was sure al-Sadir could not see coming.

His failure had been in assuming Dalia wouldn't see them coming — and why should she? Still, they had made no contingencies, had not even given their full plans to Jocelyn and Curtis. The pair back at the NSA knew where Liam and Josh would be headed, knowing that Josh wanted to track down his boss at Bearbridge and share some words, but they were busy working on the list of contestants and tracking down the other viewers who might still be at large.

His boss had so smoothly and adeptly orchestrated this counterattack, this ambush. She had known all along. How? Who had told her? If it had been al-Sadir, how did he know?

Now, they were screwed. They couldn't even update Curtis and Jocelyn — the phone they had used was back on their boat. Out here in the middle of the bay was one of the few places on earth where the mesh network was unreliable — had Dalia known that? Connection would be spotty at best, so this part of their plan was not supposed to involve trying to contact anyone.

So what had he missed? Josh tried to work through the permutations, to try to see the larger problem. He tried to understand the puzzle, all of the individual pieces, and how they fit together as a whole.

He couldn't for the life of him figure it out. As he sat in the chair across from Liam, Ruth Dalia to his left, the mercenaries closed in around them. Each of them was well-trained, none of them speaking and all of them on high alert. Their weapons were down now out of respect for their boss, but they still held them with both hands, ready. Ready with the flick of a wrist to open fire if Josh or Liam got antsy.

They wouldn't, of course. What would be the point of that? To bleed out on the deck of her yacht would almost certainly lead to Molly's own death soon after. If al-Sadir couldn't get what he wanted, he would make sure Molly would suffer.

"Why exactly are you here, Josh?" Dalia began.

"What involvement do you have with the *Escape from Eden* game?"

She stared at him, her head moving slowly as her eyes danced across his face. She was trying to read him, and he had no doubt she was quite capable of it. She had not succeeded, not gotten this far in life, without being able to read a person impressively well. "I know of it," she said.

It was Josh's turn to laugh. "They *kidnapped* me. Pulled me out of my car and brought me to a place where they killed people. Brought *my wife* there. I'm going to ask you again, *what do you know* —"

Dalia waved her hand dismissively. "Or what?" she asked. "You're going to *what?* Shoot me? You notice I didn't have my men search you for weapons. That reveals the status quo right now, Josh. You think I *fear* death, don't you? So what if you kill me? How long after do you think you'll make it? And unless you or your friend here is packing a massive amount of explosives and you plan on ending it for all of us, there's no way you're going to kill all of my men."

Josh nodded along. "I didn't think I had to bring weapons."

"A wise choice," she said. "Now, I do owe you at least some explanation as to why you were taken."

"Kidnapped," Josh repeated. "I drove a car off a bridge to try to get away. Almost died."

"Yes, that does remind me — you do owe me a car."

The H7 flashed in Josh's mind.

"Anyway," Dalia continued. "Yes, the *Escape from Eden* game is quite... serious. I disapproved of using something so oppressive and *permanent* as a solution to our problem."

Liam frowned and opened his mouth to speak, but Josh cut

him off. "So you do know about it? What exactly is your involvement with the game? With al-Sadir?"

Josh wanted to ask about the other names on the list as well, who they were and why they had all agreed to kill people as a means to find a solution to this problem of theirs.

She frowned deeply, as if considering her words carefully. When she spoke, Josh sensed both her incredible charisma and her ability to act a role. She was genuine, authentic. "As I told you, I disapproved. I thought there would be better ways. I'm disappointed to say I was wrong. *Escape from Eden* was the *only* way. The only way to find the person we needed. Little did I know that person was someone I had employed all along."

"You and al-Sadir both want me for something. What's that about? What's this project or problem you think I can solve?"

She shook her head. "Not a problem. *The* problem. Something the world is not ready for, not without you in charge of it."

"In charge of *what*? And why do you have to kill all these other contestants in order to find someone to lead this project? What good could that possibly do?"

She looked at him then, confused. Truly not understanding why Josh was here. He saw it in her face, spelled out as if reading the pages of a book. Either she was still acting, or she truly was confused. She thought he knew more than he knew. She thought he had figured something out.

"You don't understand, do you?" she asked, the concern still on her face. "This isn't just something a company can solve — some project we can simply apply computing power and human resources to. This isn't about finding a handful of sharp programmers and devs and engineers, and putting them all into a room."

"Tell us, then," Liam said. "What *is* this about?"

NEAR UMM SAID

Persian Gulf | Qatar

"About eleven years ago, our government began a program to build a quantum computer. This was hardly a new development, even then, as you well know, since many large corporations have been working toward the same goal."

Josh and Liam nodded along. Quantum computing was seen as the holy grail for computer scientists. Artificial intelligence study had shifted from being the wild west to a stable, reliable industry sector. It wasn't shiny and new anymore, and though breakthroughs happened all the time in artificial intelligence research, the ultimate goal now was to build a computer that could *handle* a true artificial general intelligence.

A *quantum* computer.

To date, the main problem with quantum computing technology was that researchers could not get qubits to stay coherent for very long. The larger machines — 200 or 300 qubits or more — were even less reliable. The finicky devices needed to be cooled to a super low temperature, requiring vast amounts of energy and resources that made progress slow. Any temperature, sound, or light variations could cause decoherence.

"As usual, our government was late to the game. But what they lacked in expediency they made up for in breadth of resources. When you can print money, you can buy time."

Again, Liam nodded. Josh listened intently, waiting for the punch line of this cruel joke.

"You of all people, Lane," she continued, "know very well that the government has not yet been able to achieve their goal, since you would have been brought onto the team years ago if it seemed like they were making real headway."

"You brought me to Bearbridge because of my interest in quantum technology," Josh said.

She confirmed this. "Indeed, as well as your expertise. The way your mind works is very much like the quantum computer everyone has been trying to build — thousands of data points coalescing onto one solution to a problem. Piecing together a fully formed picture out of seemingly unrelated items. And you've got the military background we were looking for, as well. You're disciplined, motivated. You see the goal, and you don't stop until it's achieved."

Josh frowned. "Thanks for the positive performance review, boss," Josh snapped. "But I have yet to start on anything *real* at Bearbridge. First, you implanted me with this chip — which I thank you for, by the way. It's quite the little toy. But you've kept me at arm's length from any real quantum work."

She shifted in her chair, looking once at Josh and Liam then back down at her hands. "Yes, a travesty. But my hands were tied. This same government project I am referring to brought me on five years ago, mostly for access to Bearbridge resources. They wanted an ally who would give them the manpower, the resources — the money, if theirs got tied up with congressional oversight committees — and the like. It was a board position, and I really had little power there. But I was privy to information. I was privy to what *really* happened to the project."

Josh raised an eyebrow and glanced over at Liam. Liam was on the edge of his seat, fascinated. The man clearly had not heard this story, either.

"So, did they actually pull it off?" Liam asked. "Did they figure out how to build a computer that was stable?"

She nodded, but there was a hint of fury in her eyes. "They... did not. But a quantum computer *was* built."

"We haven't heard anything about that," Liam said. "I think the NSA would —"

"In light of recent events, you shouldn't put so much faith in the NSA's ability to be at the cutting edge of security technology."

Liam's jaw tightened. She wasn't wrong, though. Liam had learned the hard way that the NSA's intelligence was not as tightly locked down as he might have hoped.

"Anyway, the reason no one's heard of it yet is that the project went black as soon as it was almost finished. It's been wrapped up tight, kept at arm's length, even from its own government."

Josh knew where this was headed. "So *what* government did accomplish it?"

"Well, technically, the United States government."

"But you said —"

"Yes, I said the United States did not build a quantum computer. But the truth is, they did everything else. All of the pieces were there, ripe for the picking."

"So someone picked them," Liam added.

She nodded. "Yes. Our government was cocky enough to think they had the project sealed up tight, that they still had the power to create something everyone in the world wanted to build, without revealing how it was done. They created everything necessary to build the world's first *true* quantum computer, stable at room temperature and capable of hosting a true artificial general intelligence. One that, left unchecked, could theoretically usher in a singularity event."

Josh was impressed, but he still held disbelief. "It doesn't make sense, though. If somebody stole the work, the US government would do *anything* to retrieve it. They would turn over every rock in every corner of the globe in order to make sure that it didn't get into the wrong hands."

"Sure, unless it was in the wrong hands to begin with."

Josh's heart sank. "Are you saying —"

She nodded again. "Yes, Lane. The project was sealed and no one heard of it because it fell into the hands of the Chinese government. They continued working on the project in secret, and I have it on good authority that they eventually achieved what the US government was so close to building. Somewhere in the heart of that country is a *true* quantum computer, most likely already hosting the world's first true artificial intelligence."

"You said it *fell* into their hands," Liam said. Josh snapped his head over at his partner. "That implies it wasn't *stolen*," Liam continued. "So the Chinese didn't *take* it, which means somebody must have given it to them."

Josh nodded. "Right — but why? Who would do that?"

A smile appeared on Dalia's face. "Well, as a matter of fact, *I* would."

CHAPTER 66
JOSH

Persian Gulf | Qatar

Josh winced. "You're loyal to the *Chinese?*"

Ruth Dalia's smile faded. "Loyal? No. I'm *loyal* to power, to success. To the promise of a future. The Chinese have been working toward this for over a century. Their leadership has condemned the West, claiming it will soon overthrow the United States to become the world's dominant power."

Liam pushed himself back into the seat, his hands and arms draped over the sides of the armchair. "And you just handed their dream to them on a silver platter."

"What else would you have done? Wait for the United States to finish, so the Chinese could simply steal it, fully formed? You know full well that's their move. If it hadn't been me, it would have been someone else. A spy, a true loyalist, even an undercover Chinese national. Somebody would have taken the project and handed it to them sooner or later."

"So why do it? A way to protect yourself?"

"Don't be naïve, Lane," Dalia snapped. Humans run on incentives. You're no different; I'm no different. All the money in the world means *nothing* if the fiat currency you've earned it in gets usurped. This was a way for me to solidify my own power in what's to come. If not for me, then for my children. My grandchildren."

Josh nodded. He hated every word out of her mouth, but he couldn't argue with its logic. The world was going to change sooner or later. No nation got to be the world's dominant power forever. Not the Romans, not the English or Spanish, not the United States. China had been waiting patiently in the wings for its chance to strike. As nasty as the regime may be, he had to hand it to the Chinese government for their ability to patiently wait until the perfect moment to strike.

And it *was* a good moment to strike. The United States was fractured, divided not down the middle but into many factions, each claiming their side was correct and true and the ethical pinnacle of the human race while simultaneously blasting the other sides for their complete lack of virtue. Media had run away with the hearts and minds of Americans — and every other Western nation. They controlled the narrative by controlling emotion; they could fabricate the response they wanted in the course of a single news cycle.

Most Westerners were looking inward, grumbling and complaining about the state of their own nations, their own governments.

None of them was looking outward. Even the US military had relaxed its stance on international defense after decades of being berated by congressional committees that sought to lower the defense budget year after year.

Whatever the goal was of this quantum computing project, Josh had to assume part of it would be handling logistics and administration for the very war that would seek to overthrow the US. The Chinese were known to be quite good at these necessary facets of war already, so whatever AI their new quantum machine boasted would make it impossible to catch up. Already he had spoken with developers in different branches of the US military, all working on some version of an operating system that could handle the next phase of modern warfare: fully automated drone strikes based on 'red flag' check systems, AIs that could pilot ships and organize attacks, planes that could perform surgical strikes without needing human pilots to fly them. All of this coordinated from a centralized hub with speed-of-light updates.

Theoretically, it was an information system so vast and so complete that it had become the holy grail of the Air Force and Department of Defense. The problem was, of course, that a single computer network would be needed to run it. Physical lag time introduced by splitting up the massive computing — even into separate rooms — would render the machine obsolete.

So if a quantum device could run the entire thing...

It was but one possible reason, one possible outcome the Chinese were after. But it was enough to motivate Josh to never want it to see the light of day.

If they already have the tech...

Dalia raised her eyebrows, and one of the mercenaries stepped forward. "Head to the bridge and activate the ship's onboard AI pilot. Deactivate the firewall. We need to start moving. Lane's coming back into the project."

"So that's it, then?" Josh asked. "I'm just a pawn in your game. Everything — from hiring me at Bearbridge to putting the implant in my head to sticking me in your sadistic game — it was all just that... a game."

"Even games can have deadly serious consequences, Lane," she said. Her voice was chill, icy. "Surely by now you know you were the one we designated for this project from the beginning. We have Dr. Jakob Antonov, the scientist al-Sadir grabbed from Palem, but his value will diminish quickly, I fear. *No one* can do what you can do. You're the most well-rounded contestant we have."

"My wife — Molly. Where is she?"

She nodded, as if anticipating this question. "She's safe, but she's being held with Antonov."

"Where?" Josh demanded.

She held up a hand. "Lane, I hardly think you're in a position to negotiate. Suffice to say she is safe — and will remain so, as long as you are cooperating."

"And if I cooperate, what of Antonov?"

And what of Liam?

But he kept the thought to himself — he didn't want to call attention to the man seated to his right.

"Once the system is up, the firewall around my yacht will come down, and incoming and outgoing transmissions will continue. We'll be connected to the outside world once again, which means we'll be connected to al-Sadir, who's standing by, waiting for me to confirm you're here. That you're ready to participate in our next phase."

Got it, he thought. *You're going to kill Antonov as soon as you can contact al-Sadir.*

A new thought struck him. "How did you find me? How did you know I was coming?"

Her smile returned, only covering one-half of her face this time. It was sly, wicked, a side of her Josh had not seen. *So she's an actress.*

"My company's property lives inside your head, Lane. Surely you wouldn't think I would give you such a gift without *also* including a way to keep tabs on it?"

Liam frowned. "So, what then? GPS? A backdoor mesh connection?"

She shook her head. "No, far more simple and elegant than that. I didn't want Josh to find out we added a subroutine that constantly pinged his location. Instead, a few lines of code embedded deep within the onboard AI sends out a tiny signal once every hour, at a super-high frequency. That's it — but it's enough for the network to triangulate your location from the unique frequency."

Josh sighed. It *was* elegant. Something he would never have found on his own, because he would never have thought to look. He realized he was working against a master strategist. He had known she was brilliant, but he had assumed her gifts were relegated to areas of business, commerce, running a company.

But she had been playing him for far longer than he had even considered. Planning this out for years, most likely.

She looked at another mercenary and pointed at Liam. "I'm sure you both have determined by now that I only need Lane. Liam — whatever your last name is — while it has been a true pleasure to meet you, I'm afraid you won't be coming with us."

Liam's eyes widened as the three remaining mercenaries raised their weapons and moved into a different position. Each placed themselves in a spot from which they could fire on Liam without stray rounds hitting anyone else.

"Wait... I —" Liam shouted.

Josh noticed something then, in his peripheral vision.

No.

It was coming from his own mind. He was being pinged by someone, some*thing*. Suddenly he understood.

As the mercenaries tensed and readied themselves to fire on his friend, Josh leaned forward and smiled.

NEAR UMM SAID

Persian Gulf | Qatar

The conversation played out in Josh's mind in the span of a second. He recognized the ping — it was Eve. He had been surprised to hear from the AI, but he pieced it together in an instant.

Ruth Dalia had provided resources not just to the US government — and thus China — but to al-Sadir to build *Escape from Eden*. Someone had to provide the software foundation for the artificial intelligence that ran the Palem facility, so it made sense that Bearbridge had written it. It was the same software in use on the H7. Josh knew the voice of Eve now, and he heard it again in his own mind.

When Dalia's soldier had disabled the firewall and reinstated their connection to the outside world, he had also booted up the piloting software — essentially a clone of Eve. Back at the Palem facility, when he had used NARA to gain access to the system, he had needed to use a username and group that mimicked that of someone who already had access to the system. NARA had executed this, and this system back at Palem had recognized him and his implant as system administrators.

But the system itself — Eve, effectively — was decentralized. This, too, made sense. Why build an artificial intelligence to run security and administration from just one localized cluster? By spreading the load around the mesh net, using physical nodes around the world, whoever had built Eve's infrastructure had ensured that losing one facility would not destroy her entirely. That she was here now meant other benefactors might be borrowing her services as well, running different facilities like the one his wife was at — or just for personal use, like running the control systems and piloting Dalia's yacht.

Simple, yet elegant.

Even better, the system updated itself regularly, ensuring all access points were kept up-to-date with the most recent version of Eve's software.

Including recognizing Josh and NARA as system administrators.

His mind flew back and forth with NARA and Eve as he had her explore his access. As expected, he now had access to just about every component of this vessel. As long as it was connected to the artificial intelligence, Josh could reach it.

And he could *control* it.

Liam was cowering on his chair, bringing his leg up involuntarily to protect himself. To Josh, the mercenaries were moving as if in slow motion, pulling their rifles higher and lining up their shots. Josh watched it all unfold as he issued the commands.

"Engines full, no ramp. Engage."

He knew Eve would be able to translate the instruction clearly — it wasn't a complicated command.

"Override safety precautions."

This twin-engine yacht was capable of laying down an absolutely *massive* amount of power, but for the safety of everyone on board, Eve would only throttle up on a slow acceleration ramp, and even then, the systems would prevent the engines from being overrun.

Except for right now.

Josh gripped the chair, which he hoped was bolted to the deck floor, and waited.

There was an excruciating half-second as the engines whined up, then power shifted the momentum from the propeller deep below, up through the hull of the heavy boat, and finally into positive forward motion.

And once that motion began, it became a *fury*.

Josh white-knuckled the armchair and watched as Liam and Dalia flew forward and sideways off of their chairs. Two mercenaries fell backward onto the deck floor, dropping their rifles. One, unfortunately standing closest to the railing, flipped over the railing and into the water below as the boat fought with the infinite power of the ocean swells and it rocked side-to-side.

The yacht's acceleration caused bottles behind the bar to fly off, some of them smashing the mirror behind it, others clattering to the floor. Josh reached down and swiped one as it rolled by. He flipped it in his hand and jumped out of the chair.

The boat was moving steadily forward now, but the swells were making it a treacherous journey. It seemed every second the hull smashed into the crest of a wave, sending shockwaves through the boat's interior.

Cracks formed along one of the walls, an outdoor light fixture swinging around above his head. This yacht was not designed for this sort of speed, especially with the swells of the ocean around them.

The first mercenary closest to him was recovering, but Josh swung the bottle down and bounced it off the man's temple. He was out cold. Josh grabbed his assault rifle and lifted it, pointing it at the other mercenary.

Now fully accelerated, the only movement beneath his feet was the rocking of the waves and the odd swell as they reached a calmer area of the bay. Josh used the opportunity to call out to the man standing now on his knees, holding his own rifle with one hand. "I don't want to kill you," he said.

The man lunged. He worked to move his rifle up into both hands, pulling it forward to aim at Josh.

Josh pulled the trigger, firing two quick rounds directly into the man's chest at near point-blank range. He had no armor on underneath his shirt. The man coughed, blood immediately trickling out the side of his mouth, and he fell.

"I said I didn't want to kill you."

CHAPTER 68

JOSH

Persian Gulf | Qatar

"Head up and find the last one!" Liam shouted. "I've got Dalia."

Josh flicked his eyes from Liam to Ruth Dalia, who glowered at him from the floor. When the boat had initially begun accelerating, she had flown down, her lighter body flopping like a fish on the deck and ending up near the feet of one of the dead mercenaries. Liam was standing over her now, holding the other assault rifle.

Josh nodded and bolted away, pulling open the door that led deeper into the boat. He kept the yacht heading forward, relying on Eve's auto-steering capabilities to ensure they didn't ram into anything else or hit land. He wondered if the boat he and Liam had come here on was still tied to the side of the yacht, bouncing around and trying to keep up.

He tore up the hallway, finding a white-walled spiral staircase. If he had to guess, this would lead up to the back of the bridge. He had never been on a yacht like this, but he figured the command station would more than likely be on the top floor.

He was right. Josh burst into the control room, only to find it empty. The door he'd entered from was centered on the back wall of the bridge, and he saw all of the controls and pilot's chair directly in front of him, below a set of sprawling, wide windows that stretched around the front of the bridge. He did a quick turn to check the other entrances — one on either side of him, both leading outside and down to a deck below that wrapped around to the fore section of the yacht.

He paused, catching his breath. He pinged Eve through NARA's connection, finding a heads-up display from an onboard computer that he could superimpose on his vision. It showed their heading, windspeed, nautical speed, other bits and bobs he didn't recognize, but he left all of it. He wanted to know if there would be any surprises. If the remaining grunt found his way to the bridge to try to wrest piloting duties away from Josh, he'd be able to maintain remote control.

He turned then to the left side, wanting to get back down to the level he had been on before in case the guy had circled around to head back toward Liam and his boss. He reached for the door handle and heard the one directly behind him turn. He whirled around, weapon ready. The door swung open, and the mercenary stepped in. His eyes were on the control station — likely trying to figure out how the boat had started moving on its own accord. His eyes moved on, quickly landing on Josh in the corner of the room opposite him. They widened, and Josh saw him bring his weapon up.

"Hold it," Josh said quickly, his rifle already aimed directly at the man's chest. The other mercenaries hadn't been wearing body armor, so it was a good bet this guy wasn't, either. He wanted to make sure he had the shot in case the man — like his counterpart downstairs — continued the movement and decided to try to get off a quick shot.

Josh hoped the guy wasn't as stupid as his friend.

"They're all dead," Josh said. "You're the last one, and my buddy's down there with one of your weapons. I don't want to kill you."

The soldier-for-hire sneered. His hair was scraggly and unkempt, wet from the ocean spray, and rivulets of seawater dripped over his crooked nose. "Yet you *did* kill them." He sounded Israeli.

"I gave them the option," Josh said, shrugging. "Look, this isn't your fight. Not anymore. You won't get paid, so the best you can do is leave here with your life. Your pride might take a hit, but live to fight another day, right?"

"And what would you have me do?" the man grunted, one hand still gripping the assault rifle. Josh eyed him closely, but let his peripheral vision focus on the man's weapon. If it even danced an inch, Josh was going to have to kill him. Josh flicked his head to the side, motioning to the doorway. He didn't want to take his eyes off the man but needed to get his point across. "You can swim?"

The man's eyes narrowed. He was still standing in the doorway, half in the room. The door closed on his left shoulder, but he made no movement to come closer to Josh.

"You want me to jump off speeding boat."

"We can slow her down," he said.

Neither he nor the man made any movement toward the controls. "Go ahead," the man said, daring Josh to move.

Josh rolled his eyes as he issued the command through NARA.

He hoped Liam wasn't standing up...

Josh braced himself, leaning toward the starboard side of the yacht, planting his right foot and shoulder into the corner of the room just inside the doorway.

Eve reacted immediately, and the man standing across from Josh ping-ponged in the doorway, finally falling backward and down onto the tiny stairwell. The stairs were narrow, wide enough for only one person, and Josh knew that the walkway below them offered hardly enough room to stand, so with the right amount of movement...

Josh narrowed his eyes, watching as the man began to stand. *"Speed up, 20% ramp."*

Eve responded by putting the engines into drive once more, only this time the power contained to a slow acceleration. The mercenary stood, fumbling for his weapon, and Josh slowly increased the ramp until their acceleration could be felt again. He only had seconds before the man would be on his feet and ready to attack Josh. To prevent the guy from just flicking his rifle up and getting off a lucky shot through the doorway, Josh stepped to his left, farther into the bridge. He gripped a handle inside the door. He could see the man's feet and left side of his body, and he shifted into position to work his way through the door once more.

But Josh was ready, and Eve was ready. The vessel's speed had evened out; they were now going almost as fast as they had been traveling before, though the waters were perfectly smooth now.

"Hard left, continue accelerating to full speed. Execute."

The boat ripped to the left, and Josh nearly left his feet. His left hand firmly gripping the handle, he allowed the centrifugal force to pull his lower body toward the bridge.

The mercenary outside was not as lucky. Unable to anticipate the boat's movements beneath his feet, the man toppled head over heels over the staircase and disappeared.

Josh ran over, grabbing the handle at the opposite side of the room, sticking his head out the doorway. He glanced over the edge.

The man was gone.

The deck beneath the stairs on the starboard side of the vessel was even narrower than he had expected. He glanced out to the waters as they sped through. About forty yards from the back-right side of the yacht, Josh saw him.

The mercenary had just resurfaced. Eyes open, shouting something at him. He bobbed around in the bay, completely helpless.

Satisfied, he had Eve back off the speed once more and brought the yacht to a stop as he descended the stairs and wound around back to the deck. He saw the lifeless bodies of the two mercenaries there and turned the corner to find Liam rubbing his head.

"Thanks for the warning," Liam said. He was kneeling, still holding the assault rifle. He had his bandaged hand covering a gash on his head, and Josh saw blood between his fingers.

"My apologies," Josh said, smiling. "Had to take care of something."

Ruth Dalia lay in a heap in front of Liam, eyes open, a dark scowl across her face. The older woman had decided it would be safer for her to cling to the floor rather than try to stand or sit while Josh was exploring the yacht's capabilities. She was not pleased about it.

"I'm assuming you took care of it?" Liam asked.

Josh's smile widened. "All good." He turned and looked down at his boss. "I suppose I'll be fired for this, huh?"

NEAR UMM SAID

Persian Gulf | Qatar

"Where is my wife?" Josh asked. Liam watched him from the chairs. The builders of the yacht had wisely decided to bolt them to the floor, and though it would be difficult to redecorate the room because of it, Liam was glad they had offered something to hold onto while Josh was driving.

He looked at Ruth Dalia, who had now rejoined them on the chairs. She had broken her wrist while being sloshed around by Josh's antics, and she was quite unhappy about it.

Her eyes smoldered into Josh's. Five seconds passed, then ten. "If you think I'm going to just give you a way to help stop al-Sadir, you're sorely mistaken," she said quietly.

"I'll worry about al-Sadir later. *Where is Molly?*"

Liam watched the exchange, wondering how they might be able to get leverage on this woman. She was powerful, but he could tell she had not planned for this. Somehow, Josh had been able to control the yacht. Somehow, due to something related to the chip in his head, he had been able to take control from the mercenary and used the boat's own AI piloting software to cause immeasurable damage.

Damage that had saved their lives. His head was bleeding from a cut, but he couldn't complain — the mercenaries had been about to put a bullet through him.

How had he pulled it off? Every time he'd asked him, Josh had pushed the question aside in favor of the more pressing matters at hand. He understood those matters truly were pressing — they *had* needed to get out of the building before it exploded, and they *had* needed to find the location of this yacht in order to find Josh's wife.

But there would come a time, hopefully soon, when Liam could probe Josh about what *exactly* was inside his brain. How it was able to take over a private yacht's piloting.

And the fact that Bearbridge had done this to him, under orders from Ruth Dalia — the implications of it were staggering. It meant her company had been working in secret, bypassing traditional safety routes and regulations regarding human experimentation. It meant they would be in a lot of trouble if word got out.

Which all told Liam she had never *intended* for it to get out. Josh was a test subject, and she had admitted to putting something in the device that allowed her to keep tabs on him. Liam shook his head. *The audacity.*

Still, he understood why Josh had been Dalia's first choice for the tech. He was the perfect specimen. He had the military training and physique, but he also had the brain of a computer genius.

What had they created? He was glad Josh was who he was and not someone like al-Sadir or Dalia. He shuddered to think how powerful one could become with the help of an onboard computer aid that could connect to the mesh net.

"I'm going to give you one more chance," Josh said. "Tell me where my wife is, or I will simply kill you, then toss you overboard like one of your hired guns."

She glared over at him. Liam sensed Josh was telling the truth — that he might actually kill her. Liam didn't want him to get entangled with something as severe as murder, but then again, her actions *had* directly led to al-Sadir's right-hand man taking two of his own fingers.

Hell, I might just kill her myself.

"You can't kill me," she said, the beginnings of a smirk appearing again on her face. She was still frowning deeply, still pissed about the change of the status quo, but Liam could see that she still believed she had the upper hand.

Josh shook his head. "That's where you're wrong, Ruth. See, You told me you have a way to track me at all times, from anywhere on the planet... that sort of thing doesn't sit well with me. I'd be *very* interested in eliminating the only person in the world who has that sort of power over me."

She didn't respond.

"Furthermore, you can tell I've had the onboard OS you installed in me — NARA — make some changes. Turns out, I was able to connect to your artificial intelligence, the one you named Eve. Smart play, using her for more than just running that facility. You decentralized her, too. I don't know if it was you, someone else at Bearbridge, or another benefactor behind this twisted game you've been playing, but it doesn't matter. I have access."

"Not full access," she snapped. "You might have administrative control, but there's no way you —"

Josh raised an eyebrow and lifted the assault rifle, then pointed it at her chest. "No way I can *what?* Hack it? Gain access to *everything* you've been working on at Bearbridge? Dalia, think about who you're talking to. If there's *anyone* on the planet who can do it, it's me. And I assure you..." He leaned forward menacingly. "I *absolutely* will."

"That doesn't mean I'm going to just tell you —"

Josh lowered the assault rifle and fired a single round through Dalia's side. She yelped, then gasped, wide-eyed, as her hands found the hole next to her belly. She fell forward, groaning in agony.

"Through and through," Josh said. "It'll heal, as long as you don't bleed out. Didn't hit anything terribly important. You forget that I'm also a trained PJ, Dalia. I've seen combat. I know my way around a rifle, *and* a first-aid kit. More importantly, I really, *really* hate it when people underestimate me."

Liam sensed a change in Josh, as if a switch had been flipped. This man was hurting, desperate to find his wife, unwilling to make any exceptions. He had a goal, and Liam was seeing what happened when obstacles found their way between him and that goal.

"I also know you've got about twenty minutes before you're catatonic. Thirty before you lose enough blood, we'll be lucky to save you. But with a basic first aid kit, like the one I saw up on the bridge, I can at least get the bleeding stopped. You'll be in excruciating pain, but... I'm actually pretty okay with that."

She was crying now but trying to hide it. Her eyes were still smoldering, narrow as they gazed up at Josh while she leaned forward, clutching her wound. "Get the first aid kit," she hissed.

"Give me Molly's location," Josh said coolly. "Where al-Sadir is going to hold her."

"I don't know it by anything other than its designator."

"What's that supposed to mean?" he asked.

Liam watched the two going back and forth, suddenly realizing that Josh may have misstepped. If she didn't actually know...

She shook her head, defeated. "He'll take her back to his headquarters. al-Sadir set it up. Told the rest of us it was safer and more secure for everyone involved if no real locations were given."

"How do you refer to it then? You just call it 'headquarters?'"

She closed her eyes, fighting back the pain. "No," she said as she opened them once again. "It's just a number. A designator, as I said." She screamed then, blood seeping out around her fingers. "I don't — don't *know*."

Josh's face snapped over to Liam. There was something frantic hidden there, as if he had just realized something. Liam looked at him quizzically.

Josh turned back to Dalia. "A number?"

She sighed, exasperated. "Yes, but like I told you, I can't even recall exactly what it is — I've never needed to tell anyone. It's never written down; it's just... a number. A number that refers to the project itself, but as a place, it refers to the location al-Sadir operates out of."

"I suggest you try remembering it," Josh said.

Liam's breath caught in his throat.

"One," she began, still shaking her head. "It starts with one. One, two... something."

"One, two, four, five, three?"

Her face shot up, staring daggers through Josh. "How — how do you know that?"

He smiled down at her. "I told you I don't like to be underestimated. Thanks, Dalia." He turned to Liam, and he stood. "Let's move to the bridge. We've got work to do."

EPILOGUE

NSA HEADQUARTERS | ***FORT MEADE,*** *Maryland*

"You sure you made the right call?" Jocelyn asked. "You could have told someone at port she was on board, bleeding out."

Josh stared at the pretty young woman. He waited five seconds before answering. "Yeah. We could have."

Liam stepped in from next to Josh at the conference room table. "What's done is done. I'm not upset about it; she was behind all of this. *Escape from Eden* may not have been her doing, but she was directly related to it."

"And your hand..." Curtis added.

Liam nodded slowly. "Right. As I said, I'm not going to lose much sleep if we hear that Dalia died. We were in a hurry, and she's certainly not innocent. Let's move on."

"Any word on that number?" Josh asked.

One, two, four, five, three.

Josh could see Dr. Roger Eberly in his mind, mouthing the numbers one at a time as the room temperature increased past the point of survival. He burned, his clothes catching fire, still mouthing the words.

He was helping me, Josh thought. *He wanted me to know.*

He wanted me to find al-Sadir.

The number was al-Sadir's designator for the location where he'd been holding Molly. All it would take was a lucky break — a random association al-Sadir had accidentally left online. One that linked the number with an actual place.

The problem was that there had yet *been* no lucky break.

Three days after leaving Ruth Dalia's bleeding body on the deck of her own yacht in Umm Said, Liam had called the group to NSA headquarters to finish what they'd started.

Curtis shook his head. "Unfortunately, no. But we've got search bots running over every line of public data. Some working behind-the-scenes to access not-so-public data. We'll find it."

"If it exists," Jocelyn added.

Josh shot a glance at her. "It exists," he said. "But we need to keep thinking. It can't be the *only* thing pointing us in the right direction. We got lucky with Kahn; we just need another Kahn. We'll question each and every one of the people on the list, the benefactors and viewers. We *will* find it."

Liam swallowed. "Josh... we were only able to cross-reference three of those names with *actual* people. And they're —"

"Dead. I know." After Robert Blake, the other two names from the list he'd found on Eve's servers had been crossed off as well. Perhaps they, too, had worked against al-Sadir in some way, or perhaps al-Sadir wanted to wipe the slate clean since there was more need for *Escape from Eden.*

"But we've got an entire floor of analysts going through public records. Land deeds, titles, anything and everything that might have al-Sadir's name on it."

"He'll be more careful than that," Josh said.

"He very likely will," Liam answered softly. "But we're doing it anyway. Can't hurt."

Josh wanted to let the tears flow. He had tried his best to treat this like work, like another job. But it wasn't. This was his *wife*. Everything in this world was worthless to him without her. His own boss had gone behind his back to take her from him, and he had vowed to track down al-Sadir and find her.

But how? There was simply *no* trail for him to follow. Nothing.

And that didn't make sense, either. al-Sadir *wanted* Josh to find him. He had laid the trap for him, sprung it, and gotten away with leverage to ensure Josh would come looking for him. al-Sadir was still working toward finishing the quantum computer the Chinese had built and had decided that Josh Lane was the right candidate to lead the project. The pieces made sense now, and so did al-Sadir's reasoning behind kidnapping Molly.

So why wasn't al-Sadir simply telling me where to find him?

Suddenly Josh sat up straighter in the chair. The others were discussing using NSA supercomputing power to broaden their web search, but Josh's mind was somewhere else.

Of course...

"Curtis, do you still have the secure feed from the dark web?"

"Of the show?"

"Yeah," Josh answered.

He shook his head. "I can get it pulled up, but it went black two days ago. Nothing on it after four hours, so we stopped monitoring it."

"Pull it up."

It had to be this simple.

Of course al-Sadir would give Josh a way to find him. *Of course* he would do it in a way Josh would be able to see easily.

Jocelyn slid a laptop over to Curtis, while Josh and Liam moved to look over the man's shoulder. He typed furiously for a few seconds until a secure connection with a remote server was made. He pressed the return key, and a window opened and enlarged on the screen, a loading bar showing progress.

"This is the *Escape from Eden* feed," Curtis explained. "The same one we were monitoring while you were in there. Except now there's —"

Not nothing. The screen *wasn't* black. Instead, it was filled with numbers.

First, at the top, were the numbers they had been looking for: One, two, four, five, three.

And immediately below that, filling the screen from left to right, were coordinates.

"Hot damn," Curtis mumbled.

"It's coordinates," Liam said, his voice shaking. "al-Sadir is literally telling us where to go."

Josh let out a sharp breath. "Not us," he said slowly. "Me. He's telling *me* where to go."

"Josh, you can't —"

"I have to," he answered. "Molly's there, and al-Sadir wants *me*. If anyone else comes, she'll die. I know it. I have to do this, and I have to do it alone."

There was a prolonged silence as each of the NSA employees thought it through. It didn't matter. Josh had already decided on his next course of action.

"Find out where it is," he said. "Just because I have to go alone doesn't mean I have to go without a plan. He'll be expecting me, and he'll have teams ready to bring me in. I want to get there with some sort of idea of what to expect. Fair?"

Liam nodded "Fair. And I think some of those upgrades you were talking about for NARA might come in handy."

Josh smiled. "Oh, I think you're right. 'Bout time we see what this little thing can do."

ABOUT THE AUTHOR

Nick Thacker is a thriller author from Texas who lives in Hawaii and Colorado. In his free time, he enjoys reading in a hammock on the beach, skiing, drinking whiskey, and hanging out with his beautiful wife, two dogs, and two daughters.

For more information and a list of Nick's other work, visit Nick online:
www.nickthacker.com

AFTERWORD

If you liked this book (or even if you hated it...) write a review or rate it. You might not think it makes a difference, but it does.

Besides *actual* currency (money), the currency of today's writing world is *reviews*. Reviews, good or bad, tell other people that an author is worth reading.

As an "indie" author, I need all the help I can get. I'm hoping that since you made it this far into my book, you have some sort of opinion on it.

Would you mind sharing that opinion? It only takes a second.

Nick Thacker

BOOKS BY NICK THACKER

Jake Parker Thrillers

Containment (Book 1)

The Patriot (Book 2)

False Allegiance (Book 3)

Six Assassins Thrillers

Primary Target (Book 1)

Subtle Target (Book 2)

Unstable Target (Book 3)

Captive Target (Book 4)

Vendetta Target (Book 5)

Final Target (Book 6)

Mason Dixon Thrillers

Mark for Blood (Book 1)

Death Mark (Book 2)

Mark My Words (Book 3)

Harvey Bennett Mysteries

The Enigma Strain (Book 1)

The Amazon Code (Book 2)

The Ice Chasm (Book 3)

The Jefferson Legacy (Book 4)

The Paradise Key (Book 5)

The Atlantis Artifact (Book 6)

The Book of Bones (Book 7)

The Cain Conspiracy (Book 8)

The Mendel Paradox (Book 9)

The Minoan Manifest (Book 10)

The Napoleon Job (Book 11)

The Embers of Siwa (Book 12)

The Epsilon Event (Book 13)

Harvey Bennett Mysteries - Books 1-3

Harvey Bennett Mysteries - Books 4-6

Harvey Bennett Mysteries - Books 7-9

Jo Bennett Mysteries

Temple of the Snake (written with David Berens)

Tomb of the Queen (written with Kristi Belcamino)

Harvey Bennett Prequels

The Icarus Effect (written with MP MacDougall)

The Severed Pines (written with Jim Heskett)

The Lethal Bones (written with Jim Heskett)

Gareth Red Thrillers

Seeing Red

Chasing Red (written with Kevin Ikenberry)

The Lucid

The Lucid: Episode One (written with Kevin Tumlinson)

The Lucid: Episode Two (written with Kevin Tumlinson)

The Lucid: Episode Three (written with Kevin Tumlinson

Standalone Thrillers

The Atlantis Stone

The Depths

Relics: A Post-Apocalyptic Technothriller

Killer Thrillers (3-Book Box Set)